The Factory

M.J. Carden

PublishAmerica
Baltimore

First printing

ISBN: 1-4137-0733-5
PUBLISHED BY PUBLISHAMERICA, LLLP
www.publishamerica.com
Baltimore

Printed in the United States of America

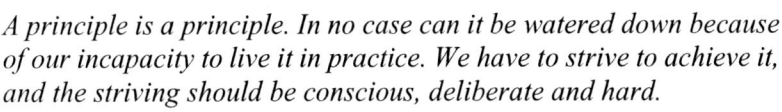

A principle is a principle. In no case can it be watered down because of our incapacity to live it in practice. We have to strive to achieve it, and the striving should be conscious, deliberate and hard.
—Mahatma Gandhi

In memory of Bridget Collings and her wonderful humanity. For Mary, John and Dan, with all the love and gratitude I can find.

To the real, principled struggle of the global class against falseness, inhumanity and barbaric exploitation. To Jack Heyman, an Oakland Longshoreman, a fearless fighter ... an internationalist!

Chapter One

Martin Cloherty had reached his destination. A rusted chorus of sirens screamed orders for work to commence. Without struggle the silence of the morning surrendered. Songless birds, startled into flight, merged with the gathering darkness of the day. It was a place where flea-ridden pigeons puffed out their chests and useless steel grey suns hid beyond the polluted skyline. And as he began to cross the road he contemplated the fortunate circumstances he now found himself in. Something entered his lungs. For the first time in his life he was free. For today, above all days, he was what *he* wanted to be, or at least what he thought he wanted to be. All around him misshapen blocks of granite rose forlornly in barren shrouds of remorseless landscapes. Nearby a solid clock tower forged its black iron fingers beyond the top of the hour. By the time he reached the kerb on the other side of the road he was convinced of his very fortunate circumstances. Overnight his wasted dreams of childhood had been realised and now his whole life stood before him written in letters of bricks and mortar. He took his final steps towards the entrance of the factory that now hung random shadows over him. His hands and eyes examined the solid beauty of brass, stone and glass that illuminated the premises of G.P. STEVENS & SONS, Electrical Engineers. Bleached by the drizzle of early morning rain the factory, his factory, spied menacingly down upon him. It was a great cathedral and he marvelled in its presence and the sanctuary he thought it might offer.

He had spent a lifetime wishing for the moment when he would be free of school and yet he had never given any real thought as to what that liberation would entail. But before this ice-cold transfer had taken place some bleak monotone teacher, forced into the role of career guidance, had vaguely asked him what he would do with this freedom. It was what he was paid to do and like everything else he passed down this line of gullible deceit with unthinking subservience. It was the way of the world. The way things were done, at least in his world. Momentarily, the boy had been fooled into thinking that such a thing as free choice existed. He prayed to hear the question repeated. Some days later he found himself sitting in the local Labour Exchange receiving the same false gift of good faith. Yet he still begged secretly to be told what to do for this was all he had ever known, all he had ever learnt.

'You must have some idea as to what you want to do?' inquired the woman behind the desk.

The question floated, wastefully unanswered as impatient queues of young eager hopefuls grew ever larger behind him mixing in contradiction with the older vacant eyes of those who knew what work and regular bouts of unemployment truly meant. Their worn eyes drifted beyond the posters proclaiming the existence of endless vacancies that adorned the walls of the Exchange. The boy's eyes shone intently in this blaze of information. One advert looked and sounded so modern, so technical. Above all it sounded intelligent. Intelligence was a word that, to this date, had never been combined with his name. The black and white posters added colour to the walls of the Labour Exchange.

ELECTRICAL ENGINEERING ... DESIGN THE FUTURE ... MAKE THE FUTURE

Although he had no idea what this phrase meant it was more the total experience of choice that mattered most to him for these were the first steps on freedom's great journey. A journey that would allow him to escape the emptiness of a life dictated by all around him, that for so long had dragged him towards the abyss of mediocrity. A mediocrity measured by persistent failure of which he had been born to escape from. For this was what he thought and this was what he thought being a man was all about. Escaping the tedium of youth. Making difficult decisions exercising choice, being free. Attempting to visualise an assumed maturity as well as the essence of this freedom; his response, or so he thought, needed to appear profoundly instant and deeply thought through. Yet it was to prove as meaningless as all that went before in his disengaged youth. Nothing was of any real consequence. He was about to discover that his experiences at school would differ little from his experiences in the world of work and the same dark forces that imprisoned his youth would continue. No real choice existed. And throughout his short life this unseen suffocating power had always been referred to as 'it' and everything that was bad was blamed on '*it*' or 'the system'. These labels echoed in his ears being passed down to him like some bleak and worthless inheritance from equally worthless relatives. But that was all in the past. He wrongly assumed it was over.

Mrs. Hyndle (for this was the name neatly scrolled on a small triangle of wood that balanced precariously on the edge of her desk) was there to carry out orders. She would never admit to this though. She was imprisoned by the patronage of those who held her future in their hands yet she revelled in this insecurity imposing her own authority over those whom she considered beneath her. She passed by them leaving a slipstream of treachery, lies and deceit to get where she was and where she thought she was going. But she was nowhere. Progress signified itself in her boundless ambition that forced smiles in the constant urge to please contradicted only by the refusal of her real wish to do and say what she really wanted. Her life slid effortlessly behind the comfort of the masks she donned. This was the price she knowingly paid to join the system, she bought into the system, she subscribed to the very same 'it' that the boy had now thought he was escaping from. And within 'it' all were imprisoned for 'it' was inveterate and inviolable. ' It' was the indefinable power of the 'system' that breathed a death of solitary greed and selfishness on all who passed its way. Locked inside the system that defined her own made to measure slavery she longed to be a child again, innocent and outrageously honest. He envied her maturity and status; she his youth and freedom. If only they could speak to each other for he was still a willing pupil. He answered the woman's question.

'An electrical engineer.'

From behind the desk she slowly repeated the boy's response, 'an electrical engineer? Let's see what we have then,' she threatened.

Reaching into a wooden box that took up most of the surface of her desk she pulled a long narrow drawer towards her to reveal an infinity of index cards. With the skill of constant repetition the woman ran her fingers from front to back, pausing once to deftly lift a single brown card from amongst the pack, picking at it like some diseased specimen. She read the contents of the card to herself and made a note in the ledger that lay in front of her. All was officious as her status demanded. This theatre of her own employment was meant to impress and set her labour apart from other more menial forms of employment and this was what she freely thought behind the leaden wall of her soul. All of this lay hidden amidst the debris of the props that proclaimed her status but she did not have the honesty, or more importantly, the freedom, to admit it or discard this fraud for the sake of the boy. Nor did she have the free will to admit that her work was as boring and repetitive as any prospective factory labourer's work. For to do this would be to truly elude her condition and this fear bolted her to the relentless routine that stole daily from her very existence. Bored with herself, hating her lifeless condition, hating the brown painted walls that closed in on her as each day passed, all was dishonesty and treachery. Nevertheless, she knew what she was doing for she only looked to herself and no one would be allowed to stand in her way or provide some useless distraction of care or attention. The box consumed her body and for a moment she disappeared from view. How she despised the human sacrifice she made every day to stay in the shameless competition of her chosen career. Like the boy she thought too that one day she would be free of this.

The rough collar of her blouse rubbed annoyingly against her neck. She became increasingly ill at ease with herself as she strangled some distant human emotion, a self-doubt, an intangible guilt made up of her own childhood nightmares. Heroic waves of lost dreams broke long ago against the rocks of a life imposed upon her. Now she always doused these pure white thoughts of liberation as instantaneously as they appeared. She was licking her thumb and forefinger as if preparing to snub out that hidden flame burning in front of her. All her dreams were dead. She was bored with the young man who sat obediently before her. It was her work to ensnare him into a pact but he had been shaped to be a willing victim and in his ignorance he longed to be a victim. Her work had already been done for her. With the brutal finality of an abattoir she dispatched the boy stabbing the neat brown card in his direction. She spoke quickly without ever again looking directly upon the former schoolboy and this pleased the boy, who offered only a taught respect to the woman. How he aspired to her station, to be like her, to join her. Yet she was killing him.

'Be there at seven o'clock on Monday morning,' she said abruptly.

As he reached the shining glass revolving doors of G.P.Stevens and Sons he became aware of the bleak absence of sound at that moment. Like the blackest night sky surrendering infinite stars to a patient gaze time dropped its jewelled curtain. So it was with this silence for the longer he listened the more intense became its existence. The air vibrated to a damp noise that whispered through the surrounding factories once the sirens had exhausted their call. The area that before had been a bustle of breathless men and women who pushed and jostled with urgent suspicion driven hard into their faces was now deserted except for this invisible steel hum that moved the walls and pavements around him. Late cyclists cut through his path with heads bowed in grim determination. He entered the main foyer of the factory and for an instant he wondered where all his fellow workers had disappeared.

'Wrong place,' the voice became louder and more emphatic.

'Wrong place!'

It was the voice of a young girl, a girl not much older than himself. She was sitting behind a large ornate bureau replete with plastic flowers and a visitor's book. Filing her nails glancing up only to check her reflection in the mirrors that encircled the reception area leaving the solitary boy to fumble in his pocket for the card given to him a few days earlier. That morning he had bought his first newspaper and as it fell to the floor he could just make out the image of a dead man lying on a concrete slab. He thought it was Jesus. The caption read, 'Che Guevara is dead'.

'Didn't you hear what I just said? Wrong place!' the girl looked away. 'Around the back, that's where you should be,' her hand pointed towards the door.

'And you're late,' she added like some final fatal wound.

He plunged the card deep into his pocket and folded the newspaper carefully, thinking of the picture of the dead man. As he turned away he gave a glance over his shoulder towards the girl filing her nails, checking herself in the mirrors and he thought how excellent she was. She fell back in her chair as if oblivious to everything beyond herself as her life ticked by to the drone of an enduring factory clock breathing over her every hour. It was now almost a quarter past seven and the light outside had begun to fade beneath the gathering clouds. He was truly fortunate. Thick black rods of rain bounced off him. He ran towards a small steel door at the back of the building. Slowly the door opened, allowing a gust of warm acrid air to escape from inside the factory and he could see and feel the steam rise from his soaking body. A small hunched figure poked through the darkness to examine the boy outside the factory. The young apprentice thought only of the immediate instant and that instant was consumed by his desperation to get into the factory. Although the man shouted above the storm that rose both inside and outside the factory the boy could hear or understand nothing.

A heavier gloom encased him in a narrow corridor of corrugated iron. Nearing the end of this tunnel shafts of light broke down the darkness as he became aware of the ever-increasing noise that crushed against him. Further down the passage great swathes of light cut into the corridor illuminating a thickening smog that swelled and fell around him. Violent rushes of burning metallic gases began to attack his senses. A new corridor lay ahead. He began to climb a rusted steel staircase with the weariness of some aged mountaineer. He was weighed down by an absent air that crushed against his lungs. As he reached the top of the stairway an iron gangway levelled outwards to disclose a vast gallery that swallowed his vision then suddenly, as if unleashed by some unseen dam, a huge tidal wave of noise swept over him and in that instant he was drowning. Then the balcony upon which he stood vibrated beneath him. Louder than ever before the factory blazed below him with the thunder of a thousand storms. An endless darkness lit intermittently by blinding explosions of light that stamped flashed sparks upon scattered silhouettes. Men and machines lay strewn across the great space below him. Engulfed in a machined atmosphere of smoke and steam he now stood some thirty of forty feet above the floor of the factory embraced in toxic clouds. Cocktail poisons burnt invisible holes the size of exclamation marks upon the lungs of all those who breathed its acid caress. These faintly coloured airs mixed carelessly everywhere in the factory.

It was impossible for the young apprentice to comprehend the cavernous synchronicity that drove back and forth in the act of production as arms and wrenched backs rose mechanically and fell in calibrated harmony. And this industrial epic held no dimensions as it squandered the imagination of the boy. But above all else it was the noise, the ceaseless incoherent noise that travelled from the floor to ricochet off walls, ascending upwards and outwards. A nuclear noise that exploded before him in its violent echoed aftershocks. Whose power bellowed throughout in mushroom waves of sound that never reached their threatened crescendo. All that lay beneath heaved with an uncontrollable anger which in turn became illuminated. Sparked into life, by the flight of a million flames that danced upon the wretched machine workers sweaty industry. Great incandescent fireworks of hot metal sprayed madly amidst their darkness like a thousand stuttering flashbulbs. In the seconds that followed this artillery of production resounded ceaselessly, remorselessly from the blackest of spectres to the richest displays of golden lights whose searching beams danced amidst even the slightest wreckless movement. Movements that collided head-on as each tiny universe of the production process united in its chaos.

The platform upon which he stood rose above three sides of the building. It was the architecture of an observatory. A prison architecture whose cell doors clung to a perfection of bricks that ran the length of the factory as if in existence only to highlight the Victorian splendour of this dressed steel walkway. Encased within these mountainous walls were four enormous extractor fans that roared out a remembered sound of lost acceleration. And the scale of this industrial art weighed its excitement heavily upon the young schoolboy who floated above a pit of furious noise and rancid gas that repeatedly stabbed at his senses. The giant fans spun in unison, engines roaring, from some unseen broken-backed fuselage. The aftermath of a plane crash. Now he struggled to be included in this wild world. Some forever hidden romantic machismo told him to endure this hero's death as it encircled him. As time passed it became his normality. He scanned his location with the experienced eye that often belongs unknowingly to the casual onlooker made comfortable through the act rather than the sight that lay before them. He pretended not to have been consumed by the fury that attacked him. Camouflaged in the role of factory tourist the boy watched as the detached onlooker would watch any maddening frenzy. Any riot or carnage. He looked through the eyes of someone hiding the enjoyment of others misfortune safe in the knowledge that it was not him. This was not happening to him. Strangers in a distance engulfed in their own catastrophe had nothing to do with him. By now he was regaining some control. He felt nauseous. He was late. The fleeting thought that they were the *underclass* came and left him without a second thought.

He looked along the platform towards the row of doors that broke into the brickwork along the length of the metal landing, printed on the first door, the words FACTORY MANAGER could just be made out etched onto a cracked wooden exterior. As he reached out to knock on the door he realised for the first time just how wet he was. He tried to shake off the water from his raincoat but as his hand rubbed against the arm of his coat a large watery oil stain appeared dripping carelessly to the floor encircling his boots in pools like thick black blood. This distraction took him beyond the door and into a room exhausted of colour. Two steel cabinets dominated one corner of the room whilst a small desk in the centre gave refuge to oil-stained papers and plans. Everything competed with lost engine parts and broken metal for vacant space on the desktop. Cigarette smoke engulfed the room emitting a heavy smog from which petty reds of light struggled to donate a reluctant colour to the room. He watched intently as cigarette ends lazily picked out flakes of dust that floated in their cheap makeshift illumination. A man faced him from behind the desk while another sat on a small stool in the corner. *Like two pigs,* the boy thought. They studied the hopeless young man who assessed this new space with grateful eyes converging upon the shadowy figures before him whilst all the time he dripped oil and water where he stood. Nothing in the darkness disclosed their intruder's focused eyes whilst his ears were locked in a background noise of thundering industry that drummed on with a cold steel violence thudding inside his skull. The man stood up from behind his desk. Compressing his knuckles into its edge. His body was entombed within a dark brown suit etched in grease-shined patches that gave off diffident reflections each time his body moved to the throb of his high-pitched voice. He yelled out his words in rapid succession as if issuing orders to a room full of broken soldiers.

'Well, do you know what time it is?' he asked.

The abrupt movement of his jaw hypnotised the boy, who listened impassively, more interested in trying to guess just how long the cigarette could stay in the man's mouth before he had to take in some air. Even the stale putrid air that scratched at their throats like knots of barbed wire. Meanwhile the other man stifled a laugh coughing smoke into the air ensuring that he did not interrupt his superior.

'It's seven thirty and you're supposed to be here at seven. Every minute you're late we deduct money. At this rate you'll be payin us to work here.'

At this point the factory manager looked over to the other man in the corner, who peered over an oil-stained cup that he clasped in both hands. The remnants of his cigarette burned steadily against the ends of his fingers dropping delicate strands of ash like snowflakes over his clothes. He nodded approval. He bowed the bow of subservience and this momentary silence ended.

'That's right, Mr. Johnson,' said the man in the corner.

'Look, I'm prepared to overlook your lateness. Is that understood?' he said.

The expected conciliatory gesture unfolded. This was the stuff of life he had endured at school and come to despise. That infinite coal face of punishment and reward. He looked directly at the factory manager.

'Good,' this arrogant assumption, 'Good.' He grunted.

Both men assumed silence as acceptance. Silence for the former schoolboy was rejection.

'Now perhaps we can sort some things out.' Johnson placed a clean brown index card on the desk in front of him. 'Is something the matter?' he asked.

The boy hid behind his silence while Johnson stubbed out his cigarette in the overfull steel ashtray as the other man allowed his stub to fall in agreement to the floor joining other cigarette ends that were encircling his feet. Johnson lit another cigarette and a bright yellow flame rose and fell instantly to flash vivid silhouettes that filled the room. For one brief moment the true fragments of colour, long lost within the room, were disclosed. And all this went unremarked.

'Look, lad, if you don't go looking for trouble you won't find it. Now just sign the card,' he demanded.

The card itself was a copy of the one given to him at the Labour Exchange with the only difference being that on his card it had printed Apprentice Electrical Engineer, on the card handed to him by Johnson it simply said LABOURER.

The young boy spoke quietly and slowly.

'I think a mistake has been made. I'm applying to become an apprentice electrical engineer.'

He landed his forefinger upon the card as if to erase the meaning and insult the boy read into these letters. Both men began to laugh loudly and the one in the corner was now standing being encouraged to laugh louder as Johnson repeated what had just been said and amidst this false flattery of laughter nothing more was mentioned in the room about the vacancy for an apprentice electrical engineer. He was what they said he was, a labourer. The boy had surrendered again. Johnson leant across the desk pushing his face as near to the boy as he could.

'I'm giving you a start. Three pounds a week....' he paused as if for impact and his voice rose, 'ten shillings for Saturday morning ... that's compulsory,' he waited again.

'Understand me?' his voice became louder still. 'We make things here

from steel, cast iron, copper and bakelite. We make them into something.'
The man seemed overcome with pride at this statement.

'Do you know what that means?' he asked

The boy did not 'know what it meant.'

'If you don't want the job leave', he said looking casually towards the door, 'we pick and choose every day. Hundreds. Hundreds, eh, Tom?' he confirmed to the other man unsure if confirmation was needed.

'But if you're lucky it's a job for life,' he stated as if no doubt existed in this statement of truth.

The boy appeared impressed at this gift, '*or was it a threat,*' the boy thought to himself.

Tom Carberry sat in the corner and he seemed to be enjoying the discomfort experienced by the boy for gone was the bold stance. Now the boy's head was locked rigidly with eyes fixed upon his tormentors and his defeat exposed itself as he suddenly realised that this was not school and he could not walk away or go home to where his parents would offer some protection, some blanket of care. Still, he tried to compose himself and without another word he surrendered to sign the brown, oil-stained index card cursing the word 'LABOURER' as he did so. His mind raced ahead with images to block out this bad situation. How he wanted to avoid it but his persecutors would not and could not relent for this was their role and their absent humanity was as automated as the machines that drilled out the barrage of discordant industry that now returned to fill his head.

'Good. Now lad, just do what you are told. Tom 'ere will take you out and show you the ropes and give you your first tool.' Both men laughed. The boy did not see the joke.

'Now you get on that factory floor and get some electrical engineering done,' he said.

The laughing continued as he was shown out of the factory manager's office. School life, as detestable as it was, now faded into a bitter obscurity. The world of work was different from his expectations. Outside the office he again swallowed the sounds and smells of his new environment. He could barely make out the bright clash of metal upon metal as machine competed with machine punctured by the screamed communications of their operators. The young labourer now looked down upon the men and women who toiled in the stench of burning oil that cooled hot metal in creamy measured spurts, that drilled and cut and shaped and dripped hydrochloric acid that in turn scraped invisible scars on their lungs and skin. Breaking storms of production drove through the factory in every direction. The old man, dressed in his long white coat, went ahead of the boy, walking quickly along the raised metal catwalk. Below him some workers on the factory floor cheated glances upwards, shouting indistinguishable insults to their fellow workers. Hurriedly they both descended the staircase leading down to the factory. When he reached the bottom step the boy slipped crashing to his hands and knees and as if from nowhere Johnson appeared jutting a fat dirty finger at the boy as he lifted himself from the floor.

'What the fuck 'ave they sent us ere then?' he screamed.

Johnson had walked this far from his office and the boy observed the call of some workers as the small, breathless piggy figure of the manager rolled down the staircase. Like some ancient chant of cowed captivity.

'Morning Mr. Johnson' … 'Good morning' … 'Mr. Johnson … Good….'

They called in a false staggered humility. And these suppressed cries of secret subterfuge varied in delivery, volume and confidence. But the impression was not lost upon the boy of grown men ingratiating themselves with their boss. But the irony was lost on the boy. For the workers it was a step towards the rolling plains of freedom. They were 'takin' the piss' and 'takin' the piss' gave them a moment of laughter and each moment of humour was a taste of freedom and revenge. He was to learn that irony and sarcasm were part of the defensive shield that many workers used—if only in this madness to secure some sanity. And it was a rich and real humour that echoed in the solidarity of working class unity—a secret language that cut through the hypocrisy and lies of the system that sought to enslave them. Above all else it enraged the management. It was reason enough for the workers to keep this onslaught alive. True to the irrelevance of this contact Johnson ignored the workers who had greeted him because he knew that behind his back they spat on the floor or mouthed 'fuck-off' as he passed. Why say it anyway, thought the young labourer, free from the power of the factory manager's office. As the taunt rang out it crashed upon his own sense of dignity and his head turned in all directions urgently reacting to the bleats of his tormentors. From behind the machinery and smoke workers looked towards this welcomed distraction straining their deformed frames to poke their badly carved heads into the face of the boy who was still on his hands and knees. In his own time he rose slowly brushing his raincoat with filth-stained hands. This gift from his mother, that symbolised for him his transition to adulthood, was now a mass of grease and oil and as he lifted his head the piercing brightness of a thousand fluorescent lights clawed at his eyes.

He now stood at the border of the factory as near to the molten core of light, smoke, heat, metal and steam as you could get without being consumed. It ran at him in one final deluge. It swirled around him rising up from the factory floor in great urgent clouds. Clouds that hissed and strangled their insipid breath in all directions forming dark mists around triangular steel girders whose perfect angles strained to support the glazed roof of the building. This was the land of the machine and the machine was king. For the machines carelessly consumed men and women as they each struggled in turn to exist in their shadows. Forced in perpetuity to line themselves up in enslaved symmetry. Endless rows of fluorescent tubing hung precariously above them. Beneath them white lines on the floor marked out the areas of each machine reinforcing the restrictions of their movement as if to prove that it was not their world but the world of the machine. It was cold steel brutality that held dominion. Bent double over, under or around the machines workers shamelessly distorted themselves in the search for detailed measurements, thickness of metal, accuracy of lathe or drill, the angle of the bend in the metal. Half machine, half man or woman. Only their shackled movements disclosed the inanimate from the animate. Those workers nearest to the staircase escaped to view their newly acquired distraction in a rare moment to steal a moment to stand up straight, a moment to lessen the noise that beat against their bodies every day. For breaks in this relentless monotony were rare but above all it was a moment to have contact other than that of the machine. This momentary idleness was the boss's gift. It was his moment. His to take away as quickly as it was given. The boy witnessed all this and hated them for their surrender. Even in this brief time he had still learned nothing.

'Thinks it's a fucking electrical engineer!' the boss yelled.

The impromptu theatre ended as the very people whose attention the boss had sought were now to be dispensed with and he turned upon them as fast as he had turned on the boy. For the boy it was school days again. A flashed memory calmed his situation. After all he was used to confirmations of power over the powerless, of bullies in the schoolyard, and for a moment he swore he could see a hanging crucifix in some distant corner of the factory but he sighed to himself as he saw it was just another distortion, an illusion, a simple mistake.

'Com'on, Com'on. Show's over. Get back to work,' was the order.

As the machines started up again normality within the factory was restored. Johnson left to return to his office. The noise and stench of burning oil returned and Carberry lit another cigarette. In the absence of the boss he was the boss and it was this protection of meaningless hierarchy that marched down the battalions of the factory in some cast iron patronage so that all men could become bosses if only for a second. If only in their mind. At all levels someone bossed someone in this place. They both began to walk the four-foot-wide gangway that divided the floor of the factory into two halves which in turn split into innumerable paths that then cut deep into the darkest recesses of the factory like lost roadways with forgotten destinations. Mapped out under the gaze of strip lighting that flickered oppressively above these gangways the strict geometry of the factory, its machines, its raw materials and its workers lived and breathed like one giant organism. Each had their own detailed role to play like the minuscule segments of some decaying insect they twitched lifelessly, remorselessly, as if with a purpose. As they approached the heart of the factory the man halted abruptly and to their right stood row upon row of brown oil-stained cards slotted into metal pockets with each card containing the oil-impregnated fingerprints of their owner.

'Here's your clock card and your works number,' he fumbled for a moment '809,' he said.

He pulled the boy's card from inside his pocket and punched it into the green metal clock that stood at the epicentre of the factory. Its prominence in this place disclosed a reverence that went beyond the practical use of such an instrument as the measure of time. For this was an icon, whose status was a celebration of the theft of time. Human time. Freedom. It celebrated the mastery of the factory boss over time itself. The defeat of the time anarchy of agricultural work that preceded the march of dark satanic mills. The capitalist's abolition of sunrise and sunset. Industrial capitalism could not exist without the rigid measurement of time, and the power of the clock dominated all activity on the factory floor. For labour time formed the vital measurement of profit. This was its purpose. The electric light had overcome nature and the clock defeated the random habits of the seasons. The boy's card banged the clock into action and faintly typed the time on one part of it. Carberry's pig eyes lit with satisfaction at this sound.

'You clock on and clock off. If you're late you'll lose pay and if you do it too often you get sacked. Now put your card in slot 809!' his self-selected guard ordered above the bombardment of the factory.

The boy leant over and slipped the card into its place and as his fingers left the card the oily image of his thumbprint confirmed ownership, or ownership of a sort. His eyes scanned the bank of brown cards before him, all had the telltale fingerprints, the signature that declared ownership, the ownership of the factory and its agents. For the first time since encountering the two men the young boy appeared to regain some confidence for perhaps now that he had submitted his card, with his fingerprint, he would be left alone. Now that he had surrendered he would be free. He tilted his head and looked again at his card. Nothing altered. His name, number and oily thumbprint all remained intact. The boy smiled in resignation to himself, but not to the factory. The man gave the card a final jab, bending it slightly further into its slot. Two oily fingerprints now marked the card numbered 809 and ownership was confirmed.

Chapter Two

First, that the work is external to the worker, that it is not part of his nature, that consequently he does not fulfil himself in his work but denies himself, has a feeling of misery, not of well-being, does not develop freely a physical and mental energy, but is physically exhausted and mentally debased. The worker therefore feels himself at home only during his leisure, whereas at work he feels homeless. His work is not voluntary but imposed, forced labour. It is not the satisfaction of a need, but only a means of satisfying other needs. Its alien character is clearly shown by the fact that as soon as there is no physical or other compulsion it is avoided like the plague. Finally, the alienated character of work for the worker appears in the fact that it is not his work but work for someone else, that in work he does not belong to himself but to another person.
—Karl Marx, *Economic and Philosophical Manuscripts* of 1844.

The man and the boy continued their walk down the central gangway of the factory, both being mindful not to wander beyond the thick white lines of strict demarcation that navigated the direction of their journey. But the boy's natural reaction was to place his feet beyond the lines and to shade his eyes from the glare of the lights that poked flaming tubes into the back of his head as he passed under them. And all the time the old man stole a look behind him, almost wishing the boy to break the futile metal symmetry of the factory so that he could reimpose it again. When they reached the far side of the building Carberry pointed to one of the many workshops encased within their own borders of white lined floors and staring fluorescent strips.

'You get ya body over there, see Mr. Williams, he'll tell ya what to do,' he said.

Not satisfied that his message had been understood by the boy, he pushed his face towards the apprentice.

'But remember me and Johnson are watching ya all the time, understand?' he added.

Carberry rolled around, then left and the thought of being free of him was satisfying to the boy, for now he felt able to assume that the worst was over. But he became increasingly aware of the stares and glances, the blinked movement behind the machines that had bothered him since his ill-fated entrance into the factory, as if wild animals hidden in the metal overgrowth were stalking some half-dead and naked prey. His mind wandered haphazardly and he still thought he was better than his imaginary hunters.

'Watch out, lad,' someone shouted. 'Keep yer eyes open!'

'Oh, I'm sorry, I didn't see you,' the boy replied, looking downwards.

'All right, just be a bit more careful,' the voice tumbled calmly and friendly towards the boy.

The worst was over. A normal human being at last, he thought, as if amidst this chaotic induction he knew or held a concept of normality. He stood back to allow his newfound friend to pass him, crippled in his struggle to pull a small metal truck containing long lengths of thick angled iron towards another part of the factory. He tried to lend a hand and as the man passed, he smiled.

'I'm looking for Mr. Williams,' the boy said.

'He's over there in the white overalls.' The man pointed towards some distant location. 'See, that's him,' he said, vainly forcing deep, reluctant breaths into his lungs. The man stood up straight and took a dirty cloth from inside his green overalls. He was about forty years of age and looked tired and drawn; the apprentice felt skilled enough in making such a judgement based upon his father's age, coupled with that look, that vacant look that now seemed to hang unwanted in the brittle atmosphere of his home. He thought his analysis was unimportant anyway because everyone looked so much older than they really were. In that tiny segment of a second he thought of his mother and how she now looked drawn and humbled by the struggle of many unfriendly and unyielding years. His thoughts ended as he turned to the man who now wiped his forehead. A grey smudge appeared and after blowing his nose the dirty cloth was bundled back into his pocket. Wrenching his back over the truck, the man began to push at his load again, but this time the young boy became aware of the enormous weight that the man struggled against. The strain carved itself across the man's face in grimaced trenches that dissected his head. For the boy the worst was over and his interest in the struggle of the stranger mattered little to him. In the midst of the incessant noise that threw clouds of steam in every direction; the stench of burning oil, the constant movement of people, machines and materials in this market place of industry he was as much hidden and anonymous as his misfortune could donate. He looked towards the place where a few seconds earlier the stranger had pointed and there sat a man leaning over a large metal desk that was situated in the centre of the workshop. As he walked ahead the screaming crash of iron bars could be heard as the load that had passed him a few seconds earlier collapsed to the floor, dropping its dead weight instantly. He looked back, then continued his walk in the opposite direction as if nothing had happened and if it did then it did not involve him. Someone screamed and workers ran from sections of the factory. Within moments other screams rang out. The boy tried to catch sight of what was happening. An accident? Shamelessly he ignored this further wave of chaos. He thought this and he knew he was wrong. By now he had convinced himself he was different from the labouring class that encircled him. What class was he from, he thought to himself and in the nothingness that encircled him his mind gave up and skipped forward.

'Mr. Williams?' he asked.

The man looked up at the young boy before him.

'What?' He looked beyond the boy. 'What's happened over there?'

The boy tried to look concerned but no point seemed to exist to this act. Williams's head weighed firmly in his left hand and as he spoke his words were muffled and indistinguishable amidst the breaking waves of noise that drowned all conversation in the factory that forced the young apprentice to assume much of the conversation.

'Whoever you are you should have been here an hour ago,' he said. 'How old are you anyway?'

'Sixteen.' He was actually only fifteen and half but it seemed more in keeping with his newly discovered maturity to add on those important few extra months.

'That's a good age to be. You look as if you've been rolling about on the floor,' he said and as the last words of the sentence unfolded another large crash somewhere else in the factory drowned out the final syllables.

'Pardon?' said the boy and in the brief silence that followed he examined the shock of silver hair that covered the man's head.

'It won't come off, you know. Like most things here those marks are there to stay.'

The boy moved closer. He did not understand what the man said. Williams lifted his head out of his hand and carried on speaking but this time he was much easier to understand.

'We'll have to fix you up with some overalls for today but you'll have to buy your own in time. Green's your colour, brown for the foremen and white for supervisors.'

His voice trailed into the distance as if he had given up on the meaning of his words. Then he stood up. He was tall and thin. The top of his body arched forward. The young boy thought the man was going to make an important point and he leant closer as if to give his fullest attention but the man was not leaning forward to make a point. Both heads almost collided, then the boy caught sight of the foreman's back with its boney contours raised up in sharp relief against his white overall like a snow-covered mountain.

'This bothers you?' he asked, almost disinterested. 'You'll hear a lot more about it soon. Anyone would think it was their problem.' He looked away from the boy.

'If only they knew. If only they really knew.' He turned to face the boy again. 'Now let's have no more about it, perhaps we'll try and get you started,' he said purposefully.

Then the man's hand suddenly jutted into the air, his thumb and forefinger joined at their tips, he turned his wrist quickly and croaked out the letters.

'OK!'

The swiftness of this movement caught the boy by surprise. As if to reinforce the action the man repeated it, although this time much more quickly.

'OK!'

The supervisor walked ahead of the young boy, arching back and forth as each foot slapped against the stone floor. His arms were tucked into the small of his back where his fingertips met at the base of his hump. His hands cradled and comforted his life's misfortune. Williams swivelled around; punching the air in front of him, the wrist twisted as the thumb and forefinger met again in one darting movement. The boy waited for the gesture to be followed by the 'OK' that the old man inevitably spluttered as he continued walking on ahead. It eventually came. Behind a small alcove in the workshop stood a row of dirty rusted metal lockers whose doors were all open, and from one of them the supervisor produced a bunch of oily rags, which he opened out and threw to the boy. It was a green overall and it stank of stale oil and damp. He gestured to the boy that he should put it on and without speaking the boy began to take off his raincoat, which was now not much better than the overalls having been covered in oil and grime after only half an hour or so in the factory. Every contact he made with his coat left an indelible mark and the care he would normally take over such things was now replaced in the knowledge that the damage had already been irrevocably done. As for the overalls, they were made for a much bigger person than himself but he made do as best he could folding here and tucking there as Williams's body jarred back into action, hands tucked beneath his hump, feet slapping against the floor.

Immediately behind the twisted rows of vacant lockers a man was leaning over a large metal sawing machine, feeding it with long lengths of four-inch-wide channel iron. Each time the saw ran across the face of the metal it recoiled back with a loud bang, like the recoil of a shotgun to reappear with its blade on the cutting face of the metal. Each movement of the blade, of metal against metal, screeched upon contact, only to be faintly silenced by a spurt of creamy oil released from a small pipe above the blade. Each contact with the hot blade released a plume of acidic smoke that rose upwards into the face of the machine minder.

'John,' the supervisor called to the man as he jabbed his forefinger into his collarbone.

'John, here's a new labourer, just show 'im round for us, get im to clean around,' he asked respectfully. 'You know, keep him safe,' he added.

The young boy was behind Williams and he leant forward simply to see if he would make his distinctive gesture to the machine minder. Suddenly the arm jutted out, fingers met and wrist twisted. The letters spewed out. 'OK.'

Not waiting for a response the foreman left. Another piece of metal crashed to the floor. The blade of the machine continued to thud out its movement, spewing creamy oil against imaginary steel. This machine could not detect metal in its presence, nor could it choose metal, measure metal or load it onto its cutting frame. At this moment the human minder had power over the limitations of the machine. The minder stood up and said something to the boy, but against the noise of the factory and the machine that continued to cut air the boy could not hear. The minder slammed his hand against a red button on the side of the cutter. Immediately the machine descended towards a halt. Within seconds, in that specific area of the factory some scarce margin of silence was unleashed. The man and boy began to soak up this space with illegal communication.

'Sorry, son,' the man shouted needlessly, 'what have they said to you?'

The boy looked up and replied, 'I thought I was going to be an electrical engineer but they say I'm a labourer and the foreman told me you would show me around, I think.'

'Well, it's a good time to start, it'll be teatime in a minute. Look, can you just give us a hand putting some of this metal away and we can have a talk over some tea,' the man said cheerfully.

The boy was happy to talk to someone, to do something at last. By being like the rest of the workers he could hide, camouflaged by work, he could make a noise and create smoke so as to blend in with the other workers, and in this he could be one with them, not separate, the same as them. He craved for this equality because he had been constantly aware of the stares and huddled conversations that his appearance in the factory had created and such attention made him feel wary and ill at ease. He bent down to touch then lift his first piece of metal but he misjudged its weight and length, causing the metal to crash to the floor. Despite the noise, his first noise, his first contribution to the cacophony that had shattered his senses since entering the factory, no one lifted a glance at his novice attempt to join the world of work. His failure went unnoticed. The man smiled at the boy. And the boy felt at one with the *underclass* albeit momentarily.

'Don't worry, son, leave it there,' his fellow worker said. 'I'll see to that. Do me a favour and grab that cloth,' he pointed towards the floor, 'just give the cutter a bit of a wipe. And be careful!' he shouted.

At that moment the factory klaxon droned above the noise of the workshops. Throughout the factory lathes, drills, metal saws, bending machines, welding torches and giant sheet metal cutting machines, a family of machines, ground reluctantly to a halt ending the bombardment of noise and smoke that had waged war since seven o'clock that morning. Since the beginning of the industrial age. A ceasefire tumbled around the workplace. The tumult of banging, sawing, drilling and shouting cascaded down inside the factory, reaching a point of almost silence as machines relinquished whatever false loyalty they had as they involuntarily spluttered their response to the collective push of red buttons. This action set in chain a remarkable explosion of unshackled freedom. Released, the screaming voices of the workers could now be heard in the void left by the dying sighs of the machines. For most of the workers their speech reflected the volume of the particular machine they minded, so the noise may have changed, but the volumes remained the same. Nevertheless, the klaxon was an all clear. A peace that allowed the noise of the workers to now fill the factory. But the workers still shouted at each other as if in perpetual competition with the machines as hand, head and arm movements accentuated the subject of their communications. Only the noise of the giant extractor fans could now be heard above the jostle of human activity. As smoke rose up from the factory floor the remembered force of the engines' mighty blades churned meaninglessly. Their use had long since past having been suffocated by years of oil and dirt. Their function was now reversed pumping filth down into the factory. And as quickly as gravity lifted the black factory air the dead fans pushed it back again. The man offered him a seat alongside himself on the metal cutting machine. He produced two rounds of cold toast wrapped in greaseproof paper and offered the boy his breakfast.

'Oh, it's all right. I'm not that hungry, perhaps I'll have a cup of tea or something,' the boy said.

'It's up to you, have you got some money?' asked the man.

'Yeah, oh I'm fine, really,' the apprentice insisted.

'I'm John Evans,' said the man, adding almost apologetically, as if cursed, 'the chargehand.'

The boy introduced himself. But he could not escape the transformation within the factory, for in a matter of seconds hundreds of people were

24

scattering in all directions as if a bomb had gone off and another was about to follow. Men and women hurled into each other as they rushed along the white-lined gangways of the factory. Some sat at their machines eating sandwiches, pouring tea from grime-laden flasks, still calling out each syllable of useless communication. Others clung to their machines, carelessly wiping spent metal and oil from rusted surfaces. John Evans broke the silence.

'So do you think you'll last a week or two with me?' he asked.

The boy returned to the conversation, 'Oh, no problem, Mr. Evans.'

The man smiled. 'Hold on a second, son, you're not at school. Perhaps you can just call me John. I think that will be enough,' he said.

The young boy was still deep in thought. He was well practiced in this art from the days when teachers would starve him of interest, leaving his life balanced upon a knife-edge of distraction—any distraction. So he could keep up with any conversation without actually listening and so his mind concentrated upon the giant extractor fans that towered over him and everything. He surveyed the workers who ran through the factory trying to escape some nightmare that only they could see. Where had the time gone, he wondered to himself. It only seemed like minutes since he ran in from the gloom outside to the gloom inside. As John Evans ate his toast the boy continued to monitor his new environment, trying to work out what fears or dangers he needed to avoid if he was going to survive in this death trap. Occasionally, the workers that passed gave some menacing stare. One knocked into him. But the young boy felt secure in the company of his older mentor. A number of women congregated nearby in the sheet metal workshop. As a couple of women passed they shouted greetings to the chargehand.

'Got your own assistant then?' one woman said. 'Fuckin 'ell,' she continued, 'things are looking up.'

The other pushed her head towards them. 'When you've finished with 'im send 'im over…. We'll give 'im something to do,' she said before running off in the direction of her friends.

'Oh, I'm sure you will,' the chargehand replied.

'Don't mind them,' he said to the boy. 'By the way, they're good people. Good people,' he said as if speaking only to himself, underlining any doubts with the nod of his head. 'That's for sure.' He repeated this as if having to confirm his own statement. As if apologising for the intimidation the factory and its workers threatened upon all newcomers.

The boy had never heard women swear before and this shocked him, but he hid his true feelings well. He turned towards the man and the more he sneaked glances of the man who sat next to him the more secure the boy felt.

He took note of the loud but inaudible screams and shouts that now dominated the floor of the factory. Along the main gangway that divided the factory in half two women pushed a metal trolley which had a huge tea urn balanced precariously on the top tray and beneath the tea urn two lower trays contained food. Biscuits and meat pies. The women stopped at one of the many intersections that cut across the gangway, allowing a queue of workers to encircle them whilst others filed across the factory towards the tea trolley as if it was a beacon. In the fury that unfolded one of the women called for order.

'Hold on, hold yer 'orses, yer gonna knock the fuckin lot over,' she yelled.

'Hey bollocks, get your hands off.... Stand back or no one will get served.... Com'on, who's first,' threatened the other woman as her face scowled into the sea of humanity that speared towards her.

Their thick bare arms pushed against their customers like prize fighters and their giant hands formed fists as big as faces. Both women stood legs apart, upright, with their fat sausage fingers squeezed into the steel handles of four giant milk jugs. It seemed that the more the women shouted the more the crowd responded. Most of the men and women in the queue held cups in their black hands waiting for them to be filled. Only occasionally someone would push too hard and cause the boiling stew of tea to splash and hiss on the metal tray or a pie to end up on the floor, leaving a mark like human excrement. The boy continued to watch in silence.

'It's always the same,' the man said. 'Every day without fail. It's not the girls' fault. Why can't they all learn a bit of sense.... Just too lazy to go to the canteen. Not that that's much better but just look at them. Anyway, there's more problems than that in here,' John Evans said to himself.

'And that reminds me,' he continued, 'you must join the union. You haven't got problems with that, have you?' he added. At this point he turned to face the boy, who answered immediately.

'No, of course not,' he paused for a moment and added the name 'John' to the sentence.

'Well, you shouldn't. You'll find out there's a lot to sort out here and with the union as well for that matter but that's another story. I'll get you a form later. But just look at that,' his head nodded forward, 'it's like some primitive ritual and the food isn't exactly good or clean. You see.' He stopped and returned to reading his paper, as if pausing for thought he finished his sentence brusquely, 'They accept it, all of it, and that's the problem.' His voice faltered in the short distance that separated them.

As the man returned to his newspaper the boy drifted again into a study of his newfound condition. His eyes mingled amongst the chaos that still encircled the tea trolley. Elsewhere in the factory varying levels of pandemonium rose and fell like long-awaited tides. Most of the women, he could see, were situated down one end of the factory in the sheet metal shop. Sitting on wooden benches that lay against the wall or standing around their great cutting machine. The women were deep in conversation, breaking off to point at men or shout blindly across the factory. He could not make out what they were shouting as their calls echoed in a peculiar way, lost in what passed for quiet within the factory. Many men sat at their machines, isolated in that moment, in some invisible sanctuary. Others leaned against walls or machinery, urgently seeking to make idle conversation—any conversation. The boy tried to identify the varied mix of people before him while he huddled himself in the shadows of the factory forever beneath the giant extractor fans that seemed always to dominate his vision wherever he looked. Yet he had not noticed that their speed had been reduced and that now he could see the huge blades rotating inside their cavernous mountings. The slow sweep of blades sent out a persistent swish as if resting in wait for the fresh mists of disfigured air to rise up once again from the factory floor.

His mind wandered aimlessly and without care. Just upon his brief introduction to the factory he thought he would never forget its sheer immensity, the poverty and grandeur of its architecture. Its absolute enormity. For a moment he became aware of the need to move himself from the uncomfortable edge of the cutting machine. He leant forward and cupped his head in his hands. Through this movement he stole glances at the women in the sheet metal shop and after a while his gaze lifted slowly and at that end of the factory he saw for the first time that the whole of this gable of the building was constructed of glass mounted upon a wall some eight to ten feet high. Thousands of individual frames of glass, no more than twelve inches square, covered the whole of this section of the building, curving to meet the roof sections of the factory. At its highest point the roof of the factory glistened upon tiny jewels of glass set in their delicate metal frames. Whispers of reflected colour faintly showered life as it existed beneath its display. And no one saw this and no one cared. The boy saw it and he thought that perhaps it could have been a cathedral before it was a factory or possibly a factory soon to become a cathedral. Whatever, it did not matter, the building was, in his view, a beautiful contradiction, a collision of art, industrialisation and human despondency. Of all the subjects he endured at school art always commandeered his respect and religion commanded his thoughts. But, did others see it like him, he thought to himself. He doubted it. He was compelled to share his observation with his friend but felt that he might think him pretentious or stupid, for after all it was only a factory. Yes, but what a factory. The small slate windows crowned its glory which until this time had been obscured by the smoke and dirt that spewed from the machines. After the extractors had grudgingly performed their duty and relocated the black air that hung over the factory the windows provided a fresh light that slowly flourished then blazed down upon the factory without him even noticing. A shower of gentle-coloured reflections trickled downwards, dancing in rainbows of the faintest light. His thoughts drifted into silent words he held only within himself to paint this scene. At this moment his happy dreamworld floated in the cascades of light that he alone had created. The young apprentice considered himself well versed in the art of observation, this was his field of expertise, and he was pleased with himself. He returned to observing the workers. The workers in their regimental dirty green overalls. Yet still he did not see himself as *'one of them'* and this was a momentary dementia that captured them all at first. But undoubtedly, given time, he would become *'one of them.'*

An air of expectation seemed to capture the movement of the workers as those that sat at their machines began to clear away their empty sandwich wrappers, dusting their machines with oily rags as they tidied around purposefully. The women in the far corner also appeared to be preparing themselves for some event. The tea trolley had long gone. The two 'tea women' with their oversized arms and oversized legs had disappeared. The men in the drill shop could be seen making adjustments, cloths in hand, mindlessly feeling the points of their drills, wrapping their dirty hands around the full shaft of their drills, turning them slightly with their hands while brushing grime away with their free hand. All these movements appeared seamless in their rough symmetry and throughout the factory the workers were all taking up their positions, by their machines, stroking them, patting them, polishing them until this process of grooming spread slowly through the factory like some great disease. No longer could the boy identify groups of workers in conversation. No longer could he hear their laughter or shouts. Expectation filled the air until somewhere in the distance a groaning noise could be faintly heard. It grew steadily. Then the call of the klaxon burst through the factory. This was what the workers were preparing themselves for, not for the end of their brief break, but for the return of work and as the klaxon reached its most piercing pitch, the machines stumbled reluctantly, rocking from side to side before sparking into action. Once ignited each machine blasted its own unique engine noise as they throttled towards production, as if tuning up in mechanised preparation for a full industrial recital. It took a few moments before every machine was operational. Within seconds plumes of smoke spurted out in all directions, rising from the machines like aged steam wagons spluttering under failing ignitions that needed more acceleration, more fuel to bellow more killer smoke from their rusted exhaust pipes. Across the factory curving shock waves of noise unfolded upwards and outwards in conjunction with black cargoes of smoke that waved upon the air. Neither the chargehand nor the boy had stirred amidst all this.

John Evans tidied around his work area as if the filth demanded the constant care, cleaning and the permanent attention of a spoilt child. By now the smoke and noise within the factory had found its natural level. A Hell of sorts, thought the boy. The man shouted towards him, killing his thoughts.

'Let's just move this iron out of the way and I'll take you to see some of the working plans that we use to make the switchgear,' he said without displaying any real interest in his words or their meaning, 'that should give you a better idea. Then we could introduce you to some of the workers.'

John Evans led the way towards the supervisor's desk in the middle of the workshop. Williams, the hunch-backed supervisor, was not there. Around the desk three steel partitions, no more than five foot high, sectioned this area of the workshop off from the rest of the factory. Hooks, arranged in neat lines, carried mounds of papers that covered most of the three partitions. The chargehand examined these before looking through some of the other documents on Williams's desk.

'Just come here a second,' he said. 'You see, this is where all this workshop's allocation gets dealt with. These are the production targets and plans for this week. I know it looks complicated but it really is quite simple. We only produce switchgear in this plant so it's basically repetition, bending copper, drilling holes, wiring instructions....' His voiced trailed off, then started again.

'Some of the men in here don't even look at the plans. So when management change the specifications someone's cut five thousand pieces of copper six inches long when it should have been six and half. That's when the balloon goes up.' He shook his head slightly. 'Everybody from the office comes down threatening to sack everyone. It can cost them dear if a mistake gets made. It always struck me as odd that we only ever discover an error after someone's cut or drilled a good few thousand pieces.' John Evans shrugged his shoulders. 'So it is important to look at the draft just to check that you're doing the job right,' he said.

As he was speaking he continued to examine the papers in front of him. The boy listened as if this brief lesson was proof that he would eventually be given a plan to work off himself and he thought this was a good development. He thought about it for a moment and could not explain his thoughts. Perhaps he would be an engineer. John Evans continued his lecture.

'All these plans hanging up are jobs that have been completed, how much metal was used, specifications and job order numbers. It looks like the accounts department is lagging behind again because most of those should have been well into the office by now. If you want to ask any questions be my guest,' he said.

The boy smiled and indicated that he did understand. Just then the old black phone on Williams's desk rang. The chargehand turned around and answered it. He gathered some documents from the desk and told the boy that he had to go up to the office.

'Look, I won't be a minute, just wait here for me. Have a look at some of the plans and drawings,' he said, 'look busy at least. That's the trick in here,' he added as he sauntered off in the direction of the office.

'Look busy!' he called back to the boy. It was the golden rule of the factory.

The boy felt embarrassed. Being left alone, he didn't feel safe. He decided to make himself 'look busy' in an effort to blend into the background. To follow the last instruction of the chargehand. Every so often he would glance upwards just to ensure that no one was looking at him or approaching this liberated area of the factory and after a couple of minutes he moved back towards the steel partitions where he would be hidden from view. Boredom set in very quickly and with his hands embedded deep into his pockets he eased his way around the partition, imagining what the boss would do if he was that boss. He muttered beneath his breath and imitated the supervisor's darting finger movements.

'OK'

'Look. I'm fuckin telling,' he mimicked, 'you get this fuckin show on the road. I want twenty thousand of them, ten of that, four thousand bendy bits, two million holes all over. Do it to spec. OK. I said OK!' the boy exclaimed.

His arm jutted out, his back bent forward and his wrist twisted. In the middle of the desk was a ten-inch nail knocked into a wooden base upon which hundreds of technical drawings were skewered. The boy eased his way gently into place and sat at the desk observing the documents held together by this un-officious nail. He surveyed the desk and began examining the process by which each paper had met its fate. 'Did Williams place them neatly on the spike?' he asked himself. No, they were too haphazardly arranged for that, he thought. He must have banged them on the spike once a worker had completed the job. But how did he avoid impaling his hand on the nail? It must take years of practice, he thought. So he began learning the technique. Again, he imitated Williams's distinctive mannerism grabbing a piece of paper from the desk, he banged it into the nail, attempting to allow the nail to run through the space provided by his open fingers. But he badly misjudged this manoeuvre and the nail embedded itself firmly into his hand and as he tried to excavate the nail from his bloody palm the pain shot through his body. His screams were all but drowned in the common tumult of the factory. He cursed the nail; the documents and the thick wooden base that all lent to the overall weight of the object. He screamed so loud that its echo lost itself in the screams of a thousand drills as they scorched into every conceivable surface of metal. He wrenched the object from his hand and threw it against the desk. Doubled over with pain he kicked and cursed his way around the supervisor's lair, oblivious to his predicament and his surroundings. To stem the flow of blood he grabbed a white overall that was draped over one of the partitions and wrapped it around his bloody hand.

Much, if not all the events in the factory had flown by the young labourer as he awaited the return of his friend. Williams, the supervisor, had come down from the manager's office and was marching through the factory with his customary flatness, hands tucked under his hump, chin pushed forward whilst the whole of his body shook as his great flat feet slapped against the concrete factory floor. It was on these occasions that some of the younger workers took delight in mimicking the foreman and shouting abuse as he passed by their particular workshop. Some workers threw metal objects or balls of grease, some spat at the old man they had grown to hate and despise. But these shows of bravado always lacked the courage of confrontation, resulting in each verbal or physical attack being followed by a cowardly duck behind the nearest machine as if this behaviour had become an unnatural aspect of the human spirit, too decayed to offer anything but token resistance. Beyond doubt Williams knew the antics that followed his presence on the shop floor, perhaps an inner dignity curtailed his acknowledgement of these events, more likely the fact that vengeance could be his when and if he chose to inflict it. This undoubted power, the workers, knew was his alone to exact. The shouted insults and the whistle and crash of their missiles had gone unnoticed by the boy. More importantly, the imminence of the supervisor's approach went equally un-observed, obscured amidst the mayhem of the machines. Williams now stormed towards his makeshift office.

Over the years that he dominated all activity on the factory floor those few workers capable of serious observation had noticed how, after sustaining more than the usual levels of abuse during his regular factory walks, Williams would make for his lair, sit at his desk and stare blankly into space. His meditation, as the workers found out, rested purely upon revenge. A bittersweet luxury that could take many forms. For he had the power to be precise as to what punishment he would inflict upon a given worker. Time and the experience that time imposes had taught Williams the fundamentals of human weaknesses, for he had worked at the factory of G.P.Stevens man and boy and he had developed an expertise that only such longevity bestows. Often this expertise would be utilised in its very basic mode. For example, the worker who worshipped money would find his overtime stopped. Lazy workers were given the hardest jobs. Such basic punishments could be complemented by a more sophisticated approach, in which Williams bade his time with individuals whilst letting them know their punishment would occur at the exact moment he chose. This more subtle approach left many workers in a state of perpetual anxiety and on more than one occasion had resulted in a tormented worker openly confronting Williams and pleading with him to end the misery he had imposed. Whatever form Williams's retribution took, his power went unchallenged within the factory—that was, until this moment. A stranger was in his lair.

The boy had returned to the desk, the white overall had been thrown back to its original site and the blood had ceased flowing from his wound. Hidden from view by the metal partitions that encircled the desk he awaited the return of his friend the chargehand; his feet now positioned themselves on the foreman's desk in preparation to play a small joke that owed something to his newfound liberated status in the factory as a *'worker'*. But as always these thoughts were only in the boy's head, locked away and hidden from reality. Although Williams had caught sight of the boy, the situation was so unique even he, with all his experience of the dark side of humanity, had to quickly evaluate what his response should be in order to maximise his power—his control. But the boy realised he had been caught if only for acting the fool and this happened quite regularly when he was at school, more the victim of misfortune than anything else. As with Williams the boy had acquired his own response mechanisms, not to impose power but to restrict its impact, and he could play the game the same as his opponent but with a surprisingly mature approach, gained not through experience but through intelligence. The boy chose mock innocence to begin with. Despite his attempts the words came out too quickly and as on other occasions, with certain teachers at school, this only led to an erratic response. Williams, for his part, lost control not so much with the boy but with everything that day and this was simply an excuse for him to vent his anger. His arched body lunged at the boy. Within a moment Williams had his gnarled boney hands around the young boy's throat, that shook with every indignity he had suffered at the hands of workers in the factory.

'You lazy bastard!' he screamed.

The words spewed out from Williams as the boy fought to defend himself. No point existed in trying to defend himself verbally, this was a physical situation. He knocked Williams's hands away from his throat with relative ease and whilst still in a state of shock from being discovered he knew he had to be careful not to go beyond any imaginary line of acceptable response. This he did. Having protected himself from Williams's attack, the boy stared hard into his attacker's eyes. Williams was shocked by the ability of the boy to not only defend himself but also by his disregard for his status in the factory. It was this refusal of the boy to accept the unlimited power of Williams that ground into the man most hurtfully, like the jagged turns of a rusted corkscrew.

'That's it, you're finished,' he cried weakly.

By now the boy felt firmly in control. Finished from what? Something he had hardly begun. The threats of the old man seemed meaningless, but the boy was aware of a sadness in the man's behaviour. A loneliness that encouraged the boy to back off and retreat away from the desk. Williams was physically exhausted, for the years had taken their toll, no matter how much he ignored its deathly progress. He lifted his head in surrender but darker forces imposed their will, and Williams arched his crooked body towards the boy in a final symbolic act.

'OK. If that's the way you want it, then OK.' His voice sank with resignation.

The apprentice felt secure in his power over Williams, and the old man knew this and hated his youthful adversary all the more. For the boy was secure in the knowledge that the events taking place had gone unnoticed in the factory. Hidden by the ceaseless blockade of noise and smoke and the partitions that now encircled them. This was between them and them alone. So often in the past the boy had experienced his greatest feelings of pain and powerlessness when attacked in the presence of his peers. It was never the actual confrontation that hurt, it was always the observed ridicule of the event that heightened the pain. The boy thought silently about how fortunate he was as he awaited the next move to come from Williams, who seemed to understand the futility of his power at that moment. But he had to respond in order to defend his right of control, his right of power. These movements that he felt were his and his alone. The boy recognised that this was an independent power, not for the boss or '*it*'. And the boy admired this old man as he returned the boy's stare, speaking quietly as he caught his breath.

'So you wanna be an electrical engineer,' he said, 'you wanna be a craftsman. Well, I've got the tool for you, son. Just the tool.' His voice fell to the floor and the boy strained to hear his words. 'Johnson wanted to give you this but I didn't.... Well, you can have it now if that's what you want. Now you come with me,' he ordered.

The old man's threats ceased to be of any real relevance to the boy as he followed him beyond the partitions of his makeshift office. Williams had adopted normal posture, with his boney hands tucked beneath the base of his hunched back. His beak-like features protruded forward, lurching ahead of his huge feet as they slapped against the factory floor, sending a shock wave that reverberated throughout his body.

'Com'on, I've got a job for you. OK,' he called.

In a few seconds the old man and the boy had arrived at a small room behind the main tool shop. Williams emerged from the storeroom mumbling repeatedly.

'An engineer?'

He turned quickly and delicately handed him the largest brush that the boy had ever seen in his short life. It was immense. A wooden skyscraper that defied the natural laws of design or proportion and its scale demanded respect for this was the brush of brushes. The boy could barely contain his laughter as he stared at the abnormality of this giant's creation.

'Your job is to sweep up this factory from the moment you enter it to the moment you leave. Sweep.' He called him. 'A ... sweep, that's what ya are, a factory sweep. Now you pick that up and you sweep and I'll be watchin you. It's the only tool you'll see in here,' threatened Williams as he started to push the boy around again but he regained his composure at that vital moment when all control can be lost and the boy watched this transformation dispassionately as the old man's voice fell nervously to the floor again in a silent scatter of iron fillings.

'No, you stay there, don't move,' he demanded without commitment.

Williams ran off as best he could in that twisted body God had seen fit to impose upon him while the boy pushed his hands into his pockets and waited patiently, resigned to his fate, no longer caring. In what seemed like only seconds Williams returned with Johnson, the factory manager, and Carberry, his assistant. By now some workers close by began to take notice of the presence of such a senior delegation on the factory floor. As the three men passed by the tool shop the two bosses had taken a vanguard position, walking side by side, with Williams behind them. It was left to the latter to shout abuse and fling his arms about in the air, telling the workers to get back to work. Johnson appeared suitably oblivious, Carberry slightly less so in accordance with his status. The young boy stood fast at the sight of these three ridiculous beings as they marched through the factory towards him. Two fat men and one thin screaming uncontrollably. Importantly for the boy, the workers in the tool shop remained at their benches, although one or two dared to look over to where the boy was standing. Realising this, he decided to throw all caution to the wind and he moved out towards the middle, where he could be seen by most of the workers in that area of the gangway, almost stopping Johnson and Carberry in their tracks. Williams pushed accidentally into their backs, hissing out an awkward apology. Both men looked around and in silence displayed their utter disdain for Williams. Johnson now faced the boy and in his high-pitched automaton speech he addressed the boy.

'I knew it, I fuckin knew it. A smart arse,' Johnson said as he looked around him for confirmation.

He looked towards Carberry, who fulfilled his subaltern role with due deference. This little man had already become a hate object for the boy from their first encounter, with his voice pathetically timid and used only to agree with the demands Johnson made of him. At this instant a distracted drill shop worker caught his hand against a drill bit that spiralled into his flesh, spewing blood in every direction, and as the man screamed the others looked vacantly on avoiding any involvement. The injured man's cries for help went unheard until eventually one of the women ran from the cutting shop and gave the man first aid before taking him to the factory nurse. Undisturbed, other than having to perform a look of angst and disapproval at this distraction, the boss's repartee continued.

Carberry looked on slyly protected within his wall of silent sycophancy. Unsurprisingly, this emphatic confirmation served only to further annoy Johnson as he peered at both men. He continued. 'It would be too easy ... boy,' he called him like some slave owner, 'so easy for me to sack you, much too easy,' now his voice grew louder, 'now I'm going to help you become used to discipline and respect for yer betters. Now I think you've heard this before but you better believe me, I'm different and I'm going to make you accept that in here you do what you're fucking told to do.' Johnson leaned into the boy's face. 'I'm not fucking interested in you, I'm interested in what use you have to the factory because without work you're fucking nothing. Williams will watch your every fucking move, you little arsehole and I, well....' At this point he paused and looked up to the roof of the factory for no reason whatsoever. The two men behind him also looked to the skies. The pause lasted a lifetime. 'I am going to make it my business to make your life a misery. So you get that fucking tool.'

At this point his body staggered towards the direction of the brush.

'And get to work, you useless twat!' he screamed.

Johnson's voice had become less deliberate and threatening although the boy remained silent throughout his tirade with his stale eyes rooted upon some distant object as if this act was response enough. This had annoyed Johnson in the office earlier that morning and he struggled to ignore it this time so as not to undermine the impact of his attack on the boy. Intuitively, the young boy knew that no response was required. The two men turned on their heels and waddled quickly back through the factory and as they passed the noise levels increased, indicating that work for some had stopped as they struggled to find out what was happening in this lonely corner of the factory. And as they rolled through the factory, so too did this noise. The brush remained throughout in the boy's hand. Williams stared at him, still not satisfied, and the boy knew this and he remained silently unimpressed with the events of the last few minutes. Both united in a twisted despair at the roles that had been dealt out to them with neither comfortable in their enactment. Williams knew this also and knew that his role in the factory had been one long contradiction that ran contrary to his own trade union history in the factory, his friendship with John Evans and his hatred of the boss. Yet this was, like so much else in the factory, an unknown history to the boy. The old man pushed past his opponent towards his lair so that he could stare into the oblivion of his sad and wasted existence.

Alone at last, the boy examined his newly acquired status that the gift of the brush confirmed. The handle of the brush was as long as he was tall and at its base the brush head was a full four-foot in width corresponding to the width of the factory's gangways. Two large iron-strengthening bars fanned out from the base of the handle to each end of the brush head. He stared blankly upon the brush whilst he pondered his immediate future and no matter how he tried nothing would alter. It was his first day at work. Everything he had wished for was invested in the world of work. His unhappiness at school was to be solved, or so he thought, by the simple act of leaving and getting a job. He tried to console himself. Perhaps this was what happens to all apprentices. He felt isolated and alone as he considered that this was now his reality. Delicately, he placed the brush against the wall and sat on a small wooden box. His head sunk naturally into his hands. Sitting back he raised his eyes glancing at the glass and steel roof as the noise of the factory banged and jostled against his body as if for the first time. John Evans had deserted him. Where was he? Why had he not returned, he thought to himself. Never had he felt so alone as he looked with resignation towards the giant brush. Suddenly, the factory siren sounded. It was one o'clock and the workers had half an hour to take their dinner.

The klaxon breathed out its last sigh and its hand deadened the machines if only for a brief spell. The boy hid away for the rest of the day. He watched the dirty hands from a distance. Watched them making everything and owning nothing. Building with their bare hands things that the factory bosses could never realise. A lumpen mass that gave the misery of their lives, their broken backs and amputated limbs, to a system that could never be their equal. Other people, he thought, were hell. He hated them and he hated their submission. They, this shattered mass, could never be liberated. Or so he thought. The boy made the usual mistake of assumption. These men and women were what they did and that was all. That was their everything. And as the factory stormed with their industry they drowned in endless tides of hopelessness. This was all he saw. That afternoon he searched for solidarity and saw only separateness. Clouds of anxious faces lost in obedience. This was what they did and this was what they were. The boy knew nothing.

Nothing of the churning of revolution that burned in the bellies of the majority. The reality of what they did held no significance for what they were. The two were incompatible. He was consumed in quicksands of guilt and contempt. Hatred drilled into his being. The afternoon blazed to its conclusion and the day ended.

The machines staggered to a halt as their minders ran towards the centre of the factory. Hundreds of exhausted hands pushed and grabbed at their clock cards so that they could punch them into the clock and prove where they had been that day. Once this ritual had been completed the workers ran towards the factory exit as if escaping death itself. Within seconds the ever-present noise of the factory plummeted towards its only aspect of silence that was a constant drumming that pounded painfully throughout the building. The giant extractor fans, although stopped, now turned effortlessly in the stale air that blew along their shafts from outside. In strict and regimented sequence the fluorescent lights that bore down upon the workers like a thousand prying eyes turned off and as they blinked the workers vanished. The apprentice continued to sit in silence. He now contemplated his journey home. What would he tell his parents, he thought. Whilst the father said little his mother was genuinely excited by the thought of her only son going to work. She was suitably impressed with his apprenticeship as an electrical engineer. He began to walk towards the lockers to retrieve his coat, the raincoat that had been spotlessly clean at the start of the day was now covered in oil stains and still damp from the morning's rain. He remembered what he had been told, that this oil, like so much else, was impossible to remove, and as he put the coat on the oil off his hands simply added to its misery. Walking past the foreman's desk the young apprentice saw Williams staring into a space where neither of them needed to acknowledge the existence of the other. Deliberately the boy ignored his clock card as it rested officiously alone in slot 809 on the metal board.

Consumed by hate, he made his way through the dark, empty factory in a silence curtailed only by the slow and slurred rotation of the giant extractor fans above him and the meaningless drumming noise that constantly prodded his body. The old man who greeted his arrival in the factory allowed the boy's exit to proceed without comment. Outside it was dark and desolate as the rain pursued its tasks of the early morning and his mind was still inside the factory and in his desperation the young boy felt also that his very soul was there too. And the hatred he felt drained him. Loneliness followed his journey home and the few workers he came into contact with he hid from, ashamed of his dirt, ashamed of his condition that marked him in his mind and, perhaps, the minds of strangers, for this was what he thought. But they too were like him, dirty and dispossessed, for they were victims also. But each victim's hurt took priority as they stole furtive glances of each other's misery, as if this act alone would give them some vengeance or consolation. That the other's pain was greater than theirs.

When he arrived home his mother greeted him excitedly, asking what he had done. Was he a success? But when she looked upon her son she felt only a mother's sadness and she comforted her son, speaking softly to him.

'Quickly, I'll run a bath for you. You look as if you've been working very hard, what with all your electrical engineering things. Go and have a bath and I'll serve your dinner up with yer dad,' she said.

It was the excuse the boy needed to get out of the way and he ran up the stairs to the bathroom. In the mirror he examined his filthy reflection and as he threw cold water into his face it became clear that the filth was not going to be removed easily, it was ingrained into the pores of his skin and the harder he tried to scrub the oil away the darker it became. His gestures became more violent as he realised that all his clothes were covered in a dusty oil that had its own telltale stench and when he removed his shirt he discovered that the filth had penetrated his clothing to cover his entire body. His mother had run the bath for him but he knew that once he entered the water that too would become a filth-infested swamp, but it was all he could do in his vain attempts to remove the stain of that day. Nothing would remove that stain. In a final attempt the boy scrubbed bleach into his skin and although it cut into his body like broken glass, some of the filth was removed. Unable to share or expose his sense of abject failure, the apprentice went straight to his bedroom, and in his loneliness he cried away the unmeasured pain of that day into a bottomless pit, into which no one else could fall.

Chapter Three

*The strongest man is never strong enough to be master all the time,
unless he transforms force into right and obedience into duty.*
—Jean-Jacques Rousseau

That night the young apprentice did not sleep well. His brain was subjected to the persistent taunts of failure. His failure made all that more painful by its immediacy. One day was all it took and his empty life laughed ahead of him, taunting him. The dreams of a world outside of his hated school had evaporated to an even darker morass as he considered the repercussions of not returning to the factory. His innocence could not evaluate the substance of such thoughts. He was unable to seek advice from any quarter. Perhaps, if he refused to go to work, this would be a matter for the police or that stupid woman who sent him to the factory in the first place. Why did he say he wanted to be a worker anyway? No options were ever open to him. Why didn't he realise this? What could he say when his friends asked what work he did? Everyone would know he was a factory sweeper, he knew how labels stuck, ingrained in the minds of others forever, he was the sweeper, the dustman, and in the fractured world of status this mattered, for even at the bottom of the heap status reigned supreme. He desperately needed to speak to someone, someone like John Evans, but even he had deserted him. At around five o'clock he got up out of bed and in the bathroom he examined the dirt on his body, the mass of dead oil that masked his face like some unwanted tattoo. Much of the dirt had evaporated to a greyish scale that paled against the redness of his eyes. He spoke to his reflection in soft but clear words, telling himself he was going to return to work, and his stomach no longer churned inside because a decision had been made. The young apprentice would defend himself as he had done at school. This was his way. He would fight back.

His father was also awake. This was quite normal. Normal for over thirty years. Even when he had no work to go to the imposed discipline of the factory clock dominated his life and as they passed each other on the narrow landing of their high-rise flat his father reluctantly acknowledged the presence of his son. A look of broken resignation etched upon his defeated face punctured by the dark and empty windows of his eyes. And this was the same face that the boy recognised as it carried its haunted presence throughout the factory. For the boy now saw that his father was no different than other men in the factory. This look of submission appeared numbed into the senses of men long versed in the run of excuses that would explain away their indifference to a life that delivered little more than subsistence and misery. The son peered into the vacuum of his father's eyes, to reach out to the man he respected above all things. This giant of a man ignored the silence of his son, merely casting his shadow as he walked past the bare bulb that blazed light in the hallway. In just a day their relationship had altered to that of fellow workers, one old the other young. The latter was yet to surrender to the dominion of the factory but the former had long ago conceded his humanity in exchange for the humility that such work, by its very nature, imposes. A deep sense of shame gripped the son and propelled him out of his home and back to the world of work.

At six fifteen a stream of industrial buses arrived to take the waiting lines of workers to their destinations. A steady flow of cold rain poured over the boy as he walked from his home to the bus stop. He welcomed its refreshing caress as it rinsed against his dirt dry face. Many of the buses were already full. When they arrived the grey shadows that were bundled together at the end of the main road pushed hard against each other with a heavy impatience. The inevitable bus arrived that would suck the boy up the staircase into a thick fog of cigarette smoke that attacked his throat, and as he coughed hard he was bundled into a seat. Inside the bus steam from the wet, dirty clothes of the workers rose like the early morning mists. The overwhelming greyness of the scene consumed him. For it was a graveyard bus. Dead people gobbled up in a capsule full of grey clothes, grey faces, and grey air cutting through the blackness of the morning, certain that on its return it would equally cut through the blackness of the night. Silence, grey and black, silence, grey and black. Some examined pictures of half naked women that beckoned them from the dirt-stained pages of comic newspapers. Others seemed locked in half-muttered discussions. As the bus shook with the unevenness of the road the boy repeated to himself, 'silence, grey and black,' in time with the jerks of the double decker. He was happy. Happy because he saw the collective silences, the collective greyness and the collective blackness of this terminated ride to nowhere. He looked to making some comment, some conversation, although each time he began the futility became obvious. Dead men don't talk. Against the noise of the engine, rain and coughing one or two women could be heard in conversation punctuated with the occasional broad laugh or hidden giggle. They were beautiful and his eyes danced with their every movement. The grey men kept their vanquished silence welded down by the guilt of years of inaction. Yet he knew nothing of their history. Nothing of their actions or their lives. In this he was different than them. He just did not realise it. That morning he was not on that bus.

That someone, that some system could have the power to impose upon people a life that wished away the hours seemed unimaginable to the apprentice. This indeed must be some great power that could proclaim freedom and democracy and yet force people to work in the most degrading and inhuman conditions. No more than prisoners locked on a treadmill existence that barely kept them alive. More bizarrely the work was killing them and yet it was fought over even though the life that these factories reluctantly surrendered clung only to the hungry winds of subsistence. In the paucity of their condition workers spoke of 'well-paid jobs' of 'so and so who had a great job—getting paid good money'. With the only real comparison being poverty. What sickness overcame people to grade the levels of poverty that their lives had been reduced to? All for a poverty wage for which they could expect to work in conditions that no one could define as humane. As if to add to their subjugation an aura of good fortune, the good luck to have such work, was pushed down their throats and shined into their eyes. This, in his naïveté, he fatally assumed meant that somehow these men and women were willing victims and this error only compounded his anger. Silent grey and black it was. An absurdity established to be destroyed. The more the boy looked upon his own condition the more he raged against the machines that imprisoned such good men and women. He raged against a system that upheld this degradation and most of all he raged against an unknown and unseen enemy which had always been called 'it'. With no humour left he endured his journey locked in thoughts of the revenge that he would rain down upon this thing that fed upon such solitude, such indignity, such poverty. And in his ignorance he failed to see that many had fought and continued to fight against this great economic, social and political swindle. Many sat alongside him on the bus, an army of rebellions. He just could not see them.

Within half an hour the bus ended its journey at the industrial estate on the edge of the town. Daylight was about to break. But for the hundreds of workers who tramped the worn pavements to their own rotten factory not much thought would be given to the glint of a winter's sunrise. Normality for them was this state. This state of perpetual darkness in which they shovelled out their lives. Despite the rigours of the previous day's events the apprentice was singularly buoyant as he walked past the main entrance of G.P. Stevens, sneaking a glimpse of the young telephonist who continued to file her fingernails whilst catching her reflection in the wall of mirrors that formed her cage. A thousand bicycle's launched urgently and haphazardly all over the place searching, prodding forward towards their destination. They weaved clumsily amongst a thousand foot soldiers with bells ringing wildly. A queue of workers formed a line in front of him to file through a thousand steel doors. The old man, seated behind his makeshift pigeon hole, watched impassively as the workers began to speed up their return to the factory. Once inside running towards the clocking-on machine situated near the centre of the factory floor. On this day his entrance to the factory was concealed as the young apprentice simply followed the lead of the collective. The factory was dimly lit but as the clock approached seven the fluorescent strips clicked, flashed and buzzed into action. And in this epileptic blaze that faltered above them workers scrambled for the brown numbered cards that proved their presence in the factory. They had to be pushed down the throat of the clock, and this was crucial for they were in the factory to do their time and time is money and money was what they wanted, even at the expense of their time. The clock was a machine and it too was king.

'Watch who yer fuckin pushin…. Hold on, will ya,' someone yelled.

And this became the collective cry but this was a mixed event. A non-event of anger and humour that the boy knew he should avoid. He stood back and waited for a quiet moment when he could punch his card. Suddenly the klaxon droned out its starting orders and within seconds the melee at the clocking-on point ceased, allowing the boy to ease forward to punch his card into the top of the clock, and when he retrieved it the numbers 7.01, written in red ink, realised his lateness. The boy, as an integral part of his fight-back, ignored this event. Of itself it simply did not matter. The barrage of noise and smoke that was the factory had already been set in train along with the course of the day, the month and the year until it would end. Made invisible by the normality of industrial chaos his task was now to locate his brush, the tool of his trade. On this, his second day, the young apprentice wore an old dark blue boiler suit that belonged to his father. He walked towards the place where he had left the brush the night before but it had been moved so he waited behind Williams's compound. Time now existed for him to observe once again the pull of the factory. The pull of its gravity. The constant ebb and flow of humanity as it bowed to the production that droned out from the machines that belonged to the factory owners. Up and over, in and out, up and down, shuffling or running along the white lines that marked out the gangways as if the air they breathed would be taken from them if they stopped or moved outside their boundaries. Yes, they functioned, he thought to himself, but it was the extraneous function of the machines they served. He was satisfied with his thoughts.

His mind wandered about the still nature of much of the machinery and how the role of the worker was to feed its disability. He considered the immoveable weakness of the machines. *If man created machines that could feed themselves,* he thought, *then workers would not be needed. But surely workers would always be in command of the machine?* His thoughts turned in his head. *If only because someone would have to turn them on or off, set the cutting tools, oil the moving parts, clean the waste product?* He muttered to himself. No, the boy had thought this through. *Man and machine need each other—robots did not exist nor could they.* He remembered reading somewhere that inventions were really simply innovations that just improved, or modified with the progress of man's creations. His naïveté gave him security. Deep in thought the boy imagined as best he could what it would be like in this factory in thirty years time. *Not much different,* he thought to himself. He thought of what the concept of technological revolution meant. For him the technology was already here, in front of him, and he was not too impressed. *What would people do if they did not work on the machines?* he asked himself. These contradictions weighed on the boy's mind as he waited for his brush to appear. The turbulence that belonged to the factory reclaimed him and ended his thoughts as he became aware of his real condition. His eyes fell from the glass roof.

'You … you should find your brush, you know,' said a voice.

Before him stood a man. A man not like others in the factory simply because he did not look old or fat or dirty or have that vacant look of defeat, which was the hateful image the apprentice now carried with him of all that occupied the factory. This man must have been the cleanest worker in the factory with his starched overalls, white shirt and dark blue tie. Even the cloth he rubbed against his clean hands seemed spotlessly uncontaminated by the filth of the factory. He was handsome with thick-rimmed spectacles and black swept back hair. Whilst being caught deep in thought and somewhat startled by the sudden arrival of this stranger it was difficult for him not to laugh out nervously at the man's staggered speech. He was able to control himself but mockery was normal and people who are different must expect to be figures of ridicule because this was the norm. A norm established and reinforced throughout his lost education and even on his first day at work, fat, thin, ugly, black, stupid whatever, it didn't really matter, for difference was the essence of amusement and power over others. It was the protector of the norm in all its abnormality. The apprentice had never accepted this but had always opted for the easy journey by joining the mob at school for fear of being perceived as different himself. Upholding a priority of sameness that existed to the exclusion of anything different and this was the paucity that contributed to his hatred of school. This was the paucity that led him to hate the factory and its workers and in this sameness he was content with his own difference. He did not laugh as a tribute to the freedom that could now be his away from the stifling repression of school. As a result of this the tone of his response was respectful.

'I know, but it's nowhere to be seen so I'm waiting for Mr. Williams.'

'But you … must look … I'll help,' stuttered the man.

Each word blocked in the throat of the man as he forced himself to communicate with the boy but with some haste the man rummaged around the area as the boy turned from side to side to keep him in view. Amidst a clash of steel and banging of metal doors the man emerged with the brush. Clearly elated and unable to pursue his feelings in words he mimed his satisfaction in a small dance that articulated to the boy his own happiness at being able to help another person. For his part the young boy observed the delicacy of the man's movement and the gentile display of a warmth so humane and simple in its silent expression, for never had he witnessed such a pageant. Taking the brush, he in turn mimed his gratitude.

'I … saw Johnson and you yesterday,' the stranger said. 'I was watching what happened. He's, sad. A very stupid man, but you must be very careful, very careful. I saw it all. I … saw it all … because, you see … I'm a toolmaker and I … see lots of things … I travel around the factory and I … see them all….' said the man disdainfully.

A longer than usual pause then preceded the man's own anger at his failure to speak as clearly as he wanted. Locked in concentration he formed his final sentence in a controlled and effective delivery that clearly pleased him and it was his statement.

'I'm Brian. Brian Atkins,' he repeated.

The young boy examined him more closely. He knew that a toolmaker was one of most respected skills a worker could have in the factory although he did not quite, as yet, understand why. The man before him looked more like one of those RAF mechanics that would run out to a recently landed Spitfire to undertake some mechanical survey. Dressed in smart blue overalls, white shirt and tie, Atkins had a permanent expression of being deep in thought. But his accentuated mannerisms, compounded by his random stammer, cruelly created another image. He was entirely apart from the nature of normality, or what passed for normality, inside the factory. The young apprentice followed him down a main gangway of the factory and as they both entered the drill shop area some workers began to shout a torrent of abuse at the toolmaker as he brushed a pathway through which the boy could follow.

'Now Atkins … go on, ya dirty fuckin bastard,' screamed one of the men half hidden beneath the iron frame of his machine.

The abuse continued as the toolmaker turned to face the boy, his anguish and hurt was clear. He quickly gave the boy the brush and with his head bowed ran off. One of the men who had been shouting abuse at the toolmaker approached the boy.

'Look, lad, whoever you are you just keep ya fuckin distance from that dirty homo,' he yelled above the din of the workshop, 'he's a fuckin monster and we don't let 'im out of his fuckin cage. You make ya fuckin mind up … fuckin stay away.'

The man used each word as if they were knives cutting into the boy, stabbing him with his meaning. He was one of the drillers and his stance reflected the years he had spent crouched over his machine. But when he straightened himself he was huge with arms so wide he held them out from his bulging stomach. His neck was lost within a mass of fat that clung to his face. Phlegm flew from his mouth as he yelled and at the end of each few words he wiped his mouth with a filthy rag that simply added more foul dirt to his face. The circling movement made with the oily cloth mixed sweat and dirt as the man coughed spit into it before wiping his grimy face. A common practice in the factory. The boy ignored everything. He turned his back and sought to return to his work area. 'Where the fuck do you think your goin? Ya little bastard!' the man shouted.

By this time a number of workers from the drill shop had gathered around the man. On seeing that he was being ignored he turned to his co-workers. It was the ritual of decline that the men responded to. For the boy violence, inhumanity and hatred were the common currencies of the factory and to gain respect some workers bid against each other's excesses. After only one day the apprentice knew this much to be true but this group could not recognise a refusal to respond and so they pursued him. However, the familiar presence of Williams soon rang out. Unfortunately, for the gang of drillers, Williams could only see that they had left their machines and that the apprentice had his brush in his hands. His hand struck the air and twisted with predictability as he ordered the men to return to their machines. This was just an interruption, an abnormal break in the tedium of prison life, expected but not condoned.

'OK, get back to work. Show's over. OK?' urged Williams.

Again the theatre continued as the workers muttered and shuffled their way back to their machines. The act was complete and servility had triumphed jointly with oppression, as both need each other, craved each other, to maintain the status quo at all costs. The boy observed and knew this and it sickened him.

'Good lad.' Williams nodded his head approvingly at the boy's own seemingly effortless subservience.

'I knew you'd see sense after yesterday,' he said. 'This place looks nice and clean. Good lad. I knew you weren't stupid. Lads just havin' a bit of fun, well, as a new lad you've gotta expect all that. Just lettin' off some steam, were they? Gotta real sense of 'umour, haven't they?' Williams did not sound convincing. He was not being honest. He knew it and the boy knew it although he refused to disclose it. The boy began brushing the gangway.

'No, just hold on, lad. I knew you'd see sense,' he repeated. 'Now just take your time, look around the factory as you sweep yer way through it. Just work your way around, keep to the gangways. Get to know people, get to know yer factory. You'll do all right 'ere, I can see it now. Good lad. OK!' beamed Williams as if another conquest had been settled.

Throughout the conversation the boy used his brush as a prop, occasionally moving the handle as a form of non-verbal communication. The brush having satisfied Williams's need for acknowledgement now turned to perform its function, and the human being that provided its motivation was both saddened and weakened from his experience. The confidence of the morning appeared to be momentary. With a newly acquired sense of freedom the apprentice sought brief sanctuary behind the workshops. Hidden by rows of disused lockers he needed time to regain the frame of mind he had begun his day with. His thoughts returned to the absence of John Evans, the chargehand, as well as the toolmaker he had met that morning, both men were so unlike the others he had seen in the factory, and whilst he felt he understood that difference he needed to confirm his belief that some element, some hidden dimension of humanity, existed within the factory. Was every factory the same? He pondered this thought as seriously as all the other concepts that floated inside his head. It was always a duty he imposed on himself to linger on those matters he failed to understand instantaneously. This process occurred often. His thoughts rattled onwards and upwards. They all manufactured goods, machine was king everywhere, of that there could be no doubt. Then it must follow that this was normality wherever the machine operated and they would be around for a very long time. At least as long as men existed to respond to their commands, that is. Such torment could end if robots replaced machines but this was just a dream. Machine was king. No, machine was the pharaoh to the slaves. His mind was a fog. All he knew was that he was no slave and that his days in the factory would be numbered. Perhaps, when the workers in this factory were young men they felt the same and as with his father they just succumbed. One day they just woke up and gave in. But that was too simple. For life, even in one so young, has to be infinitely more complex and rich. *Men and women do not just relinquish their freedom overnight.* In one day he had not relinquished his rights as a human being, but, perhaps, in two years he may feel different. This ridiculous thought passed through his brain. He collected his thoughts as they circled the giant brush that silently watched him and was now to be his regular companion. Then the noise of the factory kidnapped his senses as if to remind him of its overwhelming power. Man and machine. It was clear who held power. This would explain the behaviour of the automatons who had to evolve in the dark shadows cast by the machines. Then this equally ridiculous thought also left his brain.

It was time to survey his environment, time to use the freedom given by Williams. The klaxon wailed out its command that work should halt and as it droned to silence the cataclysmic noise from the machines followed its reluctant progress towards silence in delayed succession. Only the revolving clatter of the giant extractor fans embedded in the walls above the factory could be heard. Human noise again replaced machine noise. The boy saw no use in joining the interminable queue for tea; he was in no state to mix with the factory workers. As the routine of the factory tea ceremony unfolded near the main gangway the toolmaker could be seen making full use of this distraction to walk towards the apprentice, holding an army rucksack tight against his chest.

'I'm sorry about this morning ... I ... was only trying to help ... they always treat me like that ... I ... just ignore it,' he stopped for a moment, 'my mother's made some food, every day,' he looked up towards the roof as if for inspiration, 'it's really nice food, you know. Please have some,' implored the toolmaker.

'No, I'm not really hungry. Thanks anyway,' replied the boy. He genuinely was not in the mood to speak with anyone. 'I think I just want to have some time to myself, Brian, you know how it is,' he said.

'Yes, b ... but I thought you would like to have some company,' insisted Brian Atkins.

It seemed that the toolmaker was much more relaxed and whilst his language was still strained, it appeared more fluent than before. No sooner had he sat down when a delegation could be seen emerging from the drill shop. It was the chargehand, walking with the man who earlier had been spitting abuse at the young boy.

'Union business, now fuck off!' the man barked. Atkins was already packing his sandwiches away, ready to move off.

'Hold on, McCabe,' John Evans interrupted firmly. He tried to catch Atkins but he had gone. He turned to the boy.

'I'm sorry I could not get back to you yesterday,' he said, 'but I've got the form you need to fill in to join the union. This is McCabe, your shop steward.' He pointed to the man at his side. 'He's the convenor for the factory.'

McCabe cut across the chargehand. 'Fill it in,' he ordered, 'I'll sort out your card. Ya still wanna join, don't ya,' McCabe demanded to know.

The boy watched McCabe intently, he also watched the way the toolmaker had fled in fear at the very sight of him.

'All right, John,' the boy was glad to see his mentor again, 'of course I want to join the union,' he said. His eyes looked deep into McCabe's broken face as he spoke.

'Good lad, fill the form in and pass it on to McCabe,' John Evans replied.

McCabe was now returning the boy's glare. The chargehand made his apologies again but promised he would see the boy at dinner hour and as he left the boy thanked him. McCabe stayed.

'Look, stay away from that fuckin faggot Atkins and don't think because he's yer mate' McCabe pointed towards the chargehand as he walked into the distance, 'that he can help ya. I'm warnin ya ... friendly like.'

McCabe swayed threateningly in front of the boy as he spoke, and having made his point he left. The apprentice simply nodded as McCabe made his way to the drill shop, wiping the sweat from his forehead as his giant frame lurched along the gangway. It seemed to the boy that things just got worse in the factory—not better. The thought entered his head as to how men and women could expect McCabe to represent their interests in the factory. He was determined not to give in to any of them and that included both the bosses and the workers if necessary. The action of filling in the union form would be a vital part of this fight-back, or so he thought, and he immediately began work on it. By completing it quickly he thought this would provide a symbol of his determination to be a committed union member. Within minutes the form was filled in and he walked towards the drill shop, where McCabe now sat with a circle of workers around him. He was inviting confrontation.

'Lookin for a new boyfriend, is we?' one of the men shouted.

The boy handed the paper to McCabe and left. Then the klaxon marked his departure. A short silence followed in the workshop until McCabe burst into laughter, calling after the boy, 'Now don't you go callin any strikes now, ya in the union just come and see me if you've gotta problem. I'll sort ya out.'

McCabe stood up on the side of one of the drills, swinging against its bulkhead, shouting louder still, but his noise was now drowned out by the klaxon ordering workers back to their machines. McCabe's entourage laughed approvingly at their leader's display of intimidating ignorance until the klaxon sounded. His gang of drillers swore in unison as they scurried back to their workbenches, displaying no sign other than obedience. The apprentice regained some of his earlier confidence as he strolled away from the drill shop in the full knowledge that he now enjoyed the patronage of

Williams, the supervisor. Patronage equalled privilege and freedom was one of those privileges. He knew this and he knew that he did not have to accept it, just exploit it. Having located his brush the apprentice surveyed his environment for another time as if viewing the rolling hills of some beautiful English county. Left or right? This was his own question. A long gangway lay ahead of him like a corridor of discovery, urging the boy to survey its long forgotten mysteries and lost metallic secrets. He chose left, sweeping ever so gently as he went, making no impact upon the endless trail of filth that lay before all in the factory. The weight of the brush slowed his pace further. Eventually he came upon two large rubber doors hidden from view by the rows of machines that formed the boundary of the drill shop. He swept a mixture of oil, dust and metal to the side of the gangway so that he could push the doors open. This proved harder than he thought as some obstruction blocked them from the other side. Having laid down his brush he squeezed his fingers between the doors, managing to free one of them, and as the door opened a grimy dust poured onto the gangway, covering his boots. The boy screwed his body around the door trying to gain access to the room but his feet became buried in the deep mass of dust that now spewed onto the floor. Eventually he stumbled into the room brush in hand.

Around the edge of the room dust formed piles over one foot deep in places. At its centre a naked light bulb swayed loosely, monitoring the dust as it flew into the air, only to cascade down in dark grey flakes. The source of this disturbance stood immediately beneath the bulb. As the apprentice peered through the grainy mists of the room the figure of a man could be made out bent double over a large slab of cast iron. Two thick rubber hoses ran from a point in the ceiling to a grinding machine that the man cradled in his arms. From where the boy stood it looked as if man and machine were one, connected by thick rubber umbilical cords held high in the fog-laden air. A spaceman lost in the void carrying out vital repairs to his craft, ignoring the wild sparks that flew as he attacked iron with iron. The noise was indescribable. Contained in one steel cell the screech of metal on metal amplified itself beyond mere machine noise—it obliterated the senses. It was a noise that pushed hard against the boy. After some time had passed the man noticed the figure with the brush standing in the middle of the room. He reached to the side of the bench and pushed a large red metal button. The tool dropped almost instantly. And in the descending silence the worker too stopped. Facing the boy, his features could be barely identified as his gloved hands struggled to remove goggles that cut deep into his face. Two clear patches of dirt around the man's eyes were exposed contrasting bleakly with the darker dirt that hid his features from closer inspection. Having laid down his machine the man then removed his oversize leather gloves. The boy waited for the false silence to be broken and continued to watch intently as the little man shrank even further as he shed his protective clothing. He ran his bare hands across the top of the cast metal as if caressing a piece of ancient granite that would soon become the new David.

'Nipples, fuckin nipples,' he mumbled quietly. Aware of his audience, his voice grew louder, 'Never fuckin standard. Could be fuckin anywhere!' he shouted. 'How I am suppos' to fuckin find these fucking nipples if they keep fuckin movin em? Nipples should be fuckin standardised ... in the same fuckin place so that you fuckin know where they fuckin well are,' he complained to no one in particular.

At this point he began to cough uncontrollably, his chest heaving with every hacking bark that fought against his struggle to breathe. Only when he bent over the cast metal before him did his seizure end and with one final cough he cleared his chest as well as the film of dust that rested upon the cast iron. Arching his head forward he spat towards the floor, phlegm now dripped from his mouth as his bare hand cleared his jaw, leaving a glistening patch of wet dirt over his cracked dry skin. The dust had begun to settle and the boy could see more light breaking into the room from the bare bulb above the man's head. The light no longer swayed with the violence of the noise.

'I don't fuckin know how fuckin long I have to fuckin wait before they fuckin fix this fuckin machine,' he told the boy, 'it just keeps fuckin losin power.'

At this point he picked up the rusted grinder and shook it. 'So I've fuckin told them and ... well ... who am I? I could do fuckin thousands of these fuckin casts.'

He threw the machine down against the cast. 'If I had the fuckin right tools ... one of those fuckin modern ones ... that's all ... well ... who am I? Not a fuckin toolmaker, that's fuckin it ... not a fuckin toolmaker ... I'd get me fuckin machine if I was fuckin one of them,' he told himself.

The little man looked up and faintly acknowledged the boy's presence with a direct question as if he had been holding his conversation with him all the time.

'You got my fuckin new machine?' he asked accusingly.

'What's that in yer fuckin hand, is that me new fuckin machine?' he said, screwing his face into the darkness before him, fighting his endless struggle to define the faded shapes that always slowly danced before him. Blindness was creeping up upon him and he dismissed its presence as he did the deadly dust that cut into his lungs each day. Then the boy lost himself in trying to count the number of 'fucks' the man used between each word. As he lost count the man spoke again.

'Never really fuckin accepted, at least not in the sense of having a real fuckin craft.' His hands now rested on the cast metal before him and he looked like he was giving evidence.

'Ask them to do what I do and none of 'em have the skills required. You see, it's engineering craft. None of yer technological tools. They're not real toolmakers ... not like in the old days. How-e-ver ... if you gave them this....'

The man fought to catch his breath when another fit of coughing took its hold. The apprentice went over to a small sink in the corner of the room. He turned the tap, thinking how interesting it was that the last sentence contained no 'fucks'. No water came out. But the man had wrestled himself from this latest spasm after releasing another large chasm of phlegm from his chest that allowed him to continue as if nothing had happened. It was the way he stressed an interlude from the word 'how-e-ver' that made his otherwise aggressive and disconnected conversation seem deeply human. *More human than the rest,* the boy thought to himself. Within seconds the man was speaking normally.

'Now where the fuck did I put that fuckin disc? Sanding fuckin discs should fuckin always be put under the fuckin sanding stool,' his voiced faded into his body.

'How-ev-er ... this is the way things get lost and if I didn't....' His voice then began to trail into the walls that surrounded him, burying themselves under the tiny grains of cast metal that swirled within the room.

He was rambling, incoherent and alone, and yet he spoke as if in conversation with others in the room, even though he was still yet to fully acknowledge the presence of the boy. By now the room seemed much lighter as the dust had been given a rare opportunity to settle and the boy thought that it was little more than a grey dungeon. And as the light gradually imposed its role in the room it was clear now to see that grey was the dominant and only feature the room possessed. Even the raw cast metal had a silvery grey tone. Shapes in the room were shrouded with sheets of grey dust of which the man too was little more than a perfectly sculptured grey shape. The apprentice was immobilised as if he too had turned to stone brought on by the conquest of metal dust that threw itself over everything in the room. What reason could exist for such a condition? As the shrunken human figure in the centre of the room continued to speak to himself, larger particles of dust, unsettled by the silence of the machine, dropped noiselessly from the air like tumbling feathers. This room had long lost its shape; utility and form. This was the power of the factory and its owners to create a reality that imposed itself upon the worker. Work was a function that workers performed. Its shape, noise, dirt or paucity of humanity was unimportant. As long as it was work and, most importantly, work for the bosses. All the worker had to do was to perceive it as the means, or rather their means, to an end. In this sense the work in the factory had no reality; that the work was meaningless. As insignificant as it was backbreaking, numbingly repetitive, filthy and dangerous. It was killing the workers, yet it was still inconsequential. That the work de-humanised and alienated the being from the self was of equal insignificance. Although it imposed a tiredness that no sleep could evade, that no respite existed from, was of no importance. No dignity in this labour of humanity whose only reality was that inflicted by faceless strangers. Those who would not, could not, exist within the prison they created. For its purpose was money. Its reality was money and its justification was profit. And this was killing the worker each time he or she set foot in his workplace no more or less than a volley of bullets from a firing squad. It was the only means to the only end for this class. This class, this working class or underclass. The futile importance of these labels descended upon the apprentice like a mortal wound. . The factory was the reason for their existence. Without the factory you would have no industrial working class. The factory was mother to all their misfortunes.

Profit and power the reality and the reason. The philosophy and the religion that answered all doubts, all questions. For those who still sustained the humanity to question this un-reality it was indeed the most momentous struggle against universal power. They were heroes in a world were servility was king, pain pleasure. In a system that was able to numb and weave a complex mystique capable of drawing a veil upon its own horror. For this was the madness imposed upon the being by the masters who created reality in their own image. To accept in silence so that they might exist to repeat this torment day after day was surrender. Fearful until death that they might disturb their masters to inflict even greater horrors upon them. All so that they might toil for money. Yet within this brutal incarceration, this punishment absent of crime workers fought. Workers fought with a courage without measure. The boy could see the immensity of this struggle but he could not comprehend its magnitude. These thoughts bombarded the boy's mind as he watched the forgotten grey worker before him. The green button was pushed so that the noise and the dust could create the means of his production as well as the means of his own premature death. Nausea overcame the apprentice. But he was still able to reclaim his own thoughts beyond the hatred that he felt. He could move his body to physically escape and running towards the doors his own dust storm altered the terrain left in his wake. Suddenly the noise of the room was replaced by that of the factory, his lips were parched and cracked but it was the deepest of dark sorrows that filled his mind with an unquenchable thirst. At this moment the blinding lights of the factory replaced the darkness that had briefly imprisoned him. Now standing within the factory, its deformed normality restored, he laid his brush to one side and decided to exercise his freedom and wander away from the dangers of the factory and seek the source of its murder.

Chapter Four

There are indeed many precautions to imprison a man in what he is,
as if we lived in perpetual fear that he might escape from it, that he
might break away and suddenly elude his condition.
— Jean-Paul Sartre, *Being and Nothingness*

In the corner of the factory, resting beneath one of the giant extractor fans, the stench of stale urine stole amongst the pollution of the factory and collided with all the senses. The boy's thirst evaporated as he pushed at a thin steel door. Inside, a group of men in the corner of the room were punching and kicking a man. The man was doing little to protect himself. Unnoticed, the boy had entered, trying to at first ignore the violence. He made towards the three sinks that were located on the other side of the toilets. Two men stood by the sinks smoking. The group in the corner turned towards him and the largest of the four men lurched forward. He could see they were McCabe's men.

'What the fuck are you looking at?' one of them said.

'Nothing,' the boy felt obliged to answer.

Pointing to the bundle on the floor, another said, 'This bastard a fuckin bosses lackey and we're not gonna let him fuck things up 'ere and you better take notice. This is what 'appens to twats who try to fuck with us,' the man spat.

These words echoed with a series of thuds that filled the room, then the man on the floor released a deathly groan, the only noise he had made since the boy entered the toilet.

'OK, leave the fucker,' said one of the men stood by the sinks.

Upon this instruction the four men stood back. The smallest member of this group launched one final kick to the man's head and as he recoiled from the thrust of this blow the man's head shuddered against the brick wall of the toilet. The contact of brick with skull was recorded by a sickly dull thud and as the stricken man raised his head the boy could see it was Atkins.

'You've seen nuthin,' one of the attackers screamed at the boy.

Whilst these words were addressed to everyone the driller's stare focused upon the boy and with a motion of his hand he indicated to the others that it was time to leave. Atkins stood up, his eyes, as ever, fixed to the floor. Fumbling in the pockets of his boiler suit he produced a neatly pressed handkerchief with which he began wiping the blood from his face. Walking towards the sinks, he ignored the presence of the boy, maintaining his glance locked to the floor. Standing in front of the sinks he pushed his face against a small, filthy cracked mirror that hung precariously from a large bolt encrusted into the brickwork above. Then with his right hand he turned the single tap that was loosely connected to the sink. Water eased out of the tap and mixed with the oily slime that encased the whole of the sink. Using both hands he tried to salvage as much clean water as he could to wash the blood from his face. In the sink the blood mixed with the oil and water to form a new filth that begrudgingly filtered itself through the open hole at its base, pouring water over the floor. New patterns of filth replaced the old. Atkins bent double over the sink, punching water into his face and hair, and the boy could now clearly see the open wound on the back of the man's head, from which a dark thick red blood oozed.

'Brian, you'll need to get that seen to … it's quite open,' he said as if apologising for the cause of his injuries. Atkins ignored him and pushed his head under the tap and into the thick reddish black ferment that now filled the sink. A stream of blood trickled down on his face and Atkins tried to stem its flow by placing his handkerchief over it. Seemingly satisfied that he had done all he could Atkins stood back from the sink and began brushing the dirt from his overalls. Turning, he left. On the other side of the toilet a cubicle door opened and a youth, no older than the apprentice, appeared.

'Look at that blood,' the young stranger said. 'Atkins asks for it … I think he likes it. Asks for it and then never fights back. That's weird.'

The boy faced the apprentice. 'You're on the brush, aren't you? Been watching you. Three pounds a week and ten shilling for Saturday … you and the rest of 'em must be fuckin stupid … everyone takes the piss outta me … I've got more money than all of them including the fuckin toolmakers,' he muttered, as if stating some historical fact. With his mind still on the events that caused so much damage to Atkins the young apprentice just stood and listened.

'Do you wanna see my wages? Come and look 'ere…. Quickly!' With the motion of a gangster ready to show just how bad he really was the boy stood bolt upright in front of his peer.

'Quickly, hurry up!' he called, poking his face, angelic and innocent as it was, so close that the other boy began arching backwards.

They entered one cubicle. The boy stood on the broken pan of the toilet and told the other to do the same. Reaching up to the cistern he placed his hands inside and drew out four pieces of shining brown metal eight inches long by half and one inch thick which he passed to the other boy, who held it as if it had just been taken from a metal furnace, thrusting it immediately back into the other boy's hands dripping in rust-coloured water.

'Look, arsehole, this is wages. That's about twenty pounds worth. That's over seven weeks wages in this shit hole ... do you wanna join my company or stay with Stevens and Sons and all those other fuckin deadbeats?'

The apprentice nodded to the rhythmic tirade that the other boy beat directly into his face.

'Fine, that's right. I knew you had more sense,' the apprentice nodded uncontrollably. 'It's you and me against those shits, I need you and you'll soon realise how much you need me.'

The nods came fast and furious to the beat of the other boy's words.

'You're a copper robber now,' the youth confirmed like a priest would smoothing the altar cloth before the axiomatic transformation of bread and wine. The words rolled into one another to the beat of the boy's laughter.

'That's what you and I do and the beauty of it is that fuckin brush,' he stated as he stole huge clouds of breath.

'It's the key to the door, every door. It's the key to the stores.' He laughed. 'It's where I started, on the brush.' The boy was patting the apprentice on the back as if congratulating him.

'I'm in the drill shop now and I hate every minute of it. But you and me, we're soul brothers.' He grabbed the boy's fist. 'It's the beauty of the brush, you're no one, the lowest of the low, but you,' he corrected himself, 'I mean you and me, well we can be the richest bastards in the place. Just make sure that the stores are kept spotlessly clean.' He laughed at his own irony and all the other boy could do was nod.

'But don't get too greedy. Take as much as you can, put it in the cistern and make sure you don't block the thing up. I'll sort the rest out.' He stopped talking and looked around the room.

'On Friday we'll both go to the scrap yard and get paid,' he told the boy as he looked deeply into the face of his newly recruited conspirator.

'I'm Hasaan,' he proclaimed. 'Welcome to Hasaan and Brothers' Company Ltd. You're gonna be the richest fuckin brusher-up there's ever been,' he pronounced. Then he looked into the boy again.

He had only half listened. But the explanation of the principles of theft that the black boy had enunciated were agreeable enough. He told him his name and in that instant had signed up to a life of crime. That was the way he was brought up to understand it, but he just wanted to be free of any further distraction. The distant look that now hung from the boy's face like a steel mask bothered the other boy.

'Look! Don't be goin all principled on me,' Hasaan said. 'Don't you listen?' He leant further into the boy's face. 'They're the fuckin thieves. You should be a little bit more proud and confident of yer socialism,' he confirmed as if assured of his legal rights in this matter.

The apprentice felt comforted by this and acted as if he had understood the subtlety of his analogy.

'You and me,' he said philosophically, 'well,' he seemed to be examining the concept of the unity of two beings, 'well, we're just redistributin the wealth,' he said, 'no more no less.'

Hasaan now ventured into the field of philosophical imperatives with a vengeance, as if to test both the young apprentice and his own ability to conclude legitimacy between theft and honesty. Clearly, he had no doubts regarding this premise as his earlier agitation replaced itself with a calm and wisdom that excelled his years.

'You know McCabe?' he asked.

The apprentice nodded.

'Everyone knows McCabe, he's a bad bastard. Stay away from him and don't interfere with his business. He's got more power than the boss. Than Stevens himself. He runs the place. I'm warning you now, don't get involved.' The boy stopped as if considering the next words to use.

'He suppos' to be for the workers. He ain't!' Hasaan allowed for a further brief silence to rest between him and the apprentice.

'Now that's what I call dishonesty,' he concluded emphatically.

Both of them where still perched on the toilet when the elder boy indicated the need to climb over the cubicle, leaving the door to the toilet locked whilst they exited by the other two broken doors separately.

'See ya,' the boy called and he was gone.

Within seconds the apprentice was left alone in the toilet, his eyes and mind transfixed on the blood-splattered sink before him. For him the priority was to escape, to locate his brush, to seek solace, to retrieve some normality from the madness that now encroached his every waking minute in the factory. Work was not the freedom he thought it would be. It had stolen his friends and imposed a loneliness of individuality. His personal confidence was drained by the all-enveloping dominance of the factory. His normal state of being had been evaporated by fear. Strangled in the twisted embrace of the factory.

Time had swept by, he was hungry and the drone of the factory siren reminded him of his condition. Before the siren completed its wail, before the extraction fans had grinded to a stop, he ran to join the exodus of workers as they raced from the factory floor to the works canteen. He wanted to eat, above all else he wanted a change of scenery. He melted into the confusion and momentarily he was lost in the crowd as it advanced towards the canteen, where the tumult of the machines was replaced by an empty noise that marched with the workers. They kept their own regimented lines that so disciplined their movement throughout the factory. The canteen itself was no less a part of the factory than the drill shop or the metal cutting shop. A large bleak hall whose controlled design imposed its discipline on all who entered. Tables replaced machines in a vast expanse of horizontal and vertical lines bordered by paint below and fluorescent lights above. It was a cynical facsimile of the factory as if to proclaim that no escape or respite existed. From all according to the factory to all belonging to the factory. Cigarette smoke replaced the emissions from the machines the dust and filth were there as if by necessity. Knives, forks, plates and screamed communications confirmed an absolute dependency on noise that hid the fear of silence. The silence that might invoke a serenity to communicate as humans beyond immediate basic instincts and towards a shared experience. Whose very conclusion may challenge the existence of the factory. Oh yes, this entire building was a marvel of control architecture, a monument, a celebration of the power of capital, of the owner over the worker. Its physical proclamation of power quietly complementing its psychological power. The boss invested as much in this process as in the pursuit of profit. Profit was inexorably linked to control, they both needed each other, fed off each other, pursued each other.

As in the factory the canteen's noise rose and fell in violent bursts and the noise came to be soporific to the worker who gained comfort from its invasion. And for peace perhaps they all surrendered to it. Thus, with everything reduced to its base level, it came as no surprise to the boy that human behaviour, even away from the factory floor, had been reduced to the satisfaction of immediate needs at any cost. Each worker surviving as best they could. Obscenity and personal abuse for some had become the language of interaction, not only on the factory floor but also in the canteen, and again this hatred was their gift to the younger workers, women workers, the weak or the different. Women cooked and prepared food for the workers in the most primitive and unhygienic of circumstances and they were double victims of the bosses' inequity and their fellow workers' failure to comprehend the mechanics of their condition. Each worker seemed to have their own insult to offer the kitchen staff carried upon the venom of their own brutal cowardice as if by these actions they were expressing their own vacuous power over others. But it was all performed in the sickly name of humour—a bit of fun. A humour that helped them survive but nevertheless a humour they felt covered their actions. Within time this humour became impossible to identify—were they joking or being serious? In the end it did not matter. The factory managed to brutalise even the faintest human connection.

Language and behaviour had been replaced by the urgent need to satisfy instant demands and this process of collective debasement appeared only momentarily relieved by the rare interruption of those workers who conducted themselves with respect for others as if compensating for the behaviour of their fellow inmates. More often than not they were pushed or jostled along the queue. For their part the female canteen workers could respond for themselves but no reason existed why they should be subjected to such treatment whilst they worked. It was known that many of them would be treated with equal brutality at home, often by the very same men thus doubling the iniquity. The young apprentice lost his appetite together with his wish to mix with his fellow workers. He caught sight of McCabe holding court in the centre table of the canteen surrounded by the four men who had earlier been attacking Atkins. For a moment he felt McCabe's stare as if he was expected to pay homage at the table of a great leader.

The silence of the factory floor was sparsely punctuated by the repetitive scrape of the ventilation fans upon their wire mesh housing. All the fluorescent lights had been switched off, allowing elements of natural light to filter kaleidoscopes of faintly coloured beams across the length of the building like watercolours flushing gently over clouded landscapes. As rain hammered against the glass ramparts of the factory rhythm mixed with imagery, settling a calmness without possibility in such a place. The young apprentice wondered at the magnificence of the metamorphosis from factory to art-house, he knew it was possible, anything was possible, if only a person knew how to discover it. From the raised gangway where the boy now stood this effortlessly coloured cloak bathed not a factory but a gothic cathedral. And this was a moment in which the boy felt forced to respect the power of 'it' with its chameleon physical and psychological imprints that shimmered magically to dance secretly in the absence of the workers. To dance unseen in its vast emptiness. Such a realisation was not weakness—this recognition was part of the process of identifying the complex power relations in the factory. Not just unquestioned, but legitimised power, because it was their right to have power, they deserved their right to control, a divine right that reflected in the magnificence of religious architectural metaphors. His mind wandered. Descending the raised metal gangway, the young apprentice appeared content to walk the factory floor and bathe in the light and ghostly sounds that breathed through the dirt-encrusted glass roof of this giant facility. By the time he had reached the floor of the factory clear sunlight glistened over large cross sections of the plant, fading in and out. In the far corner of the factory a small group of workers were huddled together.

Chapter Five

He has no respect for capitalist property, because he recognises that that property is the fruit of past robbery of the workers. He has still less respect for it when he discovers that it is a means for robbing him in the present; robbing him not merely of material wealth, but robbing him of his manhood.
—W.M.Gallacher and J.R.Campbell. *Direct Action* (1919)

This was a grouping like no other he had encountered in the factory. Whilst they shared some obvious connection this physical link was disconnected and casual with each man seemingly preoccupied in his own activity. Two men were competing against each other to fill in elements of a newspaper crossword puzzle reluctantly complimenting each other as they absent-mindedly unwound the clues. Once a clue could be answered mutual satisfaction was exchanged without any real communication as though the passage of time had replaced this need. It being enough simply to know and move on to the next clue and amidst such mutuality a friendship forged through endurance could be perceived. The largest figure in this grouping sat bolt upright, staring straight ahead, listening intently to any movement or noise within the gathering like a giant beacon. A radar with its detection that configured participation, locating the sparks of softly traded contact. This man wore a large leather apron covered with holes of varying sizes that seemed to hold the deep coarse brown fabric together. The smallest member of this group, dressed in blue overalls, was Frank O'Toole. He stood, with one foot resting on a large steel anvil, his body bent over as his arms rested on his raised knee. He conducted this gathering. He was a welder.

As in a painting, with studiously structured subjects, invisible signs forced the eye to recognise elements of perspective and substance. In the artist's representation this small figure was the central character of the portrait. The men so far identified were old men, the only young worker in this framed gathering sat eating his sandwiches, listening and watching as if his very existence also depended upon soaking up every nuance, every gesture, every word. It was Hasaan. Being one of the very few black workers in the factory

61

and one committed to the study of theft, his involvement seemed contradictory. Nevertheless, he sat in silent expectation like the rest. Now the central character could be observed outlining some complex theory underlined by the movement of his hand, a look of concern, a scratch of the nose. Even from a distance our young apprentice could detect the control this man in blue overalls had over his audience. John Evans, the chargehand, was also a member of this group, although his presence had not been detected by his young charge. Clearly seasoned in the art of sophistry, O'Toole continued to talk, or rather communicate. Whilst welcoming the young apprentice to the gathering. How he did this was difficult to describe, for this was his art, it may have been a knowing look, a slight raising of the eyes, a dusting of his knee. Whatever it was everyone knew that it was a welcome to the intruder. A sign that this stumbled guest was no threat. The narrative suffered no damage through this momentary distraction as the boy smiled and squeezed in next to the chargehand without disturbance. O'Toole suffered no interruption at any of his sermons despite the nonsense he spoke.

'So,' he said with that anguished look of someone pained by the very existence of his own life in a world that offered him little compassion or understanding.

'The toolmakers think they're the aristocracy of labour in this plant,' he complained, 'the highest-paid as well as the highest status. That seems to be generally accepted, but we have to ask ourselves at what price this has been achieved. They don't particularly earn that much more than a lathe operator. If you compare them with our friend here....' O'Toole paused. At this point the talking hands of the little man in blue overalls opened as if to embrace the recently arrived apprentice. The welder adopted the confidence of a priest beckoning late arrivals to enter church. He asked and answered his own questions. This seemed to make it better for all concerned as no questions were ever asked.

'Yes, better paid,' he continued seamlessly. 'But examine the pressure they are under,' he suggested. 'No, they should be the vanguard of this factory if only because when they speak, in the unwritten chaos of this place, the majority would listen and follow them because they actually believe that the toolmakers are the bosses on the factory floor. But they're only the lackeys of the boss. They're as much to blame as Stevens ... they're his vanguard, not ours.'

A moment was now allowed by blue overalls for all to reflect upon his words. The boy was impressed by the words and he looked over to Hasaan, nodding his approval. Hasaan shook his head. In reality no one in this group held any solidarity with the welder or his words.

'Four across, yes, that's it,' interrupted one of the men doing the crossword. The speaker relaxed his persona to display his indignation at this clear lack of concentration upon his words. The puzzlers looked puzzled, so, in a very professional manner, he wasted no words on the two men.

'The sooner we realise that we all need each other in here the better,' he paused, as if waiting for applause. Then he continued with his act.

'The fact is that the majority of men are, by their own inaction and subservience, weak compared to the women who have more militancy than any section in the whole of this factory. Well, this of itself doesn't take much but they are, just look at the metal shop cutting room.' His arms pointed meaninglessly toward the cutting shop.

'They're big women in more ways than one and they stand up to the foremen, the supervisors and to Johnson himself. Only the other day they had them all down from the office. Why? Not because they met production targets but because they purposefully decided not to meet any of them. We all know it's one of the hardest jobs in the factory and the men proved they could not hold this job down especially when it came to the accuracy of the cut, they were useless. They couldn't do the job. They also couldn't cope with the danger involved in operating that guillotine. So they stopped work because of a problem, it doesn't matter what the problem was, what matters is that they stopped and this affected the whole of the factory's production. It was as simple as that.'

At this juncture the little man clicked his fingers, causing some in his small audience to look up immediately as if entranced by the content and delivery of his oration. Misled into believing that they were entranced, he continued. The boy was, unfortunately, transfixed—this was what he wanted to hear. The man in the blue overalls was the one who could deliver a challenge. *Deliver a revolution?* the boy thought. He nodded his agreement and this pleased the welder. Encouraged he continued.

'What could they do to replace them? Not with men anyway, more importantly not with women because unlike men they stick together,' he stressed.

The two men, who had continued with their crossword throughout, looked up and interrupted simultaneously. 'Is that why they always go the toilet together?'

Without any hint of anger the speaker continued.

'The bond of men treating them like dirt at home and work unites them and they all know this because they all experience the same things. Nothing complicated in this, nothing too difficult for even the most stupid to understand and it's that unity that gives them the confidence to be the real vanguard in this factory but the men could never accept this, let alone comprehend it,' he complained.

'Frank,' John Evans leant forward on his bench to interrupt the welder, 'I don't disagree with you,' he said, 'we have a union in this place that destroys any hope of unity. You know as well as I do that the root of the problem is McCabe and his cronies protecting the bosses' interests at all costs against those of the workers and you're involved in all that.' He seemed to accuse the welder. The apprentice could not understand this criticism, this attack. For the first time blue overalls looked unsure, uncertain as to how he should continue, and he looked towards John Evans as if some embarrassing personal problem had been exposed. Silence was used to ignore the point. The moment passed. The boy thought he had answered the question skilfully.

'We have to look to ourselves first. Look at us. In this factory we are just as important as the toolmakers, we control small individual processes that are vital to production.' O'Toole's voice drained slowly towards a distracted silence as he began to look around himself.

At this point in the discussion, as if the listeners knew from bitter experience that the conversation was about to descend into the repetition of a line of argument that they had been subjected to on far too many occasions, the group stood in unison and made their excuses to leave. The young apprentice was amazed by how people could react in such spontaneity without any prompting, as if they had been willing members of a ritual that had to conclude at a precise moment in time. John Evans turned to the apprentice and smiled and by the movement of his arm indicated that he wanted the boy to walk with him. As the room cleared the boy turned to observe the welder in his blue overalls as he sat down on his anvil and began opening a metal sandwich box, unconcerned by the instant dispersal of his audience. Unperturbed in his solitude.

It was to be a grand tour of this part of the factory that Evans had in mind for the boy. For in this corner of the factory the small workshops delivered specialised skills and materials to the larger plant. Each workshop had its clearly defined area of influence marked casually by metal boards, wooden pallets or steel fabricated screens no doubt erected by these craftsmen a long time ago to indicate their own individual spheres of authority. So haphazard were these units that they contravened the white lines and lights that imposed control elsewhere in the factory. A shantytown for artisans. But still the emphasis of defined spaces had been made even to the uninitiated. It was an unofficial hierarchy that found expression in this area basking in the false freedom given by the boss to this section. Only so long as it improved efficiency, increased profits and succumbed ultimately to the power of the boss would this semblance of individuality, of independence from the factory, be ignored. Under such guidelines, and this went for no other area of the factory, like some factory within a factory, it would be allowed its phoney freedom. This was just another contradiction. Another falsehood to perpetuate the power of the employer. What power it was to instil in humans the belief that they were free, that they had some element of free expression and yet be able still to sustain slavish control. Even the apprentice did not need this phenomenon to be explained to him. Nevertheless, the chargehand attempted to explain the hypocrisy. The boy cut him short, albeit respectfully, so that the point could be arrived at that much quicker.

'So you can see it? It really is pathetic but if you pointed it out, if you exposed this tragic farce, they would look at you like you've just landed,' he confirmed.

'But why do they do it, why do they blank it out?' the boy asked, knowing that no answer existed.

The chargehand stopped for a moment, as if deep in thought. 'Because they want to.'

Perhaps that's what it is, thought the boy.

A longer silence followed this definitive observation. Even the boy had not arrived at this conclusion. Then the chargehand dug deep into his pockets and presented the boy with a small book and an old union badge.

'They belonged to my son and I would like you to have them,' he said, changing the subject quickly.

The young apprentice did not know what to say but he was grateful for the gift and immediately pinned the badge on his overall. He knew the significance of the both the badge and the union book, a history of the syndicalists in the 1900s. It was a history he absorbed at home from his father and his friends. Nothing more was said. Nothing needed to be said, for this history was taken as everyone's inheritance. The chargehand took the young apprentice outside the workshops to a small lean-to shed made of bricks with a cast iron corrugated roof. This building had no door and was open to the elements at both ends. Two huge vats that the boy thought contained water straddled the centre of the floor, measuring approximately 8 foot in length by 4 foot in width.

'Hullo John, is that you?' a man asked.

'Daniel, I've brought a friend to see you,' John Evans replied.

Daniel was huge, with a shock of curly red hair and a beard, and the apprentice recognised him as the one with the leather apron who had taken part in the workshop discussion group. Daniel continued to sit in the far corner of his shed eating his sandwiches.

'Just tell our young friend what you do here please, Daniel,' John Evans said carefully.

The man in the corner sat bolt upright and began to explain that he dipped cast and other metals in the vats of acid before him. This was his job and no one else's.

'It splashes no matter how careful you are, it just splashes and the acid burns, but I'm not bothered, you see, it's how you handle the metal. It's as simple as that,' he concluded in total disinterest.

By this time the man was standing, leaning over the two vats of sulphuric acid, staring into the blank sheen that covered the surface, mumbling to himself as if the attention of his two visitors had already been lost. Both men looked towards each other, unfolded their arms and said they would meet up later. Without any further discussion the chargehand and the boy left quietly. John Evans threw a glance over his shoulder.

'Did you breathe in the air?' he asked.

The boy nodded.

'It's his punishment for being a union leader and it's killing him. That man is dying. Each day he comes to work he kills himself, or rather the work kills him,' he said as if the thought of stopping to explain would lead him into other explanations that would simply take a lifetime. They had now re-entered the main part of the workshops and were walking towards a small rectangle room whose open access was sealed by a metal cage. Inside a man sat eating at a cutting machine, wiping what looked like sawdust from the surface and blowing it onto his sandwich each time a piece came near his mouth. Evans and the boy stood outside the cage whilst the man gestured towards them.

'John, you all right, me old mate?' the man said falsely.

Again it was one of the workshop audience returned to his workplace to finish his dinner. And the boy began to think if this was some sort of elite work group who had been granted a pardon so that they could work for the boss independently of all the others in the factory. His cell, for this is what it clearly was, housed large pieces of brown plastic sheets covering a wooden resin. As the man was talking John Evans whisperd to the boy that the man's job was to cut pieces of board and he explained that this substance was carcinogenic and that its dust was lethal. Under his breath like a father to a son at the local zoo he tried to explain what was happening. He tried to explain the exhibit.

'Look at the ways he blows the stuff around,' he whispered. 'He's locked in because the stuff is so expensive and the management have told him not to let anyone in to his prison so he thinks this is an indication of just how important he is. He is another one killing himself but he's actually doing it for the boss. The ultimate sacrifice.'

John Evans turned to the boy. 'It's not just that but it's the fact that he enjoys doing it. He feels valued, he feels some worth, a purpose, because the boss leaves him alone just so long as he delivers the product on time and with no damage to this costly raw material.'

As the chargehand spoke the man in the cage continued speaking but the content was inconsequential and meaningless deserving to be ignored and whilst this seemed too abrupt for the boy he silently accepted that no other alternative really existed. The two observers moved on, returning to the welding shop where the small lecturer now stood alone.

'John, you were very edgy today. Think you're getting a bit too cynical,' O'Toole said.

'I'm not cynical,' Evans argued, 'just realistic. I don't think you realise what's happening here,' he said, 'all the talk in the world can't alter this … it's beyond solution … at least the solution you speak about and you know it.'

O'Toole looked hard into his eyes. 'No, you've forgotten your communist upbringing,' the welder replied, 'the Party would never sanction such defeatism. Look,' he said firmly, 'it's goin well, won't be long now, we'll show this boss the power of labour.' He smiled to himself, assured of his infallibility. 'It's all in the crisis of capital, you should know that, far too cynical. No room for defeatism, John, at least that's what I always say.' O'Toole leaned forward on his anvil.

John Evans appeared ready to mount an argument and it was clear to his young associate that he was angry but it was an anger that went far beyond what the welder had said—it was an anger weighed down by the burden of past experiences. Past betrayals. The boy could determine this much. At that moment the factory siren wailed out its order for work to restart and the chargehand continued to stare at the welder. The welder's response wrapped itself within a sickly smile of contentment—the contentment of not ever having to consider that he may be wrong. Perhaps it was this last thought that John Evans found so unacceptable. For a moment it seemed as though he was about to fight with the welder. The siren brought him back and the chargehand looked at the boy with an equally manufactured smile. O'Toole nodded to himself, satisfied with his thoughts and actions.

'Look, I'll catch up with you later. I wanted to ask what you felt about the workshops. Better still, let's just finish off at the sheet metal cutter, the girls will just bc starting up,' he said.

John Evans had recaptured his composure and now appeared happy to take the apprentice to the cutting room as if some answer, some sanity, could be discovered that would erase the memory of the last half-hour. Five women worked on this huge machine, which was effectively a guillotine some ten feet in length, used mainly to cut large sections of sheet metal prior to their final process of bending into the various box shapes into which the component parts of electrical switchgear would be assembled.

'John, what were you doing over there?' one of the women shouted, 'what's the politburo issuing today?' she asked.

'Is the revolution gonna begin in the tool shop or is McCabe bringin the bosses out on strike?' another woman cut in.

'What the fuck do you waste your time with them for?' She continued. 'They're the class traitors and you know it. God, I thought you had more sense, haven't you learnt your lesson yet?' she asked directly, perhaps not expecting a reply. John Evans smiled without reply.

All the women wore turbans and this gave to them an air of mystery, an air of foreign rebellion. The apprentice liked the look. The message they sent out clearly was one that fundamentally contradicted their environment. The woman who spoke first was clearly the leader of this group. Both man and boy flirted in this company but in a modest way and the women reciprocated with equal modesty, but this was their territory and they were in command.

'Norma, I was just showing the boy around the workshops, seeing the men. He has got to meet them some time,' John Evans said.

'The men! Well, that's what you might call them,' the woman replied.

'There's not a man in this factory except yourself and we lost you a long time ago. When are you gonna come back to us?' she asked pointedly. The boy was confused by this coded conversation.

'You know it's not as simple as that,' he said. 'Anyway, can I just introduce the lad here?'

'We know him,' she said, 'and he'll end up like the rest.'

'Hold on, you can't judge everyone,' said John Evans.

'Let's see then,' the woman abruptly concluded the conversation to the clear embarrassment of the boy.

Nevertheless, he introduced the apprentice to the women and the youngest stole a hard glance in his direction. The other women made light of this contact, pushing both the boy and the girl against the bulkhead of the giant guillotine. Whilst everywhere in the factory the klaxon had been obeyed these women appeared a law unto themselves and no one bothered them. Even the apprentice realised that if this was in the drill shop Williams would be screaming orders for work to commence, echoed by McCabe as he imposed his authority. But the women showed no inclination to start work. At least not until they were ready. At the moment they were talking. Addressing the older woman, whilst respectfully acknowledging the presence of the other three women, John Evans asked if they could show the young boy how they worked.

'Is that all he wants to see? Pathetic,' she added.

'He brings a good-lookin lad over and all he wants to see is a gang of women cutting metal. Is that what we've become? We're not part of this fuckin machine, ya know. We've got feelings.' The woman nodded towards her friends. 'Aven't we, girls?' she asked. 'Well, if that's all the boy wants to see then fine,' she said, beckoning to the group. 'Only once, mind you, can't have him getting too excited. Can we, girls?'

What followed was a pantomime. A copy of the supreme interface of man—or in this case, woman—and machine re-enacted with all the profitable precision that capital demands. The perfect match of human and mechanical labour. An expression of perfect capital, as with so much else in the factory, in all its horror. The optimum exploitation. But this was an act of mockery in the face of all that. Whilst the women moved in symmetry with commodity and machine they conducted themselves with some degree of human independence. This was not their being as part of the productive process, this was them performing a function which they hated. These women, far from being appendages of the machine, appendages of the boss, these women, by the way they carried out their function, did so in a statement of liberation. They accentuated all their moves and performed with a degree of syncronicity that only experience and skill could bestow. Two women left the group and went to a stack of sheet metal measuring ten feet square. With gloved hands the two women lifted the razor thin sheet and as it bent in the middle they used its own action as a pivot to swing one end of the metal onto the machine's bulkhead. At this precise moment two other women lifted the other end of the sheet, making it horizontal with the blade of the guillotine. Measuring the cutting length required against a yardstick attached to the side of the machine, all four women ensured that the metal was square with the blade. The young girl now stepped forward and, with her back to the machine casting a glance in the direction of the apprentice, quickly elbowed the large green button into action. Following this instruction the machine crashed down in immediate and quick succession with a metal safety guard that protected the blade from human contact. Instantaneously, the blade roared down, cutting the metal cleanly. The five women made a line and bowed towards the men as a large section of cut metal crashed to the floor.

Throughout this performance the chargehand had stood with his arms folded, occasionally raising a hand to scratch his chin but smiling and clearly enjoying the company of the women as they went through their show no doubt not for the first time nor the last. Both bowed in mock respect. Moving towards the women the boy wanted to show some interest in them as people but found himself referring to the machine as if that had more life in it, and his words made no sense because they conveyed some automatic respect to the metal as opposed to the workers.

'Norma, this must be really dangerous,' he stammered.

The five women looked at the boy and the youngest stepped forward bowed again and as she rose she pulled off her oily red turban to uncover a head of blond hair cut short around what the boy had already thought was a beautiful face. With a grave look at the boy she declared, 'Only if you bang your elbow.'

The boy thought she was magnificent. Beautiful. The whole group roared with laughter, then the women set about pushing and grabbing at the apprentice, who was by now beside himself in pleats of laughter whilst he tried to dodge the amorous advances of the women. Quite forgetting where he was, he turned to run but caught sight of Williams storming down the central alleyway. In the distance he saw the factory, its machines and workers; its noise, stench and filth pulled at him like a siren of the seas. But he was on an island and it was a different Williams that sailed towards them. Not the one that deals with the men. The women knew this and made no attempt to pretend, as the men would do, to be working. Unlike the men they stood their ground.

'John, can I speak, bit of a job breakin out,' said the supervisor quietly. He turned to the boy, 'Go find yer brush, lad, OK,' he said, smiling.

Williams was efficient in his words and actions and his manner rolled above the tumult of the factory like a calming wave. Even the hand gesture did not precede the customary 'OK'. This was a man achieving normality. In this instance silence was revolt and after a long pause the chargehand bid his farewells to the women and the boy walking with Williams, examining a blueprint that the foreman had passed into his hands. As the couple left the women gave out a shriek of laughter. The young girl was fixing her turban and told the boy that she might see him later. The boy's heart raced ahead of him. The women did not return to work, preferring to look down the factory at the bleak furore that had by now recaptured the factory. Like a battlefield viewed from some hidden promontory. For his part the apprentice decided, after having reminded himself, that it was time to steal copper. It was time to rob the robbers, and to do this he needed his brush. For this was his passport to freedom. It no longer mattered what people thought or said, the brush had acquired a status of its own. A magical friend that made him invisible. He waved farewell to the women and 'brushed' his way towards the stores. In the centre of the factory stood a secure cage that housed all the expensive raw materials and equipment needed in the factory, including its most expensive metal, copper. At the gate to the cage the storekeeper kept guard. Another small man intent, like the rest, to impose his absolute necessity to the great scheme of things that was the factory. He examined every docket, every plan, every inquiry with scrupulous detachment, all this the boy assumed. The brush approached the gate, followed by its young apprentice thief.

'Hold on?' a voice called.

The boy looked at the man, then looked towards his brush, this was his docket, not too much detail but still a pass to gain entry. For the storekeeper it was just another responsibility that only he could deal with. After all, this was why he was the storekeeper and no one else. Ignoring the boy, he too looked at the brush as if it would speak and make the necessary official requests for stores or tool bits. None came.

'You'd better shape up,' he said joylessly 'I'm expecting some very important jobs this afternoon.'

The brush entered the stores, followed closely by the young apprentice, and an unknown world opened up to him. A jungle of steel neatness whose metal leaves hung delicately upon branches of iron. The boy swept the narrow alleyways of the cage, searching the contents of the metal boxes that rose up from the floor like steel skyscrapers. Each item was clearly marked like a forensic catalogue waiting for the moment when their particular specimen would be needed. He wondered at the remarkable system of classification that covered the tiniest screw to the largest bolt. Every piece had its own identity with sub-classifications, clearly marked, no matter what the complexity. '1 inch by quarter metal drill, left hand thread,' he read each carefully scripted label, '1 inch by quarter metal drill right hand thread … 1 inch by quarter flat nose … 1 inch by quarter round nose … 1 inch by quarter brass drill bit,' the list was as comprehensive as it could possibly be. An industrial archive of nuts and bolts. A Leviathan of worker's control developed beyond form or reason. A celebration of skill and human intelligence beyond anything the production process could impose. So the boy thought about this wonderful display as his hands and eyes explored in wonderment. His respect for the storekeeper increased in proportion to each new filing discovery he made as he pursued his search for the copper ingots amongst the regimented rows of metal shelving. Even the writing that underlined the title given to each item was in a thick rich copper plate hand flowing majestically like quiet tendrils hanging in the air.

Eventually, the apprentice became aware that whilst the filing system was extraordinarily concise and detailed it did not provide the casual visitor with the necessary legend to locate specific items. This information, this knowledge had been withheld by the storekeeper in an effort to maintain control, for no one could enter this metal maze without first asking the storekeeper exactly where the tool, raw material or part was located. In this system only the storekeeper could inform the customer of any location. The boy smiled to himself at this further piece of self-preservation created by a worker intent on making himself invaluable to his employer. It stopped the boy from asking where the copper was so that he may steal it. But in the furthest corner of the store he discovered his treasure. A whole section devoted to copper. This library of precious metal distracted the boy, he thought only one length existed, the stealing length. As the craftsman would search for the finest detail of machined raw material with a gentle care our young apprentice rattled through the boxes of copper with ignorant speed as he rifled for the length that would fit in his trousers. All this time, perhaps through nerves, he joked quietly to himself, 'I only want the fuckin robbin' size.' Keeping a wary eye against the company spies, and for him this would mean everyone, with the exception of the chargehand, his black friend and the girl in the cutting shop, he marvelled at just how heavy even a small piece of this glistening copper could be. He eventually found the right length and width of copper for theft, 8 inches by ¼. Guilt turned his head and as he looked around he was startled to see the face of Brian, the toolmaker, pushed hard up against the outer metal cage that surrounded the stores. The blood had dried on his face but the hollow look he gave the boy only served to highlight the bruised swelling around his eyes and mouth. It was the face of a corpse, and its sudden appearance gave the boy an instant shock.

'What are you doing?' he whispered as if he was the thief and not the boy in the cage.

'Look, Brian, I'm redistributing the wealth,' he said.

'No, you're wrong and you know it. You'll,' his voice blocked, 'you'll get caught,' the toolmaker said abruptly.

Without any further communication he turned and left. The apprentice had made up his mind and nothing was going to deter him. Perhaps even the toolmaker understood this. Whatever was the truth, guilt, as normal, began to consume the boy. But it did not stop him. He quickly placed six pieces of copper around his waist, tying them in with his belt, then covering the evidence with his overalls. With the copper weighing down against his slight frame the boy followed his brush to the gate of the stores.

'Where's the rubbish?' the storekeeper asked with an air of inevitability that was not lost on the boy.

'I bet you've just brushed it under the shelving?' he said as if he had released the sentence time and time again to other 'apprentices' over the last three decades.

'It was clean, it didn't need sweeping,' the boy said innocently. 'You should have told me,' he said.

His guilt exposed itself and he thought the man saw this and for those important seconds he froze, awaiting his punishment. Unknown to him, the man did know. But he chose not to act. This was his freedom.

The boy began to see the librarian and not the storekeeper in the man. He even spoke like one. As he turned to make a speedy exit one of the pieces of copper moved. He leant forward as if to check a vital component on his brush and amidst the general distraction of the factory made his way to the toilet, the cistern and the redistribution of wealth. As he entered this stinking brick and steel hut attached to the outside wall of the factory one of the drill shop workers pushed past him. The boy thought nothing of this. Then events moved in quick succession as his crime threatened punishment and it made his heart pound like the criminal he had become. He had not worked all day, yet the filth from the factory had fused to his body. The features of his face were shadowed with deep black lines and curves whilst his hair stuck fast to his head in random clumps. Was this his punishment? His thoughts swam with his other 'crimes' and he swallowed hard to hold back an eruption of vomit. Was this guilt or just the fumes of human excrement and urine that smothered him? He gave up thoughts as he caught his reflection in the grim laden toilet mirror. His cracked reflection in the broken toilet mirror carved disparate features that aged the young apprentice the more he studied his uneven image. Water flowed putrid and slow from the single tap where Atkins had attempted to clean the wounds on his head a few hours earlier. That same congealed blood mixed with the dirty water from the tap as it leaked towards the sink. A bucket of green sludge filled a paint tin that was used by a few workers who attempted to clean themselves at the end of work. Razor sharp filings had been slipped into the cleaning agent and as the boy washed he slashed his hands and face. And in these quick instant moments he knew what was happening yet he persisted until a slow reality began to measure his pain. Blood red slits opened around his face and hands.

It was near the end of the day and a number of workers from the drill shop entered the toilet standing behind the boy. The contents of the paint tin had been especially prepared for him as part of an initiation ceremony, a right of passage, a deformed ritual which had become the unspeakable norm for all new factory workers. A normality that superimposed the brutality of employment as an aspect of tradition, pride in one's work, the need to signify some transfer from one to the next, a graduation to the darkness of these satanic mills. Some element of humour had, so it is said, a crucial role in this barbarity with tales handed down and across local factories recorded with the zeal of a job well done. The apprentice was initiated at the precise moment when McCabe entered the toilet. This finale of this brutal attack upon him lasted fifteen minutes. It was enough time for him to be stripped, beaten, covered in metallic soap and human excrement. With much satisfaction of another job well done, of proud traditions upheld, of present respecting past, the room emptied. Throughout this initiation McCabe stood and watched. He called his dogs on and he called his dogs off. Now the boy was a real factory worker. Naked and injured he slowly dressed himself and walked out of the factory, ignoring the klaxon, the clocking off and the '*running to the exit tradition'*. The apprentice removed himself from the scene burdened with a weight of guilt that contradicted his entire condition. A mass of ragged stinking cuts. Seeking refuge in obscurity and silence. The journey home held no events to be remembered. Some of the workers recognised the tell-tale signs of factory initiations, and whatever thoughts they held they hid them from each other in shamed silence. The routine scrubbing preceded the seclusion of his bedroom that excused any involvement with his family. Despite his initiation he was still not one of them, and this anger became his strength.

Chapter Six

But the animals outside gazed at the scene, it seemed to them that some strange thing was happening.... No question, now, what had happened to the faces of the pigs. The creatures outside looked from pig to man, and from man to pig, and from pig to man again; but already it was impossible to say which was which.

—George Orwell, *Animal Farm*

All the workers, it seemed like all of them, hated Atkins. Any examination of this would be impossible; suffice it to say that everything Atkins did met the necessary failsafe workers' criterion for hate. Notable exceptions to this inclusive practice could be found amongst the women workers, the young black drill shop worker, the chargehand, Williams the supervisor, and the apprentice. As a worker Atkins was the most highly skilled in the factory; a worker who moved with ease from tool room to cast metal shop. He had taught himself the intricacies of technical drawing and often corrected the many inaccuracies that found their way from the main office to the factory floor. Not for him the mind-numbing ritual of two thousand holes drilled top dead centre, two inches from the angled end of some obscure piece of metal. He was a truly free agent. An aristocrat of his class who refused the rewards of such a valued title. And this was one reason that he was hated. Because he was incorruptible, and that made him different because he didn't have a price. He was different in so many ways, least of all because once his highly skilled tool making duties had been performed he would return to building his own complete fuse boxes from raw materials to finished product. He would machine all the individual parts himself and often be seen working late into the night in the bakelite or welding shop. This work was unpaid but G.P.Stevens provided this unique talent with total freedom so long as he delivered switch-gear equipment, built to customer specification. This he always did. As he feared entering the drill shop because of McCabe's influence there Atkins had acquired his own drill machine from old parts left lying around the factory. Needless to say this turned out to be the most sophisticated and precise machine in the factory, and in keeping with his extraordinary engineering skills this machine was customised to meet only his exacting standards of workmanship. Following the completion of each handmade item of equipment that often had to be made to unique specifications for the customer, Atkins would engrave his name on the internal mechanism of the equipment. As his switch-gear and electrical boxes never required repair his signature would never be seen again once he had sealed the transmission unit and the piece had left the factory for yet another happy customer.

For their part, the bosses, who long since recognised the primary importance of Atkins to all production in the plant also hated Atkins because he confused the purpose of mass production, of single cell tasks, of the extreme division of labour, of wholesale alienation of the worker from the product. Atkins could build all the company's products from scratch. He knew the processes involved from start to finish so much so that draughtsmen from the office spied on him to learn the transfer from theory to practice. New orders or new equipment were always tried and tested by Atkins and his comments, advice or criticism were avidly sought although no indication of this was ever given. Often when he would make some comment or observation office staff or management would pretend to ignore him but once they returned to the office they would ensure that his views were acted upon. They claimed his ideas as their own for money or the pleasure provided by ingratiating themselves with the boss. Everyone knew this went on but the pretence was important. No one would tolerate any celebration of Atkins's skills. His intelligence was a source of ridicule. On many occasions company spies would monitor his work from the gangway or the factory area itself so that they might learn the methodology of his engineering prowess. They learnt nothing. He was held in the highest esteem by the management although they never let him know, and in their jealousy of this fact the workers hated him. Atkins ignored all this false patronage and for this the workers hated him even more. Yes, all the workers hated Atkins.

Elements of Atkins's work could be seen throughout the factory both in design and realisation. But through their hatred and self-inflicted stupidity the workers did not see this nor did they wish to. It was as if a great lie was in existence and to deny it would be to deny existence itself. He was more important than the boss, more important than the factory, and neither the vested interests of the employer nor the corrupt union could accept this reality. He was different and perhaps this was his biggest crime. Atkins's signature was scrawled all over the factory and this was all the confirmation needed for the workers hatred to continue unchallenged. They hated him because McCabe hated Atkins. Jealousy, envy and bigotry fuelled McCabe's hatred. 'Atkins is a fool, a stammering queer who lives with his mother,' they complained in unison. But still they could not erase the silent recognition that encircled the factory proclaiming his skill and intelligence. Hate often transformed itself into admiration and this contradiction had its cause in the madness of the factory. It was this recognition that fanned the flames of hatred within McCabe. McCabe claimed that Akins was a boss's lackey and yet no one could ever remember seeing Atkins speak with any of the bosses. No one could ever remember Atkins betraying his fellow workers. McCabe even claimed that Atkins was a scab, a strike-breaker, who worked through the last recorded strike in the factory some fifteen years ago. This strike had been led by John Evans and McCabe when the latter was a much younger and more radical man, but in reality Atkins had only worked in the factory for the last ten years. Again, everyone knew this but chose not to speak because the rewritten history appeased the employers and McCabe and made life that less complicated. Hatred obscures truth and the truth that most workers observed was that McCabe no longer worked on the factory floor for his time was consumed by union work, or rather union work of a particular sort. Much had changed since the strike and McCabe's hatred for Atkins was the hatred he held for himself but as with so much else in the factory acceptance of these contradictions delivered something, if only the equivalent of time off for good behaviour. So this complex mechanism of opposites colliding filtered the most unpalatable realities, making them appear satisfying; making good evil and evil good. This process had long ago extinguished freethinking amongst many of the workers in the factory and reality was always a victim.

That morning the young apprentice was also filled with hatred, not for Atkins, but for McCabe, the bosses and the factory. In an obvious act of defiance he arrived at the factory early and walked past the clock machine heading straight for Atkins's workbench, greeting the engineer warmly as the two damaged beings struck up animated conversation. When the factory filled the boy's time card began to stand out on its metal frame proclaiming his absence. Yet he was there and by the time the siren sounded for that morning's work to begin his card stood alone as its fingerprint oil stains pointed accusingly at all who passed by. John Evans had joined the couple immediately upon his arrival in the factory. The workers in the drill shop watched as the women from the cutting room circled Atkins's company along with the apprentice's young black copper-robbing friend. By 7.45 a.m. news of the apprentice's initiation ceremony had spread throughout the factory. The group that surrounded the boy offered a hand of friendship and support that satisfied the calculation he had made the night before. For him to fight back such support was necessary, for it proved that he was not alone and that the factory did not enjoy unanimous acquiescence. Unity existed if only amongst this loose-knit group that had come together spontaneously at the toolmaker's bench; in a display of solidarity centred upon the injuries that had been brought to bear on Atkins and the factory sweeper a day earlier.

McCabe and Johnson leaned over the platform rail that encircled the upper floor of the factory as this unique divide opened up before them. Despite the klaxon, machines had not been switched on and for a full ten minutes a fractured silence engulfed the plant. The measurement of this time was simple, it was lost production, and as Johnson evaluated the inanimate nature of his workers its economic cost banged in his head as the cogs of his double-entry book-keeping soul sent out the alarm to the cog wheels of his industrialist's brain. Every experience in his life was translated into cost centres as his entire being strove for the perfect alignment of cost-effective production and profit. And whilst Johnson struggled with economic theory McCabe was consumed by the silence and inactivity on the factory floor. Not because it represented lost production time or failure to meet necessary targets, but because the klaxon had sounded and the workers were not working. His brain struggled to excuse this phenomenon. Without looking at McCabe Johnson announced that he was stopping two hours' pay across the factory. McCabe turned to respond without knowing what to say but this was a moment for action, not words. Johnson had left to return to his office.

Now McCabe was a giant of a man. A slow physical being who had long recognised that his size, proportionately, outweighed his intellect. This Darwinian paradigm had also impacted upon his ability to communicate verbally to the ultimate point at which his body literally spoke for him punctuated intermittently with a loose affiliation of single syllable grunts. Violence was his dialogue. Johnson knew this and the workers knew this. But as with all things in this place, no one really spoke of it, no one really admitted to its existence. As McCabe stood alone on the metal gangway one could feel some sympathy as he struggled to think through his situation, but this ability had become all but extinct. Unlike an amputee, who can still locate feelings in a lost limb, McCabe knew his brain was still there, physically, but absence of use had made it all but redundant. Genetically he was more machine than man and the employer marvelled at the enormous potential that would be gained if they could replicate this entity. A factory full of McCabes would be their dream. He ran the length of the platform, stumbling down the metal stairs to the factory floor. At this point white-coated supervisors and some foremen from the various workshops had begun to fan out amongst the workers. Amidst all this activity the siren wailed a second time. McCabe and the supervisors shouted in unison.

'Get back to work! Get back to work!'

Instinct alone brought McCabe face to face with the grouping around Atkins's workbench. Their idle talk continued until the expected interruption rained down.

'You've just lost the whole factory two hours' pay,' bawled McCabe, 'you fuckin tosses. Get back to fuckin work. Now!'

As already identified McCabe had few if any attributes, but his survival instinct was very much at the forefront of his decision making process. His praetorian guard awaited instructions and in the drill shop work had already commenced so McCabe spread the word that the apprentice, Atkins, the chargehand, the black and the women had lost them all two hours' pay. After this task had been performed McCabe returned to the warren of offices that bordered the upper gantry of the factory. It was said that he had a former broom cupboard as a union office situated next door to Johnson's main office. Rumours long circulated that when the boss wanted something imposed on the workers, line speed-ups, new production targets etc. etc. he would repeatedly shout McCabe's name until he arrived in his office. For more secretive meetings Johnson would simply bang on the wall until the faithful dog McCabe responded with his presence. Cowardice and fear provided some of the main currencies within the factory, underlined by the basic instructed emotions of hatred or fear that McCabe's dominance had instilled. As a result all responses failed to be thought through logically, with problem solving inextricably linked to a three-pronged approach governed by hatred, cowardice and fear. The loss of two hours' pay was a substantial blow to any worker at this time. Those who were guilty had to be punished and the workers' immediate response was to collectively refuse to speak or acknowledge them. Thus, '*sent to Coventry*', as the expression went, Atkins's group were to lose contact with the rest of the factory. This unsurpassed stupidity would greatly improve the quality of life of all concerned. The traded insults and physical abuse suffered by Atkins, the young black worker, his apprentice friend and the women were to be replaced by silence.

Often events have an incomprehensible habit of happening. This flew in the face of those whose minds are employed in the cause of capital and labour, whose preference is to sustain their mutual hatreds through immovable dogma. For such expressions of spontaneity threatened the order of both the self-ordained left and the ultra-right. Spontaneous, often direct action was perceived as outside of any mutual understanding of the power of the system. Any attempt to unlock the anarchy of personal liberty, of human expression, of the capacity for unlimited free potential ran contrary to the interests of the phoney left and right that breathed life into capitalism. For they had long since reached accommodation in the control of all things within and without the system. They were the cancerous '*it*'. The cause and effect of all slavery. One was the system and one did nothing to fight it—nothing to truly represent the oppressed classes and cultures of the world. They were both guilty. So it was that in this tiny microcosm of the system, in this tiny corner of the capitalist world, the fragile peace of the factory was now in danger.

For fifteen years stability inside the factory was based upon a deception. This fractured bargain was seen as a betrayal, for the workers had lost their humanity in a deal done on their behalf without their knowledge or agreement. In the factory of G.P.Stevens, a tiny cog in the capitalist wheel, the price of this betrayal had increasingly diminished over the years. The gains made during the strike had withered away. Wages in the factory were amongst the lowest in the country and conditions were medieval. McCabe and his corrupt union bureaucracy had delivered industrial peace for nothing more than subjugation and the futile status donated by management's empty patronage. Thankfully, deception always has a limited lifespan, that is to say it is never infinite, pursuing as it does its own demise. So it was within the factory that this spontaneous uprising, without leadership or organisation, unleashed the years of frustration experienced but unchallenged to the majority of the workers. These telltale signs had been identified some time ago by Johnson. His response, as ever, was to drive down further the condition of each and every worker. Being the boss, Johnson saw this response as part of the natural mechanism for imposing control. Johnson could do this silently and secretly without the need for personal confrontation or discomfort. A pen, a word or a revised calculation was all that was required. Job numbers, production times, targets and what passed for a semblance of quality control could all be imposed upon the worker with due legitimacy. From the office these instructions were transformed into blueprints that transformed themselves into orders that enslaved the worker, who in turn transformed the blue ink into commodities. The beauty of this system was that it would not last forever—the workers would fulfil their reality and destroy this madness. Eventually they would be truly free—at some point they would be free.

Within this remarkable process plans and raw materials were transformed into a product that the boss, upon completion, took away from the worker and sold. The worker was essential to this metamorphosis at every stage of the production process, from coal to ore to steel to finished product. But this alchemy was not complete until the worker donated the final transformation, that of surplus value, profit, the very essence of capitalist production and the root of its contradiction for this value could only be realised through the impact of living labour, of the worker as producer and consumer. Such perverse exploitation requires extraordinary methods of control to ensure that the worker was not allowed to realise the true extent of this robbery and if they did the mechanism to curtail any opposition had to be omni-present. Frank O'Toole was the factory's expert on this process and could quote extensively from Marx and Lenin. McCabe called upon this expertise whenever the need arose to deflect from his treachery with the camouflage of socialist theory. To some in the factory the boss was the boss because they were better educated, more intelligent. Why this was obvious. If they could be bosses then they would. This was the way, the past, present and future. How could it be any other way? This level of unquestioned fealty existed alongside the workers' endemic hatred of the boss enshrined in the knowledge that they actually were no different from the workers themselves, but the superiority of the system, of the boss, nevertheless, went unchallenged to any meaningful extent. When it was challenged it died amidst the misery of treachery that came upon the workers from all sides. So the lie persisted as if any shift within this un-status quo might result in unimaginable repercussions not for the creators of chaos but for the victims, the workers. Through the ages capital and its client states inflicted this un-status quo. Even the so-called politicos feared any real challenge to the authority of the system. Those comrades who did often gave their lives either through martyrdom or poverty. So the lie persisted encased in treachery, ignorance and fear, for the foundations of the lie were deeply embedded and woven into the false reality and consciousness of all who suffered its consequences knowingly or otherwise. This was indeed a power. The power of *'it'*.

As always it was imperative that the choreography of the asylum be returned as quickly as possible, for everyone knew that breaks in production created the vacuum within which thought could occur. Seemingly, the moment had passed and the group, centred around Atkins, had dispersed lazily. The apprentice walked slowly towards the factory clock. His card, except for the few workers off sick that day, stood alone in the metal rack. He clocked off for the night before and banged his card into the clock for a second time. This action confused the crude mechanism of the factory time-piece, which spat the card out stamping asterisks rather than time on the boy's oily brown employment card. Glaring at this meaningless configuration that now defaced his card, the boy smashed his fist against the side of the square metal clock. Nearby, workers observed his actions in silence and disbelief. If work was simply a means by which workers obtained money for hours employed then it is not surprising that the recorder of this time achieved a status of importance to each individual worker. Time was money, the clock recorded lateness, overtime, dinner breaks, weekend work, pounds, shillings and pence. Its central location at the heart of the factory was no abstract consequence, for it followed the architecture of the factory, the politics of design, the sculpture of control and dominance etched into its mortar, glass, metal and space. Since the dawn of man architecture had long imposed the legitimacy of power. The legitimacy of enslavement. The complexity of such architecture encompassed the entirety of the building, the entirety of its form. So the clock was the sacristy, an altar for the keeper of time. The chronicler of this great fraud was located at the heart of the factory with its heartbeat beating the seconds, minutes, hours and days of the workers' time. It recorded their lives as would a pulse beating time, marking life until it ebbed away.

Aware of the stares of those workers close by, the boy finalised his desecration of the clock with a well-aimed grace of spit. One final metallic internal thud rattled from the clock. It stopped at 0810 precisely with smoke gently blowing through its vents on either side. A final gentle puff of white smoke rose from the top of the machine in one final gasp. At this inconceivable sight workers shook their heads, fighting with their incoherent desire to mount some response. None came. The shock of this action lasted only moments until free thought breezed through them. The boy had decided, the night before, to fight back, regardless of the consequences. At school he had been placed in similar situations, eventually learning to submit to the hopelessness of the power of authority. But this was different and he had made his decision. This was his freedom now and he thought to himself that somehow school was different. But it was the same. Turning away from the clock the boy walked his decision through the factory, he wore his decision and the workers saw this and McCabe saw this from the distance of the balcony and he witnessed this transformation in the boy, who had by now retrieved his brush, using it as a rest from which to look upwards, across the factory, to the two tiny figures stood on the balcony. Johnson and McCabe looked down on the brush and the boy. Johnson knew that the events of the morning could have cataclysmic implications if left unchecked. McCabe saw these events as simply an excuse to launch more physical abuse and fear on the factory floor. This was and would always be the key to McCabe's power. Johnson's more sophisticated approach owed much to his understanding of the complex nature of power in the factory and the needs of *'it'*. That delicate balance needed to justify injustice. By that afternoon other events took hold in the factory.

It must have been done in the lunch hour, a time when most of the workers found their way to the canteen. Only O'Toole's discussion group and perhaps some of the women from the cutting shop stayed on the factory floor. Atkins would either sit with the welder or take some fresh air on the open field at the back of the factory. All this did not matter, as the destruction of Atkins's own private workshop had been completed without anyone's knowledge. The personalised drill and lathe, the most accurate in the factory; the most comprehensive tool collection and over ten years of blueprints had all been stolen or destroyed. Those with any humanity in the factory, even those that followed the systematic brutality exacted against Atkins, knew that this would hurt him more than any physical or psychological bullying that had been imposed in the past. It would devastate him and their response was silence, mumbling silence, guarded looks, the vacant response that only guilt could inform. John Evans and the women looked for Atkins. But the moment had moved beyond their normal expectation of fear. Atkins had been washing himself in the toilets at the other end of the factory and the weary team that had dedicated so much energy to the destruction of his work station had set about Atkins for the second time in two days. The act was done with a vigour and vengeance that exceeded all previous acts of violence against this quiet and humane man. Despite their factory wide search, despite asking other workers if they had seen Atkins the engineer would not be seen until early, very early, the next day.

It is alarming that so many many people can go through life and experience many things and yet never really realise the potential of the enemy or the danger they face as if life itself was no more than a continuation of childhood; nothing really holding any great importance, and if it did, someone else would sort it out, clean up the mess, shovel the shit and make it all better again. That the creatures might pretend to be one and the same as the boss, working somehow towards the same ends. Oh, what liberation equality brings when its measure is the abyss of human paucity. Cries of 'we really didn't mean it,' or 'we never really expected this to happen, if only we knew.' As if ignorance itself would absolve these children in the men's bodies. These puerile agents who give up all responsibility so that they may hide under the blanket of obscurity, as if there could be any escape from the nature of the factory, its control or its exploitation. 'That the boss would sort it out,' that he was basically 'one of them.' What manner of confusion allows these men to forfeit their rights to others incapable of no other actions than corruption, financial, social, political, human—the tirade is endless. An infinity of abuse meaninglessly evaded in the struggle for the anonymity of the 'quiet life'. What shame in the knowledge of those men and women who have struggled against worse crimes and sacrificed their lives for freedom. How the crime becomes compounded by this feigned imbecility. This false innocence of childhood is not and never will be an excuse. They carry the guilt of all traitors. No, Atkins would not be seen until the next day for the response had begun.

Chapter Seven

*But now a new history commences: a story of the gradual renewing of
a man, of his slow progressive regeneration, and change from one
world to another—an introduction to the hitherto unknown realities of
life.*

—F.Dostoevsky, *Crime and Punishment*

The factory employed many security guards to protect the owners' property,
or what they assumed to be their property. They were also there to spy on the
workers. Often a worker, or two, in each workshop would act, usually unpaid,
as spies for the management. Beyond doubt this was one of the most
important and celebrated elements of the company's control mechanism over
the workers. Indeed, it merely emphasised the depths that some would tunnel
in that spiral of depravity that imposed the supremacy of all authority into
their minds. Often spies did not even have to be hired, they simply emerged
like great whales from the ocean. Not knowing their purpose. That evening
Atkins's mother had been thrown into panic by her son's failure to return
home. At an age that blurs reality she assumed her son had been called away
for an important job, something to do with work. As this was all he lived for.
But even the passage of the years did not give way to an abandonment of her
deep concern for her only son's welfare. That night she slept as the sentry. By
contrast, the factory's security guards never experienced any problems
sleeping. This old woman and the factory's security guards shared different
concerns that night. One held dear to the concern for others whilst the other
grabbed at the concern for one's self. At around 2.30 am the security guards
on duty were awoken from their sleeping death by a giant crash from one of
the darker corners of the factory. What they heard was the jolt of the cutting
machine slicing through the pitch silence of the factory night. Its echo was to
reverberate ceaselessly from this moment.

The apprentice had now also taken to sleeping in fits and started going
over each event of the day, memorising responses, acting out what even he
knew would be the bosses' response to the anarchy that was growing more
tangible by the day. He had taken to getting out of bed earlier than his father,

partly in an effort to avoid the resignation carved into his father's face but also to maximise the perverse excitement he was taking from the politics of the factory and the small matter of the revenge he wanted to take against anyone, particularly McCabe. That morning he knew something had happened. It was different albeit a subtle difference, and in the measure of the factory even a small alteration from the norm was significant. Above all this was the thing that awoke the security guards, that slight wander from the precious norm that the safe tedium of routine instils. For the security guards were padlocked to the same chain of iron routine that dominated all who entered the factory. Yet it was the unrecognised force of infinite repetition that protected them from the unknown. The roulette wheel that change rides upon was shrouded in the contradiction that even the routine, after time, became invisible, unnoticeable to all its participants so that change itself became part of 'the expected routine'. Tea, cigarettes, the smallest of small talk liberally dispersed with sleep was the stuff of life of the security guards, who would take the occasional sleepy walk in the factory to underline their personal commitment to its aims. Loyalty to the factory was also part of their routine. That night was no different than the thousand nights that had gone before. Why should it have been any different? Conformity, regularity, routine, repetition all helped the days and nights go faster towards the goal of payday. Any interruption was a curse upon what passed for the perfect equilibrium of the factory. The perfect equilibrium of nonexistence. The crash heard at the far end of the factory was one such curse on the unrecognised, inevitable tedium that factory life confirmed. Even for those unique occasions when something different actually happened a ritual of response, a conformity respectful of all routine, came into play. A rota of inquiry even when it had not been implemented for decades was remembered and honoured. A practice that involved even a routine of argument and failed recollection.

'I went last time!' one of them yawned.

As ever the reluctant guard, whoever that may have been, whoever had been confirmed by the routine of rare interruption, walks off cursing his luck, the factory, the job, the lack of money—the point to it all. Such moments of reality tended to last for only a few seconds. Like the distant and vague recollections of a lost civilisation recounted in folk memory and song. Of a life more meaningful, spoken of by village elders and ridiculed from the vantage of modernity in all its dark satanic brutality. Thoughts as these were fleeting throwbacks often brought to the fore in alcoholic machismo or aged sentimentality. These thoughts were discarded immediately. So it was that as the elected guard walked he confirmed his hatred of life simply because he had to walk and as he approached the cutting machine and saw death, his own attitude to life remained sickeningly and insultingly intact. From where he now stood he could just make out the figure of a man lying across the eight-foot square metal bench that stood level with the machine's cutting face. At that distance when he understood the image before him he called to the other guards. Eventually, although not immediately, four men stood only a few feet away from the headless body of Brian Atkins.

By a sense encouraged amongst the few who understood the present and respected the past the young apprentice knew beyond doubt that something was wrong that morning. Some of workers, as normal, ignored all external information that was not provided by the boss or the union. Police hung around outside the factory and inside busied themselves, as they so often do, once an event has passed. The cutting shop had been sealed off while the majority of workers fought amongst themselves in the ritual phoney good- and bad-humoured fight to clock on. No matter that the still broken clock banged out asterisks instead of time on their filthy clock cards. The fact of clocking on was recognition enough that routine had been respected and that they were safe in its embrace. Some sensed that something was not quite right that morning but silently pledged to themselves that whatever it was their routine would continue. Work would continue and payday would come. Despite the time clock not working all would be all right, the boss would make it right and if they didn't the union would. The apprentice marched past the heave of workers around the clock pondering the fundamental meaning of asterisks banged onto their cards where time should have been. Amidst the normality of chaos he could make out John Evans and the group he had closed the day with. They had regrouped, Evans, the women and Hasaan. Now they stood at Atkins's demolished workstation. Two of the women were crying and the young girl from the cutting shop acknowledged the boy's arrival with a deep sigh. John Evans was the first to speak.

'Brian was found dead in the factory last night, they say it was suicide,' he said calmly and coldly. 'But it don't add up. Too suspicious by half,' he seemed to plead.

The boy appeared outwardly to be unmoved but this did not stop the women opening their arms to him, and hidden within their embrace he took time to reflect upon the tragic circumstances that now held them together. With no further words spoken the group surveyed the factory and as they did the siren wailed for work to commence. And in response the hierarchy of automatons revealed itself within the speed they unleashed to respond to their master's call. The drill shop gave ultimate leadership under the tutelage of McCabe. The others followed. The cutting machine was now the centre of several detailed inspections involving the police, safety officers, assorted foremen and management. It could have been a murder scene. No one knew but all suspicion was drowned in a sea of hatred. After all, it was only Atkins. Tom Carberry could be seen poking his piggy face into the deeper recesses of the cutting machine, being no doubt the first time he had ever paid so much attention to the tools of the bosses' profits and the workers' misery. Although they could not hear it was clear by the grotesquely false earnest nature of his gestures that Carberry was playing the concerned boss with only the welfare of his workers at heart. McCabe, the so-called workers' representative, the union's senior officer on the factory floor, kept well away from events, preferring to marshal the workers to work.

Silently the renegade group moved to the far corner of the factory to the welding shop where O'Toole was clearly geared for work, hedging his bets between being a 'goodfella', not working in respect of a comrade's death, whilst leaving enough room for reversion to play the company hack. O'Toole, in reality, was profoundly unprincipled. As a result his life was one long hedged bet living in the shadows of the nondescript with the rare appearance into the safe half-light that provided the false image of independent thought and even courage fighting the boss for the downtrodden worker. Yes, O'Toole was that typical traitor, and he knew it and the rest knew it. As the group approached, blue overalls turned to non-working mode as the noise of the factory measured the time of the group's arrival, and when the noise was not enough to blanket his emptiness he broke the silence first.

'How can people work after that?' he mumbled unconvincedly. 'The blood not even cleared away.'

'We always knew Atkins was odd but to do that to himself,' O'Toole said, looking around his workshop anxiously.

'Suicide.' He stopped and looked towards the group that faced him.

'Must have stayed on in the factory, well, he always did that, working against everything we fought for, crept back and stuck his head in the cutter. You know it took them three hours to dismantle the machine and get his body off that rack.' The welder spoke only for himself and with a sense that he knew it. But he continued.

'The head was stuck in the basket at the back of the cutter … no matter how bad things are you don't just kill yourself … clearly unstable.' He was pleading for agreement that never came.

'But how can people work after that?' he begged falsely.

'I bet they refuse to work on that machine again.' O'Toole knew he was on his own and his mask was beginning to fall.

'Well, we all know what women are like,' O'Toole said.

He was in customary full-flow until the young apprentice finally broke his own self-imposed silence adopted when he entered the factory. Silence can reassure so much in that it inflicts upon others the responsibility to speak, judge, and infer all that this wonderful mechanism of speechless void creates. Now was his time to establish his independence. To let others make what they would of his language as it filled the void. More often than not words and actions matter little to people soaked as they are in perpetual self-justification for all they do and hatred for those who hold contrary views.

'That's a load of crap, it was your sort that killed him!' the boy yelled to the surprise of his friends.

'You and McCabe.' The boy's hands pointed into the face of O'Toole.

'Atkins was a good man. His only crime was to be different and you all hated him for it because he exposed your fuckin' hypocrisy,' the boy shouted.

Blue overalls leapt into this confrontation, spitting his hatred into the group.

'Hey lad,' then he corrected himself, 'son,' he insisted on calling him. This one word sent the boy into unknown turmoil as he waited for the insults to flow.

'I've been in this factory for over thirty years!' O'Toole yelled. 'Seen it all. I'm proud to say I've been a shop steward most of that time struggling against all odds so that little pricks like you can get a better life from the sacrifices I and other comrades made. So don't you dare attack me cos' of some fuckin madman.'

The boy now stood head to head with the welder whilst the group held back and allowed the young worker to speak his mind for the first time. Normally, in the hierarchy of factory life such events would not take place until at least ten years had passed, but these were proving unique times in the factory.

'And that's a load of fuckin crap as well.' The boy broadened his shoulders, poking his fist at O'Toole. 'Your struggle is knowing what the boss wants so that you can give it 'im,' he screamed into the welder's face. 'You represent the boss, and what's worse is that you try and cover it up with a load of political fuckin mumbo jumbo to justify why you prefer the company of bosses to that of the workers. Atkins was a good man, better than you or yer mate McCabe could ever be.'

Whilst the boy spoke O'Toole constantly repeated the phrase, 'that's it,' as if this mantra would cease the boy's attack. The boy was now moving ever closer to the welder and as the loudest 'that's it' rang out he pushed the welder over the anvil that had for as long as people could remember acted as his one-legged platform from which he delivered his lunchtime orations. Being almost ready for work the welder had his torch in one hand and his protective mask in the other as he fell back hard against the floor. O'Toole's cigarette ignited the welding torch as a heavy punch of pressure sent a spurt of flame across the room almost setting light to the group. The boy moved in and kicked the torch across the shop floor, setting fire to the dust and wood chippings that filled this end of the factory. The welder rolled to his feet and turned off the oxyacetylene bottle that was strapped to the wall.

'That's it, that's the fuckin lot!' he screamed. Now he ignored the boy and addressed himself to John Evans, the chargehand.

'Someone betta put out that fuckin fire cos I'm not and he's in breach of safety procedures and I'm reporting 'im to Johnson so you betta get yerself ready, lad, cos your fuckin Trot feet ain't gonna fuckin touch ... and I'm gonna report you to the fuckin police over there for assault and battery. That's it! That's it!' he screamed with a finality that had no reality.

Frank O'Toole choked upon his anger as the group turned away, with the young girl from the cutting shop pulling the apprentice out of harm's way. The fire in the welding shop had now caught hold, fuelling the general mayhem that engulfed the factory that day. John Evans spoke to the boy as he rejoined the group.

'Look. Everyone's upset,' he said, staring at the boy intently.

'No, John, he fuckin isn't.' The boy now turned his anger upon his mentor. 'If he was upset he'd show some respect and not start work even if it's just for a few hours until they find out what happened.'

'Yeah, that's it, lad,' shouted Frank O'Toole from a distance, 'typical adventurist. What? Stop work and lose another day's pay? Don't you wanna fuckin work?'

The boy looked over his shoulder. 'He lost his life,' he yelled.

'He took his own fuckin life,' O'Toole fired back. Gone was the softly spoken sophistry of the political tutor. O'Toole screamed amidst the fire and the smoke. 'What's your fuckin problem? Atkins was a fuckin scab and that's the end of it. He's fuckin dead now. So you piss off and let me....'

The sentence was finished by the whole of the group if only in their heads. 'Get back to work....' That was what it was all about. That was what everything in the factory was about. Getting to work, starting work, getting back to work, finishing work, returning to work. At any cost, at any price. Evans, the women and Hasaan did not feel any need to intervene, they agreed with the boy and matters had for too long been ignored or not spoken of. Now was the time to let things run their course. Suddenly McCabe stood in their path, glaring at the group before him, looking at the fire behind them. O'Toole lit another cigarette, seemingly oblivious of the need to put the fire out, being more concerned with either starting work, reporting events to Johnson or going straight to the police. McCabe's morning had been spent getting everyone to work in the aftermath of Atkins's death. In an inspired effort to keep the workers' minds off such distractions and in an effort to make up lost production the management had issued new productivity targets that morning. The workshops were to be sped up. This seemed to anger some workers more than the suicide of a comrade and colleague. McCabe shouted to his political confidant, the welder.

'What the fuck goin' on ere?' he screamed. Then he saw the flames licking the side of the factory wall.

'Fuckin 'ell get that fire out,' he shouted over their heads.

He pushed into and through the group but could not let a chance go by to make some remark.

'Regular stop work movement, aren't we? Well, that fuckin scab's death not gonna change anythin ere and your cards are well fucking marked. Help us get this fuckin fire out. Comm'on!' his voice slurred with anger.

McCabe was ignored by everyone except the apprentice, who again sprung to the defence of his dead friend but this time with a vigour measured only by his hatred of McCabe.

'Brian Atkins was never a scab and you know it.' He stood up to McCabe, face to face. 'You're the only fuckin scab in here,' he screamed. 'You bosses' fuckin lackey,' he spat into McCabe's face.

McCabe was caught between his wish to kill the boy and his psychological desire to please his boss. The fire in the welding shop was now getting out of control. His primary function was to serve the interests of the boss, the apprentice knew this and taunted McCabe to make his move.

'Fire! Fire!' the boy screamed, mocking McCabe's thoughts. Again, the actions and words of the boy surprised his cohorts as he displayed a confidence that had no fear. McCabe's body shook with indecision and his choice was simple—kill the boy or put out the fire.

'Get the hoses. Put that fuckin fire out,' McCabe yelled.

The group now left the factory by way of the acid barn. Outside the barn the huge figure of Daniel Hawkins could be seen staring out to the distance. Two workers emerged from the factory pulling a trolley carrying iron for the acid bath. Hawkins ignored this movement behind him, leaving the cast iron to be stacked with others waiting to go into the acid bath.

'We used to sit out here all the time,' the acid bath man said, still looking directly ahead, 'Atkins said it was ugly inside and beautiful outside. The grass and the trees, even the rain, it used to clean us, dilute the acid and clean the oil. That's what it did. The harder the rain the better it was,' he said calmly, 'no one came out here. Just us two.' He stopped as if to think upon his own words.

'How can they stay in there all the time?' he asked. 'That noise, that filthy atmosphere. Don't they like clean air?' He paused again, lifting his head to the sky.

'That's what Brian and me liked, the clean air. We liked each other's company and we treated each other with a respect that no one else in there would even think of.' His head sunk deep into his chest.

It was a dismal day but still a day to be outside of the factory and the group sat on an old plank of wood with their backs against the wall of the factory. The women, Hawkins, the two young men and John Evans stared into the distance in silence. Williams the supervisor came out of the factory. The group turned in unison and the apprentice noticed clearly that this was not the walk of the man who strode around the factory, arms tucked under his hunched back, belching out orders. No one moved. After him came the storekeeper and the cast metal shop worker. Other workers emerged from the factory, blinking in the sparse light, taking in the air as if it were their last breath. As they passed through from the darkened exit to the failing light of the day they seemed transformed. The nature of this transformation was difficult to identify but they were, somehow, different. The supervisor sat down next to John Evans and lit a cigarette. Williams joined the silence. Words would have to be spoken, they all knew that, but it was a moment for silence, and the longer it endured the more calming it became. Now even the noise of the factory was to be replaced by the rustle of long grass and distant trees. Four women, three men and two boys stared into the gloom of the late morning. After immeasurable time had passed Williams lit another cigarette and casually offered the pack along the group. Absently the apprentice took one, accepted a light off Williams and allowed his coughing to break the code of serenity within the group. Williams spoke and whilst addressing everyone appeared focused upon John Evans.

'The police have all left now and they've taken Brian's body away,' he said. 'There'll have to be an inquiry but it appears to have been suicide.' No one spoke. 'John, he'd made himself a tool so that he could reach the cutter's starter button as he lay on the feeder tray. I can't imagine when he did this, but the tool he made was as precise as ever. As precise as everything Brian did.'

Silence bore down upon them as they stared ahead into some unknown distance that did not lie before them. Williams continued regardless as if he knew that he had to share this rigid information.

'To kill himself in that way he had to be precise, the act itself took a lot of thought.'

The supervisor's words drifted over the group. More workers from the factory joined them as he spoke.

'It was very deliberate, they'd fuckin broken him, John, that bunch of dirty bastards had finally got to him.' His voiced trailed into the blind distance before them all.

'The police brought the tool he'd made over to me to ask what the tiny

mark was on the side, I told them he signed his name on everything he made.'
Williams closed his eyes. 'He made tools for all sorts of jobs,' said Hawkins,
'he was murdered—that's all there is to it. Murder,' he confirmed. Silence
returned adn each worker harboured their own suspicions.

Hawkins and one or two of the women gulped back tears. Annie, the
young girl, changed places and sat next to the apprentice. She too was crying
as she held his hand tightly in her own, rolling his hands, pulling at his
fingers, wringing her own hands against his. Williams continued to speak as
if unloading luggage he had not realised he had packed. Piece after piece hit
the concrete floor and he could not stop it or himself.

'It's never been as bad as this. As far back as I can remember we had
respect for each other, we stood together and looked after each other. You
and I started the union in this place and it was strong, never perfect, but we
had solidarity and we fought one enemy, not ourselves.' He turned to face
John Evans.

'I know you disagreed with me taking the supervisor's job, but I thought,
why shouldn't the workers have these jobs? We're all workers anyway and
I treated everyone the same, as if I was still a shop steward, but they couldn't
get their heads around it and while they sucked up to the boss they called me
a lackey.' He seemed to be off-loading guilt, passing it on to the chargehand.
The apprentice listened intently.

'That's part of the madness, and over the years look how they've
changed.' Williams gulped for air. 'Look how bad their conditions are now,'
he started pointing back towards the factory, 'and yet they still respect the
boss more than their fellow workers. Brian's death should blow this place
apart if there's any humanity left. But they've carried on working as if
nothing's happened.' He looked hard at the chargehand.

'John, you've got to get a grip on this, the men will look to you now.'

John Evans raised his head, pushing his chin forward.

'You've got to take control, you should never have resigned in the first
place, that fuckin McCabe, you knew what he was capable of. I know you
had problems but....'

Williams stopped short and turned directly to John Evans, while the group
listened they all continued to look straight ahead, only the apprentice strained
forward with his eyes locked onto Williams.

'John, I'm sorry, I wasn't thinking,' Williams stuttered. 'John, I'm sorry,
brother.'

The apprentice was the only member of the group not to know the
meaning of this but he knew that he could not ask, at least not at this time.
Others on the bench looked towards him as if to urge caution and remain
silent, the young girl dug her nails gently into his hands. Williams lifted his

gaze from John Evans and looked straight ahead, the silence returned, falling upon the group once more. Other workers had by now left the factory and others continued to follow them. Small groups huddled near the acid barn in the no man's land of political statement, neither really in the factory or out of it. But at least this indicated that they were not prepared to carry on working after the death of Brian Atkins. Knowing the nature of what was unfolding John Evans's group turned in almost perfect synchronicity to examine this exodus. They returned their gaze to the distance.

One of the more stupid drill shop workers came running out of the factory shouting to anyone that could hear him. 'Well, that's the fuckin lot: there's fuckin murder in there,' he yelled, 'and you lot are gonna get the fuckin sack, McCabe's doin his fuckin nut and Johnson's called a meeting for 4.30 today.' He waited for a response that never came.

'I don't know what all the fuckin fuss is about.' His voice was lost in the wind and the man was left to stand alone. Having been listened to he was ignored. He shook his hands as if they would make a response. But a new reality was unfolding and as most of the workers outside of the factory understood this. Their silence spoke of a unity not known for many years at G.P.Stevens and Sons.

The timing of the meeting was crucial, as was the fact that the management were calling the meeting—not the workers or the union. It was a reflection of the unity of the group that they required no explanation or clarification of these matters. Yes, 4.30 p.m. was a good time, half an hour of the company's time the rest belonging, belonging in the context of who owns the workers' time, to the boss, although the workers saw this as their time. Time being money, the workers always felt obliged to finish such rare meetings at 5.00 p.m. 'No pay—No way,' so many of them said. Thus, the workers were being called to a bosses meeting. Between 11.00 a.m. and 4.30 p.m. no sirens were sounded, some work took place and some work didn't. McCabe spent the afternoon off the factory floor in the company of bosses preparing for the meeting. John Evans, the women, Williams and Hawkins and the two young workers idled their day away. Three of the women joined their fellow women workers in the canteen. Evans and Williams spent the afternoon in deep conversation holding random and informal meetings with the workers. Many now sought the company and leadership of John Evans. Hawkins went to Brian Atkins's workshop and tidied things around as best he could whilst collecting personal effects that Atkins's mother should receive.

Annie took the young apprentice across the field to the tree-lined fence that defined the boundaries of the factory. They both felt the need of each other's company, the need to escape from the factory. A seamless flow of self-pity and guilt consumed the boy. It was here that he learnt of the suicide of John Evans's only son some five years earlier. The girl described the details of how the boy had moved from alcohol to hard drugs. One night he just threw himself off the top of his parents' block of flats, twenty-two floors up. She stressed it was the deliberate nature of the act that so shocked John Evans and everyone who heard the story.' She paused for a long time.

'It wasn't just drugs. It seemed coldly calculating,' she said. Another space drifted in between her words.

'He entered the lift. He was going home. He travelled to the twenty-second floor, turned the corner, walked towards the balcony, raised his leg onto the railing and launched himself over the side.' Her words flowed relentlessly to the beat of the leaves against the wind.

'All this time thinking and concluding his final act on a journey he had made all his life.' She paused again. 'He was going home and he made this detour. Familiarity, a loving family, all this measured to nothing in his determination to kill himself. A few minutes earlier his mother was talking with friends on the same balcony that night. It was a summer evening. If she had stayed out a few seconds longer she would have seen everything.' The leaves gently kept their rhythm.

'He may have just been on his way to his front door and just took the decision in that instant to throw himself over the side.' She stopped for a moment. 'In that same instant he could have regretted his actions but by then it was too late.' The wind seemed to fall as the sunshine rolled across the field casting tiny shadows on falling leaves.

'I can't begin to understand, no one can, and that's the problem.' She pondered upon her own explanation.

'Why he did it no one really knew: it was just that he had decided to maximize the pain for all that loved him. It destroyed them and John lost touch with everything. He was the real leader of this factory and Johnson respected him because he couldn't buy him out. Not like McCabe. He was on the verge of getting the women equal pay and a real wage for the apprentices,' she said. 'We had real unity then. A real solidarity.'

Annie told him how he would not recognise how good it was in the factory then. 'They were honest and dignified days. The workers controlled the factory. It was a wonderful time.'

The young worker listened intently to the lessons of this story and he respected the young girl's knowledge of life and the factory. She was more mature and experienced than him, this much he knew. And he thought now, above any other time, he knew everything. He was complete. He loved her beauty and she wanted him and showed him how to make love. Annie showed him so much more. She treated him like no other person ever had. He was a man, 'a real worker,' or so he thought. A worker who hated the boss and this hatred served only to heighten their solidarity, their love. They held on to each other against the cold wind of the afternoon and the icy breath that blew up from the factory against their handsome faces.

Understanding Annie's feelings towards the young apprentice long before she ever did, Hasaan had left them alone when he had discovered that they had gone across the field together. He had always hoped that one day she would be his girlfriend. His heart filled with jealousy and there was nothing he could do about it. For some time he sat on that wooden bench straining his eyes at the two tiny figures as they huddled beneath the distant trees. He thought how suddenly the apprentice had inherited everything and in his poisoned mind everything was 'the girl,' for even he would accept that nothing else was on offer in that cursed place. He felt that same icy breeze against the back of his body and alone his mind festered. He had to take his mind off things. For the rest of the day he did this by going around the factory sabotaging machines and altering measurements to blueprints. His hatred was satisfied by these acts. At 4.30 p.m. you could hear the sirens wail throughout the factory. Clearer than ever before.

Chapter Eight

It often happens that a factory owner does his best to deceive the workers, to pose as a benefactor, and conceal his exploitation of the workers by some petty sops or lying promises. A strike always demolishes this deception at one blow...A strike, moreover, open the eyes of the workers to the nature, not only of the capitalists, but of the government and the laws as well...But when the workers state their demands jointly and refuse to submit to the money-bags, they cease to be slaves, they become human beings, they begin to demand that their labour should not only serve to enrich a handful of idlers, but should also enable those who work to live like human beings.

—V.L.Lenin, *Collected Works.*

In the past regular union meetings used to be held outside of work and at the weekends. Once a month these were social and political gatherings at which union leaders like John Evans and Williams would report back events in the factory and take resolutions from the floor on what was to be done to further the wages and conditions of the workers. Normal attendance would be at least three to four hundred workers and most would stay after the meeting, have some food and drink and carry on discussing political and work-related issues into the night. They would celebrate and have a good time. They worked hard then and they played even harder and drank even more. Nothing mattered then because they had a dignity that rose above the abstract conditions they slaved under. It was a solidarity born of their experiences of life and it was held together by their socialism—pure and undiluted. Little had really changed in the engineering industry and factories such as G.P.Stevens could still impose 1940s wages and conditions on its workforce with impunity. Other industries experienced massive upheavals, strikes and bitter struggles, like the seafarers and dockers. But manufacturing industry struggled hard to establish their own rank and file movements against rigid opposition from employers bolted to the twisted morals of Victorian England. Primitive and dangerous conditions confronted outmoded concepts of skill; engineering pride and inexplicable respect for machinery that would have been better suited to a museum. Within all these contradictions the organisation of the workers rested upon individual leadership and solidarity in the factory. John Evans personified this; the workers knew this, the unions who relied upon people like John Evans to give them respectability and trust in the workplaces of England knew this. A lifelong communist, John Evans had been a victim of the union, employer and government proscriptions that mirrored the American McCarthyite witch hunts against members of the Communist Party and their 'fellow travellers'. This latter term covered all exigencies, making the witch hunts infinite in their scope. A catch-all crime capable of imposing devastation on all who felt the finger of hatred and vengeance tap their shoulders. John Evans was banned from holding any elected or appointed office in the union in 1955 and despite some relaxation the 'red scare' on communists or 'fellow travellers' was still in place by the winter of 1967. The bosses exploited this and they campaigned hard to undermine the work undertaken by shop stewards as the real unpaid representatives of the working class. Many workers suffered simply because of their belief in socialism and despite the personal and family ordeals this brought the majority of these comrades persisted in their struggle for justice and freedom.

Amidst these upheavals John Evans had to carry the burden brought about by the suicide of his son. His position was deeply contested, and following his enforced removal from office it was clear that the vote had been fixed. McCabe won the ballot although allegations of corruption and ballot rigging did not impress the official union despite evidence that clearly implied the involvement of G.P.Stevens management in getting McCabe elected. He was seen from the start as a company man who, seeing the writing on the wall for communists, quickly resigned his links although he still often referred to small hand-written notes, supplied by Frank O'Toole, that allowed him to misquote Marx or Lenin at meetings. McCabe was not the brightest of stars in the factory. Not that this mattered of itself but sadly he thought otherwise and was encouraged to think this way by the bosses. To secure their investment they coached him and advised him, ably supported by Frank O'Toole. Following this tuition his brief contributions continued to be shattered with mis-pronunciations, foul language, and his opt-out clause of ' you know what I fuckin mean anyway'. He dragged many of the workers down to his level. He brought shame to his office and actively undermined any expression of solidarity. But he could get the promises of good times to come and the payment of shillings here and pennies there for individual workers from the bosses. He said progress could be made without conflict, working together with the bosses and no more strikes. Simplistic static logic peppered with dreams of a better tomorrow and underpinned by violence and thuggery McCabe secured his place in the factory and his reward was never to work again on the flimsy excuse that work hindered his ability to represent the workers. No one saw his wage packet, no one saw him clock on or off, no one saw him work, and everyone knew he was wealthy, that is wealthy in the context of the poverty of the workers. But people such as McCabe do not command a high price. A slap on the back from the boss normally does the trick. The workers knew this and the bosses knew this but the ultimate deception was that no one would talk of it. McCabe's stewardship of the factory ensured the demise of democracy. No more meetings outside working hours, outside the control of the factory—free from its unblinking gaze. As a gift from the boss McCabe was able to announce meetings in factory time, 4.30 to 5.00 p.m. and within this half hour the workers were encouraged to end the meeting. With most of the workers still in the factory at 4.30 p.m. at least this ensured a turnout of some seven to eight hundred workers who were effectively locked in until 5.00 p.m. anyway. At which time the meetings would always be encouraged to end, like work, when the bosses' klaxons roared. At four thirty, the sirens again directed the workers to the canteen and the sporadic slots of production that flickered across the workshops ended.

Little work had been undertaken that day. The drill shop, in isolation from the rest of the factory, worked as normal, in fact they worked harder that day. Elsewhere men and women just went through the actions and during the course of the day over three hundred workers had drifted outside the factory to complain about everything and anything. Having been given that excuse by the death of Atkins. Throughout the factory machines stumbled to a halt as workers stretched out and rubbed the parts of their bodies that ached in their distortion to replicate the movements of the machines. Some workers cleaned down the machines that shackled their bodies whilst others treated their lathes or drills with much less respect. The majority despised their confinement. Workers on those machines that cut, bent or stamped smaller pieces of metal often found it difficult to stop their hands or arms moving to the rapid rhythms of their machines even after they had spat out their last stump of metal. Within their automated environment humanity too had become automated, human actions would become robotic as the drudge and grind of work imprinted itself upon the souls of those who succumbed. Now these workers bustled towards the gangways to make their way to the canteen. Some talked, some cursed, some shuffled—resolved to sustain their last instruction heads bowed eyes blankly staring downward. The apprentice had never attended a meeting before and he joined the women, Evans, Williams and Hawkins on the march across the factory. Annie kept close to his side and he felt confident. Hasaan had been missing for most of the day but he caught up with the group, pushing his young friend in the back and telling him how much copper he had robbed and how many machines and blueprints he had sabotaged. Union membership covered all the workers up to the level of foreman. Supervisors had their own union, a union of sorts. Little attempt was ever made to exclude supervisors or bosses listening in at the back of meetings. This open spy network was adequately enhanced by McCabe's own unique form of treachery that encouraged this espionage in the name of solidarity. Solidarity with whom was never clear. Williams had always been the exception to this rule.

That afternoon the canteen was full. Cigarette smoke strangled the air as a pale grey acrid smog hung from the ceiling sprayed a diffused light off fluorescent tubes that spluttered above them. A vacuum of air rested beneath its weight, silhouetting the mass of workers below it. As the young apprentice's group entered this huge square hall the scene formed a canvas of layered haze. Dark, grey mists sketched every crevice of the room. Noise and movement allowed the human eye to segment the scene to make sense of the image as it tricked the brain. Once deciphered, the image was set, never to be confused again. The apprentice tried in his mind's eye to return to the smudged lines but by now he was amongst the moving mass of black and grey workers, looking, as would a theatre goer, to get the best seat in the house. Annie stuck close to him; so did the rest of the group. They opted for a space at the side of the hall near the front. From this point much could be seen and heard. The workers sat and stood as they worked. In the front were the mass ranks of the drill shop, behind them the tool makers, behind them the lathes operators, cast metal shop, metal cutters, metal cleaners, assorted crafts and at the back the labourers. On the edge of the rows of tables and chairs sat most of the women workers, and the group sat near them.

For half an hour smoke and noise filled the room as the workers waited for their shop stewards to arrive. No point in conversation as the only communication that was allowed in the tumult of noise was primitive, but as in the factory many of the workers had evolved new forms of communication that disregarded the need for sentences. Although in their hearts they wished it to be another way it was as it was and they had lost the art of choice. No kindness stood to describe this futility as to really comprehend its madness, you first had to behold it in awe for this was '*its*' power, to transform humanity. The boy looked and wondered and thought about school and teachers and education, the false dreams and images of youth. This potential to achieve was offered and cynically and knowingly taken away. The working class could only envy from a distance these lost dreams perceived in a snapshot of begrudged learning. Whilst he knew little of such things the fact that he knew of their existence was enough and they had been stolen from him. All those experiences. But where did the images that lay before him have their explanation? Why was this educational genocide not

100

uncovered? What use was this blink at knowledge when the falsehood of school, the drought of learning, resulted in its robbed benefactors being condemned to such places. The boy knew that they were part of the same nightmare, the same reality. They were as guilty as the boss, the system. These phoney educationalists. The boy hated education because it failed to liberate, failed to fulfil its true potential. His reality was a reality he could not escape from and they knew it. 'They fuckin know it.' He gritted his teeth and wiped his brow. He looked at the dirty, oily rag that had become his property and he saw that he was no different from the rest of humanity that filled the canteen that afternoon. But he still did not blame the workers—he respected them and hated their tormentors in all their varied forms. At this point the keepers of the keys of the asylum entered.

Johnson entered first. Carberry scuttling behind him. McCabe and the shop stewards committee entered next, there were at least twelve of them, one being the local union paid official, Ken Jacks. This man received the wrath of almost everyone in the room, and according to the women he only turned up to take things off the workers and agree with the boss. After a few seconds another man entered. He was different to all that had come before. Everyone in the room knew that this man was, in their language, 'a big boss'. Indeed, he was a 'big boss', it was George Pearson Stevens, the factory owner's son, who, as is often the case in these situations, to avoid confusion, always took the name of their father. Three chairs had been laid out in the front of the room, these were taken by G.P. Stevens Jr., Johnson and McCabe. The rest moved to the back and when they sat down the crowd lost sight of them. The piggy face of Carberry could just be made out rising up and down, arms waving, shouting to various workers.

'Show some respect. Shut up! Sit down. Don't you know who this is? Show some respect!' he yelled to no one in particular.

But none of this could really be heard and although silence fell on the room when they arrived this silence was a noise in itself. Workers mumbled, shouted, nudged, cursed, regretted everything and regretted nothing. Some became stronger and some became weaker. Some stood and made clear their hatred for the boss or for McCabe. You could not hear, but these expressions of dissent rose from the body of the mass in quick succession and had it been allowed to continue no doubt every worker would have eventually raised their physical being in revolt against the symbols of authority that now sat before them. It was a courtroom and a fight arena. As ever, their tormentors knew this and Johnson stood bolt upright, arms extended, hands palms up, as if to calm the baying mass. Some pockets of silence emerged but it was left to McCabe to close the door on this small revolt.

'Com'on—that's it, keep it down, let's listen to what Mr. Johnson has to say. Yeah. That's it....'

Amidst the cursing and insults that flew around the room McCabe conducted himself admirably with only the occasional covert physical threat to particular individuals. He managed to do this by turning the whole of his body in front of Stevens and Johnson and mouthing threats that, whilst you could not make out definitively everything that was said, clearly included the words 'fuck' and 'kill'. This was the McCabe that the workers knew best and when this was realised he sat down with a sickly smile directed towards Johnson, who now stood up for a second time. The thumbs of both hands were balanced on the edge of his oily waistcoat pockets and as he spoke his fingers opened and closed as exclamation marks for his audience heaving inward and outward. Johnson spoke in his usual high-pitched voice that ran in spurts with the cadence of a man making constant demands. He stood for a few seconds and waited for the noise to cascade to a level that he found acceptable, then he spoke.

'We are as upset as everyone to hear of Atkins's death and Mr. Stevens junior has written to his mother.' He stopped and seemed happy enough that this pause spoke of respect. As the moment passed he thought to complete his sentence. 'Stating the same,' he continued, 'we know it wasn't pleasant this morning but we have got a business to run and by God that's what we intend to do.'

He looked into the deep middle distance. After a few moments he started up again. McCabe's eyes drilled into the floor.

'But it seems that a small group of people don't want to work here anymore and they're causing problems through the whole of the factory ... they know who they are and we know who they are....'

Johnson was sweating profusely and had released one of his hands from his waistcoat to allow him to bang the table. McCabe and Carberry exchanged cigarettes whilst Stevens junior looked into the heart of the room, clearly disinterested in the entire proceedings. Johnson continued.

'Christ, men!'

At this the women catcalled Johnson.

'You know what I mean,' he complained, 'we see the figures in the office every day when you've all gone home and the last two weeks have been dreadful, that's why we sped up. It's your job we're lookin' after and if you don't wanna work here then let us know.' He looked around the room expecting someone to own up. In disappointment he trundled on.

'But we intend to deal with that and I know some of you are expecting a wage rise this year, well, we've had to tell your representatives, your union man here,' Johnson turned to face the union boss. It was a meeting of bosses. He bowed and turned to the crowd.

'Mr. Jacks.' His voiced trailed off wearily.

Jacks smiled towards Johnson as if to underline their relationship. But the workers knew what was going to be said next, for they had heard it all before. Again, some jumped to their feet randomly across the room, screaming dissent at the platform. Others kept their heads bowed, this group sat mostly in the front, where workers from the drill shop held the majority. The women kept their own discipline, watching events as they unfolded, passing comments to each other and pointing at the platform before them as well as the ranks of silent sheep that lay near the front of the hall.

'That's it, shout as loud as you like. Speak to your union official. He agrees, better to keep the work here than lose it abroad,' he shouted above the shouts. 'This is real business and our market won't allow us to pay higher wages. No one wants these old switchgear boxes anymore; demand is down,' he called out, 'but if we cut costs we can keep most of the jobs here. That is your decision. You know what to do....'

It was meant as a statement but in some other way it was a question. A question that left control over telling people what to do hanging in the minds of the workers. And if they had wished they would have challenged this thought, yet they did not. Of course they knew what to do—they knew that better than any boss.

With that Johnson, Carberry and Stevens junior left the room. Stevens leant over to Jacks, the union official, telling him something, and everyone knew it was a threat irrespectively of how cultured the gesture seemed. Pandemonium erupted throughout the canteen and now it seemed like everyone in the room wanted to have their say. Some of the women taunted the men, who sat silent when the boss was there and were now shouting as loud as they could. But this was the normal pattern of events for meetings of the workers, rare as they were, these days. Hawkins walked to the front of the room and his huge frame and undoubted strength commanded silence. He raised his hands above his head, then turned to Jacks and McCabe, his face contorted with anger.

'No meeting,' he demanded, 'should take place without a minute's silence for our dead comrade.'

Amidst the chaos it was clear that the drill shop workers wanted no such thing, besides it was now almost five o'clock and they wanted to agree with whatever McCabe told them and go home. For a moment Hawkins stood alone. Annie's grip on her apprentice's hand loosened as she and the rest of the women marched silently to the front of the hall. At first, this line of some sixty women met with the normal insults that these workers had endured for too long. Their determination was apparent to the crowd. Men stood in solidarity with them and their number grew until they were the clear majority in the hall. With heads bowed the minute's silence had begun and because workers joined at different moments the minute extended itself until silence stole into the room. And when the women were ready they raised their heads and returned to their seats. Immediately noise engulfed the room again. McCabe and Jacks screamed for order, then the workers disciplined themselves, telling each other to keep quiet so that they might now hear the depth of treachery that was about to be unleashed upon them. A silence descended, rolling from the back of the hall to the front. McCabe spoke.

'I've got nothing to say. You've heard Mr. Johnson. There's no other way, unless you wanna strike, then we would all get sacked.' He was about to close the meeting down. He genuinely felt he had said enough. Now his anger began to rise. He started shouting.

'The committee met with Mr. Stevens junior!' he screamed.

A hush folded itself around the room. People now waited to hear what the deal was. What the compromise was. What the sell-out was. But they were to be disappointed.

'It shows ya ow important it is when he gets down here from London. Yeah, shout as much as you want. We wanna keep our jobs ere so the committee's recommending we accept no pay rise this year and see if we can negotiate deals within the factory.' Screams came from the floor.

'It's only what we've done in the past few years. So let's give it a go and close the meeting. Is that agreed?' Again the room erupted.

Jacks the union official then stood up and made it perfectly clear that the union would not be supporting any action against the company. He spoke of the government, the white heat of change, of union power being at its height, of regular meetings in Downing Street between the union leaders and politicians and the massive strides being made by organised labour. The workers could not just throw that away on a selfish pay claim. After all, he stated, 'inflation was looming'. Now the room shook with a hatred that surprised even the most experienced of trade unionists. Workers from the drill shop spoke first whilst cries of 'take the vote' reverberated through the rafters of the canteen. It was difficult to hear what was being said with the constant flow of noise around the room, and the way in which some of the workers communicated made it often impossible to understand a word being said. Sometimes they shouted so loud when they spoke that their words linked into one long drone; others spoke so briefly that the listeners had hardly any time to comprehend what was being said. Laughter, hatred, threats and cries of support wove this language of noise to an anarchic conclusion as if the contributors suddenly realised the futility of this senseless barrage. Noise levels began to reduce. McCabe wanted it to continue so that he could intervene and abandon the meeting, claiming that the workers wanted to accept the shop steward's recommendation.

Whether through exhaustion or lack of oxygen the workers sat and waited to see what might happen. Fragmented hecklers dispersed around the room continued to attack something, someone, somewhere but their cries were indecipherable. One of the women from the cutting room marched again to the front of the room and began to speak but she was greeted with a wave of insults so she turned and climbed onto the raised platform that now contained the steward's committee. This action alone brought some concept of order. Margaret Harvey had been at G.P. Stevens for almost thirty years and this, of itself, demanded respect even though, in the eyes of many workers, she was still a woman earning pin money doing a man out of a job. But her husband had died years ago, leaving her to bring up a family of five children, so in the twisted logic of bigotry she could expect some time to speak. Any other woman would have been thrown off the platform. The men also knew that she had more courage and dignity than most of them, so a silence of note fell on the hall. Margaret Harvey also happened to be one of the best speakers in the factory, articulate and knowledgeable. She spoke directly to the platform and dismissed them as corrupt 'lackeys of the boss and the system'. McCabe she blamed for the demise of radical trade unionism in the factory, claiming that the loss of John Evans, as convenor, was a tragedy. Then she addressed the main body of the hall.

'The death of Brian Atkins was a direct result of victimisation.' Her finger pointed around the room and up to the platform. 'Oh yes, you can go on denying it. Well, as a woman I can speak with some authority of being victimised in every sense of the word, why are women paid less than men?' she asked. 'We do the same work! Why can't women work overtime? Become toolmakers?' She paused for a few seconds. 'Be elected as shop stewards? Some of you might treat your own wives disgracefully but you're not going to do it to the women in this factory,' she shouted.

'So we know about victimisation, systematic abuse, and we saw it happen with Atkins, men in this room, men, so-called men on this platform, look at them, take a good look because you won't see them for another year ... and they know it—and they know the guilt they carry for killing Brian Atkins.' She stopped and seemed to examine the walls of the room as if they too shared in this guilt.

'They even had the audacity to call him a scab. Them,' her finger pointed again to the platform, 'calling anyone a scab, but they did, and men in this room knew that was not true but peddled the myth—a minute's silence! You should hang your heads in shame for the rest of your lives. But men like you learn nothing, so now we have to accept a wage freeze, a wage cut more like it. The highest-paid man, outside of McCabe that is, takes home about £11 a week. £11 to feed and clothe and pay rent. I work damn hard as a woman and I take home £7, with four kids on the floor…?'

'OK, Queen, you've had enough,' McCabe spat from the platform.

She turned directly to face him. 'Fuck off,' she said calmly, 'I'll finish when I'm good and ready.'

Her hatred for McCabe was self-evident.

'Look at that apprentice over there. (Annie gave her young lover a nudge) £3 10 shillings a week? Some of them work harder than any of us, it's just cheap labour, and Stevens wants more of them. Mr. G.P. Stevens junior, oh yes, they wheel him out to frighten everyone.' She leaned over the platform. 'The big boss, well, the big boss is just gonna get into his chauffeur-driven Rolls and go back to London while you think about how to pay your rent or buy some decent food. No, it's gone on too long now and we should stand our ground and fight for real wages and conditions, but you all know we're gonna have to get rid of McCabe before we can do anything.'

At this the room exploded in division.

'Oh, yes, that's what I'm saying. We need to bring John Evans back to lead us against the boss and to unite the workers in this factory!' she yelled above the crowd.

As the tumult in the hall raged Margaret Harvey returned to her seat. Workers standing at the front screamed incoherently in support of McCabe whilst towards the back of the hall workers applauded the woman's contribution. McCabe again called for order.

'Well, now you know,' he said, 'do ya wanna have a vote on who wants to get the sack cos that's what she's talkin about?'

McCabe turned to the welder, 'Ere' Frank, you respond.'

O'Toole walked to the front of the platform. This was often a common practice at meetings where a rank and file speaker got the better of the chairman, it was a reflex response to bring on his 'best player'. McCabe always did this on those rare occasions when his authority was challenged. Not that that had happened much recently. The welder was gifted in the dark arts but familiarity had long bred utter contempt. His words now carried little impact amongst the majority of workers. He was one of the many who could speak for hours and command interest, even respect, until that is people actually listened to what he was saying. Then it was apparent that the words were simply words and in the conjunction of sentences it amounted to nothing other than verbal nonsense. Most of the workers knew this. McCabe in his stupidity and arrogance refused to see this, refused to understand the mechanisms of transformation that had been unfolding in the factory over the last few years. His tarnished political ambassador had been exposed to all bar those whose lives were regimented by the numbing dogma that scratched the surface of exploitation and masqueraded as opposition. Frank O'Toole addressed the meeting in much the same way as he addressed his small lunchtime study group. At first some workers claimed they could not hear him but they soon sat down when they concluded that little real point existed to listening to him anyway. The welder, it seemed, ignored the entire hall, such was his confidence in his art of communication. This, like the man, was a first-person singular speech in which I, me and mine dominated. As in the past he always referred to notes and in his arrogance the notes were rigidly adhered to irrespective of arguments raised from the floor. O'Toole considered himself to be McCabe's second-in-command, a dream combination of brains and brawn. Perhaps this once was the case but now it was a view he shared only with himself. Now the workers could predict his speeches, shout out the conclusions to his sentences and mimic his odd priest-like gestures as he spoke. It was in this state of exposure that this small man now spoke.

'Brothers.'

The women led a disinterested response of 'what about the sisters?' but sadly Frank O'Toole knew little of correction or alterations, as his prepared text dictated his speech. He looked to his grubby piece of paper for an answer to his tormentors and saw only the script of his and others' treachery. It was to be yet another flawed history lesson.

'All my life I've devoted to the struggle of the working class, our aspirations to replace capital with labour.' He paused for celebration. Something tumbled through the room but it was not celebration.

'This road is long and hard. This is why we call it the struggle, our struggle. Until we reach our goals we have to struggle with the chaos of capital until it becomes its own gravedigger, and at this moment we will achieve the conclusion of our struggle. We know problems exist ... but Rome wasn't built in a day ... trust us.... The union is our union and we must respect its democracy and its officers, they are our leaders and without leadership, strong leadership, we have anarchy. Stevens is a hard boss but a fair boss as well. Let us negotiate from a position of strength.' These words seemed to please him and he continued oblivious as ever to his falseness.

'Mr. Jacks is an experienced negotiator for the union and they don't come much higher than him,' he called out to the hall, 'united we stand and,' he held his breath as if for effect but it seemed to all that he had forgotten his well-trodden vocabulary, 'divided we fall.' The words as ever were unimportant, empty, and no one really listened. They tumbled to the floor wastefully.

The vast hall finished his short contribution for him after interrupting at every available moment and as blue overalls provided many such moments the platform was left in no doubt as to the feelings of the workers. Even McCabe understood the writing on the wall although it was still very vague to him. Perhaps it was at this point that bedlam detonated. It was now almost seven o'clock, most of the drill shop had already left with the assumption that McCabe would carry the day, not with any great oratory but with that naked aggression fuelled by management and union threats that so often 'did the trick'. But the time for tricks had long passed and had not the canyon of space left by the drill shop workers at the front of the hall, reinforced with tables and chairs, been there, then Jacks, McCabe, Frank O'Toole and the rest of the committee would have been attacked. As it was the gap between the platform and the workers served simply to underline the division between these two distinct groups. One or two younger members of the committee tried to intervene on behalf of the workers but McCabe pushed them back. A cry rang out from the back of the hall, no speech, no analysis, no mystique of 'real politik'. Simply a word that encapsulated the wish and demands of the workers in that hall that night.

'STRIKE!'

At first some workers did not register the cry immediately, others repeated the call until this one word found itself repeated and as often as the word was spoken the louder came its rendition. It seemed as if the room would explode with this word. This single syllable rattled to the beat of feet and hands as they banged against the hall.

'Strike! ...Strike! ...Strike! ...Strike! ...Strike!'

Like thunder it rolled over the workers back and forth like a tidal wave and its force lifted the room and the people within it.

John Evans sat silent. He was a man revisiting experiences from his past. Annie and the apprentice banged the floor with their feet and called in unison. Hawkins, the young black drill shop worker and the rest of the women from the metal cutting shop sat silently. Margaret Harvey looked across to John Evans, both raised their eyes and shrugged their shoulders. The group now stood and made their way out of the canteen behind the rows of workers filing out chanting that word, the word that brought them together in unity, the word that gave them true freedom from their oppressors.

'Strike!'

As the room emptied the pale of smoke that had hung over the hall throughout the meeting began to fall slowly and the committee, on their platform, became lost to sight in the deepest of grey hazes. McCabe had left earlier, dragged away by Jacks, to meet the management. Stevens junior had not left the factory for he understood the potential for rebellion amongst the workers. But he did still expect McCabe and Jacks to deliver on time as usual. Both men had scurried to the factory manager's office, only Johnson and

Stevens where there. As soon as they entered the room the owner's son knew what had happened. It was written over the union official's face. McCabe's face was blanker than normal. Calm and purposeful the owner's son spoke to Jacks.

'You had better not tell me that we have a strike,' he said as untold time elapsed before Jacks summoned up the courage to answer him.

'Well,' the union official said as if no other word would do.

Before Jacks could make up his apologies for his members' behaviour Stevens had put on his coat and was about to leave the office. Before he closed the door he turned to Jacks and gave him a look of cold derision.

'I will shut this factory down at 8.30 in the morning if every worker is not making switchgear by this time,' he said as if disinterested in his own statement.

Johnson waited a few moments, keeping his gaze fixed firmly to the floor as if studying some slight imperfection. He then left without exchanging any words with the other men in the room. Jacks looked at McCabe, who said he would sort it all out in the morning. Jacks knew otherwise and he left the room. McCabe stared into the empty space before him, ignorant of everything.

In the factory the young drill worker had separated the apprentice from his girlfriend long enough to show him just how much copper he had managed to steal in the mayhem of the day. Both strapped each other's waist with as much as they could carry in weight. Darkness had descended hours earlier outside the factory and a blanket of soft snow covered the ground. Both boys were able to blend in with other workers in the factory. Many assumed that a strike would start the next day and wanted to immobilise their machines or collect their belongings before they went home. Fred Williams, the foreman, John Evans, the chargehand, Daniel Hawkins, the acid bath man, Margaret Harvey and Annie, from the metal cutting shop, all waited opposite the factory for the boys to emerge. Cold, hungry and wary, they huddled together. Each copper bar weighed at least two pounds and Hasaan had taken his opportunities that day to steal more than both boys could carry, but despite the weight stashed against their bodies movement inside the factory towards the steel exit door was slow but possible. An added bonus for the young thieves was that all the security guards had been designated other duties as a result of the late meeting and this, they knew, would give them a relatively free passage out of the factory. Problems only began to materialise when both boys encountered the snow and whilst they trusted their group to protect them they knew they would never condone theft, even if it was from the factory. Both boys did not want to disclose that they had bundles of copper slabs strapped to their waist. Recognising the dangers that the snow brought for both of them they negotiated their exit from the factory with a great deal of skill and a balance only youth provides. Unfortunately, other workers were leaving the factory at the same time and it was a law of probability that contact of some sort would eventually be made. It happened as they weaved their way across the road. A group of young apprentice toolmakers began throwing snow at the boys and in an effort to avoid this attack they attempted to move and run at the same time. This action proved fatal for both boys, who, whilst advancing to the middle of the road, fell with the solid descent of two narrow brick walls. Neither boy could lift themselves off their backs as the weight of the copper heaved against the absence of any grip on the covered floor. Eventually one of the boys managed to roll over and get to his feet whilst the other lay prone in the middle of the road with traffic held up on both sides. Williams knew what the problem was and so did the others. John Evans and Annie ran across the road and lifted the dead weight from the ground. Silent looks expressed the dissatisfaction of the elder members of the group as Annie and the two boys navigated their way to the nearest bus stop.

At eight o'clock Annie and the two boys arrived at a local scrap metal dealers on the edge of town. Hasaan was first on the old metal scale watching intensely as the dealer balanced the ancient mechanism that would disclose the weight of the boy to subtract it from his hoard of copper. He was used to this routine and the games of the owner. Even in theft there is still more to steal. Hasaan knew he never got a good deal but he was happy with the money he normally got from the dealer. The scrap metal yard was pitch black and only the street lamps provided some sense of shadow in the darkness and as the scales crashed down the man began to mumble some curse to himself, then he spoke to the boy on the scale.

'You're about eleven stone, aren't ya? Well, let's call it a tenner,' he said.

Hasaan demanded that the copper be weighed separately. 'I got fifteen the other week and this is twice as much, you robbin bastard,' he argued.

'Take your fuckin stash elsewhere then ere!' he shouted to the other boy.

'You get on the fuckin scales,' he said to the apprentice and before he even got on the scale the scrap metal dealer had announced his price.

'Now that's what I call twenty pounds' worth, take it out, lad, drop it there.'

Hasaan now went straight up to the merchant and confronted him.

'I've got exactly the same amount of copper as 'im, what are you fuckin playin at?' he yelled.

The man pushed into his face.

'Take it or leave it—make your mind up.'

Whichever way the calculation was examined, the boys and the girl knew that this was almost over ten weeks' wages—and worst still, the scrap metal dealer knew this. As both boys argued with the man Annie stepped forward and grabbed the money now being waved by the dealer. Both looked at her and told her to give him the money back. Looking them in the eye, she said she would wait for them outside and in a panic they ran after her, shouting abuse at the scrap metal dealer as they went.

'What are you doin, you've just cost us a tenner?' Hasaan called.

Annie stopped on the pavement and faced two angry young men.

'Look, it's late and I want to have a drink and something to eat. Here's your money, give it back to him and strap that copper back around your waist. Here's your money, go on then,' she said.

The snow was now falling quite heavily on them. Hasaan snatched the money from the girl and ran back towards the scrap metal dealer's barn. Now out of sight a crash of broken glass and cursing rang out in the dimly lit street. The three ran off down the street away from the dealer, who was now chasing them. Thirty pounds was a lot of money and the three spent much of it that night on drink, food and a nightclub. For a few hours they ordered whatever they wanted and bought drinks for who ever they wanted. It was an experience none of them had ever had and they did not expect it to arise again, at least not in the near future. That night, as the young apprentice observed Annie, he thought that he loved her. Loved her if this meant he wanted to be with her all the time, then yes, he loved her and had done so since he first set eyes on her.

Chapter Nine

*The technical subordination of the workman to the uniform motion of
the instruments of labour, and the peculiar composition of the body of
workpeople, consisting as it does of individuals of both sexes and of all
ages, give rise to a barrack discipline, which is elaborated into a
complete system in the factory, and brings the previously mentioned
labour of superintendence to its fullest development, thereby dividing
the workers into manual labourers and overseers, into the private
soldiers and the N.C.O.s of an industrial army.*

—K.Marx, *Capital*

Some workers arrived at the factory very early in order to set up their picket
lines. Workers going to other factories on this vast industrial estate ignored
the disruption to what passed for their normality. Some came over to find out
what was happening. By 6.30 that Friday morning over one hundred workers
stood in the icy snow by the main entrance of G.P. Stevens & Sons. It was
over fifteen years since the last outbreak of industrial action and now, as then,
its leader was John Evans. He had been one of the first to attend and whilst
he did not claim the role of leader he knew from experience that the mantle
of responsibility would eventually fall upon his shoulders. This was not
arrogance but inevitability. Some braziers had been lit and the workers
huddled together with an air of great confidence, examining every aspect of
change that affected passers-by, the road, the sky, the traffic, even the cinders
as they glistened in the braziers. This behaviour reflected the cavernous
fracture with the regimentation of factory life that any strike imposes. In this
sense, like any prisoner or conscript, suddenly cast to the outside world, the
trauma of freedom collapsed against the abject feeling of loss and exclusion
from the cold comfort that repetition and routine provides. Eyes darted back
and forth as if waiting for the boss to come out from the factory and invite all
the workers back after recognising that a dreadful mistake had been made.
Some workers stood uncomfortably close to the factory gate, shuffling ever
nearer in the vain hope that they may be sucked in without a trace from the
abnormality of the picket line for the normality of the production line. Many

of the workers who arrived at the factory were clearly equipped for work and joined the group nearest the gate in the twilight world of the striker-worker. Some simply crossed the picket line and in its newness, like the snow on the ground that morning, these first steps into the factory found their treachery lost in the novelty of it all.

All was contradiction. McCabe and Jacks had entered the main office at about 6.45, ignoring the workers who stood as vacantly as guards on ceremonial duty. They in their turn allowed them to pass unhindered with the equally vague view that they were going in to negotiate a victory or a defeat. Something in their heads accepted this action. It was their habit. They were still factory workers despite standing on a picket line. The tumult of transformation was yet to hit them. Hundreds of workers stood in the street outside the factory that morning, only a handful of workers had crossed the line. Margaret Harvey and John Evans answered questions fired at them as different groups of workers nominated one amongst their number to seek information, any information. Around these two individuals a further grouping had emerged, many of them being shop stewards, who by their silent proximity to Harvey and Evans had rejected the corrupt leadership of McCabe. The apprentice and his girlfriend arrived late on the picket line, looking tired from their late-night celebrations, they too clung to the group around John Evans. Frank O'Toole used the main entrance to join McCabe and Jacks. This was a time of symbolism, when the language of the body spoke clearer than any words. The more practical workers on the line, who had not surrendered their freedom to the factory, revelled in their liberation. For this 'wildcat' action, as it would no doubt be considered by those whose luxurious liberty allowed them to avoid the conscription of industrial life, would impose a unique opportunity upon everyone. Some of these workers took control to ensure the organisation of the practical sustenance of the picket line, heat, shelter, food and drink. As if by magic the rudiments of a long stay outside the factory walls were being established without supervision, without orders, without bosses and without authority.

For five hours the workers stood outside, then, at 11.00 o'clock, some commotion by the main entrance announced the presence of McCabe and Jacks. John Evans was ushered to the front so that he may be best suited to hear and respond, if necessary, on the workers' behalf. Such was the air of spontaneity that now inspired those workers outside the factory. Because of his history and because of his integrity his leadership seemed randomly thrown up by the crowd. The apprentice was overwhelmed by the speed of these proceedings. He could not have dreamt for more. In his mind the revolution had started. Yet his dream confirmed he still knew nothing. McCabe stood on the steps of the factory and made an effort to lean on the brass bars that adorned the stone staircase. He looked somehow subdued, and this image of silence persisted as Jacks proceeded to speak to the workers who gathered in front of him. The apprentice stood directly alongside John Evans. Looking beyond the figures before him he could see the young receptionist. Her life, unsurprisingly, had altered little, and despite the commotion outside she continued to prune herself in the mirrors that reflected her image, waiting longingly for nothing.

Jacks was not a man to welcome the invasion of union members on his precious time. His life was not too dissimilar from that of the young girl behind him. He had an image of himself that surpassed reality and he preferred to consider his self-worth in the presence of those whom he thought, without doubt, to be his betters. They were his mirrors. This left him only one option but to seek the patronage of the boss class. For they were the people he respected most, not the dirty unkempt workers whom he claimed to represent. For them he had long despaired. He had risen above this mayhem because he had proved himself better. This was what he thought. He long held the view that the choice before him was management or full-time employee of the union, for no difference existed for him in this choice. Whilst he chose the latter he flattered himself to think he could transfer his abilities of leadership to serve enterprise and profit more directly at any time. The impressive figure that Jacks had cultivated now stood before the workers. He wore a tie, and in this world that made him a figure to be respected. Well respected or hated. In short, he wore the costume of the boss. And for Jacks this was his normality. Now the comfort of dealing with the bosses was being replaced by the nausea of the mob, who knew his every treachery.

'I need to tell you it has not been easy in there, but, after some time and some serious negotiations, I am happy to tell you, brothers.' He had started his betrayal.

The cry rose from the sisters and the brothers of the sisters together. A united cry.

'And sisters!'

'As you like,' he muttered under his breath, 'comrade McCabe and I have successfully reached an agreement, you can all go back to work now,' he announced. He turned to go back into the factory. McCabe had already disappeared from the scene. Pushed forward by a group that now encircled him, John Evans spoke for the first time. He spoke quietly and calmly amidst the cries of the workers.

'Brother Jacks, could you just explain what that agreement is?' he asked.

'Ah, Brother Evans,' Jacks replied, 'wondered when we'd hear your voice again—it seems such a long time. No, I can't. You have to go back to work first. You were supposed to have been sacked at 8.30 this morning—I've just saved your job,' Jacks boasted.

John Evans's voice grew louder. 'Just explain what deal you've cut with the boss. I think we deserve that explanation.'

As the shouts of 'agreement' rose amongst the crowd of workers Jacks turned his back to walk into the factory offices. As he reached the doors he turned directly to John Evans, clearly replicating the actions of Stevens the night before.

'That's the deal. You're back in the chair, John. Get them back in here for 11.30 or you can explain to them why they're all fucking sacked. Do that favour for us eh, Comrade,' he said, smiling.

Fred Williams, the only supervisor on strike that morning, lurched forward, cursing Jacks and telling John Evans that he now had to address the workers. But the workers themselves were organising this event and within minutes the movement of the crowd, now totalling several hundred, eased him to the top of the steps. Even before he spoke the comparison between Jacks and McCabe and John Evans was stark. This was a modest, quiet man who had never lost the respect of the workers in the factory. They saw him differently than people such as Jacks and McCabe, but it was this difference that frightened them, because his integrity could lead them, or so they thought, towards all manner of principled disaster or victory. Now they had to make a choice. His experience was assured.

'Well, sisters and brothers,' he began, 'most of you heard, they will not tell you what they have agreed but if we don't return to work within twenty or so minutes we are all going to be sacked. Listen, the choice rests with you— you don't have to be told the implications of your actions; but whatever we decide we stick together either out here or in there. It's time to decide....'

Workers in the crowd shouted their determination that they wanted to stay out, some wanted to return so that the negotiations promised by the union could start. Each view was momentarily argued on the snow-covered pavements outside the factory. The divide amongst the workers varied from issue to issue, person to person, but general agreement had long been reached that something had to be done to redress the balance of power inside the factory. Atkins's death and the treachery of the union only forced matters along. They had given too much away. On this the majority were agreed. Evans had a style that undervalued almost all events of the moment, and while in the crowd heated arguments were exchanged his manner and ability to weave together complex differences brought calm upon the workers.

'Little point exists to arguing about what's wrong,' he told them, 'we need to make a decision, because once you've gone back in you all know what to expect. Perhaps we can do both? It's Friday and you're all due to be paid.

Let's see if they are going to pay us and let's see for ourselves what the agreement is between Jacks and Johnson,' he suggested.

His thoughts rippled through the crowd and when asked to vote the majority decided to go back inside the factory. United again, the workers returned to their workplace, pushing through the police lines that opened like giant vaults. This and nothing else seemed too important at the time. It was a phase, another phase in the struggle. About one hundred workers had already entered the factory that morning, and as the strikers came in from the cold this group were gathered in the drill shop listening to Johnson, Carberry, McCabe and Jacks. It was clear that they were taking orders to proceed with as much work as possible despite the absence of the majority of the workers. The factory remained in darkness as John Evans led the men and women along the corridors and onto the floor of the factory. While the workers congregated in one section of the plant Evans, Williams, Margaret Harvey, the apprentice and his girlfriend marched towards the management and the union. Jacks and McCabe stood close to the men who had crossed the picket line as if to underline a solidarity of sorts. Johnson stepped forward and asked Evans what he wanted.

'Well, obviously we need to discuss with you the agreement you struck with our union and we also need to know what arrangements are being made for the workers to be paid,' Evans said.

Johnson turned to Jacks and McCabe, then looked towards the growing group that now stood before him.

'Oh no, John, it's not as easy as that, you know quite well that we talk to the official union, not any rag-tag thrown up by a mob,' some of the group began pushing forward, 'and if the men want payin' they can get back to fuckin work,' Johnson ordered.

John Evans directed the same question to Jacks and McCabe. Absent stares provided, or at least they thought so, a reasoned explanation for their actions. He turned towards Johnson.

'It seems perfectly reasonable that the men get paid for the work they've done and that we be given the details of negotiations between the company and the union, Mr. Johnson,' he repeated.

The men who had entered work early that morning mainly kept their heads turned or bowed away from the stare of their fellow workers who now confronted both the bosses and the union. One or two men from the drill shop, known supporters of McCabe, felt invigorated by the direct interest shown in them by their newfound sponsors, calling out to Evans that that he could lead his army back out of the factory and to the dole office. Johnson told these men to shut up, then turned to Evans and asked if the men would be going back to work.

'The men and women need an answer to the two questions I've already asked,' he said.

'Well, that's that. Unless we see some productivity no one gets paid. I've gotta factory to run and that usually involves men making things,' Johnson stated.

Johnson returned to informing his workers just what was expected of them that morning as welders, drillers and lathes operators identified their skills. Frank O'Toole appeared to be using his own organisational skills to direct this operation. It seemed all too well organised. John Evans was now talking in earnest to his small group of helpers and it was agreed there and then that they would direct all the workers to the main wage office and demand their pay packets. From that moment the strike would begin. It is at such moments that leadership acquires a value often beyond the individual or individuals who find this mantle thrust upon them. Little explanation was required for the workers who milled around the main area of the factory, they followed that which they needed most—leadership. The wages department was not big but it employed at least five clerks, who were now beset by almost the entire workforce of G.P. Stevens. As usual on Friday their wage packets had already been deposited in the company safe ready for distribution at the end of the day. The head cashier, an elderly man, who had known John Evans for many years, expressed his sympathy for the workers but told their leader that he did not have the authority to pay strikers out. Margaret Harvey stepped forward and instructed the cashier that if he did not start making arrangements to pay out the workers, then he and the company safe would be thrown out the window. This threat caused much laughter amongst those workers who now stood on the top of the gangway outside the wage office. As their numbers grew they snaked down the metal staircase and poured out on the factory floor. Laughter tumbled down the line. Even the cashier laughed.

'Put in such a charming way,' he said, 'how could I refuse. But I must speak with the boss first and confirm that this is all right.'

'No, it's not,' Margaret Harvey insisted. 'Who does that money belong to?' she threatened the wage clerk.

'It's the company's money,' he said without question, 'money that will be paid to the workers when it has been agreed,' he added forcefully.

'No.' Margaret Harvey stepped closer to the man. John Evans stood aside.

'It could never be the company's money because they keep tellin' us they have none, so if they have no money where did it come from?' she asked with equal force. 'It could only come from the labour of the workers,' she answered, 'and the fact that they built things that were sold for money and that's what's in the safe. So let's just have our wages. Now!' she demanded.

Left with no real physical options but to concede to her demands, the cashier asked for a few minutes to get the safe open and have his staff ready to pay the workers their individual pay packets. Cheers rang through the factory as the news of this impressive victory passed down the line to the factory floor underneath the office balcony. Some of the men at the top of the staircase had never been in the cashier's office before and this was the first time they had seen the company safe, they had heard about it and joked about robbing it, but this was the only time they had actually seen this green, brass and steel box that contained the very essence of the factory. This was what it was all about, so they had been told. It was what they worked for, and their awe matched that of Catholics beholding the sacristy, it was the body and blood of the bosses. Rumour past down the line that the workers at the head of the queue were actually breaking into the safe. This sent loud cheers throughout the line. Within minutes the workers were picking up their pay slips and word was also passed to the workers that after they had their pay slips they should go to the canteen for another meeting to decide what to do next.

This whole process took over one hour to complete and in the canteen the staff had already begun to make sandwiches and soup for the workers only for the first time no one would be charged. By this action alone a tangible transformation had already begun to take place. Men helped the women in the canteen, men treated the women with respect and even some of the women began to treat the men with a respect of sorts. Nevertheless, the transformation was marked and everyone saw this. Some disliked the change, others revelled in it. A shop stewards committee was busy being formed on the platform where the night before mayhem had ensued. A number of good men who had been shop stewards under McCabe's leadership stood alongside John Evans, Fred Williams, Margaret Harvey, Annie, Dan Hawkins and the two youngest of this assembly, the apprentice and Hasaan. The apprentice had spent all his time that day bolted to the side of John Evans, watching his every move learning, and wanting to protect him. He now stood at his side in the centre of this larger group that had now grown to around fifteen people and at his side stood Annie. For him this was the revolution and he was to make sure that he missed nothing and was involved in everything.

John Evans called the impromptu meeting to order and asked the group to elect a leader that would be acceptable to the whole factory. One of the former shop stewards moved that John Evans accept this role and this was agreed amidst a great cry from the majority of workers. The chargehand then explained the situation as he saw it. It was unlikely that they would find out what agreement Jacks had reached with the company until it was too late. The workers would have no option but to continue their action and the event in the wage office would obviously incite a response from the management.

Johnson had about one hundred workers on the floor of the factory and his intention was to start work. No doubt he would then contact the Employment Exchanges to get more workers to replace the strikers. But it was imperative that the workers should start the strike inside the factory and that the tactic was to occupy. The committee would also have to acknowledge the reality that they were fighting both the union and the bosses and this strike would be deemed unofficial and wildcat. Nothing could happen unless they carried the majority of the workers. Members of this newly formed committee exchanged ideas as to how best to realise these objectives, as the basic principles outlined by John Evans were met with a resounding endorsement. Plans would have to be made to ensure that the workers occupied the whole of the factory and secured all the entrances. Production would continue under the regime of a workers' co-operative. John Evans looked up from the table and saw that the canteen was now almost as full as it had been the night before. Many of the workers were now queuing for food at one end of the hall. Outside the sun shone, cutting swathes of golden light into the canteen, and despite the snow it was warm and the workers felt that warmth. Evans turned finally to the group assembled around the large table at the front of the canteen.

'Sisters and brothers,' he said, as ever stressing the word 'sister', 'it's important that we respect each other, there's no room for rhetoric—these men and women are going to have to make perhaps the most difficult decision of their lives here this morning. Let's show some respect and leadership here. Would any one else like to address the meeting?'

The group agreed that it be left to John Evans and Margaret Harvey to explain the issues to the workers. By this time the hall was full, not with the anger and hatred of the night before but with a calmness eased by the satisfaction that these people themselves had made a decision, had exercised a choice. They had done something that was not the result of an order or command. Not imposed from above but delivered from below. Light passed through the room casting no shadows. The newly formed committee lined up in front of the workers. One of the elected shop stewards came forward and asked if any other workers wanted to serve on the strike committee. One or two came forward as more cheers rang out from the workers. Then he asked if the new committee could be endorsed by the meeting. More cheers rang through the hall. Then he asked if the meeting would endorse John Evans as the convenor to replace McCabe. Louder cheers erupted. At this point John Evans stood and addressed the meeting. For many years he had been the convenor of the plant, he was a respected trade unionist, renowned for his integrity and ability. When he spoke he commanded a respect; a respect that could only be earned through long years of practical experience. His first task was to inform the hall that the funeral of Brian Atkins would be held on Tuesday at the local church and it was important that as many people as possible showed their respect. Evans felt that yesterday's minute's silence was not genuine and that the man who called it had no rights in this matter. Everyone in the hall rose and when the minute passed Evans addressed the workers again.

'This is not going to be easy and we have difficult decisions to make. Your committee feel that we have no option but to strike. But we continue it from inside the factory.' He paused for a second.

'We occupy!' he shouted and the workers responded with those very same words. The cry bounced off the metal beams in the roof of the factory. 'Occupy!'

Again loud cheers rang out, rolling through the hall from front to back, and so began a lengthy debate as to the validity of the tactics being recommended. The workers had already nominated people from their own departments to speak on their behalf and this reduced the normal routine of repetition that such meetings generally encouraged. Some workers were confused. Some were frightened. Some asked plainly stupid questions as to what they would be paid if they worked during the occupation. As they spoke the detail of the tactic became clearer and the more practical amongst the workers volunteered to ensure that food was available, some volunteered to oversee security, others just let it be known that they had particular skills that even their closest friends were unaware of. This group would paint or write leaflets, design posters, make banners. It was agreed that each worker would pay a shilling a day for food and drink. Rotas would be established to cover night shifts and as each responsibility was outlined cheers rang out as particular workers were nominated for specific roles. Jokes flew across the room regarding the ability of some nominees to actually stay awake or be relied upon for certain tasks. After only half an hour the workers were decided and they clapped and cheered when John Evans told them to take up their respective positions in the factory but only after the committee had reported its decision to the management. Under no circumstances would violence be tolerated, this was to be a peaceful, dignified but determined occupation. He asked everyone to be patient, stating that what he had to say to the company would only take a few seconds, after that 'we will take control of our own destiny,' he told them. At this every man and woman rose to their feet clapping, whistling and cheering. Such outpourings of pure emotion, of liberation, contradicted the cold reality that they had, to all intent and purposes, already lost their jobs, lost the only means possible for them to provide for their families. Now the euphoria of freedom was to sustain them together with the strength that only a real unity of the human spirit can bring.

The transformation was as complete as it was instant and like prisoners surveying the demolished walls of their cells they had a vision of freedom and of the possibilities, the endless possibilities, that lay before them. For they had been released. The light in the room seemed brighter than ever.

Chapter Ten

*...a movement of liberation not only of women but of men by women.
One of its most basic aspects is its opposition to military and financial
models of organisation, to the power of money and giant
organisations. It represents a will to organise one's own life, to form
personal relationships, to love and be loved....*
                                —Alain Touraine. *Le Nouvel Observateur 1978*

Annie kept hold of her young apprentice as he stood at the side of John
Evans. The whole committee left the hall marching down the gangways
towards the drill shop. McCabe and Frank O'Toole were examining some of
the machines along with most of the workers who entered the factory that
morning. McCabe was in a rage as he turned to face John Evans. They had
all heard the news as it rattled down from the canteen.

'So ya think ya can just replace me,' he shouted, 'well, ya welcome to it
cos you're all gonna end up in fuckin prison. Johnson knows you've
sabotaged these machines and he knows who's dunnit. Who the fuck do ya
think yer are?' McCabe demanded. 'I've told yer all this factory's gonna shut
down. What are you gonna tell the men? Don't worry, lads it's the fuckin
revolution.' He started to laugh. 'Yer a gang a fuckin dick 'eds. Well, I'm
tellin ya we'll get these machines to work soon enough,' he screamed.

John Evans remained calm. 'No, McCabe,' he insisted, 'we're asking you
to leave the factory now, you and these men here. They can stay if they
want—they'd be welcome to. But if you don't leave, then we have no other
option.' The hidden threat hovered above them.

At this McCabe lifted the giant spanner he had in his hands and came
towards Evans. Hawkins stepped in front of him and stared darkly into
McCabe's eyes. McCabe was a big man, overweight and wholly incapable of
any rapid movement, but still his presence always proved domineering.
Hawkins was bigger and stronger. McCabe knew this. His power in the
factory had all but disappeared overnight and his disparate army, once a fine
example of adherents to the system, now looked torn and shattered. Evans
repeated his call to McCabe, who turned to his ramshackle gang.

'I'm gonna see Johnson, you lot stay put,' he ordered, 'take no notice of this crowd,' he turned to the chargehand, 'I'll be back, Evans, and it's you that'll be leaving—not us,' he threatened.

O'Toole ran after McCabe, avoiding all contact with Evans, who now addressed the men gathered in the drill shop. No women had crossed the picket line that morning. Evans explained without malice that the men had a fairly simple choice to make, either they occupied or left immediately. One of the men said that he was waiting for McCabe to return and the others remained silent and still. Evans and the rest of the committee, as well as some of the men and women who now joined them from the canteen, knew that it was imperative that they clear and secure the factory as quickly as possible. It was a decisive moment when hearts can weaken. Minds can be changed and doubt can destroy the courage to act spontaneously. Such moments were key to all events. Some of the men joined the group, the majority cursed and swore at Evans and the workers who stood with him. Whatever psychology took place at this moment, reality would possibly record that it was the simple majority against the minority that mattered at this instant. Corralled in the drill shop, Hawkins ushered them along the gangways like a policeman on crowd duty. Behind him workers provided authority should some doubt this singular officer's powers to enforce his will. Within seconds about seventy workers had grudgingly been funnelled out the factory. It surprised few that this group obeyed these orders with such timidity, for orders were all they knew. For the other group a different world encircled them—for they were the ones now giving the orders. The steel doors slammed and bolted behind them. Again the celebrations of the workers resonated throughout the factory. From the balcony that loomed over the factory floor the figures of Johnson, Carberry and McCabe could be seen. Johnson shouted down to Evans and with an air of unaccustomed good manners signalled that Evans should come up to his office.

Johnson was conciliatory. He recognised the situation for what it was and knew that the balance of power at that very moment was precarious to say the least and he had to judge its potential. He had already dismissed McCabe's role in this complex equation. Evans was now the man to deal with, if only for a short duration until normal power relations returned to the factory. His world was one of inevitability, for he expected his word to be obeyed. Normality was his power, the power of capital serving the interests of the owner. Stevens had left instructions that he, Johnson, should act to regain control. Concessions could be made and despite the constant repetition of wage restraint the deity of money was perhaps the most unimportant element of worker employer relations. Yes, wages had to be constantly driven down with the lie that financial management was the essence of good business, but control mattered much more. The whole system rested upon control and without it the system would collapse and in this context money meant little, but it had been rammed into the workers' minds that money was the god of all gods. The trade union played this macabre game because it kept them away from the politics of their true relationship, coupled with the fear that if they replaced wage claims with demands for greater control of the production process they just might possibly challenge the real power of the employer class. Money was the smokescreen, the falsehood that protected everything and everyone except, of course, the workers. But in this contradiction of realities they were unimportant yet vital to the whole process of exploitation. Evans knew this madness and awaited the bribe as he walked up the metal staircase.

'Look, John,' Johnson said as he held out his hand, 'we need to sort this mess out quickly, the men can have wage negotiations but they have to return to work now before—well, I'm sure you know what I mean.' It was said in a fatherly way although Evans had rejected his hand. Without care Johnson continued.

'Bring them back and we can sit down like reasonable people and arrive at the normal compromises that I know we can make,' he said.

Johnson had been given a free hand to reach an immediate settlement. G.P. Stevens junior had accumulated massive savings on the cost of wage labour in the factory thanks mainly to McCabe's ability to deliver. Whilst such additional profit, a profit upon a profit, was always quickly gobbled up by the capitalist class, their obsession with double-entry book keeping, the measure and record of profit and loss, allowed them to write off annually the surplus they stole for themselves from the workers. Nevertheless, if money were needed for a contingency to speculate it would be found. This was one of those rare occasions in which some of that wage labour surplus needed to be ploughed back and invested in human capital as opposed to dead capital. This latter element of dead capital, costed for new machinery, had never been called upon as with most engineering firms they still relied on the machines that had made armaments during the war. In fact, some of the machines used at the Stevens factory dated back to the First World War. So, in a strictly economic assessment of the financial strategy of the factory, money was not an issue especially in relation to who controls the factory. The invisible hand of the market economy could rule as long as this rule was in the control of the capitalist. As Johnson spoke Evans became more agitated. He knew that many of the workers would be impressed with this apparent offer of a wage rise or rather the offer of negotiations over a wage rise. This, he knew, would not solve the long-term problems of the workers, for they needed to regain some control back in the factory, but Evans was under no illusions; this was not the revolution but it was an important opportunity that had to be taken to regain influence and reclaim dignity for the workers on the shopfloor. Above all he wanted this to be known by Johnson, that the workforce was bidding for control.

'No. That's not the issue,' he said. 'Atkins was a victim of the issues and that's to do with a lot more than wages. We need to establish, here and now, the basic increase on wages. We need now to agree an agenda for those conditions that have to be improved for the workers in the factory. This we can do in five minutes. You know that and I know that. Will you agree to this, Mr. Johnson?' he asked. At this level of awareness they were both ambassadors of capital. Evans knew this.

Economics is a truly dismal science but contains a symmetry of mathematical beauty in which the logic of numbers, no matter how random, creates calculations from which may only be concluded a given set of answers. It has a breathtaking aura of fundamentalism about itself. This is to say that provided with a set of figures an infinite number of given calculations may only conclude with one product—that being the correct answer. Unlike so much in life there is a comfort in having a problem for which only one correct answer applies. That is, the answer you want. On the face of it this may seem somewhat dismal but satisfyingly dismal without doubt. In such a predictable world one would assume that the trick would be to make this predictability all encompassing. This is where the capitalist moves beyond knowing the answer to mathematical equations and enters the unknown vast uncharted and variable waters of the human condition. Sadly, the introduction of this unknown quantity, this unknown mass, obliterates the axiomatic nature of capital's mathematical foundation as it drowns in the suffocating act of offering sane explanations for insane exploitation. However, in order to account for this unknown, the capitalist has to give it some value so that in effect x can be incorporated into their wonderful world of numerics. The only way to provide x with a value is to impose it, control it, defend it, protect it and above all ensure its value is the lowest common denominator in relation to the rest of this economic conundrum. In other words, to extract the potential of human expression from human labour. No one but the capitalist must know what the value of x is. Now, despite the whole panoply of the State being made available to ensure the value of x, the destruction of all human potential, even this sophisticated and brutal racket of protection at times, fails to impose its will. This was one of those times. Evans awaited Johnson's response. At this crucial moment he chose to add his own personal influence upon the value of x. Conciliation flew out the window in his outrage at the arrogance of Evans, of the workers, to challenge his power to impose the proposed value of any settlement.

'I've contacted the police and informed them that your mob have stolen money from the company's safe,' this power to call in the state was a vanity that Johnson could not hide. 'Arrests will be made. Those not in prison will be walking the streets,' he said.

At this point he looked over the chargehand's shoulder and shouted at the committee and some of the workers, who now crowded on the edge of his doorway. 'You're all fuckin sacked, now get out of my office and get out of my fuckin factory, you're all fuckin finished!' he screamed. The mask slipped gently from his boss's face.

'No,' replied Evans, 'it's you that has to leave.'

For a few moments a great expectation filled the room that begged someone else, or something, to enter and correct the chaos of this situation. No one would really ever admit it, but deep down they all longed for a normality no matter how much they hated it. They would not, including Johnson, have been human had they not wished to avoid the outcome of their actions. Not through cowardice or political naïveté but because at that moment they challenged everything that had been pushed down their throats from infancy. From the time before infancy—to their forefathers. The apprentice stood alongside Evans and thought that he was in a school play. Whatever thoughts raced through individual minds, this was not a normal situation. Within those few seconds, as if frozen in time, nothing did materialise to alter this reality. Hawkins, robotic and responsive to the inherent need to act, moved forward. Johnson muttered that he had not heard or seen the likes of this ever before. Hawkins's shadow cast over him. McCabe looked and acted like a beaten dog. Carberry constantly wiped the sweat off his round face searching for something to do, something to say. But as with so many his role was to do what he was told. Perhaps that was the problem for all of them. They were waiting to be told what to do. This was all that was expected of them. But nothing happened. The longer they waited the longer nothing happened.

The three men pushed past the workers as they stood at the doorway reaching beyond the raised metal gangway down towards the factory floor and out of the factory. No doubt they were on their way to summon up the forces of capital to regain control. Some workers held their heads downwards as if embarrassed by their actions with silence offering them some anonymity for the crimes they were committing. Johnson and Carberry pushed downwards amongst the faces that now were deaf to orders. Deaf to their control. A crime was being committed but no one could identify it. Criminality being determined by those in authority from school, to State, to law, to Magistry, to police, to factory owners. Yes, they knew they should be proud of what they were doing but the concrete burdens of imposed authority weighed heavy on every man and woman. One of the workers on sentry duty at the steel door allowed its metal bolts to break the silence that now arrested the air inside the factory. Guilt froze its inhabitants. When the metal door slammed all guilt was lifted. It stopped breathing for them. They were free. And in the instant of this realisation they understood that it was, in the end, all meaningless. The factory, the boss, the state, the power, the means of control. Because it only existed while they accepted it. They gave it life. You could touch the air as this free thought rested upon them. Again, the workers cheered in victory as they were truly free of their immediate tormentors. The apprentice and his girl pushed past the workers in the office and peered over the raised gangway to look down on the majority of workers as if to check that the factory had indeed been liberated. This was the case. And he was overwhelmed by the act.

It was Friday afternoon. The call went to all the workers that they should again report to the canteen. That afternoon the wintry sunshine held, bathing the factory in a glowing spectrum of random shades that bounced reflections off the deep reds, greens and blues that adorned the livery of much of the aged machinery on the factory floor. Men and women busied themselves in this warm winter sunlight that enriched the spartan décor of the canteen area. Fresh tea and sandwiches were hurriedly made and handed out as the workers walked leisurely into the room. No more running and pushing, no more forcing food into their mouths, looking at clocks, looking over their shoulders. No more awaiting the siren's orders. It was as if a new civilisation had been born that day without any person knowing. For it all passed without comment as if people were too embarrassed to acknowledge the perverse sickness of their previous life. At one end of the room the committee, now numbering about twenty workers, sat and busied themselves with their newly acquired responsibilities. Tea and sandwiches were brought to their table as they were to other workers as they sat and talked quietly over the events of the day. People welcomed each other and spoke differently for the first time. A new respect emerged spontaneously, urged on by the serenity of the factory, as if the building itself lent its support to the actions of the workers. Men and women spoke of their aspirations for the future, the problems that needed to be solved, the way they would like the factory to be run - now that they were in control. John Evans was ready to address the workers again.

'We all want to thank you for the magnificent way this whole occupation has been conducted,' he told them, 'it's very important that we maintain that discipline and especially the dignity and respect we have to show each other as fellow human beings. It's almost five o'clock and we know many of you will have to travel home to see to your families, but we have to recognise that we also need to defend our occupation. We need everyone to give his or her names into Annie and her new husband....' At this the hall erupted into laughter and jeers.

'I'm not sure if we can organise a wedding as well as an occupation,' he joked 'but we have to respect the needs of all our comrades.' Laughter rang out.

'Sisters and brothers, from this list we can draw up a rota to cover the occupation for the weekend. We expect that some will be able to do longer hours than others because of personal circumstances but everyone has a contribution to make. Some will be greater than others.... Again, we have to respect that and not complain amongst ourselves. We need volunteers to repair the building.' A loud cheer rang out.

'There are that many holes in this place the police would have no difficulty in pouring in anytime along with the rain,' he said.

'Not ever!' came the response.

'We need to clean this filthy factory up!' he called out. Loud cheers again rang out.

'The toilets! The canteen! The working area!' Like an architect building a new city, a new civilisation, John Evans listed his dreams.

'We need artists to make banners and people who can use a typewriter,' he shouted, 'we need workers who can use the stencil copier to make leaflets,' the cheers ran thick and fast on each word.

'We need volunteers to feed us all and yes—we need workers who can lift the blueprints form the orders in the office and supervise work in the plant. We want to nominate Fred Williams for this job, is that agreed?' he asked them.

Now some workers hated, or rather acted out a hatred for Williams, not because he was a particularly nasty or bad man but because he was different and the new regime of respect made this unacceptable behaviour. Some of the workers were slower than others at responding to change and they made some remark or other when this was announced but such words and ideas had been instilled by McCabe and the management. Other workers looked back at them, critically calling for 'a bit more respect.'

'We also need some workers alongside Fred,' John Evans asked, 'so when you give in your names please identify what you can do, what you would like to do and what you will not do. I think that's everything—does anyone have any questions?'

Discussion groups sprang up throughout the hall with impromptu group leaders explaining some of the finer detail of what was being said like a group of translators. This lasted for a few minutes when one of the drill shop workers stood up at the back of the hall. Now as in all these situations it is very difficult to know when people have genuinely changed or whether they are spies or agents provocateurs. But the benefit of the doubt must always be given. The man was recognised as being very close to McCabe and some of the less forgiving amongst the workers asked why he was not with him. Order was requested and received. The man spoke.

'Did I hear right? We are gonna continue to make switchgear?'

A response flew around the hall, 'Yeah, that's right,' the workers told him.

'How can we do that?' the man continued. 'Where do we get our supplies from? Who's gonna pay us? What pay will we get? Do you think they're gonna allow us to stay 'ere like some little Soviet?' The speaker waited for an answer. His arm pointed towards the platform. 'You lot on that platform better be very careful,' he warned, 'we can't operate a factory like this without the bosses and you know it. We need negotiations and I'm moving that now. Take the vote,' he called.

Some in the hall mouthed muted support for these comments, others began to shout the man down. John Evans put it to the vote that negotiations be requested. With only ten or so agreeing to this, the idea was thrown out.

'Well, that is the clear answer, and unless we have any other suggestions the only road forward is to occupy or stand outside in the freezing cold. Let's have confidence in our abilities, we made this factory and we created everything in it. We don't need bosses to tell us what we already know and they don't have a clue about. We know this all to be true. Let's not punish ourselves any further, it has been a long day; can we agree on the committee's recommendation? Raise your hands.'

With this a sea of hands punched the air and men and women held each other and cheered as they proceeded to present their names to the apprentice and his girlfriend. Name, skill and preference were noted for each worker alphabetically as it was agreed that the workers would no longer have a number but a name. It took a long time to record all this information and organise the weekend shifts for the workers, but others helped the two young clerks and within hours seven hundred and twenty workers had officially signed up to join the occupation. A minimum number of two hundred workers would be kept in the factory that weekend to cover days and nights. They had more than enough volunteers. Teams of workers now scoured the factory, replacing broken windows and doors, cleaning the toilets and the factory floor. A small group of workers sat in the office examining new contracts for which blueprints existed. One or two did an inventory of what raw materials existed in stock. Hasaan began repairing some of the machines he had sabotaged and even went to the extreme of returning some of the copper he had stashed away in the toilet cistern. Others cleaned the canteen and took stock of what food would be required over the next few days. The apprentice wanted to go home and have a bath and return to the factory later that day. He left Annie collating her list of those in occupation.

Within an hour he had returned regretting that he ever made the decision to go home. For the news of the occupation and dismissals had been on the local radio and his father left him in no doubt that he opposed all such actions, telling him to go back to work. As he looked at his father he saw the face of McCabe and O'Toole, that fear and bluff. The act of being a man in a man's world as they saw it yet not meeting either criterion. His mother, or so he thought, agreed with him, but she was little different than his father. Why would she not speak up against his hypocrisy? Locking himself in the bathroom the apprentice struggled to make sense of his emotions, secure in the knowledge that at last he had found something in his short life that gave him hope for the future. He had discovered others that thought like him and he compared this discovery with the times he had read books and shared the knowledge that a writer could disclose innermost feelings that only he had thought possible. Despite everything he was calm and collected. Confident. He told his mother that he would be out all the weekend because he had been voted in to do a most important job. She held him close, gave him some money and food, and he left. His father looked in disgust at his mother and shook his head in silence, returning to watch television whilst she continued in the kitchen. At eight o'clock he was standing in the darkness outside the steel door to the factory. Every worker had been told the password to enter the factory. The young boy banged on the door and whispered the word 'comrade'. Bolts screeched against the metal on the other side of the door and a face appeared. It was the same old man who opened the door on his first day in the factory. He looked cleaner, younger and generally more agreeable.

'OK, son, hurry up,' he said.

As the boy entered the factory he could sense the transformation immediately. It now smelt like a hospital as workers continued to clean walls and floors, and when he passed them they welcomed him. Running along the metal staircase and up to the offices he glanced over the metal balcony down to the floor of the factory. Subdued lighting allowed him only to make out the vague forms that moved slowly beneath him. Some workers slept in neat rows along the wall, others read quietly. Some talked quietly in groups whilst individuals could be seen cleaning machines or checking blueprints. Workers marched to and fro, passing documents, exchanging words, returning to some other part of the plant to continue their work. But it was the music. That music—that led an air of the surreal to this new factory. Apparently, as he was later to find out, it was Mozart. His immediate reaction was to find out its source and disconnect it from the mains. To him it was church music, the queen's music or at worst the music of the upper classes. This was all he knew. It was only in this search that he was forced to listen. Softly the music rose from a small radio below the main balcony upon which he now stood. The same music flowed from inside Johnson's reclaimed office. When he entered the room he could see members of the committee writing, studying documents or talking quietly with John Evans.

'Hello son. Everything all right?' John Evans asked.

'Eh yes, fine, thanks. What's that funeral music on for?'

Dan Hawkins's huge frame took up much of the corner of the office. He stood up and placed down the book he was reading. 'Don't tell me that an educated lad such as yourself has never listened to music before?' he said.

'That's not music. And if it is it's bosses' music,' the boy replied.

'It's Mozart and I think we expect you to learn to appreciate it,' said the acid bath man. The boy sat down next to a small boiler heater fixed to the wall smiling that stupid smile that we often think covers all manner of embarrassment. He kept quiet. He was trying to think of something to say that may ease his burden but quickly realised that all he could think of was to insult most of the people in the room. He never said it but his eyes disclosed his thoughts. That these men and women built like carthorses with the strength of oxen, hands like hooves and backbones like industrial wrenches could have any interest outside of the beasts of burden they had become. He thought it and was ashamed of his thoughts. His young friend, Hasaan, sat on the floor in the corner and could not stop himself from intervening in the conversation.

'And we all thought you were an academic, it's fuckin Mozart,' he said with all the experience of an Opera fan. 'Ask yer wife Annie about it, she's one of our experts,' he added.

The figure of Hawkins blocked out the little light that was in the room as he stood over the boy.

'For a moment I was thinking that, well—perhaps you thought that people like us, well, to put it bluntly, that people like us have no brain, no ability to rise above the filth we have to work in,' he spoke only to the boy, no one else could hear. 'How very, very wrong we can all be, my young friend,' he said softly. 'We have people in here who have the most creative and artistic abilities. People who all have an expertise in whatever field they have chosen from fishing to the study of architecture. The fact that they treat us like oily rags does not automatically make us that way.' He studied the boy intently. 'But I'm sure you wouldn't think in such a bigoted way?' he added sharply.

Hawkins poured the boy a cup of tea and asked him if he had eaten. The boy could barely look the man in the eye. His shame was complete and yet Hawkins made his observations so quietly that hardly anyone else heard and the boy thanked him, equally silently, for this.

'Oh I'm fine and I've got a bag of food and some money as well.'

Tired, he closed his eyes and soaked up the soft blanket of tranquillity that had now befallen the factory. John Evans was explaining that the workers had to begin work on Saturday morning.

'Otherwise they would be bored and start looking for excuses to give up—we need to keep everyone busy,' he said. Enough plans existed for at least a month's work and all the raw materials were in the plant.

'It is important that we stick to the schedule outlined at the meeting. I don't think the police or the company will bother us this weekend. Just as long as they know that we are not wrecking the place. Their spies will keep them well informed,' his voice trailed softly around those still awake to listen.

One of the men in the room asked did he have any ideas as to who the spies might be. Margaret Harvey lifted her head from some of the documents she was examining. 'Look.' She leaned forward. Without her turban and overalls she now assumed the role of a manager. 'It could be anyone and normally it will be the person you least expect. These documents we got from the company file—they highlight just some of the things that were going on. Receipts for payment to McCabe for work he never did.' Some in the room began to take notice. 'Money paid to the union as membership dues. But I just did a simple calculation and it doesn't add up, even assuming eight hundred members the figure's way too high. The welder, security guards, drill shop workers, even Jacks is on the payroll!' she exclaimed.

One of the men in the room asked to see some of the documents. 'It can't be,' he interrupted, snatching at some papers.

In a matter-of-fact manner the woman concluded that none of them understood the real depth of corruption that was going on in the factory. The men she named had been costed, whether as payment or wages—they had their own accounts. Not much but still a sizeable figure taken over the year. The documents then got passed around the group. Beethoven was playing on the radio. By now the apprentice had fallen fast asleep. Annie returned and sat on the floor next to the boy and placed her head on his shoulder, then closed her eyes. Carelessly they slept while the factory planned and worked amidst them. Being mindful of their sleep, members of the committee quietly examined the documents and files that now filled the office. Margaret Harvey appeared to be co-ordinating this operation and every so often she would snatch a document and make a note of its content. After several hours she quietly called the room to order.

'John, look at this,' she said.

All the documents were supposed to record the contracts that had been concluded by Stevens to produce switchgear parts or completed units.

'We know that we only have four or five main customers, who then sell them on as a supplier—but look here, look at this, one of the main suppliers is a company called Glens and they're owned by Stevens junior.' She scanned the paper for a few seconds. 'We dispatched over 600 switchgear units to them last year and no invoice appears anywhere. He's robbing his own fuckin company and look at the other directors listed for Glens. Jacks is named here. He's a director and the union is listed as a shareholder. What's all that about?' Then she pointed towards another paper. 'It's a report from some laboratory somewhere down south, it's informing the company that bakelite, dust from cast metal and some of the other shit we use here is carcino.... What's that, John?'

'Carcinogenic?' John Evans interrupted.

'Yes, that's it, carcinogenic,' she repeated, reading directly from the page.

'Likely to develop cancerous tumours unless replaced by less harmful raw materials or manufactured in the strictest environment ... providing full safety wear and on-site cleaning facilities to all workers who have any contact....' She put the papers down. 'John, this is amazing!'

Perhaps it was tiredness or the ability of the factory never to raise any surprises. The group in the room appeared to show little interest in her detective work.

'We need to think this through,' said John Evans. 'Don't let any of this out of the room for the time being. We need to use this to our advantage,' John Evans said forcefully.

Hawkins looked straight at John Evans as they bent over the papers before them. 'John, we have a duty to all involved—to let people know,' he said.

'I know that,' Evans replied. 'Look, the company will say that these are only views, not hard and fast data. They'll say it's all perfectly safe. We need to pursue it further, under no circumstances should we work with this stuff we'll lock it all away in the morning. Let's just sleep on it. Margaret, you need some sleep. In fact, we all do,' he said.

At this the people in the room sloped back against the walls, trying to make themselves as comfortable as possible. Within minutes the murmur of each person breathing replaced conversation. Dreams replaced thought and the factory slept. The apprentice became conscious of the sweet smell of the young girl's hair. She slept whilst he gently caressed her. She soon stirred from her slumber and kissed the boy delicately on his cheek. They left the room, taking care not to disturb any of its occupants. As they reached the steel balcony that overlooked the factory floor and surveyed the scene beneath them. By now most of the workers had found a place to sleep. Over two hundred bodies spread over the floor of the factory like a vast campsite, the light barely strong enough to cast out the pitch darkness. Above them a clear starry night shone through the glass roof with the moon providing its dull haze for the factory. The young couple found an empty room and pretended to be older than their years, making love together for only the second time in their lives. The apprentice said he loved her and she smiled and held him close, their inexperience locking them together, comforted by their embrace. Such sleep for all in the factory was fitful and sporadic and the circumstances predicted that they would not sleep the whole of the night. By four in the morning some workers were in the freshly cleaned canteen having breakfast. Soon the level of organisation in the factory was revealed as workers prepared tea and toast and delivered it throughout the factory to the grateful army of occupiers. The young couple were awoken by the sound of voices in the rooms next to them and soon rose to join them. Both sat in their respective places on the floor and listened intently to the debate that may have been going on for hours. The committee and some of the workers appeared wide awake as they thrust into a complex argument about the occupation, work, capitalism and society. It was now approximately four thirty in the morning. One of the older shop stewards was speaking and he seemed to be in a minority, as almost everyone in the room appeared to be shaking their head as he spoke.

'Well, just think about it,' the man urged, 'your assumptions are based on your reality that things are going to stay the same. I don't know, stay the same forever?' he asked.

'I don't think you're saying that,' he answered his own question. 'So you accept to some degree that things will change. This factory hasn't altered since the war. Talk of the white heat of technological change and we all think of spaceships and robots.' People in the room looked blankly ahead.

'I remember the unions supposedly becoming more democratic only because real democracy was here on the shopfloor and they knew they'd be left behind, so rather than have us outside the tent pissin' in they brought us under their control. And the government told them to do this because the union barons could not deliver their members. Could not *sell them out*. It was obvious that power lay on the shop floor.' Some people nodded in agreement.

'Look at the darkness they were moving out of,' the man continued as if given the right to speak for the first time in this life, 'bans and proscriptions on communists holding any office in the union and that included anyone they didn't like—fellow travellers they called them, because of some phoney cold war between capitalism and communism, and if we had a choice what would we want?' Some in the room waited for the answer.

'But no one really asks us,' the worker continued, 'they couldn't give a fuck. So where is the democracy in that? Have you seen what's been happening in some factories in the Midlands? The owners are shutting down and selling their pre-war machines to Asia. They reckon there's more profit in closing down than retooling. So what happens to the workers? They are now unemployed and the factories they used to work in no longer exist. The Japanese are going into mass production in a big way and they reckon they'll be the big industrial nation soon replacing Britain and America.' Some workers in the room began to look for some distraction but the worker persisted.

'OK. Union membership is higher than it ever was but has our power increased and are they any less corrupt than they were in the 1930s and the 1950s? I don't think so,' he answered. By now workers were entering and leaving the room randomly. Some in the room looked at each other, suppressing laughter at this political onslaught. The worker pursued his monologue.

'Yes, the papers talk of wildcat militancy and they will probably accuse us of that and put it down as a communist plot and what's the solution? Money. That's all the union's can go for, they haven't got the bottle to talk about control, taking real control. You get a fuckin rise in pay if you're lucky and the cost of gas and electricity go up more so it means nothing. Don't be surprised if the government bring in laws to reduce the power of the unions.' His voice began to rise.

'This occupation is a real challenge, but how many other workers would have the guts to do what we're doing? We have to spread it. That seems like an impossible task, and the political groups?' He looked around the room. 'Well, they'll tell you what to do. They're good at that, as long as they don't have to do it. It's not gonna stay the same, and who the fuck in their right mind would do what we do for £11 a fuckin week? It's a fuckin insult,' he said angrily.

As he spoke others wanted to interject. Finally a pause for air allowed in another speaker. 'So what are you sayin?' one of them said. 'No point exists to any action by the workers? That we are all doomed in the future anyway as machines get sold to Africa or wherever?' The speaker looked around the room. 'No point in getting out of bed. I'm forty-seven, I've got eighteen years of hard graft left in me and no bastard gonna rob me of that. Fuck the future, fuck the spaceships and those fuckin robots. No one can do what I do—I'm fuckin safe,' he said as he looked for someone to challenge his statement.

'Isn't it funny that it's the labourers who worry all the time. Get yourself a fuckin trade, man,' he said, 'make yourself wanted by the boss. Japanese?' He spat his words out as if inviting some confrontation, 'They make plastic toys for Christmas crackers, don't they?' No one laughed at this last comment as the worker continued.

'Are you honestly thinkin that they'll become engineers like some of us in ere? Look, I use a micrometer, I measure the smallest distances known to man, and what I can't measure I judge with me eyes. Then I set the tools to make the cut, each one exactly the same. Don't tell me a machine could do that.' He was pleased with his words. 'Even the boss wonders at our skills sometimes. You think they can get rid of craftsmen like me?' he asked.

'Yeah! That's right and your precious boss doesn't want you, now does he?' the previous speaker replied loudly.

'Look, when this ends, give it a few days, we'll be back and working more overtime to make up contracts. That's the system. That's the way it works—it's not that bad,' the worker said as he leaned back against the wall of the office.

'My parents didn't have running water. It's getting better for each generation, and if the system collapsed there'd be riots in the streets.'

'Yes, and more fuckin police and army to deal with it,' came the reply.

'They're not gonna give up their power easily and if they can get the Asians or whoever to make things cheaper then they'll do it. Those skills of yours. Have you seen the new lathes and drills and tool making equipment they have now?' he asked. 'A monkey can do it. I was reading the other day that they want to do away with apprenticeships….'

'They'll never do that,' the other man interrupted.

'Why not?'

'Cos industry needs trained workers, skilled men,' he said confidently.

'That's fuckin crazy talk,' the other worker replied.

'It's the cost of labour, that's the key. Everything is geared to reducing the cost of living labour, and if Asian workers replace us then they'll be replaced by others, and so the cycle of exploitation will go on until nothing's left.'

'Is that what they told you to say at your last meeting?' the other asked.

'Fuck you, you arrogant bastard, my lad, at home could do your job. The last time you did anything skilled was on the fuckin bog. You can live out your life thinkin nothing's gonna change and when you least expect it….' He paused and turned towards his fellow workers. 'Say you did get the fuckin sack from here, what would you do?' he demanded.

'Go the labour Exchange and pick up another one,' the man answered.

'What?'

'Like a packet of fags? What if we all do that?' he asked. By this time people in the room felt the argument was going nowhere. But the two protagonists continued.

'The employers are gonna have a field day picking one from 800,' the other said, 'and he's not gonna pick the trade unionist, is he? Not the one who thinks for himself—sorry, and herself,' he corrected his words looking around the room for agreement—a sign for him to continue. None came.

'He'll want some scabby bastard like the seventy bastards who crossed the line this morning. Look, I don't wanna argue, but I can't accept this romantic vision of the employer constantly wanting to look after the workers. If they say the system is profit, is capitalism, then it's like declaring a religion, you know you can identify between different faiths because of the way they practice their religion but they all have a god. So when the capitalist says I want profit you know it's not just for one day. It's forever and it's for whatever cost.' His hands started to punctuate his words.

'If monkeys are cheaper and more able then monkeys it will be. African tribesmen, child labour, slaves, nothing's new, it's all been done before. It's not a question of if,' he pleaded. Without pausing for breath he carried on. 'It's a question of when. What wages will you be drawing if your job's getting done in Hong Kong? Oh, and don't be under any illusions, all these workers will carry on the struggle in their own countries because exploitation doesn't have any basic wage level or condition of employment. A crime is a crime in any country in any culture and exploitation—Capitalism? Well, that's the crime. But eventually all workers will know this and that's when they will rise in rebellion,' he said with surety.

'You're a fuckin manic depressive,' the other man growled.

'And you'll end up being an arsehole that would do anything to protect themselves, anything.'

'We're here, aren't we?'

'Just about,' he replied.

As the heat of the argument rose Hawkins sat quietly, his huge frame curled up in the corner. From being the unknown acid shop man he had become, in the eyes of the workers, the respected and thoughtful leader he had always been. He closed his book over and spoke for the first time.

'It's important that we consider the theory but this is our reality at the moment and all our energies have to be spent on defeating this employer. We have a great responsibility to the workers we claim to represent,' he said almost coldly.

John Evans continued to examine the documents that were being uncovered from the files of G.P. Stevens. Margaret Harvey sat at his side highlighting relevant passages. The young apprentice and his girlfriend were cold and hungry. The magic of their condition, as they listened intently to the debate, became a reality for them and they where in a world of their own. Two of the newly self-appointed canteen workers entered with a pot of freshly made tea and a mountain of toast.

'An army fights on its stomach and the generals stand behind them giving orders,' one of them said amidst thanks and laughter, 'but we still thought you might like some grub anyway.' Laughter filled the room as the 'generals', large and small alike, shared out this welcome gift. Talk now returned to the practical matters of the day. The two protagonists had left the room. It was almost six o'clock in the morning. One of the strikers entered the room. He had been on main door duty when the police knocked.

'Perfectly civil, perfectly civil,' he stated to himself, 'they've got Johnson with them and they just want to come in the factory and check that no damage has been done. They give their word,' he added, convinced of their sincerity.

'Just the sergeant and Johnson,' the worker confirmed excitedly, 'what do you think? Sounds all right to me,' he concluded doubtfully to himself.

Some of the workers in the room rose immediately, shouting towards John Evans that they could not be trusted and how it would be stupid to let them inside. Others agreed. John Evans felt that the strikers had nothing to hide and nothing to lose from such a visit. If the police were planning to storm the building they'd do it anyway. Perhaps they were looking for another way out. Perhaps they did not have the numbers to deal with the occupation. As normal, in the new situation of the strikers thought replaced anger; discussion replaced shouting the loudest. After a few minutes the group agreed that the police and Johnson be allowed in. This decision was passed on to the workers, who where now congregated in the canteen. Their response differed little from that in the room earlier. The consensus agreed with the committee. John Evans and Margaret Harvey were nominated to show these unwelcome guests around the factory. They walked towards the main entrance of the factory, where they both waited while its steel bolts were pulled back. A gust of cool fresh air caught their faces as they walked together into the crisp winter morning. Two police cars could be seen embedded in the fresh snow that had fallen that night. A police sergeant shook their hands and asked if they could see inside the factory. Johnson clearly did not enjoy this situation, for it was his view that the policeman was acting far too well mannered with people he considered to be little more than criminals.

'Mr. Johnson here reckons you've done a lot of damage in there,' the policeman said, 'now I don't share that view but let's have a look all the same,' he ordered.

Harvey and Evans had no need to speak as they turned towards the factory. The visitors entered the factory. Johnson behaved as if nothing had changed, marching ahead towards his office. Margaret Harvey called him back and took great delight in informing him that this was the workers' factory now and he had no rights to go anywhere unless she agreed. The group kept together. Throughout the tour the policeman and John Evans were in deep discussion about everything other than the factory. They spoke about family, the weather and football. With little time for Johnson, the policeman was grateful that the woman kept him in check. But he had had no knowledge of what the factory was like under the authority of Johnson, so he could not make any judgements as to whether improvements had been achieved under the occupation of the workers or the bosses. It was clear to him as he walked leisurely along the gangways that no damage had been done in the factory. Johnson knew this from the moment he entered, but like a ferret in a hole he rummaged for some sign, some proof that would reinstate his authority. In reality the policeman was interested in nothing. Evidence of recent repair work on the fabric of the building was obvious and the more Johnson saw the more his anger raged inside. John Evans asked the sergeant if he would like some breakfast and he agreed. This provided an opportunity to leave Johnson with a female worker in command. She began ordering him about and calling him 'comrade Johnson', much to his astonishment at the audacity of any employee, former or otherwise, making fun of his position. The fact that she was a woman only compounded the felony.

When John Evans and the policeman reached the canteen even he was not too confident as to how the workers would respond. The sergeant was greeted by the newly appointed canteen staff and served with eggs, bacon and fresh coffee. This could not possibly have taken place without some humour, and the sergeant appreciated that and when he asked how much his breakfast cost the workers' informed him that it was free. He placed a bright half-crown on the table and asked them to put it in the strike fund. As the sergeant ate his breakfast more small talk ensued with the strike leader. However, both men knew that the real point of the conversation would have to be reached at some stage. The sergeant spoke first.

'John, you can imagine what's going on out there. Stevens wants us to clear this place at any cost. My bosses are the same bosses that you've got. They drink and eat in the same places and they're in the same Masonic lodges,' he said. 'You know this?' he added gravely.

John Evans was unsure if it was a question or a statement. He remained impassive, aware that it was just a tactic—somehow he was expected to believe that they were the same. He waited to be told how the policeman's father was a factory worker as well. That always seemed to happen whenever he came across some patronising apologist for the system. So they were the same. He kept his thoughts to himself. The man kept speaking.

'As far as I'm concerned no damage has been done and I don't know what it was like before you took over but I can imagine it was the usual shit-hole,' he said.

John Evans refused to be drawn into the conversation.

'My father worked in a factory like this.' Again the policeman waited for some response. Evans smiled to himself.

'I've got my job to do. It can be unpleasant more often than not, and if they blow their tin whistles, like dogs we'll respond. John, I'm almost retired, I don't expect you to agree with me or think I'm a nice fella. I won't be if we come in here smashing ordinary people around, good people as well.' He looked across the canteen. 'You don't wanna hear this but it's my job,' he finished his breakfast. 'Anyway,' he said, 'I tell you what, that was a fine breakfast.' He pushed the plate away and asked, 'is it always this good?'

John Evans resigned to smile. 'Only since we took over,' he answered.

Both men shook hands and on the way out of the factory they gathered up Johnson, who was being harangued by a number of women on the factory floor. The policeman spoke to Johnson and told him, quite emphatically, that no damage had been done inside the factory and it was clear that a great deal of repair work had been undertaken by the workers. Enraged, Johnson was physically removed from the factory by the women and the police sergeant. That day over three hundred workers had arrived at the factory by 7.00 a.m. They all seemed to pass Johnson as he was being ejected from the premises. He thought they were returning to work, which they were, but not the work he controlled. For this was liberated work.

By 8.00 a.m., after the fresh shift had breakfast, work commenced in earnest. Contracts, whose deadlines had passed weeks ago, were to be completed and new orders for switchgear parts or full assemblies were to be met on time. Fred Williams and his new team of assistants ensured that the workers each had given responsibilities for which they took control. Matters changed rapidly inside the factory during the occupation. Not only did the factory look cleaner, it was cleaner. Scaffolding had been erected during the night around the giant extractor fans that had long ceased to perform the function for which they were intended. The broken wire mesh had been replaced and the blades of each of the fans had been thoroughly scraped clean of decades of polluted oil, grime and dirt. At 8.00 a.m. the team assigned to repair these fans announced that, whilst they had not finished the work completely, they wished to turn them on. Crowds of workers gathered and cheered as the giant rotors turned. No longer did they beat against broken wire mesh, no longer were they dragged down by decades of silted filth. They turned swiftly and cleanly—silently, above the halls of the factory. They extracted air from the factory and as no foul air had been created for a number of days it was difficult for the workers to judge just how efficiently the extractor fans now worked. Their repairers knew this, and to prove it, if proof was necessary, they attached red ribbons to the outer wire mesh and when the rotors whirled the workers could physically see the strength and power of the refurbished rotors as the ribbons flew in their draft. At no time in the past would they have ever considered the possibility that one day they may stand beneath those huge extractor fans and cheer and clap and marvel at their beauty. But on this morning they did just that.

They had achieved a reality in which they ordered their lives, their decisions, their wishes, and in the process they began, that Saturday morning, to achieve production targets unheard of in the factory's history and yet they worked less. They were more relaxed, they conversed, they ate properly and they breathed clean air. Not surprisingly the noise in the factory had been reduced substantially as the truth emerged that much of the noise had been created by those workers who wanted to look busy, wanted to create the impression that they were working, and noise was the key because for the boss silence was non-production. Noise was production and the more noise that was made the more it appeared that production was actually taking place. As the workers greeted and spoke with each other they too grew in stature. They had eluded their tormentors and proved to themselves it could be done. Having been condemned to a life of drudgery, of imposed inadequacy, this achievement knew no measure for those who experienced it. And they knew that this was good. A revolution in more ways than one. The giant extractor fans turned majestically, filling the factory with the purest of air, and their blades scythed through what was left of the old factory to make way for the new. Annie and her young apprentice stood on the raised metal platform from which they could see directly into the vast chasms of engineered metal and steel that lay behind the extractor fans and for the first time he understood the real beauty of the workers' abilities, the skills and knowledge required to produce such industrial masterpieces. She had discovered the marvel of the workers' engineering achievements a long time ago and she smiled at the boy's realisation.

Chapter Eleven

To go on strike is to deny the existing distribution of power and authority. The striker ceases to respond to managerial command; he refuses to do 'his' work. A new dimension of living can thus be revealed to the striker; an existence in which 'ordinary' people are able to control events and command the attention of 'them'. The experience of this new reality can transform the striker's perception of normal life. What was 'normal' can no longer be regarded as 'natural'. Attitudes towards work and authority become critical as opposed to acquiescent.
—T.Lane & K.Roberts, *Strike at Pilkingtons* (1971)

Work on that Saturday concluded as it had begun, at a sporadically leisurely pace. The last workers to complete their quota finished around eight o'clock that evening. Some workers had left the factory to buy beer and whisky, for it was felt quite natural that they deserved to celebrate their heroic actions, and celebrate they did. They danced and sang throughout the night and by three o'clock a small group were left to consider the reality and philosophy of their actions. Eased from inhibition by the naked honesty that alcohol delivers, the conversation ranged from religion to communism, from the history of the working class to the future of that same class. That night over three hundred workers occupied the factory. They now controlled it.

John Evans had taken the opportunity to go home to wash and change his clothes. He invited the apprentice and his girlfriend Annie to share a meal at his home. Workers could come and go from the factory as the police pondered the demands of the bosses to reclaim 'their' factory. In their inactivity the workers could exercise their freedom. John Evans lived in a small council house with his wife quite near to the factory. She was a quiet and attractive woman who clearly shared the political commitment of her husband, and when her guests arrived she sought an array of detailed information about the morale and practical condition of the strikers whilst her husband washed and changed. They had moved from their high-rise flat immediately following the death of their son. When he entered the room his young adjutants were drinking bottles of beer as they vividly described the events of the last few days to his wife. The room was simply decorated but the walls and cupboards contained icons of working class political history. Evelyn Evans not only shared her husband's politics; in some way she appeared more intense on the practical struggle of the workers as opposed to the theoretical. Shelves of books fully covered two walls in the living room. Marx, Lenin, Trotsky, Gramsci, Luxemburg, Irish history, the works of Jack London, Sartre all competed for space. On such a cursory glance it was a revolutionary's library that both Evelyn and John Evans referred to at points during the conversation. At one stage they contested the views of Marx and Lenin, hurriedly turning pages of well-worn books to unfold a particular passage or the relevant quote that would prove beyond all doubt that one was right whilst the other must therefore be wrong. At first our young couple suffocated their desire to burst out laughing, assuming that this would be disrespectful in the company of such serious-minded scholars. But it was they who poked fun at each other, disclosing to their guests that politics can be both humorous and stimulating. As the evening drew to an end tiredness complemented by the careless condition that honest company invokes released John Evans from the heavy shroud of pain that seemed at times to haunt his very existence. Turning to his wife, he remarked how much the young apprentice reminded him of their son. His wife agreed but told him not to embarrass the boy. The apprentice pulled from his pocket the union badge given to him by John Evans on his first day in the factory. Evelyn Evans smiled the most distant of smiles.

'Oh good, you haven't lost it,' she smiled, 'it belonged to my father. You can't get them now, not for love or money,' she said as she held the badge in her hand. 'Yes, a real collector's piece, and our son wore it with pride. As you will, I'm sure,' she said to the boy.

Having satisfied what seemed like the most distant of memories, the woman rose to her feet. The party ended. Annie slept that night in the spare room with her young lover and in the factory the last few strikers eventually gave in to the deepest sleep.

As the night's freshly fallen snow crushed under their cold feet three figures stood outside the factory half hidden in the heavy silver mists of that winter's morning. They had all slept well and looked rested to the worker who opened the steel door in response to the code 'comrade'. For the second day the three marvelled at the transformation that had been undertaken within the factory in such a short space of time. Breakfast was being served in the main canteen and they joined over two hundred workers for this first meal, which was 'better than anything you'd get at ome'. This was now the stock response to any food that was served by the volunteers who took responsibility for the welfare of the workers. Whether this was a genuine response to the nature of the food being served or whether it was amazement that something half-decent could be served in the factory mattered little. Perhaps it was simply the exhilaration of change of control of taking personal responsibility for the entire factory without a boss in sight. Yet, ironically, the workers were better bosses than the bosses. For they were more disciplined. Stricter in the interests of the collective. But it was an authority that breathed gently and equally over every worker.

John Evans received instructions from the different departments. Williams, who now assumed the role of foreman, manager and even 'boss', explained that everything was going well and that day only six hours' work was required. Dan Hawkins had been trying to contact the various customers in relation to completing their orders and they seemed to be oblivious to the fact that the G.P. Stevens factory was now under the control of the workers. He had even succeeded in getting a number of outstanding bills paid to the factory. Margaret Harvey had continued to examine the company's files. Evidence continued to emerge which showed that the union had been even more deeply involved, at the highest level of the factory's management, than they had previously expected. The union had shares in the company. Hasaan had been placed in charge of reclaiming waste metals and raw materials together with the proceeds from sales of any scrap metal. He excelled in this line of work. When he had finished giving his report to members of the committee, who had by now joined John Evans's table, he dug deep into his pockets and pulled a wad of notes out, slapping each note on the table as he counted it. Workers counted with him and when the figure reached £87 they called on him to hand the rest over. But it was all in good humour and in response the young worker made his final gesture placing a crisp £20 note on the table. The money was accounted for and placed in the main office safe.

At eight o'clock workers began to leave the canteen to start work and it was noticeable to all that silence, or rather a quietness of sorts, produced a calming, dignified resolve to this movement of human beings as they independently chose to resume their labour. No siren was needed and later that day it was ceremonially disconnected. Those members of the committee who did not have work tasks in the office also returned to work on the factory floor. John Evans gave Annie and her apprentice their first lessons in how to use a lathe whilst other workers not directly needed for that day's production exchanged their skills in an effort to replace those workers who chose not to take part in the occupation. Hasaan had always wanted to learn how to weld and so this skill was being delivered to him by a rather short but very smartly dressed worker whom the apprentice recognised as the dust-covered cast metal shop worker. He asked Hasaan if the man appeared strange to him.

Hasaan felt he was quite normal, intelligent and good fun to learn from. As the apprentice examined the man from a distance the transformation filled him with hope and a resolve that proved beyond any doubt that the occupation was a victory on a host of different levels.

That Sunday a new shift of workers entered the factory, allowing those who had protected the occupation at night to go home and rest. Each worker gave their name to a number of volunteer staff, who then issued instructions as to what work was required. The factory clock had been dismantled and removed shortly after the siren had been disconnected. That day the warm glow of the winter's sunshine cut through the factory, producing vivid shards of light that layered the entire floor of the factory. No longer could the giant extractor fans be heard beating against metal and brick as they turned and ground against the filth. Now only the faintest rustle of breeze exposed their purpose. For now the air in the factory could be tolerated amidst the elements of smoke and oil that were a natural by-product of the work undertaken by this army of occupation. Noise levels had been reduced to such a pitch that individual culprits found themselves being lectured on how to work without creating the mayhem of noise that they had long associated with the process of production. It was also observed that some workers whose monotony of repetitive movement continued long after they had left their machines could now reclaim control of themselves. They were now adopting a less rigorous approach to production. They maintained productivity levels but only produced enough quantities for that day. This allowed them to balance their working time in a much more humane way. They controlled the machines. Life in the factory reflected the rapidity of change since their decision to occupy and the speed of this change affected everyone. Some men were deeply concerned as to what fate awaited them, but they found solace in their freedom that they celebrated with a vengeance. Some felt the occupation would not last too long, as the police would eventually act on behalf of the employers. Some simply followed the last command, unable to liberate themselves from the bondage that imposed servility as far back as they could remember. None of this was admitted or spoken of. Now was the time for solidarity.

During the course of that Sunday morning many of the workers' wives had brought food to the factory that had been donated and collected from the local community. In the canteen they prepared a feast in that invisible way in which workers, once given the opportunity, take control for themselves wholly and independently. Silently, their guests, women, children, trade unionists and comrades, gathered in the works canteen helping to prepare this Sunday meal. Somewhere around two o'clock men and women from the factory floor eased their machines to a conclusion, vacantly assuming their freedom to choose when and where to stop work. Eventually, quietness tumbled lazily through the factory. Each worker appeared to be greeted as they entered the canteen with wives, friends and children running to join them for what was a meticulously prepared celebration dinner. A table had been set aside for the committee and their families but John Evans and others decided that this was inappropriate. This committee would share the same tables as the rest of the workers. This threw some panic into the unofficial organisers that was only suppressed by the notion that the canteen staff should take the table of honour that had been placed at the front of the canteen.

Threats of closure, mechanisation, redundancies, wage cuts and increased productivity had circulated this small neighbourhood for almost two years. Many of the local factories produced goods for the same customers and with each being a link in the local production chain fear rose that one closure would result in other factories following suit. It had long been the local custom for one employer to push ahead with increased production targets and wage cuts whilst the other employers watched how the workers responded. If change was left unchallenged then similar cutbacks were imposed in neighbouring factories. If change was challenged then this loose federation of employers would share any costs incurred to defeat militancy before it impacted on their factories. Everyone knew that these local employers met regularly to plan such strategies. Free Masonry played its usual part with local Chambers of Commerce, corrupt politicians and councillors supplemented liberally by the trade union and church hierarchy. None of this was any surprise, it was merely the great and the good doing what they did best. Plotting and plundering in pursuit of self-interest and the power of capital. The preservation of the status quo. For the reluctant leadership of this occupation they realised that power was the key. In the industrial setting, collective bargaining, or free collective bargaining as it became oddly known, meant little if it could not be punctuated by the exclamation that if progress was not made, workers would defend their wages and conditions at all costs. The official union chewed over the potential of replacing conflict in the workplace with conciliation. The role of the independent arbitrator, as if such a concept could ever really exist, was to create that mysterious middle ground. That place in the meaningless ether where the greed of the capitalist class meets the interests of the workers. It never existed and the workers saw their wages and conditions undermined at every turn. Trade union education became a cottage industry as many union leaders fell for the flattery that they too could come in from the cold if only they brought their horny-handed membership with them. Their behaviour was ascribed as dysfunctional, being the result of poor educational standards and overly large foreheads. You could educate the dysfunctionality out of them whilst sacking those who suffered the hereditary version of conflictual relations with capital. Shop stewards needed to be educated in the use of body language, percentages, self-financing productivity deals and how to behave at consultative meetings with employers. Talk of workers on the board served to confirm this end of conflict terrain now being willingly explored by union leaders dulled by fine wine and expense account lifestyles.

As ever ermine cloaks awaited those who arrived at the swill bucket on time. Royal ascent was given to numerous reports on the industrial relations 'anarchy' that faced Britain. Devlin inquired into militancy on the docks whilst Donovan mused upon the pluralist principle and the positive image of the 'responsible shop steward'. A cottage industry flourished as the study of industrial relations became part of mainstream university curricula. Doctors and professors of industrial relations dined long and hard on irrelevant concepts of workplace organisation, made all that much foggier by their romanticism for all things working class. Man on the moon status was delivered to those few academics that actually ventured to one of those quaint northern cities in which the existence of factory life was known to proliferate. The official unions had to control their membership who exercised 'unofficial leadership' on the shopfloor. Politics had no place on the shopfloor as industrial capitalism claimed allegiance to modernising Britain's dark satanic mills for the good of the economy. Whilst industry needed to be modernised so too did labour. As with so much contemporary thought the push towards 'modernisation' was mistaken as radical, even revolutionary, focusing no less upon the transformation of industry benefiting both the worker and the employer. Banishing to the dustbin of history out-moded concepts of conflict betwixt worker and boss. Yes, these were heady days, but many workers were old enough to remember similar 'transformations' utilising the same language and terminology encompassing time frames as distant as the turn of the century to the period of the Second World War. Not much is new in history, especially when young men assume originality in misquoting older men and history. Once the language of self-justification had been exhausted it was just another matter of reducing further the costs of living labour. This was a global and timeless phenomenon. Meanwhile the labourist apologists for capital wove their weary web as they succumbed to the flattery of being treated as important and valued members of the bossing elite.

Most workers knew that the extraordinary heroic history of trade unionists was made not by the bureaucrats in their tatty suits but by the workers themselves in opposition to them and the factory owners. They could never ever remember more than one or two unique struggles in which the union leadership fully supported their members in strike action. This was their magnificent movement, kidnapped at its birth by the ruling class. Anger always corresponded with the increasingly reactionary nature of union leaders, but the workers expected little more. As the right-wing lurch continued unabated this was contradicted by the right-wing media image of these very same people whom they labelled 'the left-wing union leadership'. Confusion reigned as right-wing union leaders were identified as wanting a revolution in the workplace. This was never the case. Their revolution was the personal one, to become a union official, to have status, personal wealth, to become a Justice of the Peace, an Alderman, a councillor, a Member of Parliament and then, true esteem, a genuine ermine cloak, a seat in the House of Lords. Above all they perceived themselves as different from their class, above their class and they knew their role was to control their class on behalf of the ruling class. The primary buffer upon which individual freedom terminated in the cause of *'it'*. Most workers knew this and hated them for it. Rare exceptions to this rule existed, but their rarity bordered upon extinction.

Given air to breathe, silence to inquire, time to think and comfort to converse, all men and women may express their innate ability to comprehend their environment. The trick is to impose an environment that contradicts their human development. In their freedom the workers in the canteen on that Sunday spoke of all manner of things affecting their condition. They all understood the contradictions they now confronted and they understood fully the power that would be used to defeat them. All around debates and arguments ensued, but most were agreed that no option other than that they had taken was viable. Their torment had to stop at some time, and the longer it went on the worse their condition would get. No amount of explanation or excuse from the bosses or the union's leaders would convince them otherwise. After all, they were not on strike. Union leaders never took part in strikes, so what would they know. But this was a fragmented unity, and in that canteen on Sunday it was clearly observable that the doubters found solace in each other's company. They sat at the extremes of the room, talking furtively of how they could evade this bad situation. Some, lacking the courage to exercise their right to discuss their fears, waited for their own moment to strike. The leaders of this struggle understood this scenario only too well and took account of the small number involved who could not shake off the terror that freedom brings. It was clear that this Sunday was to be a day of rest for the occupation that had now acquired a routine of its own in just a few days.

The strike committee took the opportunity to plan further elements of their strategy. Rest days and rotas were rewritten. Basic needs such as food and drink were planned for the next four weeks. Arrangements were made to ensure that the morale of the strikers held firm. Bulletins would be produced and meetings would take place every day to report back on the situation. That afternoon John Evans received a phone call from Jacks, the union's full-time official. He spelt out that the occupation was doomed, that the management had sacked the workers involved, and a new workforce would be hired.

'So, what's the union's position?' Evans looked across the room to his fellow committee members as he asked the question.

'That's it. You're fuckin doomed, John, and you know it,' replied Jacks, 'but this is the moment you've waited for, isn't it? Well, you've got it now.' Jacks was confident in his tone. 'Well, you know the rest of it. I'm meeting with Johnson tonight and I've been told to cut a deal for our members, about a hundred I think, that didn't join your band of losers. Oh, they'll be all right, that's for sure,' he said.

John Evans did not display any emotion. 'Good luck then. Give our best wishes to Johnson.' He placed the receiver down carefully.

'I'm sure you got the message,' he told the others in the room, 'you are all doomed,' he repeated, 'so let's continue to meet our maker.

'Margaret and Dan,' he called out, 'where are we up to with the leaflets and contacts with other workers in the local factories?' he asked them.

The planning continued into the night both inside and outside the factory. The strike committee and the workers set about the task of establishing support and solidarity action from other workers in the area. It was as much in their interests that once a struggle had begun it had to be fought and won. However, most workers fall into that human trap, that natural state of seeking to avoid confrontation—avoid bad situations. It would be a difficult challenge indeed to locate why we as humans tend naturally to this state. Confrontation can never be avoided at all costs enough to say it is not our natural state if given free choice. Given absolute choice, conflict can never be the voluntary human act it is so often portrayed as. It is an imposed state not freely entered into. Yet this conflict has been humanised to justify the violent conflicts necessary to impose an iron will for the cause of the ruling elite. Once conflict erupts against this iron will it is met with the often-silent revenge and unseen brutality that belongs to capital. Such power that does not require statement is *the power*. The power that creeps through the night to produce a second sky that clouds reality as its desire takes it. Deeply black or silver gold, its form dictates response as if the gods in the heavens were angered or pleased. A deterrence of this nature requires no explanation as the magnitude of its capacity knows no limits other than that exclaimed by mass rebellion, total rejection, the equalising force that revolution brings. Nevertheless, this sleeping giant watches every move, every gesture or response has to be noted in the context of measuring the threat whilst establishing the punitive revenge necessary to protect the *'it'*. Control was what it craved.

G.P. Stevens and Sons was not the centre of the capitalist universe yet it was a factory that required protection. Risk assessments would have to reflect a measured response both to protect and deter any further acts of rebellion elsewhere. Stevens Junior was back in town and from this darkness he took refuge and strength. The system would never tolerate strikes or any other acts of defiance but they positively encouraged wage-militancy. Occupation was a rebellion that faced up to the power of capital by capturing one of its pawns, and as such it could never be tolerated. Occupation was never about money, it was about challenging the very essence of the capitalist's power. To challenge capitalism over money was to play their game. It was perfectly acceptable, tolerated and often welcomed as a vindication of capital's all-enveloping greed. Everyone, in this context, could be seen as capitalist. To want money and want more money was a genuflection to capital and its ways. Occupation was bad. But these men and women knew what they were involved in. Above all they were practical people. They could build canals in the desert.

Jacks was to meet Johnson, not to threaten to defend the workers at all costs but to receive instructions as to what he and his union were to do next. Johnson also took instructions as to what he had to do next. Neither man had free will. Smothered as their lives were by the grace and favour of capital that made their treachery worthwhile. The sale of their souls did not capture too much value on the open market as supply outstripped demand. Such individuals, in their millions, bought into the system of their own volition, letting it be known to all that their lives, their free will, no longer existed. And for this they received valueless trinkets that shone and glimmered only in the blackness of their souls. In keeping with class and status the two met in a small hotel bar on the edge of town. A throw-away symbol of casual wealth and high status to the employing class built amongst the rubble of industrial poverty they created. Johnson had arrived first, establishing control over this neutral territory. The numbed mind of Jacks failed at every given opportunity to realise the theatrical tricks and games that powerful men play. He bungled into the hotel foyer, thinking to himself how important he was to be called at such a late hour to such a fine hotel. Yet the hotel was a cheap fairground design badly in need of demolition. The lateness of the hour chosen by Johnson was an indicator of power. Jacks would never understand this sophistication, whilst Johnson was stupid enough to think he did. A fly landed on the stained fake copper table that pressed hard and uncomfortably against Johnson's knees. He studied its movements as Jacks walked towards him. Mindful not to let him stand over him he beckoned the workers' representative to sit down in front of him. The fly escaped.

'This,' Johnson's voice trailed off in the distance for a few moments, 'well,' he looked across the room, 'it's gone too far. Have you spoken to your

General Secretary yet?' he asked.

Johnson did his best to look comfortable, relaxed, in control and angry at the same time. He leant back to fold one arm and cup his chin authoritatively in his fat hands but this action only emphasised the precarious balance his bulging frame had on the small low-slung chair he had chosen from which to conduct this conversation. Even he began to feel that he must have looked ridiculous from where Jacks was sitting. He began to sweat profusely in that ghastly stale atmosphere that pumped lifelessly in all dead hotels. Fainter than air the piped music poured from beer-stained speakers in the corner of the room. Johnson was a buffoon whose arrogance failed to observe that people existed who were even more stupid than he was. He was one of those many people to whom status mattered more than money—well, almost; and this imposed a concept of public service within which he revelled. A Justice of the Peace, leading member of his local Masonic Lodge, an acquaintance of the Lord Mayor. All confirmed his arrival upon the stage of history, albeit a very local history. This in its turn evoked a deeply inflated vision of his every personal action being perceived for future posterity, and he wondered to himself, prior to Jacks's arrival, how such an important person as himself would wish to be remembered at this critical moment. As he thought this his mind replayed the idea of this 'moment in the history of his career as a leader of local industry'. He enjoyed this thought, if only for that moment. The fly returned and Jacks responded. Johnson stared down upon the fly.

'Uh … oh,' Jacks spluttered towards a reply, 'well, he's not too pleased and he's told me to do everything in my power to get the men back to work. But I told him about Evans and he's not happy.' He thought to pause. 'Knows 'im from long ago. Stubborn—not too intelligent,' he observed.

At this last word both men looked each other in the eye for the first time to confirm that they were both intelligent and that one of the main causes of dysfunctional behaviour rested beyond doubt with the lack of education amongst the masses. For both men this also confirmed their lowly place in the hierarchy of society. Jacks was allowed to continue as Johnson returned to the fly.

'To put it bluntly, Mr. Johnson, my General Secretary has instructed me to reach an immediate understanding with yourself,' he was addressing a mass meeting, 'through Mr. Stevens of course. We need to be partners in this, as it does not help the company or us,' he said, very professionally. Johnson was almost impressed.

Jacks straightened his tie, lifted the papers he had in his hand, leant across the table and swotted Johnson's fly. Johnson scowled at Jacks as he leant further over the table to wipe away the blood-stained carcass of the deceased fly.

'Dirty things. Here, let me clean that up for you, Mr. Johnson.' Johnson pushed Jacks's flaying arms away.

As Jacks had repeated what he had been told to say by someone higher up the food chain, so too did Johnson. He disclosed what he had been told to say, with the only difference being that Johnson had that little edge of intelligence that made it appear that he was making all the decisions on these matters. Except for one interruption as a waiter asked if the men would like to order something, to which Johnson replied, 'No!' with a derisory wave of his hand. The waiter glowered at him.

The factory manager unveiled the plot for dealing with the insurrection at G.P. Stevens and Son. Without surprise Jacks agreed to everything, offering suggestions as to how the union and one hundred or so workers may be used to break the occupation. In exchange Johnson promised that the union could recruit any new workers brought into the factory. Johnson kept one vital piece of information to himself and this was a decision that had been taken some time ago. Of itself, this one piece of information answered many questions. As Jacks squirmed and ingratiated himself with this representative of the ruling class simultaneously his union's membership inside the factory uncovered what Johnson had excluded from their conversation. This vital piece of information would unfold in time.

When Johnson had finished speaking a silence gripped both men as their mutual ignorance and stupidity strangled the short space between them. Johnson was waiting for Jacks to leave whilst Jacks waited to be invited to dine with his fellow leader. How he longed to discuss other matters than those relating to the dirty labouring mass he was forced to suffer his life with until he was free of them. His freedom would come, or so he thought, through rapid promotion in the union or through the simple transfer of his undoubted prowess to the ranks of company management. This was an ideal moment to present his qualifications for such treachery. He had done it before under similar circumstances and he would do it again in the true traditions of sycophancy and betrayal. To think such thoughts takes the average human being only a fraction of a second and in this fraction of life's space he looked at the man opposite him. Johnson, because he was the same viperous wretch as Jacks, thought only of escaping from a man whom he considered ill-fitted to be seen in company with. Another fly landed on the edge of Johnson's table, bigger and blacker than the first. Jacks stood up and thanked his tormentor and left. Johnson crushed the fly with his fist, wiping the remains upon the chest pocket of his waistcoat.

Despite the expectation of treachery it is always its depths that elude us. The workers were under no illusions regarding the expectation of treachery, it was its form that concentrated their minds. No manner of explanation will

153

ever deliver the darkness that curdles beneath the surface of men with power for they have to use it and defend it. By one o'clock the factory slept, except for a few workers who guarded the entrances and the usual revellers determined to drink until they had had enough. In these circumstances the workers were in control. The factory had been secured for a second day. Annie and the apprentice settled down for the night. Never had he felt so free. Never had he felt such contentment and she the same.

Chapter Twelve

He kinda scratched his head an' he says: 'Mr. Hines, I ain't been here long. What is these goddamn reds?' Well, sir, Hines says: ' A red is any son-of-a-bitch that wants thirty cents an hour when we're payin' twenty-five.' Well, this young fella he thinks about her, an' he scratches his head, an says: 'Well, Jesus, Mr. Hines. I ain't a son-of-a-bitch, but if that's what a red is - why, I want thirty cents an hour. Ever'body does. Hell Mr. Hines, we're all reds."

—John Steinbeck, *The Grapes of Wrath*

That Monday morning the crisp white snow outside the factory had been degraded to a grime-laden icy dirt. Nearby, workers' houses choked under the weight of a familiar black smog. A second wretched sky encircled the factory that refused to admit the light of the day. Inside the factory the workers were woken by a growing disturbance outside the plant. This was to be the second time John Evans's sleep had been broken. Earlier Margaret Harvey had awoken him to tell of her latest discovery from Johnson's office files. Dan Hawkins was already up and preparing some tea in the corner of the room that doubled as the office and bedroom for most of the committee. The apprentice respected the company of Hawkins and he mixed his role in the occupation between the burly thoughtful presence of the former 'acid bath man' and John Evans. Annie had already left his side to work in the canteen preparing breakfast. One of the drill shop workers who had kept guard during the night came into the room. He had the look of a man who did not quite know how to report what could be either good or bad news. In his confusion he decided it was bad news.

'John, they're all out there and they're tryin' to break in,' he said, 'I knew that McCabe bastard wouldn't let us get away with this. He's an evil....'

No point seemed to exist for him to finish the sentence. The man sat down as if this very thought scrambled his mind. He was given a cup of tea by Hawkins, who calmly asked him how many were outside.

'It seems like hundreds and the police are there as well,' the man answered confidently. 'They're gonna' rush us, John ... I know they are,' he concluded.

Fred Williams went along the gangway with Hawkins to reach a point at which he could just see the front entrance of the factory through a skylight. They reported back their sightings. John Evans led a small delegation so that they might see for themselves. They could make out the figures of McCabe, Jacks, blue-overalls, Carberry and most of the eighty or so workers who refused to join the occupation on Friday. The police were out in large numbers, mixing with the crowd, checking entrances and doorways, searching for a way in. Behind this wretch of workers, police and management stood the sergeant who had entered the factory the day before. Little needed to be done immediately as the building was as secure as it could be made. Evans and Hawkins spoke together while the committee and others drank coffee, exchanging different insights into what response the occupiers should exact. At around seven o'clock John Evans asked the committee to meet in the canteen. As they gathered themselves around the table, John Evans was keen to ensure that workers who were not officially members of the committee should be made welcome around the table. He had always been supportive of the concept of open meetings and accountability. This was an opportunity to realise his rank and filist preferences. Coffee, tea and toast lay randomly on the table at which sat the committee and behind them rows of workers. They were all listening intently, whispering an opinion to a colleague, generally relaxing as they too took breakfast. Hawkins spoke first as John Evans opened the meeting. At this point Annie squeezed in next to her boyfriend, placing a plate of fried eggs on the table. The plate was passed around quietly as Hawkins spoke.

'I don't think this gathering outside the factory is too important, just as long as we are content that the access points are secured,' he said. 'We need to be doubly vigilant on this. Make no mistake, the union, management and police will be acting as one and they will have met over the weekend to plot their collective response. The big problem for us is to ensure how our comrades get into the factory this morning.'

He pondered upon this point as his audience accepted the pause to think with him. After some time he continued.

'We can't get hold of over three hundred men and women in little over an hour. They won't be aware of the scabs until they get near the factory,' he said, 'we have got enough workers here now to continue our occupation but we won't be able to leave and return as we have done over the weekend.' Some of the workers shook their heads at this thought. Hawkins continued, 'We took extra rations in over the weekend and we should have food for a couple of weeks if we are careful. We know how it makes people feel looking at those scabs out there but that's something we'll have to live with.'

At this he turned to John Evans and Margaret Harvey. Smiling, he announced that all production targets had been met, but some news had been uncovered in the office and perhaps Margaret Harvey should explain this. When Hawkins finished a debate opened up on the report he had given. John Evans asked for silence as he looked towards the worker from the sheet metal shop. Margaret Harvey was an industrial woman. Both in stature and physique, her intelligence had long been accepted by the majority of workers, and whilst they did not like to show it too much they respected her as a person. Being a woman in this factory, as with all factories, was a major obstacle to being thought of as anything but less than a man Unlike Hawkins she stayed seated. In her hands she held some official company documents. Workers seated around the table leant closer, listening now more keenly than before at this physical evidence, whatever it would mean.

'Since the start of the occupation we have been examining all the company papers we can find,' she said like a detective, 'we have uncovered some interesting stuff. Two key pieces of information cannot be kept a secret any longer. These documents involve all our futures. One document refers to a decision made on the factory and the other relates especially to the way Stevens has been killing us with some of the raw materials we have been working with over the years,' she concluded.

Although some noise emanated from around the canteen it was a calming early morning noise that mixed with the smell of cooking food, coffee and tea brewed in the newness of a fresh day which, of itself, was comforting. But when the woman mentioned safety dangers being confirmed alarm rang around the table, rolling out to the rows of seats that now encircled the committee members. For years the workers had complained about numerous ailments, injuries and illnesses that they believed related solely to their workplace. Whenever they went to their local doctors they were never asked where they worked or what raw materials they handled and if the worker offered this information it was more often than not dismissed as irrelevant. To see the company doctor was recognition of mental rather than physical illness on the part of the workers as he was paid by Stevens and did exactly what the company wanted him to do. This resulted in sick workers having their condition exasperated, leading to other health complaints. The workers knew too well that many of the illnesses associated with working in the factory would never come to light for many years, by which time it would be too late. In the twisted dementia of industrial life, that had altered little since the First World War, personal health and well-being was a brutal lottery in which life expectancy reflected the work you did. Bizarrely, some workers seemed to thoughtlessly accept this threat of premature death as part of the job. With some workers this was reflected in the machismo of 'men's work', or, more aptly put, 'real men's work'. So one could see workers clearly struggling with the onset of undetected illness working in an environment that openly aggravated their condition. Often men knowingly encouraged their children into this carcinogenic nightmare, aware that they may already be showing some symptoms of an illness related to the poverty and poor housing conditions brought on by factory work and the low wage they received. Their communities also suffered illness brought on by the factory's freely spewing all manner of abuse into the local atmosphere. The union was at best ambivalent to these consequences of work and at worst they actively ignored the complaints of their membership in the cause of capital. Argument, claim and counter-claim echoed around the room and as if in respect of the workers' long-held concerns in this area, no real attempt was made to silence this display of disgust. Eventually, the woman continued.

'We all know about the health dangers in here, we've known for a long time, bakelite, acid, oils and chemicals. Look at the difference on the floor with just the fans working properly,' she exclaimed. 'We'll never allow such disgraceful conditions to continue again. We know it from our personal experiences, from our families, friends and fellow workers, cancer of the liver, emphysema, asthma, skin cancers, asbestosis,' she rattled the list off. Looking around the room, she said, 'No one we know ever dies of old age.'

She paused and looked gravely into the distance before her, not looking at any one individual, preparing her audience for even more important information. 'But what we also uncovered may mean, ironically, that we may all die of old age.' Some of the workers looked at each other in puzzlement. Harvey continued, 'Last night, comrades, we found a file that involves the sale of all the machinery in this factory to a metals company in India.'

Now the calmed atmosphere of the morning vaporised as the room erupted in disbelief. With a purpose she had gone straight to the point in expectation of the furor this information would create. A wave of workers physically crashed against the table, pushing those who sat at the front forward almost onto the table. Chaotic responses collided around the canteen, with accusation and disbelief competing for a sanctuary that could never exist. For every thought they had was invested in that factory, which in turn shackled the decisions of life to the metal beams that sustained its structure. So, drenched in fear, they blamed the committee assuming that they knew all this when the occupation started. Some blamed McCabe, the union and the bosses. Blame itself, within these instants, offered some respite to the confusion of thinking of a life, of a world, without the factory. Such was its power despite the illness it inflicted upon their lives and within this cruel contradiction the workers confronted each other. The apprentice clung on to Annie for fear that she might get hurt. He could not believe the transformation that had exploded amidst the expression of one sentence. The fragility of the workers' solidarity exposed a weakness. The weakness he had seen in his own father's eyes, that distant curtain of emptiness from which fear itself holds the key to unlock more fear which comes to represent the natural state. No! Even with his lack of experience in these matters he could understand that this was no conspiracy. They had spoken of it often enough. It was in the books that John Evans had given to him. As hard as he tried he could not rationalise the hatred that now surrounded him. Suddenly a space opened around the table as the figure of John Evans stretched out above all in the room.

In the distance a new shift of workers could be seen running into the factory, cheering themselves as they arrived. A battle had been fought outside the factory with the forces of reaction as the workers in the canteen had been confronting each other. Evans held his arms out into the distance, motioning to the growing mass of workers for order. The two factions glared at each other. One from the hatred of knowledge that the factory was to close, the other from a resignation that the scabs they confronted outside would also suffer the consequences of closure. With the madness complete, the young apprentice surveyed the room that was now as full as it had ever been since the occupation began. He looked directly behind him and witnessed the medieval behaviour of men and women cut loose, disengaged from the only reality they knew, and in turn he tasted real fear for the first time. Next to him was Annie, above them stood the figure of John Evans standing on the table, arms held out as if attempting to touch a distant figure in the hall. An inevitable quiet wandered through the crowd as they struggled to regain re-admittance to their lost world. Whoever could deliver this commanded silence, only one worker seemed to accept this challenge. This man stood before them, his back rigid, legs apart with both fists punched deeply into his sides. He stuck his out jaw and took one breath of extraordinary length that he seemed to hold in his body for as long as was humanly possible. From his jacket he pulled a piece of paper. Now he waved it in front of the workers, opening it out with both hands. Men at the back pushed forward harder as if were possible to see what the paper contained. These actions mesmerised the crowd in their deliberately slow evocation as when the conjurer exaggerates his final movements as the prelude to some amazing display of magical dexterity. Everything about John Evans was different as Annie and the young boy observed. His voice scattered amongst the workers who by now stood or sat in stunned surrender lest any mark of individuality may impose a responsibility upon them.

'Well,' he said in a loud voice, 'perhaps we should have kept this information quiet like others did.' A hush fell urgently upon the room. 'Yes, the union knew all about it, and it appears that they were in talks over a phased withdrawal of work from the plant over the next six months,' he paused for a moment, 'they knew about it months ago,' he proclaimed.

As he spoke a normality returned to the room whilst the workers breathed in a comfort within which they could attempt to evaluate their condition. Spasms of immediate response had evolved amongst these workers whose life chances brought about the need to act quickly in all matters of preservation. As their lives proved more precarious than most primitive reflex actions satisfied all measure of daily contact with others. The common ailment of industrial deafness brought on by the constant pounding of steel upon steel created exaggerated body movements ill suited to any normal circumstance that they may, on rare occasions, come into contact with. So it was that, as John Evans spoke, this mass of humanity continued with the rapid body movements and singular speech of the factory floor. Amongst the workers individuals emerged who acted as translators or expert 'signers', capable of imparting the information now being offered by John Evans. Cries for silence served only to drown out further the dreadful message being delivered. Eventually even the most industrially hardened workers adapted to the new environment that the canteen now offered. Even if the speaker donated a million words to this assembly, their ability to truncate life to the barest syllable, to summarise the most complex statements to words of one or two syllables, rested upon their need to survive. Yet this in itself was an amazing ability. However, this did not stop the cynicism of these workers' lives from regularly punctuating what they heard with their own distorted versions of reality. The speaker ignored the constant distraction of his audience as he fought to be heard and understood. Pockets of resistance to anything that complicated the simplicity of working life with its constantly revolving routine were repelled at all costs. No manner of fabrication or twisted irrelevancy was ruled out by some workers as they struggled to make sense of the madness that invaded their lives. For the system always ensured that blame rested everywhere but not with it. Not with those whose only source of power rested upon chaos and savagery. Words and events for many of the worst-affected workers all had their own built-in source of understanding that could be translated into that base mechanism capable of matching the world view much sought after by the bosses. They looked to translate reality into their own world order.

The name of a foreign country gave rise to the automaton response of hating all things different. Like most factories in the area, this was a predominantly white workforce who in the main suffered human difference as they did change; with unwanted and inexplicable fear. Although many of those who worked in the drill shop hated the in-built prejudice to all things different that McCabe had sought to underline as part of his job, they had often let the worst excesses of this discrimination go unchallenged. The subtext of this fear, hatred and ignorance continued throughout the meeting, and although it was limited to the usual known minority within the factory, its existence cast its shadow upon the wheels of human progress whenever they turned. Ignorance was an excuse and a reality that such persons chose, as if their sub-standard being was above all other forms of existence. Of itself it brought deliverance of that longed for routine of life that evaded all complexity and ruled out the need for change. The need to make decisions or choices that for many was the domain of the 'boss'. This, some often boasted, was not for 'the likes of them.... That's why we have bosses'. Others sought solitude in being the 'man-child'. Life in this condition was simple and uncomplicated. Some rested on the platform of being the professional 'goodfella', they were the ones that everyone 'liked' but no one could remember why. They were clever enough to coast through existence, never saying too much about anything. Come times of hardship or difficulty they tended to crumble like rotten wood. Another group, the 'tough guys', well, they tended to get going when the going got tough. The revolution that was the factory sought would change this.

Imposed upon by mountainous falsehoods, the climb was truly insurmountable for some unless given the ropes and oxygen of repugnance, courage or something better. And so, in their confusion, the man that now stood before them was not a boss or an official of the bosses' union, so his views had to be ignored. He did not wear a tie. Worse still, for some, he was one of them. In his despair he knew this to be their reality and that they might never escape from it, but he spoke to those who had long displayed their wish to elude the condition so beloved of the system. It was to this other meeting that he spoke. This involved the majority, and whilst they often sought comfort in the simplicity of factory routine, they knew that a larger life existed outside of the strangling futility of the factory. A life far more complex than one could imagine. A life uncorrupted by exploitation and false reality. It was a life in which they had respect for each other. A life in which decisions and choices collided with a galaxy of freedoms that made it possible to make both collective and personal decisions. This was a life worth fighting for. John Evans had by now folded the paper and returned it to his jacket pocket. The proof of its reality had been accepted.

'This answers the question as to why our conditions have deteriorated over the last few years,' he said, 'why no investment in new machinery or repairs to the plant have been actioned. They knew it and the union went along with them.' Loud cries rang in the room.

'Run the plant down, that's what they did,' John Evans replied to the calls flowing upwards, 'to compete involved investment and they couldn't be bothered.'

People shouted 'Yes' or 'No' as the feeling struck them.

'Stevens is just cashing in his money, and to avoid any claims from the workers over redundancy payments,' he cried out above the noise, 'he's just engineered a dispute so that he can offload all of us at no costs!' he shouted amidst cheers of agreement and rejection.

In just four days the workers had been able to witness the misrule of the system, the company and the union. The physical atmosphere and the general condition of the workers had improved beyond recognition. Now, knowledge that the company was going to close the plant down left them all without purpose, because this was the only life they knew. Yes, many hated their existence. Some loathed the sacrifices they made to receive a wage packet whilst others knew no different and wanted for nothing more than the blanket that servitude provided. In this absence of dreams the latter led amputated lives in which the magnitude of their fear of change had immersed them in the deep void necessary to function as a factory worker. Now these two groups faced each other for the first time. Some thought the boss, even at this late stage, would take pity upon them and save them from the consequences of their momentary freedoms. One group, who had physically fought with the 'scabs' outside the plant, savoured the irony that their loyalty to the boss would be rewarded in much the same way as those who now occupied the plant. Nevertheless, the news weighed upon them all like death.

As speeches go John Evans had long perfected an art of dialogue in which he was a most able exponent. He spoke as he lived his life, questioning everything before him. So each statement found itself hung on deeply personal threads. He prodded and pulled at these fine links as if weaving a complex fabric. And through this process was his means of evaluating every substance of his thought. Unless remarked upon, this skill went unnoticed, as workers assumed the artistry was within their own powers of understanding. Understatement replaced rhetoric as the speaker explained the dilemma they all faced. No easy options availed themselves, as closure was as much as final as could be achieved. As weapons go the decision to occupy had been proven correct. The information that now lay before them would have been locked in the corruption of both union and management until an announcement had to be made. The occupation would have to continue and the workers would examine the potential to establish a co-operative based upon the customers they now had, as well as looking at diversifying some areas of production. On hearing this, some workers released the usual tirade that simply confirmed the bosses' right 'to be the boss' by some divinity. A divinity that proclaimed the state of human advancement as predetermined under the authority of the employing class. Co-ops don't work. You can't have an island of socialism in a sea of capitalism. This seemed to condemn everyone to slavery outside of the revolution. John Evans hated these contradictions almost as much as he agreed with them.

As he summed up the options available John Evans informed the workers of the need to attend the funeral of Brian Atkins the following day. This presented a problem, for if the decision were to continue the occupation, then enough workers would have to protect the factory from the police and Stevens's workers. No other member of the committee spoke as it was agreed that their chairman had explained everything to the workers, and after he had finished praising the 'dignity and courage of all the workers' John Evans received the acclaim of his audience. Within this acclaim many workers simply received the mechanical understanding of what they mistook as meaning. For some no subtext existed. Long removed from the need to evaluate information for themselves their world had only one axis. That of obedience to the last instruction. Any process that began from birth and consistently imposed itself in life, reinforced itself through existence, was bound to impact upon the imprisonment of free will. Such a process left its indelible stain on the confidence of people to express themselves. Only a larger foolishness would mistake this nurtured state as any indication of stupidity. John Evans knew this to be a truth of factory life and he respected the potential within all beings to eliminate the influence of the system and escape its crushing of the human spirit. A man can speak moderately well for long periods of time and feel understood by his audience, but the audience may only acknowledge minute areas of understanding from any protracted dialogue. Many factors weave their way through communication, and the language itself may only play a minor part as the life chances of each participant meander through their own labyrinths of perceived realities to seek understanding. So it was with John Evans's speech. He spoke for almost one hour, answering questions, calming doubts, fielding interruptions and insults. Always being respectful, never expressing frustration or anger. In all the words he chose to use the message was stark and simple and perhaps could have been expressed in a few moments. The wrath of the ruling class was against them because they had organised against '*it*'. They owed it to themselves to stand and fight for a higher principle that appeared futile against seemingly overpowering odds. This was the nature of all struggle. The men and women who faced him knew this, but the retribution of the employing class was not a sophisticated or complex tool. Once out of the system that the employing class controlled, re-entry often proved either difficult or impossible. Without a wage, no matter how paltry, each individual life in the hall was threatened. It was a time for stating the obvious, and when John Evans stood down from the table many workers stole the opportunity to remind their fellow workers just how bad things were and how much worse they were likely to get. Seen as a natural consequence of all meetings, negativity pulled them through that vital optical event in which their eyes were opened beyond the normal limitations of their existence. A darkness had been lifted and its consequence blinded many. They understood the brutality of their lives. They knew their oppressors and they knew how to fight them.

Hawkins was the strategist and he responded to the fears that overshadowed the workers' trust in themselves and of themselves. His physical presence alone gave strength to the workers' cause as well as his practical analysis of what needed to be done. Like shovels in the air, his worker's hands mixed concrete ideas as he built the edifice upon which this struggle would develop. No room existed for those who doubted their own abilities, they should go outside and join the others as this struggle would become more difficult. In his own way he simplified their condition in the irony of being sacked whether the workers were inside or outside the factory. Loyalty and disloyalty to the boss was rewarded with the equal devastation of a raging fire. Hawkins was considered an equal to all in the factory and he behaved as such a role demands. But his intellect penetrated far beyond simple working-class caricatures of industrial solidarity. This workers' worker was a contradiction that proved the nature of a class capable of moving beyond the imposed corruption of the system. He was the embodiment of progress and it was his integrity that informed the struggle from this moment. Whilst all eyes and ears followed John Evans's intellect, their hearts beat to the inspiration of other men and women amongst them that day.

Chapter Thirteen

But the hands of one of the partners were already at K.'s throat, while the other thrust the knife into his heart and turned it there twice. With failing eyes K. could still see the two of them, cheek leaning against cheek, immediately before his face, watching the final act. 'Like a dog!' he said: it was as if he meant the shame of it to outlive him.

—Franz Kafka, *The Trial*

Sadly, the apprentice thought his transition complete. He bathed in the flame of those around him. He was now a person who claimed to be representative of men and women much older than himself. But this was only in his own mind. His opinion and help, or so he thought, were sought on all manner of things, and at the funeral of Brian Atkins he had been chosen to be one of the coffin bearers. This he considered to be confirmation of his acquired respect and maturity. Annie had noted how her changeling had begun to unfold. She was displeased by what she saw. She had worked at the factory for five years and understood the complex relations that contributed to its whole. Whilst she declared a love for him her life had taught her much of the need to recognise the onerous responsibilities that diversity brought and that existence encircled a three-dimensional burden that could not be simplified through meaningless gestures of self-importance. This was the crime she saw in the boy. Thus, the boy was exposed amidst the customary flow of denials that confirmed, at least for the girl, his guilt. Overnight, he became a sophisticate through the experience and struggle of others. False ghosts appeared before him as he rewrote his own existence and played out a role no less ingenuous as those he claimed to rise above. Equally, his guilt for this crime was compounded in her eyes. Hawkins and John Evans had also become aware of the peculiar changes taking place within the boy. But they aired caution as a parent would to a son. Much closer than others, the girl soon found herself the centre of his critical defence. 'She had changed, not him' was his retort. Yet it was his voice that grew louder and longer in the company of the strike committee, not hers. With his behaviour being widely interpreted as being 'childish', the committee left him alone. Within this circle he was able to lose himself in a human diversity that he chose to use on one hand and ignore, as Annie observed, 'when it suited'. At gatherings of the committee she noticeably sat distanced from the boy, as if avoiding a contagion.

Outside the factory the other workers stood huddled together, having listened to Johnson, Jacks, McCabe, O'Toole and a police inspector promise them that their right to work in the factory would be upheld and that the occupation would soon end. For this group of workers were yet to find out that a decision to close the plant had been taken. Suitably invigorated, the crowd dispersed that afternoon, having been given instructions to return at 8.00 a.m. the next day. Unconcerned, their management leaders shared lunch in a nearby hotel. The threat passed like a battalion of clouds. A small police presence punctuated the absence of the workers outside the factory. Inside repairs continued while in the office plans were being made to attend the funeral. Talk centred upon the risk to the factory if too many workers left the factory at the same time. Numbers would be limited and extra workers would be on guard for the whole of Tuesday. John Evans suggested that he should speak to the police sergeant in an effort to achieve an amnesty whilst the workers attended the funeral of their dead comrade. It was customary in these aspects of workers control that democracy is defined as the endless use of speech as the true evaluation of free expression. This may be the case, but in such circumstances the furniture of reclaimed freedoms does not simply rest upon the rearrangement of the bosses' office desk or chairs. The philosophical imperatives are lost in the assumption that a 'way to behave' has already been fashioned by the ruling elite and that this is a design without equal, flawless. Within such a steel box some workers long for the days of the boss when life was much simpler in much the same way a drug addict churns internally for the source of normality that addiction brings. At these highly politicised moments for the working class their political masters rant frenetically against all concepts of workers control as meaningless signposts on the road to a revolution that will never happen. They too yearn for the normality that the capitalist brings to the arena of class-war, for them the system ensures perpetuity. The existence of the enemy, not their destruction, becomes paramount. Thus, the game continued as some less mature workers played at being bosses and revolutionaries without understanding the grisly connection that embraced both faiths. Talking to the police to seek an amnesty for the funeral raised images of class collaboration that flew headlong against the principles of the occupation as a political act. The debate was exhausted beyond exhaustion, and the committee deferred to the leadership of their new boss John Evans. Other matters of importance suffered from the post-mortem approach now adopted as symbolic of democratic freedom and leadership. And victory fell to those without human emotions. To those capable of sitting it out. As if waiting for death to impose a conclusion, these meetings re-ignited themselves whenever a natural calm broke into the room. More seasoned artisans took the opportunity to leave and re-enter the endless meetings as their patience and stomach allowed. The young apprentice took his opportunities to challenge the leadership of his friend as he yelled about 'selling out' the political principle of the occupation. Annie listened in horror and left the room with John Evans. They had made their decision and contacted the police outside, who in turn called the sergeant at his home to speak with the strikers' leader. Meanwhile, for a newly emerged elite, the infinity of debate continued meaninglessly in the offices above the factory floor.

Without his uniform the man looked as any other man. But like concrete, his role remained supremely solid and intact even without the formality of his absent insignia. This was the phoney war and this was informality personified. Just two men seeking a reasoned way out of a difficult problem in the best traditions of capital. The sergeant was inside the factory, sitting at a steel desk strategically placed near the tool shop. When he entered the workshop he made his way around the desk. He represented the owners of the steel desk, so he should sit on the side of authority, from which he could conduct his interview with the strike leader. John Evans was tired and ignored the puerile staleness of role-plays. The factory was reasonably silent, disturbed insignificantly by the occasional noise, not too dissimilar from that of an empty darkened theatre preparing for a finale of splendid potential. Only echoes could really be heard. The policeman was determined to air his officialdom in the face of the worker as if he had been brought in for questioning. Two games now played in the factory. Democracy upstairs—deceit downstairs. John Evans supported his chin with one arm. The policeman sat with fingertips barely touching, ruminating on life and the universe and the man who now sat before him. It was his act. Picking up a micrometer from the table, the officer examined it with its own precision. His countenance altered its state to a police exhibit—part of the crime scene. For his role the workers' representative pondered upon the theft of his tool—of his livelihood that now balanced precariously in the probing hands of the policeman. No longer the understanding figure that he had cut only a day before, this man was now operating under 'order mode' and the rules had clearly changed. The officer made reference to the instrument before him, that for his knowledge of such things could well have been a rusty nail.

'These workers have some skills,' he said patronisingly, 'never my forte. Not the practical sort.' Abruptly he changed the tempo of his opening remarks. 'But it matters little. The skills of these workers,' he thought about his words as if they were more profound than he had originally intended, 'because now they are trespassing on property that is not theirs,' he stated bluntly. 'It's my job to uphold the law,' he said. Then he waited for a few moments and added, 'at all costs.' He coldly warned John Evans, 'This unofficial action can only lead to a bad conclusion. Take my word for it.' The officer pondered his own words again with a false and heavy countenance. The act was complete.

John Evans looked through the man, declaring no intention to play his role. For him no question existed as to whether he would seek some respite from this actor. A cold silence dangled above the interrogation such as it was. He was as much a tool as the micrometer he had discarded aimlessly a few seconds earlier.

The policeman interrupted the space before them. 'Now, I believe you wanted to speak to me,' he said gravely.

The worker leant across the table, and the officer, no doubt fearing for his safety, startled back in his chair. John Evans now held in his hands the symbol of skill, status and hierarchy amongst his own community. The micrometer separated the worlds of both men and they knew it. A cold silence froze moments of time as they both struggled to control this lost space. John Evans eased his body across the table.

'Could you possibly imagine how long it takes before any worker in this factory can hold one of these in his or her hands?' he said as the micrometer glistened like a spaceship in the makeshift light of the factory.

'Could you imagine?' he asked the policeman, knowing that the answer was that the couldn't. 'Do you know it measures to thousandths of an inch?' he said firmly. 'More respected and revered by the bosses than any worker. This instrument holds a science of its own. You could not imagine its significance. Could you?' he asked again. A brief pause allowed both men to consider the small scattering of sound that tumbled around the factory.

'No. You don't know. You answered that when you came in here.' John Evans sat motionless as the policeman stood.

'This is a bad affair and we will end it swiftly.' The interrogation had ended and the policeman turned to leave.

With the mannerisms of the actor exiting the stage the policeman was gone. The worker sat quietly by himself and considered his condition. Now he looked more closely than ever at the tool before him. Examining its steely brilliance and timeless design. Weighing its delicate power in his fingers. Its tiny calibrations and small curved steel form proclaimed its brilliance. The tool balanced gently around his fingers. He looked at it as if it was the first time. But it wasn't. He grabbed tight hold of the tool in his fist, for it was only a tool, and flung it deep into the darkest recesses of the factory. An empty recoil plotted its journey as it bounced off metal machines and shimmered in the darkness that now embraced the factory. All was silent. It was gone from sight. Only echoes remained, and it seemed like the whole factory was filled with echoes at that moment. John Evans felt a cold caress enter and then leave his body. He stood up, choosing to return to the meandering words that drove, peddle hard down, into the early evening as the strike committee considered the meaning of everything. John Evans called Hawkins out of the room. They could deliver the decisions of the group as they were announced. The young apprentice was holding court on the vagaries of the workers' struggle, his energy and determination drained the strength of all about him. Annie had long since left the meeting and sat reading in her loneliness, distracted by anger for the naïveté of the boy within whom she had placed so much trust. As the night took hold Evans and Hawkins unscrewed the lid on a bottle of whisky that had languished in Johnson's office drawer. A gift from some supplier, content that bribery always lubricated the wheels of commerce and industry. Across the city a policeman examined his meal, lifting edges of food in a forensic study with his steel-plated knife. His wife waited anxiously, consumed as ever by a guilt-ridden fear that only other imprisoned innocents could comprehend.

The plan was fairly simple and reasonably basic. The workers were to attend the funeral and a number of them, approximately one hundred, were to keep the factory secure. But even this basic simplicity could not halt some on their journey towards political self-autopsy. Numerous decisions and non-decisions were made deep into the night like a country born from revolution, new laws rattled endlessly from great rhetoric and all required immediate invocation. Papers were typed and copies leapt from the steel drum copier that now communicated to the workers, the labour movement and the community directly. But before each document could be published it had to run the gauntlet of endless revisions and edits because a certain word, or collections of words, did not suit individual madness. In the end documents were published with the originals stamped 'with reservations'. This averted blame for many who would have liked to have spent a few more years deliberating the position of a certain adverb or noun. Nevertheless, in the impossibility of the situation a new factory was in the process of creation, and the committee marvelled at their newfound abilities. The apprentice learned quickly that control of communication, or attending to any menial task within the group, projected self-importance and unveiled power. It was he who mechanically typed each memo of a decision and it was he who transferred it to the cylindrical printing press. It was he who stamped 'with reservations' on each original. He did this function with great pride. Nothing moved unless he had some involvement. He had learned quickly and men and women noticed his advancement. He now had two political minders who had arrived at the factory that day to offer their political group's support. These three vaguely argued that the workers should not attend the funeral that day. That this would place the occupation at risk. But nothing came from this 'line'. Now it has to be said this particular group lay beyond the extraordinary political support delivered by 'real comrades' of every workers' struggle. These groups provide a complex local, national and often international network of support and they had an energy that was capable of lifting all industrial disputes to a different plateau. They were an invisible army without whom all workers' struggles would be doomed. A minority of sectarian groups could often undermine even the most heroic struggles of the industrial working class with their unfathomable intrigue and hatred of all things different. They inhabited their own void. A political black hole.

Men like Hawkins knew the dangers associated with giving too much involvement in the direct processes of the workers' struggle to those outside of it. In the most part they knew little of such struggles. In practice he saw them as often drowning in an ocean of their own political text and theory. The theory that portrayed the necessary blueprint of all workers' struggles, in all industries and in all countries. Rigorously they protested their unquestionable theories as if overcome by some delirious religious experience that donated to them and their members the key to the struggles of the working class. In exchange for this precious knowledge, humour, human relations and respect for the very workers they claimed to support vaporised in the heat of their own limited commitment. Paranoia eased the web of treachery they saw in all workers' leaders, whilst some genuflected in the presence of officialdom that the paid leaders of the union represented. The apprentice had made the arrogant mistake of talking too freely and they claimed this convert for themselves, massaging his inexperienced ego. Making him one of their own. These two odd-looking characters sat in the corner, making endless notes and consulting on the substance of every contribution no matter how innocuous they may have been. Every so often they called the young revolutionary apprentice over to suggest a line that should be fed into the group. Never would they directly intervene, as this would have resulted in the committee realising the practical purpose of their infiltration. Physically and intellectually they behaved aloof from the natural state of the workers. Their presence was suffered by some in false respect for the apprentice, who, albeit for only a few days, was at least a factory worker.

Hawkins and John Evans sought release from these torments of the struggle. They had seen it before a lifetime over and as young men they too took on the role of the young revolutionaries whose own struggle was at first to please then to control. So they sat where they sought sanctuary near the welding shop on the simple wooden stool where they had spent so much of their factory life, silent and grey. It was now dark in the factory and only the light cut from the offices above the factory floor etched out the figures of both men. Like some great searchlight each time the bottle lifted and flushed against the glasses bare bulbs struck their glaze. Momentary glimpses of this meagre light reflected their faces to each other, and both thought of how they had aged but neither spoke of this. After all, it was just a glimmer. Now was a time to consider the moment and both men were brothers whose honesty shackled them to the constant disappointments of life and in this honesty they suffered. The alcohol served only to oil the huge engines of this honesty so rare. Yet they battled with every sentence, confronting the bourgeois nature that seemed to encroach like an unwelcome guest upon their age and the experiences that came with their toil. In youth they had experimented with the trial of party membership and both confirmed the religion of their experiences. Yet they had long ago discarded them as irrelevant to the reality of struggle for a working class excluded from the intellectual luxury of contemplation without hunger. Intellect without survival. Theory served only to distance reality. For those with this theory lacked reality, and those with reality so often lacked theory. It was this personal struggle that they had both embarked upon, thirsting for knowledge to comprehend the conditions that encircled their lives. No such marriage was to be contemplated as power rested with theory, the real mechanics of power, in which the imagery of word and deed overwhelmed the reality of struggle. Whatever failings they had, they never betrayed anyone, they never gained from their struggles any more than other workers. They never profited from the poverty of their own class. And in this sense they were good men.

Both were obsessed by the future. The current struggle they saw in the fixed term. This was all that was required. Concepts of technology replacing workers at the point of production raised issues crucial to their struggle. They agreed that the present systems of production would develop and that certain skills would be replaced. The evidence for this was all around them even in their antiquated factory. In its Marxist sense the removal of living labour from the production process was inconceivable. They both wanted it to happen and believed it was more than possible, but then the entire process of exploitation would be turned upon its head. New industries would inevitably evolve replacing the old, and the capitalists would ensure their perpetuity by constantly reinventing themselves. Their conversation was slow and relaxed as they exchanged argument in a form wholly distinct from the debate that still ensued in the gangways of offices that overlooked the factory floor. The principle was the focus of this dispute and in this sense its tactics were predetermined. The occupation would continue and the workers would fight the employer's decision on closure. That was the principle which refused to accept the immutable power of the owner to dismiss workers without the fleeting thought one may give in choosing between coffee or tea. Endlessly examining or re-examining the situation served no real purpose for them. The solidarity of all workers in the area was paramount to the success of this particular struggle, and it was hoped that over the next few days these workers would close their factories in support. All things were possible and the lead had been given by the workers at G.P. Stevens over the last few days. Neither man expected the official union to pursue such a course of direct action, and so again they would find themselves in conflict with the very organisation established by the workers to represent the conduct of their life struggle. As it stood their life had little room for further deterioration. Above them applause could be heard, no doubt for another fine speech in which presentation camouflaged substance.

John Evans recounted his meeting with the police sergeant, whom he felt may have allowed his humanity to supersede his role. It often occurs, he continued to explain. He never really believed it—he just said it. Hawkins shook his head.

'John, forever looking for that recall of humanity in people,' he said, 'it will be the death of you and you know it.' He looked into his comrade's eyes. 'The die has been truly cast, this you also know, why try to escape it? When workers unite and stand up for themselves, the panic buttons get pressed all over the place,' he closed his eyes briefly, 'and often we don't ever quite know how deep this goes. Rest assured.' He paused for a moment and looked towards his friend and tipped his glass in salutation. 'The files on you and me and a few others will be getting well thumbed as we speak. They have to crush us, we have to be crushed,' he said almost joyfully. 'Sometimes I think we want to be crushed. But that doesn't mean we're wrong, we were born outside the walls of '*it*', never to be admitted.' He continued laughing. 'You hate them more than you will ever admit because you seek some higher philosophical meaning.' The light cut in amongst them. 'As if some justification for their behaviour could make it more able to be understood. That's plain stupid, my friend.' His laughter died. 'When will you accept the hatred that exists for the likes of you and me and those workers who have sacrificed everything to take up the struggle?'

John Evans smiled innocently as if caught in the act of some meaningless misdemeanour by a correcting adult. His friend continued.

'Look, there you go again. I think your catholic guilt....' He stopped himself and smiled at this thought. 'That's it!' he exclaimed. 'The 'guilt' can't get you to accept any behaviour without some plausible reason. Constantly living in the expectation that your enemies are going to sit down and explain why they want to destroy you. Look at your young apprentice up there. Christ, if we had a penny for every prediction we've made in the past then we certainly wouldn't be stuck here.' His voice grew gently angrier. 'He'll end up like the rest of them. He'll end up wanting to be a full-time official of the union and justify it in the way that he wants to carry the fight forward. And then? Well, you know what happens then, like his two new mates, they become dependant upon the system to give them the lifestyles they crave for. The struggle is no different than a factory to some of them. It's where they work.'

John Evans shook his head again.

'Oh yes, they'll quote Marx, the struggle and invoke the memory of the Tolpuddle Martyrs, but they need the patronage of the boss class to maintain the myth of their existence.' Both heads shook in disagreement with each other. 'They need to protect the boss to protect their struggle. To keep it going. They have to have the enemy, the beast that has to be destroyed—but not today,' he said, 'no, it's never today.'

'No,' interrupted John Evans.

Leaning forward and claiming the little light that was now left between them, Hawkins pushed his comrade's arm. 'He's not your son and he won't give you a reason for his actions either.'

This final comment sparked a response. John Evans poured the last drops of whisky into both glasses and sat back, allowing time to pass between himself and his friend. The sparse light that had been disturbed by their slight movements stabilised, casting two dying silhouettes. John Evans took his cue from this even though exhaustion had crept upon them both and it was demanding the discourse to conclude. He spoke in deference to its power.

'You're not right all the time. The boy will have to stand alone and learn for himself,' John Evans retorted. 'He'll be all right,' he confirmed. 'No. He's not my son and I don't want to adopt him. I look for justification, the reason why we do things. Why shouldn't we get a reason for an action?' he asked his friend. 'There's the irony, eh?' he said. 'Even my own son didn't give a reason for his actions.' He paused again as if weighing his words. 'It was all so decisive, all so planned out. Then the guilt.' He looked ahead. 'That self-inflicted misery of failure that eats at you every day in every loose moment when your mind is not preoccupied with some inconsequential event. You've got children and you know what I mean.' He seemed to be examining his words but decided to continue. 'You never lost any of them!' he almost shouted. John Evans regretted doing this. But he kept going. 'That pain that enforces the constant need for blame. Yes, I need to have answers. I fuckin demand them,' he said angrily.

Hawkins listened as he had done on so many other occasions to the same outpouring of self-blame. Silence breathed between them. Both men

173

eventually slept where they sat. Upstairs the lights stayed on all night in the committee room, where the apprentice and his two political commissars analysed the darkness away.

That morning a fresh fall of snow covered the streets outside the factory. Hawkins was awakened by the cold that steadily brushed up against him. He opened a small window in the welding shop, allowing more frosted gasps of air to enter the room like a breeze of frozen butterflies. Across the road he saw one police car shrouded in a bleak, soundless mist. The creak of the metal window woke John Evans, whose body welcomed the cold air. It pressed against his face. Elsewhere in the factory the movement of men and women could clearly be heard as they assembled by the main entrance. They would leave the factory together at eight o'clock that morning and had been instructed not to get involved in any physical struggle with the police or any workers who may be outside the factory at that time. Hawkins informed his friend that they just had time for some coffee before they were due to leave. In the canteen Annie welcomed the two men, who looked tired and worn as they walked towards her. She brought them coffee and toast and sat quietly with them as they ate. No words were spoken as none were needed. Opposite them sat the young apprentice with his two new friends, still deeply entwined in the dialectic of a political breakfast. Hasaan and Margaret Harvey joined Annie's company, making some observation about the changeling boy, who kept looking over his shoulder suspiciously as one or the other of his lieutenants leaned across to fill his head with their ideas. Hawkins suggested that they were now cast as 'class traitors' and should expect to be denounced at the next meeting of the 'people's court'. This brought laughter to the table, causing all three revolutionaries to look over their shoulders. Margaret Harvey thought the group had signed their own death warrants for laughing at breakfast time, commenting 'that this was not the way cadre members should behave in front of the proletariat.'

Annie kept her silence as she stared at the young apprentice who had now replaced the badge given to him by John Evans with a small red star placed strategically on his coat collar. She thought upon the stupidity that immodesty and arrogance imposes when first adopted. Time would help the apprentice to assume his true nature without anyone ever having the knowledge that once this young man was not a prisoner of ambition and personal ego. How she longed to injure her lover. Her friends knew her mind and occasionally gave her a gentle nudge back into their company, and for this she was grateful. For his part, John Evans refused to comment openly about his former charge. The workers made their way towards the factory entrance, joining others already awaiting the order to leave. Again their discipline and dignity was a vision to be marvelled at as other workers cleaned around the factory, preparing things for their return. Along the corridor the workers could feel the steel door open as its vibration released spurts of icy rain against their faces.

It was the old gatekeeper who maintained his post throughout the occupation that now energetically called back to the workers that the coast appeared clear, to which he added, 'As clear as he could see and that wasn't much,' as if this last comment would free him from any guilt should there prove to be hoards of police waiting for their exit. Everyone knew this to be the case, but they did not comment.

Outside their way was clear except for the singular police car that lay embedded in the snow. Reluctantly two policemen left the warmth of their car. The first line of workers streamed delicately from the building like an open gash in its side. Despite the icy mist all was clarity in the street as the dark mass swarmed in greater and greater numbers. The police turned hastily back to the security of their car. The sky hung low and deep upon the factory. A white sun failed above them and all the nearby buildings paled to insignificance, smothered in silence and frozen humility. They had finally succumbed to a sense of guilt for the years they dominated such crooked and forlorn human figures that now paraded before them. Even the cast iron clock was held prisoner by the ice, causing its mighty fingers to surrender unseen at three fifteen that morning. The slow animation of the workers moved in unison with nature as if its own icy breath was in solidarity. Ragged dark winter clothing of every description shielded the workers. And as they pushed their way through the snow, nature gave way to the mass of the workers who arched and snaked their way forward.

The flat road ahead took on the imagery of some invisible incline, a mountain pass. Other factory workers shouted their support as they passed by. Some opened factory windows in an effort to shout their solidarity as this flight from their condition strove forward into hidden wildernesses. Their failing echoes, soaked up by the snow, breathed only cold silence. The young revolutionary, for this was his new role, was flanked on both sides by his two primary commissars, who independently and secretly thought this 'was what it must have been like when the Bolsheviks stormed the winter palace ... blood on the snow'. One of them shared this image with his charge, who thought this a great image to conjure with although he had only a limited idea what his political guides were speaking about. But with this encouraging information he pushed further to the front until after only a few moments he was there and his mind was satisfied that his body led the line of workers in all but name. This gave his rickety mentors the excuse to march at the front as the workers made their way to the funeral. When the last of them ran precariously from the factory, one could hear in the distance the steel door of the factory slamming shut on the outside world and it sounded secure to all who heard its muffled grave noise. Within minutes police and workers who refused to take part in the occupation arrived, too late to act out their own roles of opposition in this snowbound theatre.

Most of the workers lived close to the site where all the factories had been located, and Atkins's house followed this rule. John Evans, Hawkins, Margaret Harvey, Annie, Hasaan and the young revolutionary had to go into the house. This meant that at some point they would have to break from the main group of workers. Hawkins nominated himself for this task, marching to the front and thrusting a gloved hand upon the boy's shoulder, he told his two comrades in unmistakably blunt tones that 'it was time for them to leave.' The boy looked to his invigilators to seek a comment or political analysis, but before the act could be completed Hawkins had dragged him around, forcibly marching him back to the group who now waited on the pavement. In the silence enforced by grief and respect they made their way to the home of Mrs. Atkins. Hawkins knocked hard on the door and the small, diminutive figure of Atkins's mother welcomed them all in giving each a gentle embrace as they entered her hallway. Dressed in black, she cut an all too common figure of working-class motherhood aged by the brutality of her life's struggle, physically bent by the weight of her burden and yet undiminished by her experience. Her eyes exposed the fire in her soul.

'John, Mr.Hawkins, Margaret, Annie, it's good to see you all and this,' she said holding the young black boy's hand, 'must be young Thomas and....' Looking towards the revolutionary, she gave a mother's welcome. 'Brian spoke so much about you.' Her voice trailed away into distant thought.

Revolutionaries embarrass easily, and yet this old woman had seen and taken part in more revolutionary activity than he would ever comprehend, and the entire group, except for him, knew this and understood the meaning of this moment. A moment that was lost to him. She had welcomed them into her house and it was as ever a statement of her class. A small group of relatives huddled in the living room that was almost as cold as the air outside. A single-bar electric fire meaninglessly secured heat to itself. The elderly woman apologised for the lack of warmth and joked that her husband was a coal miner before his customary premature death and would not have countenanced electric fires.

But they wouldn't let her have a coal fire, she said, 'it was bad for your health or something like that. I forget now,' she said, smiling to herself, 'I thought the cold was worse—perhaps that's what'll kill me,' she added thoughtfully. 'The coal,' she repeated to herself.

Everyone was introduced to each other and some tea was offered as Annie busied herself in her usual thoughtful manner except, that is, when it came to her lost and unrecognisable love. Hawkins produced another bottle of whisky and presented it to Annie to ensure that everyone got a drink to fight off the cold of the day. In time the woman urged everyone to enter another room in the house, where her son lay inside his coffin. She treated the closed casket as if it were some rare antique. At one point she leant over the coffin, stroking its darkly varnished lid, fiddling with the brass ornaments and crucifix that adorned it. And in her mind she was convinced that he had been the victim of an industrial accident. No one could imagine her condition as she continued to talk and behave as if her son was still amongst them, full of the life that had been stolen from him. John Evans left the room and cried silently into the mocking cold of the electric fire.

Eventually the funeral car arrived and the old woman wept quietly as her son's coffin was unceremoniously manoeuvred through her tiny home. His friends waited diligently for the family to leave the house, and as they approached the flimsy garden gate two figures greeted them, huddled together against the drifting snow. It was the political aides. As Hawkins swept ahead to greet them, John Evans urged patience. Annie grimaced as the young boy made his excuses, saying he would walk the short distance to the church with his dismal comrades. As the group reached the funeral car the old woman tapped on the window, calling Annie towards her. As the window wound down, she thrust five pounds into her hand.

'Take it for the strike fund,' she said quietly, 'those men wouldn't understand, it's a mother's love. I know how much they cared for Brian,' she said. Then she repeated herself again as if to confirm her words and her belief, 'A woman's love. Men don't think like that. Just do me this one favour without a word.... There's a good girl,' she said unknowingly.

Annie leant forward without saying a word and held the frail woman as if her life depended upon it. When the cars rolled away she could just make out in the distance the figures of three people caught in animated irrelevance and she began to cry uncontrollably. The funeral passed with cold efficiency. Over four hundred workers attended and in their black mass, etched overwhelmingly against the pure white snow, they became one huge dark cloud covering space beyond every horizon. As the coffin was lowered to the ground his mother took pride in her son who she now knew, for it had been confirmed, had so many friends and was a respected worker. This was her only wish at that moment. The workers allowed her dream to live forever. Some cried with shame and this was how it should have been. For a brief moment the apprentice revolutionary returned to reality and held Annie close as if to extract the goodness of her life for himself. This was a brief selfish moment and she knew it. In the time it took to bury Brian Atkins the police and the scabs had regained control of the factory.

Chapter Fourteen

You are not here! The quaint witch memory sees, in vacant chairs, your absent images, and points where once you sat, and now should be but are not.

—Percy Bysshe Shelley

When the workers returned all was lost. Not enough of their comrades were left to protect the factory. They now held together, expelled to the road opposite the factory gate. Before them lay the remnants of a struggle to defend the occupation. Blood rested in the road, and on the pavement its evidence indelibly marked the snow. A murky red virus stained the events of that morning and bore witness to the dark suppression needed to establish the false law and order of normality to the factory. Lost in desultory shock, the mourners took time to realise not what had happened, that was easy to see, but how to physically respond. A line of blue encircled the factory, providing a level or legality of protection that the workers were forever incapable of achieving. Snow flaked from the sky and froze their vision, merging sheets of diffident greys with a concrete drabness that appeared secure and serene under the jurisdiction of its owners' reclamation. Some of the workers ran as much as the snow beneath them would allow as if the order to charge had been given. And if it had then they would have attacked. All was lost. Yet they continued in disarray. Waves of dark blue moved forward to welcome new violent opportunities of confrontation needed in these circumstances to reaffirm the rights of the vanquisher who now had control of the factory. Not for themselves. This victory was concluded in the name of the system. They had fought to give back control to '*it*'. And this made them no different from the vanquished. Both were losers. But the police commended their minds to the corruption that justified their actions in the struggle to uphold the law.

Shadowed images stooped against the cold wind, seeking the remnants of a unity that had once made them invincible, if only for a few brief moments of their lives. These monochrome figures merged as ink-dark stains under the landscape. Over one hundred workers had been arrested and taken away so that an equal number could enter the factory to reclaim the control of the owners. The faded blue lines of police prepared themselves in the expectation of some response. They moved reluctantly away from the warmth scattered by the workers' smoking braziers that littered the pavements outside the factory. Locked in despair the workers fused together, feeling some comfort may be found within their frozen unity. An overwhelming sense of their community wrapped around them as they struggled to realise the latest turn of events that now placed them outside the power that control of the factory had given them. Lost in the desolation that defeat imposes, they busied themselves in the effort needed to keep warm, waiting in silence until all the workers had arrived at some unrecognised meeting point. As each new group or couple filtered into the growing crowd, the same questions drove into the group, to be met by the same answers as to why and how the occupation had been lost. The usual recriminations emerged as frozen breath battered against tired and worn faces. Blame appeared again as the only reason for this pointless repetition of recrimination aimed at those who allowed the police and the scabs to take over the factory. Dan Hawkins called again for quiet as John Evans stood in the centre of the crowd. A difficult silence tumbled around the group, allowing him to ask a number of workers exactly what happened. One of the foundry workers near the front came forward, taking time to look his comrades in the eye before he spoke. Pulling a black woollen hat away from his face he addressed the gathering crowd. It had been his job to co-ordinate security in the factory. He opened his hands as if to catch the murmurs of abuse that grew the longer he stood before them.

'John, we did everything we could,' turning around, he shouted to the workers behind him, 'yeah, that's right and you better believe it. Go and visit your comrades in hospital if you need any proof.'

Nods of approval in the crowd indicated to others who could not hear too clearly that this man could not be insulted or blamed with ease.

He continued, 'We carried out all the agreed plans once you left the factory but the police and the scabs battered their way through the milling and acid rooms. We couldn't hold them back. They poured all over us. Those filthy scabs.' The crowd muttered abuse and frozen breath rose amongst them in clouds.

'Most of them just stood and watched the police working out on us. We reckon about twenty were put in hospital, some of them were women. We carried on fighting outside the factory and at one point we almost got back in but they just kept coming. The police kept bringing in reinforcements until they cleared the factory.' The man stopped for a moment.

'John.... Some of them that got taken in the ambulances are badly hurt and about sixty have been arrested.'

The worker replaced his hat and melted back into the crowd. Around two hundred workers now gathered some distance away from the factory. Behind them the young revolutionary wrestled with the hushed instructions being given by his mentors, who pushed him to where John Evans was standing and in the pause that the strikers' leader took to regain his thoughts the young worker made clear his intention to speak. John Evans smiled his reluctance and stood back. The stage now belonged to the apprentice, and this sudden realisation made his body one solid mass, unable to speak. He made empty gestures as if these mute communications conveyed all he wanted to say. An angry unease closed in on him as many of the older workers challenged the right of someone who had only recently been employed in the factory to speak at such a moment. It was not his right or turn to speak at such moments. But they did not need to speak to indicate this unwritten rule of the workplace. The boy knew this—everyone knew this except his two revolutionary consultants. To them this was a chance to promote the party line, to steal a march on other political groupings that supported the occupation. This was a vital component of their dogma. The boy shivered in the vacuum where he stood, fully realising that if he was to be heard then now was the time to speak. His head jumbled sentences that even he could not comprehend, being the end result of almost two days' indoctrination at the hands of his political masters. They stood near the back of the crowd, oblivious to the reality of the workers that encircled them.

An air of arrogance was always with them as they assumed within themselves the knowledge and answers to every molecule of the workers' struggle. Both now stood intellectually above the mob and this was confirmed in the elevated persona they adopted. For all their talk of workers' rights they assumed the role and body language of any aspiring boss, greeting all interaction with a condescension that dismissed any view that did not fit the pattern of their party line. No humour existed for them. They had no fun. One looked to the other in the space that now saw the boy's lonely figure amidst the crowd struggling to speak, and they confirmed their collective displeasure at the boy's abject failure to repeat the party line that they had so assiduously injected over the last two days. Now the boy spoke, hesitantly at first, like an old car starting on a cold morning. Once sparked, he roared the engine well beyond its immediate needs. He looked older and his innocence, once so striking, seemed replaced by a nervous suspicion of all around him. The workers saw this and understood its meaning. Dishonesty rose from his presence and in shame Angie looked down, glaring into the melted snow beneath her feet as if urging the ground to swallow the boy whole.

'We can't just stand here.' He looked towards John Evans as if this unwanted link gave him some authority. 'We can't just wait here. We have to confront the police and regain control of the factory. We have to fight the

lackeys of the system and those filthy scabs to regain control of the factory.'
He looked towards the sky. 'We have to get back inside and we have to do it
now. We can call for a mass picket,' he shouted out the false originality of his
claim. 'We need the political support of the left in this to fight the class that
will oppress us forever until we organise their demise.' He looked for the
acclaim of his audience.

'Victory to the workers! Victory to the working class!' and his voice was
the same as the welder's and so was his message.

With a clenched fist raised high above his head the boy awaited the
promised acclaim of his fellow revolutionaries. Silence dropped heavily upon
the workers as they visibly hunched their bodies against the coldness of the
words that spat in their faces. A fraught stillness now occupied itself amongst
all the workers, who seemed physically amazed that their expectations had
been confirmed in such a stark manner. The girl had by now raised her head
and stared menacingly at the boy, who still awaited the acclaim of the
workers. From the back of the crowd that now surrounded the boy faint
noises pushed through to the front as the workers spoke to each other, as if
looking for confirmation that they had indeed heard the boy correctly. Self-
analysis wove its way in every direction until one of the older workers leant
slightly towards the boy and asked him in all sincerity whether he was '
taking the piss'. In his brief ramshackle discourse he had managed to alienate
everyone before him. Singular expressions of anger now coalesced to become
displays of hatred towards the boy. The crowd gave the old man at the front
the authority to express their collective will. He reluctantly pushed forward
further whilst leaning back precariously against the first line of workers. He
spoke more directly to the boy, raising his voice and turning his head to
involve the crowd in his invective.

'I don't know what fuckin planet you just dropped from,' the worker
looked nervous but his words came fast and confident, 'but feel free if you
wanna go fight with the police. You've just heard what happened this
morning and all you can think is that we just pile back in and somehow the
police will allow us to regain control of the factory.' A gentle breeze rose
around the crowd.

'Now if you can get a few hundred of your political army to stand
alongside us then no problem,' he shouted. 'Everyone will have a go then, but
on this fuckin planet we have to deal in realities and if you don't know?' he
asked the boy directly. 'That's not gonna happen. Oh, we might get a few
good comrades to support us. But today? Now, and in the numbers we need?
No fuckin way!' The man lurched forward, causing the boy to topple
backwards. His finger pointed directly into his face.

'Look, lad, we may look fuckin daft, and I don't want to be too disrespectful cos' you have a right to your opinion, but some of these men and women have been fighting bosses all their lives and this is not the first time we've stood out here with the police guarding that fuckin factory. They may have won this battle but it doesn't mean we've lost the war,' he stated matter-of-factly.

No response really came from the workers. The young revolutionary stood motionless in the shrinking space that was, only a few seconds earlier, his platform. John Evans still felt some sympathy for the boy and hoped that this experience would form part of his education. As he stepped forward the boy was ushered to the back of the crowd by his political masters, who quietly heaped praise upon him whilst attacking the ignorance and cowardice of the workers. Passing through one section of the crowd he caught a glimpse of Annie, whose expression of hatred appeared in the faces of other workers as they helped jostle him out of the way. The figure of John Evans now sought to offer a way forward to the workers as he explained that little time for discussion existed and that some action was needed. He reminded the workers that the decision to close the factory still existed and that this involved the one hundred workers who had fought alongside the police to reclaim the factory for the bosses. The same bosses who would ultimately sack them. They were still members of the union and a meeting would have to be called in light of events over the last few days. The struggle was to continue. As the darkness of the afternoon encroached upon the crowd that had now been joined by workers from other factories he spoke clearly of the need for unity.

'None of us really expected the response to be quite so determined, but we can't turn back time. The struggle has to continue because we have no other options even if we decided to go back in on the bosses' terms'....'

At this point the workers heaved a unified cry of 'Never....'

The speaker continued, confident in the unity that was now being reborn within the workers.

'Well, that's right,' he replied, 'what would be the point to go back in and wait for the factory to close down?' he asked. 'No. We have to continue the struggle and that means regaining control of the factory, but the first step is to organise a twenty-four-hour picket on these gates starting at 7.00 in the morning. We're all cold and wet, it's nearly four o'clock now.' He seemed to plead with the crowd. 'Let's go home to our families or whatever so that we can think about what is to be done.'

Another loud cheer rang around the crowd, and without confirmation being needed, the workers began to disperse in the direction of home or the nearest bar on the factory estate. This was the nature of all decision making amongst these men and women that to some extent relied upon their natural instincts for honesty and justice. In reality their reliance on instinct proved to be an implacable ally serving their class and community. It was obvious to all that more consideration of their situation was required, but why punish themselves further by staying outside the factory, in front of the police, reliving their anguish with each movement of the unfeeling tower clock. These workers could comprehend most situations before they unfolded. They had an instinct for life that had been imposed by the mechanics of their existence and it was this unique industrial instinct that ensured their survival against overwhelming odds. Absent were the falsehoods of role that raised one man above others for no more reason than the quest for patronage at any cost. These workers understood the absolute of unity, no matter how fractured this was at times. In the world of rigid discipline, hierarchy and control that they inhabited it was ironic to observe how they were capable of acting independently without the need for following order after order. They had a style that could build castles on the highest mountains if they so wished. Despite the emptiness of their condition that afternoon the workers held together in a unity shaped by the cruel lessons of their factory lives. Then, this black seam of hunched and worn workers moved off, marching in irregular columns past the police lines that encircled the factory. In their eyes contempt swelled as the police stood their ground, forcing the workers to move in and out of sporadic clusters of uniformed men. Darkness had already folded its embrace around the area and within its shadows some workers pushed past or stood head to head with the police. Other workers calmly asked their comrades to keep moving for fear of more arrests, further reducing the number of workers available to fight another day. Inside the factory a sparse light threw itself over rows of tall metal windows that lined one section of the factory. No sound or movement could be heard. The tower clock had been repaired as if some urgent priority upon its significance had been uppermost in the minds of the local factory owners. Its cast iron fingers continued to struggle against the movement of time.

That evening a celebration took place, for nothing could detract from the sense of unity that now brought these workers together. Most of them took refuge in a pub located on the edge of the industrial estate, and it was here that individual groups set about the task of rebuilding their struggle following the failure of the factory occupation. Such events were riots of good fun, plenty of food and, of course, always plenty of drink. Each man and woman looked after their comrades, and more than anything they knew how to share. These groups reflected the alliances that had been sustained through years of working together. John Evans, Margaret Harvey, Annie, Hasaan, Daniel Hawkins and Williams sat together as usual with other members of the committee and representatives from a number of the workshops. Directly opposite them sat the young revolutionary accompanied as always now by his two political commissars. Workers from other factories on the estate would drift in and out of the pub that evening, seeking information on the police action that day, asking what the union was doing and offering any form of help they could. Having received the information they wanted and confirming their solidarity with their fellow workers, money would be pushed into strikers' hands, telling them to get a drink and not to worry as other workers would soon be voting to support their actions against G.P. Stevens.

Support from any quarter was a valued and respected commodity amongst all workers in struggle. Local and national political groups and activists provided all manner of support to these workers in struggle. For them it *workers right or wrong* and gave life to the strikers that night. And this was reinforced throughout the evening as workers passed through the bar exchanging their analysis or critique of all matters industrial. Many of the workers who had been arrested that day or hospitalised found their way back to the pub telling their stories like veterans of some distant military campaign. The workers talked of all manner of things but most animated their hatred of the boss, the police and their union. Most of all they condemned the scabs who took the factory back for the employer. Many of the workers appeared content to remember how they had saved some of the scabs from being sacked by the boss that they now lined up in solidarity with. This contradiction found many differing explanations, some of the scabs had been good men, but in the history of short lives the actions we undertake invite instant judgement and it is upon this brief scale that a lifetime can flounder. Like labels on a box it is the label that denotes both purpose and description. These men were scabs, now and forever, and the fact that this label was only uncovered on any particular day proves meaningless, for this is what they are. This is what they have always been. Scabs. This is what they will always be.

The young apprentice revolutionary sat submerged under the weight of his political mentors as Annie lifted herself from her own deliberations to watch her former lover. She was betrayed and such betrayals instantly imposed a similar redefinition, a transformation and re-interpretation of the betrayer. At such moments all human emotions suffer extreme mutations. She could hear extracts of the animated discourses that now enveloped the bar so the analysis of a 'scab' that one group was having mixed simultaneously with the conversation of another section of workers proposing to reoccupy the factory. Each conversation weaved its way amongst the workers as if the topic of conversation had been freely chosen. She repeated to herself noteworthy phrases overheard unintentionally 'once a scab always a scab' and as she looked across the table to the three figures locked in almost silent dialogue, muttering to herself 'once a bastard always a bastard'. Her eyes drifted back towards her comrades but her attention focused upon the boy. Physically he had transformed his appearance. She thought how shifty and sly he now looked. Indeed, he had taken on the appearance of the two cretins who now flanked his every move.

Margaret Harvey noticed the girl's distance to all around her and, nudging her gently, brought her back to the table. She smiled and whispered to the young woman, 'Just look at those bastards, what's he thinking of being with those two? You know what they're like, they've got no sense of loyalty or humour for that matter. Well, that's his problem,' she paused for thought, 'but I feel like going over there and grabbing him by the throat,' she added threateningly.

Amidst the noise both women were free to talk although they continued to play their part in the conversation of their immediate company. The older woman held an anger for the boy, who had abused her young comrade. She clenched her friend's hands.

'You've seen it all before, Annie. I'm just so sorry for you. He's got the religion all right. Let's just hope it's only for a short time, otherwise that boy's gonna fuck up real badly,' she concluded.

Both women fell back into their chairs and looked directly ahead. It now appeared that the three figures in front of them had merged into one as the secrecy of their plots fused them together. This furtive group had also caught the observations of others in the bar that night as workers expressed their own concern at the audacity of a boy who had only worked at the factory for a few days, speaking as if he had some understanding of their condition. He earned acceptance only so long as he had the support of John Evans and other respected workers in the factory, and this proved his fatal mistake. The former apprentice turned revolutionary knew what the other workers thought of him now that he had decided to pursue, what he termed, or at least his advisors termed, 'the politics of direct action'. But this was the expected response when workers fell behind the vision of real political leadership. Hawkins, Evans and Williams epitomised the reactionary leadership of the occupation who ignored the real wishes of the 'rank and file' and failed to organise within the union to achieve maximum solidarity. For without the union's support the struggle would be lost. Yes, the unions were bureaucratic and reactionary themselves, but it was the job of revolutionaries to capture vital positions of control before any real defeat of capital could be sustained. This was 'their' theory. Intermittently the boy would defend his former friends or independently challenge the political meanderings of his erstwhile comrades, but this was met with either mentor gently breaking down each component part of his belief as if it were a mathematical theorem that could only have one possible conclusion. This conclusion would signify its approach as the mentors raised the volume and speed of their speech, often underlining what the other had said or was about to say until this dual crescendo crashed down on their captive. Each element of this process owed more to interrogation than analysis, more to indoctrination than free thought, and as such socialism appeared as a meaningless element of the debate. They began with a conclusion and pasted on the analysis that it matched. A prisoner of his own deceit, the young apprentice had made his pact and even if he did steal glances across the room towards Annie, his own refusal to turn back or break free incarcerated his being in the vacuum of his unremarkable warders. The trance of this bizarre threesome was occasionally broken as workers banged into their table or made some remark about the apprentice's speech that afternoon. And as the night progressed, liberated by alcohol, open arguments and attacks upon the two political commissars unfolded. Whilst none of this came to any physical conclusion, the three could reaffirm their revolutionary status in the midst of a mostly reactionary workforce that cried out for rank and file leadership or, put more succinctly, their leadership. This was the world they saw. This was the world they saw to create.

Most of that night Hasaan sat deep in discussion on the next steps that had to be taken in the struggle but he too had been watching the group and the longer he observed them the more hatred he began to secretly harbour. He watched his former friend and looked towards Annie, whom he had long admired and wanted to be more than a friend to. He had also watched how the young apprentice had everything delivered to him upon his arrival in the factory. No racism for this white heir. Despite whatever hardships his former friend may have experienced they could not be compared to the years of abuse the young black worker had suffered. He intensified his glare into the group that became everything he despised in his short life. Again it was the transformation from friend to enemy that rewrote the past. Now everything was viewed through the twisted lens of hatred, and like so much else it was this hatred that dictated all subsequent words and deeds. He stood and walked towards this newfound symbol of his hate but rather than confront his own inner hatred he leant forward and stared at the two figures that locked on to the sides of his former friend. Now he wanted to think about what words could penetrate the deepest pain to all three and as he sat opposite them he considered that he knew exactly the words to use. But in the distance that marked the space between the two opposing sides his mind had been erased by a hatred that pulsed through him and he could not pull back. Addressing the two ends of his fellow worker he calmed himself with the prod of a question to which he already knew the answer. His face filled their company.

'So when was the last time you two were on strike then?' he said violently. 'Or when was the last time you two worked in a factory?' He waited for an answer even though he just wanted to kill them all. He felt his pulse race and his heart pounded out of control. 'Or are you both fuckin professional, full-time revolutionaries?'

Yet this was no original line of questioning and the three looked up in a union of silence and disinterest as if having heard some old joke that lacked humour even in its original telling. In the void that now enveloped him, the young black worker could only stare more deeply into the three faces that now challenged his hatred. But he could only detect a response from his lost friend, who clearly wanted to speak but held back in trained deference to his political captors. The label now applied to his former friend was no longer as clear as it was from a distance and in his eyes a warmth exuded and sought some communication. In these moments that passed he was compelled to disclose his innermost feelings like a card player whose bluff had been called in a movement of the eye. He realised that he did not know or understand what lay behind the false masks of all three as they elected to allow the noise that was in the air to fill the emptiness between them. The black youth thought to himself how he could expose their falseness, yet he knew they would not unfold in any form even a tacit recognition of the label. He then realised that they could even put up a spirited defence of their actions. He felt unable to challenge them and he was weakened by this and the two revolutionaries knew this. It was a dance played out in time whose rules were determined by sectarian hatreds fuelled by the infinite 'isms' that proclaimed the true faith, the one and only religion. And everyone claimed the answer. The true measure of the axiom, capable of rendering all logic or conviction false. Both used the moments before them to confirm the pointlessness of entering into any dialogue. In fact, the whole confrontation was a meaningless sham in which only the personal satisfaction of the act could be exchanged either at the time or in the future as if it were a trophy. Yet they all wanted to serve the working class and they all had some contribution to make. But the fog of distrust claimed them all. Attention was being drawn to their table as observers took note of the figures in the corner locked in silent inaction. In his anger Hasaan heard and saw movements that did not take place, as the void cried out for interruption his hatred filled with the imaginary challenges of those behind him. His friend sat back and unfolded his arms, seeking some conclusion to the matter and in the slow-motion signature that mapped out this brief moment of conflict the aggressor was forced to speak again if only to break the deadening silence.

'I don't know what games you're playin now but be sure you're not at school anymore and I've got a good idea where these two are gonna lead you,' he said directly to his former friend. 'Your real comrades are the workers you should be with now, this is their revolution, if only you could see it. But it's your decision,' he said, almost pleading with the boy.

He stopped at this point so that he may have escaped any further time with this irrelevant grouping that he only wanted to fight with anyway. The three looked up and his friend nodded his head, claiming that he was as much a part of the struggle as any worker and his two comrades had every right to support workers in struggle whether 'the workers understood this or not'. This signalled the end of the strained confrontation that the drill shop worker had initiated more in some adolescent proof of a machismo much admired by the workers than any real search or inquiry for some answer that may have locked itself in a vault of reason forever out of his reach. He returned to his seat next to Annie and made some gesture to indicate that he had done what had to be done, but she evaluated this as little more than men, or rather young boys, acting out another futile role which she had hoped would be lost in the realisation of the occupation. In the realisation that they were indeed free. The night drew tired shadows around those workers who stayed in the bar that evening. Many had begun to leave to ensure that the orders issued during the night could be met. And in a discipline common to their class it was seen as their duty to turn out on the picket lines at the right time. This they did.

Within these discussions that erupt at times of workers' struggle a unique freedom of expression provides a pattern of thinking that at times would appear to the onlooker to be anarchic and dislocated. For it was only in times of struggle that workers are truly free. But in reality it was a process that established its own structures capable of rationalising the most complex of dilemmas. The workers knew that their struggle involved the union as well as the employer underpinned by the police and the political economy that would do whatever was necessary to protect capital at all costs. In this corruption rested the deep irony that imprisoned the workers in their organisation whilst equally imposing upon the union the need to at least act out its role as the representative organisation of the working class. A dark magistracy loomed over the detail of the workers' condition that marked out their struggle as futile and lost in a litany that daubed all workers who challenged the naked power of capital. This of itself ennobled the principles of the struggle. This was the workers' language, embraced physically and intellectually, for without the inevitability of the struggle everything was incorporation, the betrayal of the self to nothing more than the last order. Order demanded the destruction of the human spirit, the imprisonment of individual freedom. Because, with the individual and collective free spirit intact, capital could not survive. Capital reflected itself in every dimension. It smothered every layer of its power upon its suffocating servant. In this matrix of obedience every betrayer held an equality of guilt, and no measure existed for ultimate betrayal. The very betrayal of the self. This crime against the self and others was a treachery without equal. Within the freedom of the

189

struggle betrayal attacks workers from every angle in order to crush all thoughts of rebellion.

With the gangrenous institutions of the state intact, the sickness of conformity confirms its ascendancy. Like some embarrassing illness. Its obvious existence is denied to those who identify its stench, they are disclaimed as outsiders, madmen or communist agents determined to destroy the freedoms that capital confers. The freedom measured in each misery inflicted by the turn of the key. This was the struggle whose easy opposite was betrayal. The deference to seniority, the innate lust for patronage to sell the self for whatever price the invisible hand of the market dictated. To act out the role. To stand in the way of such a beast is the true measure of this class that now set aside all they knew to pursue their struggle. To plot against the creature was inconceivable. These men and women had the impact of their daily struggle carved deep into their faces. Their bodies racked by the poisons that industrial production exhaled in its avarice to reduce costs and increase profits. For the instruments of production fulfilled their gifts to the workers in the form of cancers that invaded their internal organs, celebrated in the remorseless deaths of young men and women before they could allow old age to free them from the torment of these dark satanic mills. So the struggle became marked in the abject theft of their physical, moral and economic being, and this spat at the workers in every experience of their reality. How they would long to experience some respite that could provide some different perspective upon the system that consumed them. But they struggled daily to exist whilst daily, in the factory, they struggled to improve and free themselves of their condition. That they surveyed their environment from such a perspective simply reflected their reality and their wholesale rejection of '*it*'. To respond in any other manner would be as illogical as the system itself. They were always in a state of rebellion, they had to be to survive—to escape their role.

By ten thirty that night the bar had exhausted all but a few of its customers. Annie prepared to leave and again glanced over to where the three figures had hung together throughout the night. Their seats had emptied earlier as secretly and furtively as their plots. Dan Hawkins, John Evans, Hasaan, Margaret Harvey and Annie had long finished the preparations for the next day, and the detail of this would be reported back to the workers at a mass meeting to be held outside the factory the following morning at seven o'clock. The group wrapped themselves against the cold and having said their goodbyes walked into the night. Passing the factory, they caught sight of ranks of police and private security guards as they encircled the building. Only the light cast by the flaming braziers gave form to the factory and its protectors. Black smoke billowed haphazard shapes up to the night sky and the white moon seemed somehow stronger. Nothing moved in the factory. The strikers had won. Production, profit and ownership had ceased. They were free.

Chapter Fifteen

When democracies have gained a certain stage of development, they undergo a gradual transformation, adopting the aristocratic spirit, and in many cases also the aristocratic forms, against which at the outset they struggled so fiercely. Now new accusers arise to denounce the traitors; after an era of glorious combats and of inglorious power, they end by fusing with the old dominant class; whereupon once more they are in their turn attacked by fresh opponents who appeal to the name of democracy. It is probable that this cruel game will continue without end.

—R.Michels, *Political Parties*

John Evans sat quietly on the bus that morning with his head leaning heavily against the window, his eyes closed in opposition to the endless distraction of his fellow travellers. Many on the bus knew him and as they took up their seats each worker would convey a respectful greeting that would always be returned. His solitude was his own as he thought through the rage of the night and the endless sparks of analysis that wove itself towards a strategy capable of challenging the power of the employer. Embers of hatred and anger burned inside him as he now took the opportunity to examine the consequences of the workers' condition. It was always his practice to establish exactly the reality and to turn this reality into its opposite. This process would include every proposal to challenge the perceived logic that always seemed to dictate an immediate response. Such immediacy, he had found from experience, was always the last option ever to consider. So now he concentrated upon the contradictions of the workers' condition. He smiled to himself as he considered the infinity of these contradictions and how much easier life would be if only the workers could accept what the boss and everyone else told them to do; but this was not real life nor did it reflect the perpetuity of the human spirit whatever obstacles the class of authority threw in its path. The documents uncovered during the occupation clearly indicated the Stevens family's wish to close the factory down once it had sold off its machinery. That was why they pre-empted the dispute that led to the occupation. The

193

position of the union was as normal. They sided with the employer class and the one hundred or so workers who had now re-entered the factory. But they could not avoid the reality that they also represented over six hundred workers now locked outside the gates. Once the workers inside the factory realised the plans of the company to close the plant, then one would imagine the union to experience some difficulty, not for the first time, in squaring the circle of their own corrupt contradictions. Thus, John Evans concluded that much of the night's discussions had centred upon refusing to complicate the workers' condition any more than necessary. They had to recognise that the struggle must continue amidst the knowledge of closure and the implications of their union membership. No other conclusion could have been made given this reality. He smiled to himself again as the simplicity of the struggle declared itself.

Condensation from the window ran down his hair, seeping past his ear, filling the space between his collar and neck. He quickly straightened himself surveying the grey murky drabness of humanity that surrounded him. Some element of sorrow dampened inside him and he gritted his teeth, lost in the thought of the great deceit that drove the workers ever more towards the abyss of mechanical misery. Someone came on the bus, dragging in the wet winter cold with him like a rotting corpse. John Evans shuddered and allowed himself a brief moment of hatred for all that encircled his existence. As he peered into the morning's darkness, flat concrete rectangles of factory units stumbled past. Smudges against the window's condensation. Grey human figures bent forward against the elements to reach the gates that guarded their exploitation. All day they would be cold and wet. It was all he could take as the cancerous smog inside the bus consumed the last remnants of stale air. Absently he stood and made his way off the bus, some workers who recognised him told him that it was not his stop. He tried to explain but found this heavy task too strenuous. Finally, the bus stopped momentarily, then cranked into the distance, pumping exhaust fumes in every direction. John Evans bent double to allow a wretch of vomit to pump from his mouth.

By six thirty that morning over three hundred pickets stood outside G.P. Stevens's factory. The snow of the last few days had now all but cleared. To the workers that morning it was colder than ever. Police lines marked an invisible equator that the pickets recognised in its humourless irony. For if this line was not crossed every morning at seven o'clock then the workers would be disciplined, lose pay or lose their job. They went through with this because they needed the money now they were being stopped from doing both. Beyond the line some sixty workers had been bussed in about half an hour earlier and they were locked in behind the lines of the locked-out. Not surprisingly, most of the police were immune to any concept of irony or

194

injustice as they pursued the internalised logic of 'only doing our job' and in the limitless emptiness of their souls orders gave them some purpose in life or, put more succinctly, a clear role. A 'no questions asked' life whose predictability offered the sanctuary of following the next order. Freed of all complication that human existence confers, they sought comfort and status in this vacuous excuse for life. Face to face with the workers their discomfort was tangible. Only barrack room solidarity enforced their role above that of the workers. Being the direct disciplining arm of the class, they had much in their role to impress. In the lines of police and workers that faced each other that morning there were people on both sides that knew the irony and knew the struggle that pitched themselves against each other on that bitterly cold day. Effectively, it was these two groups, who comprehended both the nature and the importance of this confrontation, who would defend their corners. Braziers followed the pattern of police and workers' lines but the latter ensured they were as far from the police as possible. Other braziers had been placed on the opposite side of the road, where some of the workers and their wives had begun establishing a small mobile teashop for the pickets. It had only taken a few minutes for John Evans to reach the factory, and in this short space of time the frozen air had dispersed his nausea, freeing his mind.

Inside the factory a leadership of sorts had unfolded as if to mirror the developments that had taken place during the occupation although the absence of principle and some concept of justice sharply contrasted with the psychology that had driven the decisions of those workers now locked outside the factory. McCabe's brutal presence grasped the moment that, as usual, sought communication through the diminished figure of 'blue overalls', the welder. Corralled into the drill shop, the workers were again told of the sacrifice they were making to maintain work in the factory against 'the commies who had now got what they deserved'. McCabe spoke loudly above both the silence of the factory and against the cowed subservience of most of the workers. An overwhelming sense that something was 'not quite right' circumnavigated the ghostly vacuum of the machines and the abstract location of the workers idly standing by. No longer beset by the urgency of manufacture whipped into a frenzy by foremen, chargehands, supervisors and managers alike. Wretched in their false environment, most of the workers appeared to be on the precipice of overwhelming distraction, unable, more than ever before, to comprehend the space around them, no matter how familiar it all seemed. All was darkness. So it was against this confusion that McCabe attempted to explain the condition of the workers in much the way that John Evans did only a few days earlier, but there any further attempts at comparison concluded. As the workers shuffled guilt with fear, each strove to find something, any excuse, for why they were not working at their

195

machines with all their fellow workers as they had done for as long as they could remember. Warm, uncomfortable rushes of betrayal clung to each and every man, for they were all individuals now and amongst them no women stood. The workers eyed each other suspiciously as McCabe imposed his presence, unaware of the human tumult that now faced him. He was the sergeant major addressing his regiment before they went over the top at the instruction of some imbecile conveying an order on behalf of some equally invisible imbecile officer. No emotion, no feeling, all that mattered was the last order in the conveyor belt of hierarchy and that was what he was carrying out. Without question or doubt.

'Well, you've gotta a job to do unlike those soft bastards outside in the piggin freezin cold,' he cajoled. 'Johnson and Jacks will speak to you all in a couple of hours and in the meantime we gotta clean this place up and repair any damage that's been done to the plant and machinery.' His fat arms spread and closed. 'Is that clear?'

No one would dare attempt to say that this was most unclear, and when McCabe had said that they would have to 'clean up the factory' almost every man raised their head to look around the gleaming factory that they had stolen from their fellow workers. Most strikingly, the repairs to the huge extractor fans that encircled the factory epitomised the clinical state of cleanliness that the factory now basked in. McCabe saw them looking around but assumed that a pigeon or a rat had distracted his loyal union members. No questions were asked as Frank O'Toole sneaked forward as if the need for clarification had embedded itself in the mute response of the workers. McCabe physically pushed him back and told him that any 'political theorising' could wait until later. Wiping his face with his customary oily rag, McCabe pulled his head forward like an animal about to mount some deathly attack.

'What are ya waitin for? Clock on! Get to work!' he bawled into them.

McCabe turned abruptly and made his way up the metal staircase towards the manager's office. Such usual behaviour still created a ripple of note amongst the workers as they were left floundering as to their next physical move despite the instructions discharged by McCabe. However, in the absence of any social or political cohesion few options availed themselves. The factory clock had been removed during the occupation so that order could not be obeyed. The men could not 'clock on'. No work could be done because no plans or work sheets had, as yet, appeared. No facilities were available in the canteen to have coffee, tea or any food. The food was available, it was just that the women canteen workers were outside the factory. Not one worker had the will or inclination to solve this absence themselves. They awaited further orders. In their freely entered-into relations they were solely dependent upon the boss, who saw no particular reason to reward the loyalty of these men. Most sat around and some took the time to observe, possibly for the first time, the very nature of their workplace. The unreality of their current condition provided a uniquely rare vantage from which they could finally see their prison. But these were movements of the moment. Within a few minutes the silence and the inactivity bore heavily upon this workforce without work, orders or bosses. From the gantry that loomed it presence above the factory floor McCabe and O'Toole could be seen staring blankly ahead, throwing occasional glances down to the floor of the factory. Staring blankly at the pristine ventilation shafts that encased gleaming fans. Paralysed, all animation was suspended as these loyal beings gasped for the oxygen of orders, and they knew that was what they were there for, even though they detested it. A familiar guilt consumed them. Outside the noise of the crowd could be heard.

Any movement on a picket line is always significant. By the very nature of the police movement will only occur once an order has been given. Basking in their freedom, workers on the picket line move when they want, as they want and with whom they want. This is their freedom. So when police moved to create a corridor opposite the entrance to the factory, the workers instinctively pushed against their will. True to their roles, both sides directed themselves appropriately, scuffles, swearing, pushing the odd missile, but the numbers did not exist at this time for the workers to overpower the police. Some sporadic fighting with the police did materialise but these were minor skirmishes, sparring. At eight thirty Jacks was driven into the factory in the back of a police van. He could not be seen by those pickets who managed to curse or punch the van as it sped past them. Once this act had been concluded, normal roles, albeit somewhat fractured in places, returned to the picket line.

Jacks had an extremely high opinion of himself, derived from his belief in the system that provided for all his needs. The system had chosen him above all others because he had the necessary personal skills and ability to rise to high office in the union. Rewards underpinned the responsibilities of high office because, as he often told his friends, 'how else can the firm,' which was his expression for the trade union, 'ensure that only the best people would be attracted unless it paid the highest rates of pay, company car, expense account, phone bills and home loan facilities?' All these staples of status ensured the primacy of talent to hold down such an important role. Important as depicted by wage and in its simplicity everything followed. 'The fatter the paycheck the more important the status,' he thought to himself. Often he would confide to others his pride at being chosen capable of representing the union and the membership in its relations with the employer. His skills were transferable and his career, or so he believed, could have taken any direction, be it with management or union as in his limited world view of life no palpable difference existed between these two great monoliths. At this point most workers would have agreed with Jacks, albeit for wholly different reasons. Here was the complete man who questioned nothing but performed his functions as the true functionary would be expected. To reach this nadir Jacks had been one of the first union activists to relinquish all links with the Communist Party when he himself was a factory worker. Yet Jacks, like so many others, relied wholeheartedly upon this membership and the respect it engendered to gain prominence in the factory. With the Trade Union Congress' imposition of bans and proscriptions on Communist Party members or 'fellow travellers', he quickly distanced himself from his past. His betrayal had begun a long time ago. Frighteningly, for all the workers who came into his contact, some shared Jacks's view and they performed yet another vital function of the system, of '*it*'. An endless conveyor belt of unlikely aspirants. Jacks wore his role like a suit of golden armour that allocated Jacks, the man, status. And it was this nonsense that shimmered in the minds of those workers as unfortunate as himself. For these were his natural constituents and he served them with ease as they demanded nothing in their urge to function as others may decide. How they dreamt that one day they may aspire to join him. Those who didn't dream death's dream suffered incalculably for defending their rights, their democracy, their trade unionism and their class.

A leather bag tucked beneath his arm added gravitas to his demeanour as he ran from the police van imagining some damage that may befall him, but he was already inside the loading bay of the factory. His fear, like everything in his life, was unfounded. This was occupied territory and the police ensured his safe passage as if he carried the insignia of chief inspector. This was no man that stood before them cloaked in his role. This was the bank manager, the waiter, the politician, whatever the role may be, whatever the role may involve, the uniform, the garter, the cap, the insipidness of doing what was expected in that role. Whatever that may be. The role was the cloak of deception, the ultimate falsehood. And there he stood, this balding, uninteresting failure of the soul. Jacks straightened his tie and smiled nervously to a young police officer, fearing that his deception might be uncovered. It had but he was safe. Jacks made his way to the manager's office. Which was what he did whenever he visited the factory. As rare as this event was he hardly ever needed to come into direct contact with the membership, who, after all, only paid his wages. Such minor details of reality floated weightlessly on Jacks's shoulders and he never once gave this fact a minutia of thought. At the top of the gangway McCabe and O'Toole could be seen overseeing the deadness that now stalked the factory floor. The union official was not one for detail and he paid little attention to the still silence that pervaded the entire factory. He was there to meet Johnson, nothing more nothing less, so any gaps in this process were simply distractions to role fulfilment. McCabe dug his elbow into O'Toole, who gave out a spluttered cry followed by a direct complaint to McCabe, who by now was walking towards his union official. McCabe hoped that one day he would replace Jacks and join the union's payroll and in this process Jacks's patronage was essential. This explained, if this was needed, McCabe's wholesome sycophancy to all who could deliver the prize he yearned for. Jacks knew this and was indifferent to anything or anybody beneath his order in the great food chain of life. He spoke with the expected tedium of authority.

'I take it all our members are in this morning?' he said to McCabe.

The conversation, like so much talk within the food chain, resembled a tennis match with serves and returns based upon opportunities to exact each role. McCabe took out his black oiled rag as if it were an insignia of office. A holy relic of his working-class industrial qualifications. Not from any sense of pride but as an indication that this was his current role, which he wanted to dump as quickly as possible. His aspirations went beyond his insignificant condition. His factory employment was simply a staging post of career, a launching pad to greater significance. A low-level role that one must always encounter once the decision to ascend the ladder of fortune has been accepted. The rag was dragged meaninglessly across his chin. It was an involuntary movement.

'Oh. No problems in that department,' he said cheerfully. 'It all went like a military exercise this morning, everyone is here ready for work.' His mood changed to one of businesslike efficiency. 'I spoke to the men this morning and they fully support the union's objectives. Fully support. Full support. Yes. That's right,' he stumbled.

Jacks moved past McCabe and peered into Johnson's office. No staff had entered the factory yet and all the offices seemed as deserted as the factory floor. Nothing could happen until Johnson arrived to give out the orders for the day and those that were to follow. The last thing Jacks wanted was to be caught in conversation with McCabe or any other workers, simply because he did not want to. In deference to his importance he turned to McCabe.

'Look,' he said thoughtfully, 'obviously we need to discuss some matters and I'm here to meet Johnson. Then I can report back to our membership as to our next moves.' Patting his leather briefcase that had remained under his arm since his arrival in the factory, Jacks continued, 'I need to read some documents and think a few things over so I'm just going to take a quiet walk around for a few minutes and then we can have that important chat. I want to hear your views on what needs to be done,' he said to McCabe, and as a light shone on McCabe's face Jacks rewarded his peasant underling. 'Is that all right?' he asked.

McCabe could not contain his delight at this recognition of his role in the great scheme of things. The brutal exterior of the man dissolved instantaneously to make way for the new role demanded by this rare opportunity to sell the self.

'Well,' his huge frame shrunk into the words, 'I keep my eyes and ears close to the ground, the rank and file, that's where I am. I've got a few ideas, Mr. Jacks,' he seemed to plead. 'Oh yes, we've gotta keep this place open, that's for sure.' The topic moved haphazardly onward.

Free to leave, Jacks made his way directly to the men's toilet, where he was to sit for almost half an hour, locked into one of the brightly cleaned and refurbished cubicles that had so painstakingly been reclaimed by the workers during the occupation. Sat with his newspaper resting on his knees in a moment's distraction Jacks surveyed the toilet in all its brightly cleaned elegance and thought to himself what a good employer Stevens was and how ungrateful the workers were for not realising this. Complaints about facilities such as the toilets in the factory were as unfounded as any other criticisms the workers may have had. The moment left him, and in that self-righteous assurance that arrogance and ignorance so often justify Jacks moved his fat rectum in a final comforting motion. As he pulled the chain, slabs of stolen copper moved in the cistern, blocking the toilet from flushing. He ignored this moment. His shit stuck in the pan. It did not matter to him. He stood and looked into the crystal clear sinks before him and the rows of clean soaps and towels. An expression of the workers' control that now cleansed the factory. Yes, he thought to himself, what ungrateful bastards the workers were. He walked past the sinks, pausing only to capture his reflection in the crystal clarity of the recently fitted mirrors. In the distance he could hear the pickets and police clashing again. This, he assumed, signalled the arrival of the factory manager. He left the toilet with the germs infecting his hands and everything he touched.

Outside, thick needles of sleet rained down as pickets and police pushed and fought against each other. One trying to create space for the manager's red Jaguar to enter, the other wanting to hold the line on this intrusion. Hasaan found himself in the centre of one of these skirmishes purely by accident. In an effort to protect himself from being crushed or thrown under the line of police vehicles rushing towards the factory gates, he began punching blindly into the police ranks, who in their turn had begun similar moves once the order to push back the pickets had been given. Some of the older, more experienced workers on the line saw the difficulties that Hasaan was getting into and they physically pulled the youth away from the police, losing him in the ranks of strikers that now congregated in this area of the line. One policeman, who had taken the full fury of Hasaan's fists, called out to his colleagues to 'get the little black bastard' and this call to arms gave fresh impetus to the force of numbers that the police now engaged to secure the entrance. Snatch squads threw themselves into the thick of the action, extracting pickets like teeth. The individual pickets' physical size lent an order of priority to this process and it was all the big men on the line that warranted the interest of at least four policemen at any one time. Dan Hawkins and John Evans, having overseen the welfare of Hasaan, now found themselves struggling to hold their positions on the line. Some of the workers held on to some concept of fairness in this situation and absurdly attempted to make some lighthearted interventions until they realised that this was no feeble exercise in free speech and law and order. The moment dawned upon them in the form of dark red blood as it spat at them from across the faces of several pickets as truncheons thudded the nearest skull. The British bobby did not seem so quaint from close quarters.

Amidst the chaos and disorder of these events on the picket line senior police officers could be seen and heard as they edged around the tumult of confrontation shouting commands, ordering arrests and pointing out 'key troublemakers'. This latter definition now focused upon the oversized figure of Hawkins, and when the order was given two policemen lunged forward in an attempt to grapple the acid bath worker to the floor. But Hawkins was already losing his own grip inside the melee of police and pickets. The considerable weight of the police attack on him served only to topple him over. Truncheons rained down upon him for no reason other than his size and the fact that they knew he was one of the leaders of this strike. Other police dragged at him from behind. At the very moment when the entourage of police vans and Johnson's Jaguar cut through the gap created at the factory entrance Dan Hawkins's huge frame collapsed. His body half onto the road. Whatever the outcome of this train of momentary events, the result was a simple imposition of fate. It happened. The full force of the police van ploughed into his upper body. Other pickets and police suffered injuries as the packed weight of humanity released itself in one fatal recoil. The driver of the van had attempted to stop, but it was too late. A group of about twenty pickets and police now lay across the edge of the pavement and the road. Whilst the chaos continued a police officer tried to give some first aid to Dan Hawkins, but his fate had been cruelly sealed. In that instant of disaster when all human perception slows a dark equality surfaces that levels the role to that of mere human. Such momentary acts are throwbacks to a lost civility—a lost humanity, and of themselves they are meaningless acts unless constantly repeated, which, for the most part, they are never. When the final ambulance had left the scene a marble cold silence traded amongst broken human frames. The pickets waited aimlessly outside the factory wasting their time. Outside of this inner circle the admirals of the role, the gatekeepers of '*it*', stalked their prey for any sign or weakness—any sign of retentive humanity that escaped the role. Humanity and orders do not relate so well. Any police that showed concern were slapped into line. The apprentice finally showed himself on the picket line. His two revolutionary minders by his side. And his hatred broke through the silence demanded in solidarity with the senior police officers as they called for the primacy of the role, the primacy of order, to be reinstated. It had no meaning.

Inside the factory the news from the picket had yet to filter through as Johnson watched Jacks enter his office. His arms stretched out on the large table before him, his entire form rigid, and in his mind he thought how this one meeting could be kept to its briefest timescale. Jacks fumbled his way towards a small chair that had been placed some distance away from the desk. Unable to configure the meaning of most situations, Johnson's impressive use of body language and role was to prove wasted upon Jacks as usual. Despite the fact that he knew this, he was unable to escape this formality. Johnson sat impassively, intent on not speaking first. The seam of silence that now filled the room struck fear into Jacks, who quite literally waited for permission to speak. In the corner the well-rounded figure of Tom Carberry was pouring tea into two delicately crafted china cups, one of which he now placed in front of Johnson. Once this function had been performed he took up his post on the small stool lodged in the far corner of the room. Both men lit cigarettes, and when Johnson took his first taste of the tea he looked towards Jacks with the darkest intent. This was the permission Jacks required to start speaking, but he allowed the moment to pass, interpreting Johnson's steel glare as potentially an invitation to have some tea. The union official floundered, lost in a mire of confusion as the realisation of his unwelcome status suffocated all the false notions he held about himself, his role and his significance in the immediate scheme of things. Wiping his brow, Jacks shattered the pause.

'Well … Mr. Johnson,' he began, 'I am pleased to say that most of the workers got into the factory safely this morning and things seem to be quite well organised downstairs. Just waiting for the worksheets and all. So it is important that we discuss how we are going to turn events and make this factory something we can all be proud of.' His words found no audience and in the silence that followed he felt the pressure to continue.

'These are difficult times, so I am not too sure where you would like to begin?' he suggested.

The question hovered in the stale soup of acrid air that now consumed the small room in which these three men had gathered in the full regalia of their governance to discuss great matters of the moment. Jacks had exhausted himself and a cruel thirst now overcame him. He looked straight at Carberry, whom he felt much more comfortable with in relation to the roles he wrongly assumed they shared.

'Don't suppose there's any chance of a cup of tea … eh, Tom?' he asked confidently.

Carberry's fat face rolled forward, for he did not share the assumption that both men had some equality that could be mistaken within any concept of kinship. His eyes flashed disinterestedly at Jacks, adding further to his discomfort. It was some time before he moved himself to get the tea that the union official convinced himself he so badly desired. Johnson approved of this minor drama as it ate into the depleted figure that Jacks now struck. A look of shocked betrayal sketched itself on his eyes. His mind raced through the realisations that at best things were not well in the office of Mr. Johnson that particular morning. A reasonably unclean cracked mug of tea eventually found its way to Jacks, who gulped at his thirst, and as his embarrassment exposed itself like an open wound nothing was left of his role. Nothing was left to hide behind. He attempted to salvage his soul as he caught the briefest of contact with the two men who now encircled their prey.

'That reminds me of one of the things we need to get sorted,' he mumbled unconvincingly, 'yes, canteen facilities. But I know you'll be aware of all this,' he gently suggested to his boss.

He voice disengaged itself, mechanically fading in the knowledge that no one was listening, and in this absence crucial to all communication it had shut down beyond the control of the speaker. Abandoned in his nakedness, he silently called upon Johnson and Carberry to reinstate his role. He pleaded silently for permission to reclaim the security of his mask. And they looked upon his exposure and watched his nakedness vaporise all the pretensions that now, in his solitude, made him no more than the lowest factory hand. Jacks choked on his shame and the incredulity that Johnson played a part in failing to respect the rules of the role game. Now he attempted to regain some element of composure but he knew it to be lost forever. No longer was he the representative of labour juxtaposed to Johnson's servitude to capital. No longer did the sham balance of partnership between the two exist, at least in this room. Jacks was drowning. Sinking fast in that dismal realisation of his true insignificance. Johnson had waited in his lair and his only consideration had been the choice of timing the kill. His victim was begging to be released from his agony. Carberry stubbed his cigarette on the floor. Johnson moved with absent cunning.

'No. I am not going to discuss canteens or how good my workers are for being so kind as to come into work this morning,' he replied. 'What the fuck are they doing? Listen!' He cupped a hand to his ear. 'Can you hear any machines working?' Jacks was motionless.

'Can you hear anything being produced?' the boss asked the official as Jacks's eyes drilled into the concrete floor beneath him. 'Noise equals production in a plant like this. What the fuck are they doing down there? I know the rhythms of this factory. I can tell what noise equals what production targets.' He thought about his words and liked them, he liked the idea, then he turned to Jacks.

'Canteen?' His voiced had now raised its pitch. He was screeching. 'They want us to fucking feed them? No!' Johnson yelled. 'You seem to have forgotten the deal we have here. I provide the work, you provide the labour and keep it in check. What the fuck happened?' His finger pointed at Jacks like an executioner's rifle. 'You lost control. That's what happened.' He fired his words straight at Jacks.

Johnson's voice notched up a decibel with each sentence and the more he caught sight of the crestfallen figure that Jacks had become the more he despised him. The decision had been taken to close the factory down and this had been conveyed to Johnson at two o'clock that morning by the owners. One final task had to be completed and it was this task only that brought Jacks to his office that morning, for no other reason existed for their relationship to continue. How he despised everything that moved inside the factory, and his hatred of the very concept of the workers having any rights whatsoever left him in a state of apoplexy. The union movement that these ingrates held in some religious esteem was no more than a communist cesspit that should have been outlawed long ago. Nevertheless, in his interminable hatred of the union nothing surpassed the venom he reserved for its corrupt agents. Jacks epitomised this hatred in abundance. Feeding off an organisation that they had no personal, intellectual or principled connection to—selling every facet of humanity to fuel the insatiable appetite of capital and their own personal ambition. Even the vacuous persona that Johnson had long embraced shuddered at this cruel betrayal and deception of men and women whom he loathed yet still respected for holding a principle. Yes. They were the enemy, but what did that make Jacks? He secretly admired the men and women stood outside his factory that morning, for at least they had something, some style, some loyalty, some belief. Jacks and his followers had nothing and deserved nothing. What was about to befall them they deserved, and inside his mind he laughed at the thought that they and Jacks would probably thank him for sacking them, being 'ever so humble as they were'. They might even buy the boss a gold watch. It would not be the first time, and Johnson could not hold back his twisted humour that laughed in the face of the so-called 'workers' representative'. If only he had a real gun to put them out of their miserable existence.

He looked again upon the figure that was dying before him and he saw uselessness in its full flower of redundancy. A man who could not produce, measure, cut, weld or make anything in his factory, yet he claimed to represent people who had all these skills. What Lords of Misrule could make such things possible? How he wanted to strangle the cause, and yet he knew that he was part of the cause. The cause was himself. The system he upheld at all costs, for this thing was the '*it*' that determined all in its wake. But these were passing phases of the moment in hand and he was personally well catered for by the system and he wanted it to continue to reign supreme for the protection of the superior over the inferior. Clandestine concealment camouflaged from inspection or exposure allowed this great betrayal to pulse unhindered at every level of the social order, and nothing could be lost or taken away lest this great confidence trick would collapse like a pack of cards. Because despite the size of this beast, '*it*' was indeed a fragile mechanism. Johnson's mind meandered further into its darkness as he turned finally to face the beleaguered Jacks.

'The responsibility for what has happened rests with you, your union and your so-called members,' he told him, 'they closed the factory when we had customers to serve, and those customers are no longer there.' He lectured Jacks, who nodded with the prodding finger of guilt. He seemed happy to accept responsibility, accept guilt.

'The factory is closed because you closed it.' Johnson opened his hands as if he was blaming everyone and Jacks sought comfort in this.

'The deal is quite simple. We require workers who can finish whatever orders we have left. Assuming we have any customers left. Then they can dismantle all the machinery and pack it for export. This should take three weeks, and after that our relationship is finished. If you don't want to do it we can hire gangs in.' He looked at Jacks, then continued with his orders.

'The wages will be cut in accordance with the fact that we are no longer producing anything.' He stopped and paused for a minute before picking a random figure that was lower than the one Stevens had given him. He cut further the cut in wages simply because he could and simply because he hated Jacks—not the workers.

'Let's say seven pounds a week.' It was a random figure.

'I am informing you that I want some of the workers outside to come back in because looking at the dross we let in here this morning,' his hands made circles for some unfathomable reason, 'they couldn't do the work we require!' Johnson had begun to laugh.

'This is not negotiable, because as far as we are concerned we no longer employ anyone. They all sacked themselves.'

205

Jacks thought this was a question and he was about to answer before Johnson stole the space in his words back for himself.

'Inside or outside the factory, it's a labourforce, not a rabble where some think they can please themselves. Now that's agreed?' The question was an order and delivered as such. As the words rattled out Jacks's body shook with each sentence.

As the knife twisted deeper into the soul of his very being, Jacks grew pale and drawn as his two tormentors faded from view. How he wished he was not there. How he wished he had taken up the numerous management posts he claimed to have been offered in the past—how he wished he was dead. He wanted to survey the humour in what was being put forward. He longed to turn on his negotiating skills that he never ever possessed anyway to bargain down, to freely negotiate and calculate the workers' meagre pittances based upon the company's ability to pay. He looked across the room at the obese figure that was Tom Carberry, a man he used to buy beer for and concede workers' rights to. He looked to him in a vain attempt to ingratiate himself into the company's management team. How he longed to be a player. A player of note. Now he hated himself and longed for anonymity to release him from such burdens that he knew he was always incapable of dealing with. He had known about the threatened closure for over a year and yet he thought he could buy his way out of this by offering Johnson everything he wanted, from redundancies to wage cuts. The inevitability of closure never really sank in as he considered the matter of little consequence to himself personally. All he thought about was himself. This was the standard measure he placed upon all things. In every circumstance Jacks dealt with life based upon the last instruction, the last order, the last demand, so that he may be seen as the obedient bag-man the system always has a place for. He had been betrayed, having betrayed so many before having at first betrayed himself. Is this what it had come to? Never having any semblance of revolt or contradiction, he was submerged in the greatest of frailties, fearful that any sudden movement may result in his spineless body, fragmenting limb by limb. A nausea like no other overcame him and he bent double as if to hold down the vomit he had been filled with, not just here and now, but over many years as his despicably pointless life flashed before his eyes like streams of explosions. He clasped his hands to his ashen face and seemed to be speaking. Johnson asked him to speak up. Stuttering nonsensically, he directed his words towards the floor that now opened up before him. Johnson, lacking sympathy or concern, told him to speak up, and Jacks repeated the same indecipherable words until their meaning was eventually heard.

'How long do I have?' he implored like a condemned man. Johnson responded before this briefest of sentences had been completed.

'You have until eight o'clock in the morning.'

In a broken hospital across the town Dan Hawkins released his last breath witnessed by his wife and three teenage sons. In the corner of the ward Annie Reilly clung to John Evans and Hasaan. Margaret Harvey cried openly, for she had once loved 'her quiet man' in some distant unrequited factory romance that never really ended. Fred Williams stood close by, conducting his presence with a reclaimed sense of dignity that returned with the events of the last few days. Now he was standing tall and straight.

Jacks left Johnson's office cowed and demoralised for no one but himself.

Chapter Sixteen

To consent to the plunder. To empty your pockets of rage, along with your other belongings, before you enter your infinite cell. To sell with the best of them, to kiss principle on the cheek, pat principle on the ass....

—Jack Hirschman, *You're Being Assed*

If he was to continue to get paid by the union, if he was to continue to function, if his careerist adventure was to be sustained, Jacks had to deliver his last instruction. As he stood on the gangway overlooking the endless repetition of lifeless machinery that lay before him he briefly contemplated his immediate future. It was a process that did not take too long, as his consideration only involved himself. Yes, it was a mess, but he had never become embroiled in complex strategies of analyses focused upon solving such dilemmas. For he was a functionary. In the interests of himself he had to continue, and in the momentary contemplation of his interests he considered that he could sail through his last order by simple observing events, for whatever happened he would still have his job. Standing opposite the recently refurbished air vents, he surveyed the giant extractors fans as they turned effortlessly in their production of clear, clean fresh air that brushed pleasantly against his face. Jacks felt more than recovered from his trial and as he turned to walk down the metal staircase all he could think of was how ungrateful the workers were; always complaining about the bad air, lack of ventilation and toxic fumes, yet these fans, and he looked up to them again as if to confirm his revelation, worked perfectly well. Jacks blamed the very people he was employed to represent. If justification was required for his utter contempt of these people, then it was written everywhere he looked, with his boss eyes feeding his boss mind with images of comfortable numbness. Within a few metal steps of the factory floor McCabe and O'Toole confronted Jacks. Both men appeared as if waiting for the disclosure of long-awaited good news but they also had information to impart, and McCabe barged into conversation with Jacks, thinking this knowledge gave him some unequal advantage.

209

'There's been murder out there!' McCabe shouted. 'You wouldn't fuckin believe it.'

Yet Jacks would not believe it because he was not interested.

'The police got battered and that acid man, Jenkins, Harkins or whatever his name is. Well, he's dead. That's for sure. Threw himself under Jackson's car or something.' He seemed satisfied that he had conveyed his message. He sounded unsure of himself but this never mattered before to him or to Jacks or any man locked into the world of self-centred surety in which every action, event or statement became diluted to meet with the demands of their hollow existence. Frank O'Toole, standing behind McCabe, could just be heard saying: 'Hawkins. Dan Hawkins. That was his name,' he said.

A slight anger could be just made out as he stepped back further from the two men. Jacks made no comment at the news as he began to inflict his authority over the men in much the same was as Johnson had done some minutes earlier and in the silence that followed McCabe spoke again as if this pause would invade his ordered blur of life as he needed it to be.

'So it's all sorted then? What does Mr. Johnson want us to start with?' he asked. 'We'll have this place runnin like a Swiss watch in no time at all,' he seemed happy, 'the men are all ready,' he was really happy.

'Look, there they are,' he said with a child's excitement. McCabe pointed to a group of men who looked more like a vanquished army than a lean and hungry workforce. Jacks failed to lift his head above the sinister distant stare he had fixed upon them as McCabe's thought process mirrored that of Jacks and he assumed that some humour or play acting was being unfolded before him that things were not quite as foreboding as Jacks's demeanour indicated.

'So when do we start then?' he repeated. 'Is Johnson commin' down to speak to us?'

Jacks was back in control and he would reap revenge for his treatment at the hands of Johnson. He thought that now he would teach these cretins a lesson once and for all. Looking directly at McCabe, he spoke in an air of almost complete disinterest as he answered his questions in a single syllable.

'No.' The delivery and the pause caused maximum impact. McCabe looked inquisitively at Frank O'Toole, then turned to Jacks.

'No what?' he grunted. 'What went on up there? What are ya sayin?'

Coldly Jacks proceeded. 'It's finished. G.P. Stevens is closing down and I'm calling a meeting tonight at seven o'clock in the union hall for all employees including those outside so that you can all make your minds up,' he said.

McCabe could no longer contain his fury and whatever ambitions he held to follow Jacks's path of betrayal were forgotten as his base nature unfurled itself. His voice boomed in the vast emptiness of the factory acting as a siren call for some of the workers to move towards the staircase.

'Hold on, what the fuck's goin on ere, we stood by this company crossin fuckin picket lines to get in ere and now you tell us he's shuttin the fuckin place down,' McCabe screamed into Jacks's face. 'How the fuck do you work that out?' He waited for a reply. None came. 'We did what we were told. We fuckin delivered and he thinks he can just get rid of us like that? And you fuckin agree with him,' McCabe continued to await a response from Jacks. Fast and furious he spat out his words.

'Then you tell us that fuckin crowd outside are gonna get invited to a meeting. Well, this is one fuckin fight you're not gonna sell out. After everything I've done for you?' He looked at Jacks as if he would rescind everything that had happened. This, he knew, was not possible. Yet still he hoped in vain. 'And that twat Johnson? You and that rat think you can just pull the plug? No, you've got fuckin problems, not us, mate,' McCabe screamed as he reached the point were physical violence often punctuated his conclusion, and as his anger rose Jacks began to pay slightly more attention if only for his personal safety. But his manner was still arrogant and distant, and this alone compounded McCabe's hatred. Yet Jacks stood in silence, defying the pushes to his shoulder that McCabe injected as part of his dialogue. Jacks looked toward some of the men, then turned to face Frank O'Toole.

'It's out of my hands now,' Jacks said with the finality of the gallows. 'Let the lads know about the meeting tonight,' he said disinterestedly. 'We'll sort it out then.'

The food chain was now partly completed as the hierarchy of betrayal withered its way down the ranks. Only the workers remained left—awaiting their instructions as usual. Awaiting their customary betrayal by others not like them, not with them.

The diminutive figure of the welder wanted to pursue some political trade union debate about agendas and how the union's rulebook would be applied to such an extraordinary meeting. Jacks knew this and held up the palms of his hand like a soldier surrendering and this signal was recognised in the reflex acknowledgement that this was the end of the argument. Only the noise of men arguing amongst themselves in the distance could be heard as Jacks made his way out of the factory. Instantly they understood the betrayal that was being exacted on their behalf. Suddenly, across the length of the factory, a crash of metal slamming against concrete broke through the dead atmosphere, followed by the cries of a group of young men and women running through the factory from the welding shop area. They carried banners pronouncing 'Victory to the Working Class' and 'Support the sit-in', which they placed over the metal sheerer in the corner of the factory. A red flag was unfurled and draped from a wooden pole lodged into one of the drill machines. Then this group, of about ten to fifteen, ran towards some of the workers inside the factory led by the young apprentice, his two political confidants and their supporters, who carried with them the dreams of storming the Winter Palace. Dressed in black and red, looking tired yet fired with energy, the young revolutionary held his arms as far apart as physically possible, halting any further advance from his comrades in arms. He was now facing McCabe, Frank O'Toole and the thirty or so workers behind them. They were the advance guard to reclaim the factory for the workers, but the apprentice was the only one amongst his supporters who worked in the factory, and it fell upon his shoulders to claim the occupation now reinstated as the two groups faced each other, convinced of the need to fight this battle to its conclusion. When they squared up to each other, the invading group became aware that perhaps things inside the factory were not as they presumed. Hesitation, on behalf of the intruders, froze them all in their tracks until they stood their ground some four feet away from their perceived enemy. Their young leader had, following his vigorous political induction, now developed a great deal of personal confidence, and this was further enhanced by the hatred he harboured for McCabe. This helped the momentary impasse to be ended abruptly as he took authority and leadership by the fist. Straight and firm he stood before McCabe, whose earlier confrontation was still impacting upon his limited intellect, providing the boy with even more advantage than he could have hoped for.

'Listen, McCabe, we're reclaiming this factory on behalf of the workers, and the occupation has been reinstated forthwith,' the boy said slowly but confidently. 'As workers you can join us or leave,' he looked around the group beyond McCabe, 'that's your choice. But in a few minutes those valiant comrades outside will follow our lead and regain control of the means of production once and for all.' Now he was speaking with an authority that surpassed his years. 'We will not compromise upon our demands, so make your choice,' he stated as though reading from some hidden presidential text.

McCabe lulled himself into the satisfaction of being reasonably impressed and the humour of the moment was not lost upon him. Now the opportunity presented itself for him to regain some composure, and when the boy finished he turned and looked towards the workers behind him, then towards the group that encouraged the boy to continue, which he promptly did.

'Everyone knows the role you have played in this factory, and that period is over,' the boy said. 'You crossed a picket line. In the struggle against capital some events may never be ignored, and the establishment of a picket line signifies our historic and heroic struggle as a class,' again he was speaking as if quoting directly from some forgotten working-class novel.

'It's a line that may never be crossed!' he shouted so that all could hear. 'You crossed it. You are no more than a lackey of the boss,' he said directly to McCabe.

McCabe cut across the boy. 'Look, lad, are you takin the fuckin piss or what?' McCabe said quietly so that others could barely hear his words. 'You takin control of this factory?' he asked with a deal of sincerity. 'Be my fuckin guest.'

At this the young boy's supporters cheered and clapped. They had won the day and in an emotional outburst they began hugging and kissing their fellow comrades, calling upon some of the other workers to join them. Some began to sing the Internationale. McCabe had by this time turned to leave the factory and as he pushed past some of the workers who blocked his path he shouted over their heads towards the group as they celebrated their victory.

'Hey! Sweeper, brush boy,' he called. The apprentice revolutionary looked towards him.

'Oh you can have your victory, just turn the fuckin lights off when ya leave.' McCabe shouted across the factory.

Jacks was about to leave the factory too. He looked over his shoulder and shook his head at the scenes he had just witnessed, still convinced as ever in the divine right of authority that he, Jacks and Johnson held. A further clamour of noise announced the arrival of a considerable police snatch squad who had followed the young revolutionary's group into the factory, and within moments they had surrendered their struggle without any significant contest.

On the picket line the numbers had almost doubled as workers from nearby factories began to join the former employees of G.P. Stevens on the line. Political groups and activists swelled the ranks of some five hundred workers who now challenged the police cordon that stood between them and the factory gates. But the atmosphere had altered dramatically since the death that morning of Dan Hawkins. The workers and their supporters taking every opportunity to confront the police, who in turn enforced rigid discipline throughout the line. The police were outnumbering pickets two to one. The small number of police inside the factory had taken responsibility for the main door and office entrances, and one senior officer asked Jacks if he needed to be escorted from the factory. Jacks felt no need for this, as he had to speak to the workers and inform them of the meeting that evening. Any abuse he expected to receive would prove inconsequential to himself. Inside the factory the lighting remained sparse and as the steel door opened, the light from outside blinded him, providing a confused vision of the bedlam of noise and movement immediately ahead of him. The sight of Jacks leaving the factory had an instant impact as the pickets drove forward into the police lines, attempting to get to Jacks. Hatred rained down as police encircled him for his own protection, and the nearer the pickets got the clearer the abuse became. Other than that Jacks could not make too much of events as they unfolded before him. Behind the police lines he was able to walk towards the main entrance of the factory, where he intended to stand on the steps and speak to the workers. Behind him police frog-marched the group of political activists who had so briefly held power in the factory towards a number of police vans. Proclaiming their own contribution to the struggle as they were bundled away from the picket lines, some of the workers cheered, but most did not understand or know for what reason they cheered or shouted, for their action was taken without their knowledge or agreement. The plot had been hatched the night before as the three 'conspirators' sat in splendid isolation. Once this action had run its course the picket line swarmed towards the figure of Jacks as he marched decisively behind the lines of police towards the main office of the factory. Jacks endeavoured to stand as far up the small marble staircase as possible, allowing the brass balustrade to act as some firm support to hold on to should this be required. A contingent of police offered further protection from his members as they began to congregate some feet from their paid union official.

John Evans had returned from the hospital some hours earlier and held an impromptu meeting with the workers informing them that their comrade, Daniel Hawkins, had died as a result of his injuries. He had been a respected trade unionist and comrade in the factory for almost thirty years and had suffered considerably at the hands of the employer, who, as with so many real union activists, ensured that his working life was as miserable as possible. He was a skilled lathe operator but following a short strike over working hours Johnson marked him as a communist wrecker who would have to be dealt with by the company. The workers protected Hawkins in various solidarity actions, although after some years Johnson, supported by Jacks and McCabe, was able to concoct enough disciplinary charges against Hawkins that eventually one was bound to stick. Finally, Hawkins was offered a choice of dismissal or work in the acid bath shop as part of the union-backed 'compromise' aimed at solving this matter of 'company discipline'. Hawkins could have left the factory and taken his trade anywhere, but he chose to stay and fight rather than allow the employer to prove to the rest of the workforce that they and the union held total power over all who entered its gates. Now he was gone, his physical stature, his integrity and above all his socialism would be lost to those within the factory that so benefited from his generosity of spirit. In many respects an element of selfishness marked workers' attitudes towards Hawkins in so much as they felt secure in his genuine commitment to their cause, as workers. His life was self-evidently devoted to their struggle and even his enemies would not have denied him that epitaph. Hawkins was part of that tradition of working-class existence that bred an inner sense of value beyond that measurement that sought dominion over every individual. Others would no doubt replace him, but the waste of such a life left a coldness unlike any natural element that now opposed the workers as they huddled together in silence to reflect upon the life of a true comrade. From this moment intermittent skirmishes rolled in and out of the picket line as every police movement or change of officers sparked off some new fear, some new reason to confront the enemy. Now Jacks stood before them, surrounded by the icons of their exploitation and misery. With eyes darkened by mistrust and hatred, nothing that this union official could possibly say would convince them that their reality was effectively not real. Labour and capital confronted each other, and the sight that afternoon appeared distinctively to those who wished to see within the layers that unfolded before them. Workers on the streets, lines of police and security guards, the union's representative, the factory. Nowhere to be seen were the representatives of the company. This spoke volumes as the concrete expression of the workers' reality. The fact that the true representatives of their misery were absent magnified the bizarre role of others more than prepared to defend the citadels of capital against all threats. As ever, the dirty work of '*it*' was being done by its servants—its victims.

Again, John Evans was brought to the front of the workers' lines so that he may hear directly what Jacks had to say. So there he stood implacable, elevated above the workers, whereby his absence of movement provided statuesque qualities as the afternoon light declined to omit even the most meagre grey metal shades. In this role Jacks was irreplaceable. No other could perform such a function for the system like some specially bred species locked into the pursuit of singular outcomes. Neither G.P. Stevens, Johnson, Carberry, the police or any other servant of '*it*' could provide such abject servility whilst possessing an immense physical and mental immunity from their actions. Amidst the thrusts of abuse thrown from the pickets Jacks did not flinch, causing even some of the police to wonder what possessed a person to such individual heights of social vacancy. Jacks was aware that the workers would eventually want to hear what he had to say, so his conclusion needed little evaluation other than to maintain a stoic front. Inevitably the noise broke down into sections of cursing, which in turn dwindled with repetition as voices lost the protection of anonymity that the crowd always provides, and in this process individual abuse tumbled in self-conscious inaudibility until stillness descended upon the workers. Workers changed their cries to a demand for silence long after quiet had been achieved. An empty breeze blew around them. The police lines relaxed perceptively, as did the lines of workers as they faced each other with the indifferent figure of Jacks raised between them. With his hands excavating deep inside his overcoat pockets, Jacks pushed his face into the crowd as if challenging them to pour more insults upon his person. In a final act of defiance he raised his arm slowly above the crowd, using this movement to pre-empt his address. Not the greatest of speakers, Jacks always kept his sentences short and uncomplicated.

'Well,' a hurried silence fell amongst the crowd, 'you can call me whatever you like, but if you want my advice I'd leave all your revolutionary stuff until tonight.'

With no further wish to proceed any longer than necessary, Jacks simply announced that a union meeting would take place that night at seven o'clock in the main union hall at which the union would report back to its members. Perhaps, within their expectation, the brevity of Jacks's address had disappointed the workers, and their only response was to revisit the noise levels that had greeted the union representative a few seconds earlier. Irony was not lost on these men and women who were experienced in the tragedy that Jacks's version of trade unionism had visited upon them over the years. Without reason some workers still clung to the role of authority that Jacks represented. This role, in their subconscious, could still be capable of salvaging their future in the form of some deal, some new treachery that would provide some with work, and in contradiction to their reality they held hope in this empty figure before them. Jacks harboured no dilemmas or misgivings about his role, and in the fury of that moment, Jacks sought refuge with the police, who escorted him away from the factory now that the deceit had been set in train. For, from its onset, the conflict with the company had to be concluded by whatever means possible. A strike was a symbol of failure for the union, and it was this view that Jacks held firm in all his dealings with employers, and despite the difficulties of the day Johnson had provided an escape clause that gave him what he wanted. Prepared to accept any cost towards conclusion, the deed was more or less done, and all that was needed was for Jacks to ensure some pretence at democracy that would empower him to finalise this particular event.

John Evans was calm and subdued as he examined the craft of the betrayer. His examination followed the lines of police, the obscured images of McCabe, Frank O'Toole and the rest of those workers who fought with the police to cross a picket line as they now stooped low as if under some great weight, ambling slowly behind the hidden shield that each policeman provided. Then his thoughts turned to men like Atkins and Hawkins, whose shadows cast greater light than such men and their excuses could ever imagine possible. Yet these men would pass into the obscurity of death, absent of any real respect that their lives justified even from their fellow workers. For without the privilege of role they were destined to live and die in bitter obscurity. For in this swindle the measurement of a life had been reduced to the label that could be placed upon them and greatness had no descriptive powers for the class of workers beyond the margins of that class that ruled all. And inside the class many evaluated worth in the same way that their enemies did and so a sickening duplicity invaded workers like a canker capable of remembering their own heroic comrades as some barren grouping that had no real value because the only value system they had was that provided by the ruling class. Heroes of the ignored class, the class that made all things possible to man confined to the despised death of that deceptive rabble who controlled all. Anger tightened within him as his eyes wretched towards the workers that now began to encircle him and he knew that to some he was no more than the option embodied in Jacks. A dealmaker that may deliver what some of them cried for in the poverty that had shaped them. But many workers understood the nonsense that was being played out before them. They had seen it before and suffered its consequences on too many occasions for them to consider that any justice may be delivered to them. Nor did they seek justice. The employer did not exist to deliver justice or dignity but they imagined that they could create a virtual world in which this was possible and to some that gazed upon it this was enough. For the majority it was not. Yet they worshipped comrades that had gone before them and Hawkins was their hero and all their names would live forever in their hearts and in their memories. This was the only way it could be. This was their reality.

The chargehand cast his weary eyes furtively as if in one glance he might see death itself and amidst the crowd he watched his former young apprentice return to the line with his two political commissars behind him. Behind these three figures marched the group that had occupied the factory so swiftly and so briefly. Inflated by their struggle they rose above all the workers stopping just short of John Evans. Enthralled within an ecstasy of the hero's role that they themselves took as their rightful mantel they stood awaiting the acclaim of the workers. And John Evans celebrated in his mind the unsung life of so many real heroes who gave their life so that others may advance to a better world. The lines on John Evans's face gouged deep ridges across his temple as he stared at the young revolutionary. His response was to glare back as would a young officer about to replace a worn-out general. All these actions took place within a matter of seconds and the scolding stares of John Evans had been lost in the crowd as workers looked to him for leadership. In his mind he considered the question as a tragedy of the workers' condition that should not require either asking or answering. For the malady of '*it*' sank deep into the confidence of many workers even though they did never lose the courage to fight against the inbred self-doubt that haunted their every act of defiance. In the faces he examined he saw many that had led valiant struggles against the employer and supported other workers in their struggles. He respected them and felt ashamed at their infinite betrayal by others.

Trade unionism was in its most influential phase, so some said, and yet the seeds of future treachery had been sown from their inception. A constant struggle ensued between the leadership and the led. The former strove to improve their own condition beyond the class they claimed to represent whilst the latter sought to move beyond the denominator of wage slavery. And all the time the official union basked in the glory of heroic struggles that had, more often than not, been fought without their union's support. More often than not they opposed all opposition. Caught in the mid-stream of betrayal, the union leadership moved lightly amidst both worlds and, having two paymasters, ever mindful of past and present deceptions, ever fearful of exposing their true intent. Some battled for their class and their class only, finding themselves increasingly excluded from the gravy train of influence and power as they confirmed their willingness to occupy the past and future glories of revolutionary labour. This betrayal had begun before the birth of general unionism in 1889 and their representatives invaded the movement with their class betrayal of pseudo modernism in which, forever uncomfortable with conflict, they forged pacts with capital. Explained away with a confused intellectualism that appeared to offer the spoils of revolution without the struggle, these intermediary bosses spread division and defeatism with every act they pursued. With the passage of time they openly assumed the rigours of serving capital as if this was the true struggle to fight, ever so softly and meekly, whilst always allowing the sovereignty of capital to prevail. Each decade brought their movement closer to their maker as they assumed the collar and tie, the suit, the houses, the fine tastes and mannerisms of the boss class. This imagery of betrayal would soon be celebrated openly in the victory of style over content as it evolved in the official unions under the aegis of a 'new unionism'. The age of conflict was over, they declared. And for many it had never really begun.

The workers would maintain the principle of their movement for all time yet and they would fight more heroic battles in which the great battalions of the vanguard would challenge capital directly. But always they would have to fight the betrayers within their own movement. And they rose up like some spectre condemned to undermine all opposition so that the State may prepare its defences without fear of defeat. Rank and file movements struggled to reclaim their unions as the organisation consistently embarked upon ever greater betrayals that shone more light upon the chasms that they dug between themselves and the workers. Sham democracy, phoney elections, patronage, career, bribery and corruption reflected the structure involved in maintaining this pact with capital. Now, with so many cloaked in ermine and coronets, these union leaders basked in their arrival on the septic scene of social and political power that betrayal donated. From this vantage they called for others to have their vision to climb upon the faces of the dispossessed as they had done, leaving behind little more than a muddied boot print. The iron heel that crushed the human spirit.

So the workers looked upon this circumstance with contempt and hatred, planning the day when they would sweep away this insanity. John Evans knew that the meeting called that evening by Jacks was simply another act in the theatre of deception that the union undertook to uphold the lost virtue of accountability towards its membership. Most of the workers knew this also and yet they were to be powerless to ignore this debasement of democracy, for to do so would be to disinherit the principle of the struggle. By now John Evans was surrounded by his unofficial committee and the workers. Despite his tiredness, he summoned up an inner strength to address the workers, whose own resignation drained him, leaving only the empty veins of self-doubt. But still, he had nothing but respect for the people who stood before him.

'Sisters, brothers. You know as much as we do,' he looked towards Margaret Harvey, Annie and Fred Williams, 'it's a mass meeting tonight that if anything should prove interesting. Perhaps we've been sacked, but what's the position of the others who followed McCabe and Jacks into the factory?' He looked around the crowd.

'They're going to get sacked when Jacks actually tells them the truth.' Cheers and shouts rose up from the crowd. 'The truth that we found out applies to all. So we have the workers divided as usual by the officials and the employers when, in reality, all we had to be was united.' A single cheer rang out.

'But that's the way it is and it's not the first time, so let's not blame anyone else for this condition, this is our struggle and comrades are free to make their own chosen conclusions,' he said.

At this point one worker stepped forward and asked him what he wanted them to do. The question cut through him, screaming defeatism and fear, and he wanted little more than to eradicate this in-built self-doubt. He contained much of this anger.

'Comrades! It's your decision. You're free. Make your own choices.' Again he surveyed the crowd. 'You know everything there is to know. Our struggle is against the conditions that Stevens imposed upon us all, so let's not lose sight of what this is all about. We'll see what happens tonight, and the main thing is that we continue united.' Shouts of approval rolled down from the back of the crowd in uneven spasms.

'I think we should take some time off the picket and make sure we all attend the meeting,' he said, almost sighing.

A cold wind breathed through the crowd as they accepted the subdued guidance of their unofficial leadership. It was not a time for speeches but such moments floated in the sky for the zealot intent on pursuing the line, and John Evans dropped his gaze as his former young apprentice pushed forward to the front of the crowd. Behind him stood his two political mentors. The young boy refused to look at the chargehand and again addressed the workers directly. Some had begun to leave the line already in a determined act of refusing to take part in any further discussions. Others appeared more interested in the welfare of Dan Hawkins's family. The young apprentice had gained much in confidence, and unlike John Evans's self-conscious delivery the boy rose, proclaiming the virtues of the workers' struggle and the next step that had to be taken or rather the political decision behind the need to take a particular course of action. Cries of derision rose as workers again questioned the right of the boy to assume so much that he could even contemplate the leadership of their struggle. The boy and his by now increasing band of political mentors and followers ignored all the signals before them, choosing, through preference, the oblivion of ignorance that eradicated the need to consider anything other than the last instruction. In this way they differed little from the enemy they claimed to destroy. 'More meetings!' was the cry.

'More talk!' shouted the boy. 'When what we should be doing is breaking through the police lines and occupying the factory. Our supporters have just done this and it was only the scabs and the police who forced us out, but with greater numbers we can do it and claim back what is ours,' he called out to the workers.

At this point he looked towards the darkening sky whilst he awaited the expected acclaim of the workers, and the longer he waited the more distant their approval seemed. He openly invited praise as if he were a Shakespearean actor having completed a faultless soliloquy, but the only recognition he received staggered from amongst his own as workers turned their backs in increasing numbers. Imagination propelled his revolutionary fervour until he spoke only to himself and his claque in a voice that rose beyond his increasingly reduced audience.

'The union will support us but we, the genuine rank and file, need to give leadership. Not defeatism, like what we've listened to here. They should step aside and let those with the ideas steal the moment for the class.' A ripple of applause floated upwards. 'Let's get back in the factory and then we can go to the meeting tonight and tell our union that the real struggle has begun.'

The young revolutionary was now addressing more police than workers as he stole a glance at John Evans, who looked with a heavy disinterest upon the boy, then turned and left. Then other workers raised their voices so that they might be heard, but the boy could not understand any view that differed from his, and as he spoke he pushed leaflets into the hands of those around him. Some fell onto the wet pavement, blending the black ink into faint grey patterns. With this the group collapsed into itself as the young revolutionary's supporters pushed forward to repeat the argument, spit the line, shout the pogrom of pathos, intent on demanding infallible acquiescence as if to hear was justification enough for belief. Such discipline insisted upon the natural state of blankness, that void in the eyes that reflected the empty souls of those satisfied only by the exaction of orders and instructions. For, with noticeable exceptions, they could follow any orders with impunity from whatever source, they flowed with ease, and as the police pushed forward to end what had already concluded they marched as directed towards a bleak distance away from the factory. With rage only for the workers they set about their withdrawal. Now only the police remained in the faltering darkness, protecting the bricks and mortar that was the factory.

Chapter Seventeen

...it is not the man that is wanted. It is rather, the function he performs and it is the skill with which he performs it for which he is paid. If a man's skill is not needed, the man is not needed. If a man's function can be performed more economically by a machine, the man is replaced.

—A.Gouldner

The union's meeting hall was situated near the centre of the town in its head office. It was a grand affair that of itself owed its design to the factory system its membership toiled in. As if this design eased their insecurity by proving to the onlooker that they were truly part of the same system, deserving of some measure of respect. So in this propensity to mimic their oppressors, the union hall was as dismal as any factory exterior could be, and internally the building resembled the aftermath of some long-run conflagration with browns and creams coating the internal brickwork that was dissected by huge ducts of rusted steel as it encircled every room, pushed through walls to provide some element of internal heating. Pipes and rectangles snaked the insides of the building, spreading ceaselessly down towards a subterranean main hall like the roots of some great gnarled oak. With room to fit over five hundred people, this was the only facility the union had to offer its membership outside of the 'professional service' provided by its full-time paid officials.

By six thirty that evening crowds of workers massed outside the building as the common preference was always to delay entry into the union hall for as long as possible. Political groups selling their newspapers offered genuine support to workers in struggle provided they 'followed the line'. Some held the slogan 'workers right or wrong' and they simply celebrated and supported the act of rebellion. Snow peppered the cold and bleak figures that ambled in silent groups, avoiding the interest of those who wanted to cross-examine, analyse and redefine their struggle from the comfort that false political elitism always provides. Now the figures of members of the strike committee mingled anonymously with their fellow workers, exchanging the smallest of talk in the eyes of some asking about family and friends, reminiscing about romanticised old times. And as the minutes stole themselves towards the hour the crowds standing outside the union building grew ever greater. John Evans, Margaret Harvey, Fred Williams and Annie could be seen moving from one group to the next while at the main entrance the young revolutionary thrust leaflets like hot coals into the hidden hands of passers-by to the cry of 'workers united'. His two political managers seemed happy with their arrival on the industrial stage, shuffling leaflets with ignorant confidence. Eventually clumps of workers moved towards the entrance of the building, filing down the heavy staircase towards the main hall. Absent of any expectations of what lay before them. And as they left the snow came down harder, clinging to all that lay beneath its cover.

As John Evans entered the building he looked up at the union's tributes to activists and officials over the last one hundred years. It was impressive and inspiring to him as he recalled the names of good comrades he had had the privilege to know. Some names spoke disaster and treachery to him, but this was to be expected. He noticed how the biggest betrayers of the class had the memorials equal in size to their crimes. One had a bronze bust. He caught sight of Dan Hawkins's name, embossed in gold letters, and a flood of memories crashed inside his head. He stood for a few minutes as the flow of workers pushed past him. The low ceiling of the meeting room swallowed up these teams of workers as they flowed through the short, dimly lit concrete staircase until they too became ensnared in the steel and cast metal root system that undulated haphazardly throughout the room. At its furthest point a small stage rose above the line of metal seats. Upon this stage was housed a small wooden desk, behind which sat the huddled figures of Jacks, McCabe, Frank O'Toole and a clerk from the union. His place was to record the events that would follow. He was much older than the others, and before him lay a leather-bound book that when opened took up much if not all the space on the table. Sitting a short distance away from the other three, his dark solitude captured the vision of the workers as they looked inquisitively towards the 'top table'. The unknown union official added the mystique of officialdom and a gravitas that appeared deserved without reason. Jacks sat impassively between McCabe and O'Toole, listening with a vacant air as he stared aimlessly in front of him, watching the room before him fill to overflowing. Workers stooped into the room, whose low ceiling seemed to push down upon them.

The hierarchy of the hall reflected the meeting that had taken place some days earlier in the factory, for directly in front of them sat the eighty or so workers who had crossed the picket lines to break the occupation. And they were mostly McCabe's men. Behind them a no man's land of some three rows of seats remained unoccupied, forming a natural barrier between those who struck and those who worked. This meant that large numbers of workers had to stand on either side of the hall or in front of the staircase, and in the mean light that strained from the lamps hanging from the ceiling everything appeared colourless. Noise and smoke filled the room instantly while the physical hatred for the easily defined 'scabs' blazed through the air with an unrefined prejudice. And yet the focus of this collective state were no less workers than those sat behind them in judgement. Some had a trade union pedigree beyond that of many who now sat and judged them. Within the majority that filled the hall many realised this, and they looked to those amongst their number who lacked the history of struggle of some they now screamed 'scabs' at. What they did and why some crossed the line would remain a mystery to be reduced to a detail of a moment's action that now condemned them as they sat in a bleak wilderness at the front of the hall, with only Jacks to look up to. Many did look to him for something, if only the means to cut a deal, to fix a compromise, to tell the boss that some of the workers shared their 'vision' and would do whatever they wanted to preserve the inevitable status quo. Their fixation was that a deal could always be done, but they had to indicate beyond any doubt that they were willing elements of that deal. The vacancy of their stares was all they had to offer as a symbol of their abject surrender. Within this simplistic exchange Jacks held dominion, although his only struggle involved the delivery of the deal, no matter how shoddy or shameful, and it was this dismal process that occupied his mind as he stared into the fog that now absorbed the tiny line of space between the workers and the ceiling of the room whilst shame consumed a minority of the 'scab' workers who sat before him.

Somewhere near the middle of the meeting hall sat John Evans and most of the unofficial strike committee. Hasaan sat next to the elderly figure of Fred Williams, with Annie close by his side. She scanned the room, looking for her former love. Then she caught sight of him, lost in intense discussion with his two mentors as they mapped their next strategy, and for a moment their eyes met empty of reason. She looked away. His two political tutors had no real right to be in the hall as they did not work in the factory, and whilst some workers had objected to their presence no further action against them seemed to have been taken. Eventually a calm descended upon the room. The union clerk stood and asked the meeting to stand in respect of the death of Daniel Hawkins, and he oversaw a minute's silence. In this minute you could feel the breathing mass and touch the anxiety of all. When this had been completed, the official returned to his ledger and beckoned to Jacks to begin the meeting. Jacks stood up and called for order. His fists crashed against the table, causing the other union official to pick up his pen for fear that it might bounce from the table, and with pen in hand he waited to record Jacks's words in the ledger. Clearly nervous, Jacks could rely upon his stolid ignorance on all matters human or political. To him it was the deal, always the deal, the cut and thrust of shabby compromise in which the employer is given everything and the workers nothing. Within this one-sided equation, Jacks had long found comfort knowing that the only personal price he had to pay were verbal insults of the union membership he betrayed. The union would always be satisfied in the preservation of partnership. Jacks was bulletproof as he stood to face almost the entire workforce that once was G.P. Stevens, Electrical Engineers. He was the future their movement could expect, and only a few in the hall realised this. Jacks squandered his life in ignorance and self-interest and as with so many like him did not comprehend the brutal and treacherous future his actions would predate.

'OK, brothers,' he said.

About two hundred women cried in unison, 'and sisters.'

Now the usual nervous good humour that tends to mark the opening salvoes of such tense mass meetings had been acted out as custom decreed. Jacks smiled that lonesome way when people without humour or emotion respond to other people's laughter, never quite knowing its purpose. Cries of derision filled each space in these proceedings in combat with other shouts of support 'for your union' while some just called for 'quiet', that they may actually hear what was being said.

One worker broke through the chaos and was allowed to be heard when he spoke directly to Jacks and said, 'We know what you're going to do here tonight and we know that you knew that the factory was going to shut down anyway,' the room erupted with this one sentence.

Jacks shook his head whilst Margaret Harvey shook the document that proved he was lying. But truth is always the first casualty, and the power of denial establishes all manner of confusion and doubt, and so it was in this instance, and Jacks had little time for the truth. Lies are often so much more interesting than truth and in the hatred so many carry with them lies are the preferred record. Perhaps in the end the truth or the lie is simply what people want to hear. Thus, facts and reality floundered endlessly on the battered rocks of unbelievable denial. Everyone knew why he was there. He knew why he was there. But the truth of their realities became lost in a quagmire of denials and histories rewritten. A few seats away from the man who had challenged Jacks sat the young revolutionary, who was reminded of the article in the newspaper he had read on his first journey to work. It seemed so long ago now, and for the first time he admitted in the secrecy of his own being the confusion that battered inside him. He stared at the old man who continued to expose Jacks's corruption, speaking like a barrister representing a class action of which he was part. Above all, he carried a dignity and

226

serenity that contrasted so overwhelmingly with the behaviour of the union official and McCabe. His two political mentors had already defined the speaker behind his back and gestured to their mental captive that he should ignore what the man was saying.

'Mr. Jacks,' the man continued almost studiously, 'I have been a member of this union for almost forty years.' Respect for the man rolled idly through the room, for, like prisoners on life sentences, longevity was the key to some level of respect. 'My father paid my first subscription. He gave me a book of the history of this union and I understood its significance immediately. It spoke to me in words that expressed everything I believed in even as a young man.' At these words the boy looked towards the man as his own thoughts crashed around his own introduction to trade unionism delivered by his father and later by John Evans. He fumbled in his pocket for the badge he was given and squeezed it tight, as if this action would make everything right again. He tried to catch a glance at the young girl but she stared straight ahead. The old man continued his speech. Jacks continued to look towards the back of the room, his eyes glazed with boredom, as the union clerk recorded every word.

'I still to this day cannot find the right words to express the liberation I felt in my soul from that moment.' His words drifted around the room and when they were understood stumbled claps embraced the man. 'Now you stand before me and I know what you are going to do. Not simply because you've done it so many times before but because lies have become your language in a vain attempt to cover up your actions and the role of the official union.' Shouts rang out but it was impossible to understand their meaning. The old man was unconcerned.

'Many in this room have seen the document and know that you have known this for some time. Known that the factory was going to close, and you stood by and did nothing. That says more about the future of our great movement than it does about yourself.'

At this point the man paused, and in the silence that had now floated delicately around the room one could be forgiven for thinking that only himself and Jacks were present at that moment.

'Mr. Jacks, I feel, and I hope I am wrong, that not only do you simply represent your own interests, but more frighteningly you may represent the future of our movement. That being based upon the betrayal of the membership. Their class in exchange for your seemingly endless struggle for compromise and respectability,' the man looked around the hall, 'a place at the table, Mr. Jacks!' His voice fought his emotions. 'You do not represent me in any matter you represent betrayal, you represent patronage and you represent corruption. Most of all your hypocrisy represents the future for us all, unless you and your sort are removed. No! You do not represent me in any matter,' the man said.

At this, he sat down, and in the silence that had captured the hall, some women at the back began to clap, and this moved through the hall until every man and woman, excepting many who sat at the front of the hall, clapped their approval. The revolutionary failed to appreciate the man's speech because his twin cadre had told him not to, but he suddenly recognised the man as the one who worked in the stores and had been responsible for the beautiful copperplate writing that gave every item its own classification. In his ignorance this proved that the man was not a revolutionary like himself, because how could he be? He was a boss's lackey, if only because he was conscientious in his work. The work that belonged not to him but to the capitalist. This was proof enough for the narrow sectarian mind that the boy now paraded to himself and others. Content in the correctness of his political analysis, he looked disdainfully towards the old man and in this action his behaviour mirrored that of Jacks as the union official strained to disregard all that the man had said. Jacks continued without faltering, ignoring any potential to reply to the storekeeper.

'I'm here to represent every man in this room,' he said, to which the women demanded that he correct himself. Reluctantly, for fear that they would not have let him continue further, Jacks quietly added, 'and every woman.' Loud cheers rang out at this meaningless victory for equal rights.

'So I don't want any divisions here tonight, because what I have to tell you involves everyone in this room. I've reported all this back to your elected committee.'

At this point the room rose to challenge this statement, as the workers understood that by this Jacks was placing legitimacy with McCabe, who the overwhelming majority of workers had rejected by their action in occupying the factory. It was McCabe who had come to symbolise the rotten borough of both factory and official unionism. Jacks handled the onslaught with customary disinterest, which served only to infuriate whole sections of the room as they took the opportunity to vent years of anger and frustration at the figure who now poured confirmation, if any was needed, on all they knew. But Jacks was undeterred.

'There's no room in our union—yes, your union, that's right, it's your union—for any unofficial movement.' Some cheers struggled for recognition in the front of the hall.

'Your representatives are here in front of you showing real leadership, and they support everything that's been agreed,' Jacks said. By now the room turned in on itself, and only in the front of the room did silence now reign. Most of these workers were from McCabe's drill shop, and Jacks played to this audience with the occasional foray into the distance beyond as his hands and eyes worked themselves into the crowd.

'You can shout as much as you like and you can call me all the names you like. I'm getting paid good money to stand here in front of you. It's your money! I'm on overtime now! So keep it going.' Again he managed to anger everyone with his arrogance.

'You'll soon have to accept that you want to hear what I have to say. That's my job. Negotiating on your behalf. That's my work!' he confirmed.

Jacks had begun laughing, and this merely incited the crowd, as he expected it would. But even this tumult rose and fell in its random anger, and Jacks awaited the moment to pursue his objective. McCabe and O'Toole sat impassively alongside him whilst the union clerk scribbled notes endlessly into his ledger. Jacks continued, 'This is one union, a members' union, a democratic union.' Silence fell on the hall.

'So I have a duty to tell you all what the agreement is. I met with senior management over the last few days and we have had detailed and tough arguments about what has gone on. I have to tell you that the decision to occupy the factory was ill conceived. It should never have happened, and those who led it have to take the blame for everything that followed. You challenged the management's right to manage and the owner's right to have his factory protected.'

Again the noise levels peaked as Jacks openly challenged not only the occupation but also the fundamental principles of trade unionism that many in the room had lived their lives by. Throughout Jacks's speech John Evans sat motionless, appearing to those around him to be lost in thought as he surveyed the bleak defeatism that betrayal cuts through a workforce whose trade unionism is so steeped in the strongest of working class traditions. To Jacks, the meeting was going well, as he continued effortlessly to spin the blame for everything upon the backs of the workers. His voice boomed monotonously without soul or meaning, and the shame that John Evans felt for his organisation, his union, drowned his very being. For what class did Jacks belong to? His imagination may lift him to the upper portals of the middle classes or even higher, but this was his imaginary world, constructed of people who suffered his presence only as long as he could deliver the subjugated class with as little fuss as possible. In the mind of John Evans the class traitor was always going to be more guilty than the ruling class for all the injustices visited upon the workers, because at least the latter remained rigidly locked to their own social ranking, determined by the power they wielded over others. Many workers in the hall just hated Jacks and everything he stood for, and their solution was simply to replace him with someone else. Not considering that the malaise went any deeper than the individual. Such processes of replacement gave form to the hypocrisy that masqueraded as democracy whilst maintaining the culture of class betrayal that had in some part always been the incorporated role of official trade unionism. This culture was growing inside an increasing number of unions as they reaped the short-term benefits of a stool at the high table, as the old man had said, where they could trade principle for personal advantage. John Evans fought his rage as he glowered at Jacks, who had by now begun to arch from side to side as he delivered the bosses' instructions.

'Oh! You mightn't like what you hear but you brought it on yourselves and it's no wonder that the company have taken the decision to close the factory!' Jacks screamed the last part of this sentence and repeated it for good measure, 'Close the factory, yes, you heard!'

Uproar unleashed itself and the chaos now spread to the front rows as those workers who thought themselves immune came to the belated realisation that Jacks had somehow thrown them into the melting pot of deceit. In the deafening storm that now filled the hall Jacks continued unhindered in his work as McCabe and O'Toole sunk beneath the torrents of abuse directed towards them.

'It's too late complaining now, you all had a job last week,' Jacks said, 'what did you expect?' He looked up for the first time and his voice raised itself above the crowd. 'Johnson says the factory closes in three weeks time.'

People in the hall shouted that they could not hear him. More likely they did not believe the words that they had heard. Jacks obliged them and repeated the same sentence. Chaos opened up from the centre of the room and spread out like an explosion.

Unable to continue, Jacks sat down, at which point the heads of McCabe and O'Toole closed in on Jacks as he issued some meaningless instructions. He looked straight into the eye of the storm he had unleashed. Within seconds Frank O'Toole rose to his feet, causing the noise levels to increase and then fade vaguely as some workers grasped the possibility that he or anybody could salvage them from despair. He had been a shop steward when John Evans was convenor and had proved himself capable of any treachery that could be explained away by the most tortuous routes possible as a Marxist act. Dressing always in blue overalls both inside the factory and outside, he had convinced himself that this was the attire of the working-class radical, complete with flat cap and muffler. As usual he would speak endlessly from prepared notes irrespective of any changed circumstances in events. But above all he was renowned as a man of little more than a political cliché. Unaware that Jacks was going to ask him to speak, he was not only unprepared, in terms of his usual written text, he did not know what he should be saying. Thrust into the open mire of deception and exposed to every examination that he had studiously avoided whenever possible inside the factory. This little man rummaged through his past political diatribes. The ones he always kept in the pockets of his overalls. He searched for a parachute, any escape hatch that would release him from this nightmare of instant exposure. And for a few moments he examined one or two well-worn documents with the greatest of severity, as if this adopted role would enhance legitimacy and truth to what he was about to say. Without further prompting from Jacks, he engaged his mouth without any support from his brain. Trade union speak was his natural conversational mode, and in a momentary gap that eased the storm of sound inside the room he stood alone. More confident and capable than Jacks would ever be, he spoke automatically as his clichés joined seamlessly in the meaningless jargon of which the workers had become familiar.

'Comrades, sisters and brothers, this struggle is about our unity in achieving our just aspirations,' he said convincingly, 'and Brother Jacks, our official union representative, has clearly stated that negotiations with the company have not been fruitful.' This was as good as it was going to get, and the workers knew this.

'But that plant cannot function without engineers and we have to be conscious of our collective responsibilities so I ask you,' he paused for a second, 'in respect of our historic movement, to accept the difficult recommendations made by our official in a spirit of unity.' A loud jeer tumbled around the room.

'Our aspirations may never be met in full under the weight of exploitation that puts profit before justice, but we must continue to seek a negotiated settlement at all costs and this means that we must....' As expected, blue overalls was now on automatic pilot. A deathly silence staggered around him, imposing its force more than the uproar before it, causing O'Toole to stop speaking as he searched the room for the possible cause of this silent calm. He looked across towards Jacks, who deftly ignored him. A toolmaker stood up and burst open the silence.

'What are you fuckin talkin' about? Just acceptin' everythin'?' he said, 'what kinda of fuckin leadership do ya call that?' he screamed.

Around the hall other workers unleashed their anger as the welder began speaking again, oblivious as ever to his audience. The noise rose until it seemed to the four figures on the platform that they would be consumed in a fire of lost hopes and dreams. They were losing control. Jacks pulled O'Toole down into his seat and indicated to McCabe that he should now address the meeting. McCabe had sat through the meeting without seeming to be involved. His mind ran through his ambitions as he glared into the distance. Time had passed him by for long enough, and his place on the union payroll had now escaped him finally. This much he realised over the last few hours.

He wanted to kill Jacks, who he now blamed for all the lost dreams that fell before his eyes. All his life he had waited for the call, for the job for life that would eject him from the mire of the factory. Everyone expected that one day he would be the next to fill any union vacancy. He had stood long enough as he watched vacancies unfold that he felt should have gone to him. Jacks had long ago begun to represent to McCabe everything that destroyed his career advancement, and yet he had no qualities whatsoever to impress himself upon this assumption. Nevertheless, he considered himself adequate to the challenge of joining the union's food chain, especially when he knew the calibre of those that went before him. Now he saw his ambitions float down some distant river, moving steadily away from his grasp with each word that Jacks spoke. He looked at Jacks, indicating clearly that he had no wish to speak. Why should he help bail this bastard out, the bastard who had stood in his way for so long, he thought to himself. His escape from the mundane toil that sentenced the majority to a bleak and lifeless existence had been halted by this empty being, who now choked on his anger at this refusal to help in the betrayal of every man and woman in the hall. McCabe remained motionless whilst Jacks stood again. The tumult in the room grinded slowly towards him. Intermittent shouts of abuse were thrown at him. Jacks could speak in the knowledge that the majority still wanted to hear the detail of his treachery. Looking down towards McCabe, the union official demanded that the workers recognise the finality of the position. But all eyes looked towards McCabe's refusal to speak.

'Because of what you did the factory is going to close down, and all we need now is to sort out which men are going back to work to dismantle the machinery that the company no longer needs.' He looked into the body of the hall.

'It's about a month's work, then that's it.' The finality of his words were driven home into the very soul of the workers. And his every word was listened to and understood. Jacks stole his moment.

'Everyone else in here sacked themselves when they went on unofficial strike. That's what you have to decide tonight, and those who want a few weeks' work?' he asked. 'Then turn up in the morning and the company will let you know if you've got a start.'

It was this final detail that caused the hall to implode. The union official who sat throughout the meeting scribbling notes into a union ledger glowered at Jacks as he now sat, head cupped in his hands, smiling nervously to the crowds that faced him. Clearly unhappy with the way the meeting was being conducted, the union clerk left the rostrum walking down the middle of the hall, shaking his head in disgust. Some workers took the opportunity to scream their hatred at the man as he walked past them, and when he answered them he showed that despite his position in the union he was as much a worker as they were. He turned on them and told them that this was not the trade unionism he had been brought up on, and how dare they link him to what Jacks was doing. But this was a minor event, as the hall reeled in a swell of hatred and disbelief that united the whole workforce.

Jacks remained seated and began repeating the question, 'Is that agreed then?' This phrase raised itself in volume as Jacks challenged the first few rows, louder still to the middle, until he stood again and shouted to all in the room, 'So that's agreed then, is it?' Pandemonium erupted, and whilst Jacks got his answer, all was confusion as the workers stamped their power upon their union official. To the amazement of all involved, Jacks then left the room by a side door near the stage. He had left the hall with such swiftness that some workers were shouting as if he was still conducting the meeting. As more workers became aware of what had happened they turned to each other and shouted their various and longstanding grievances against the company, the union, Jacks, society and life in general. For at that moment everything was merged in the ferment of instant realisation that they had been forced to lead their lives in poverty, a humiliating poverty that now swallowed their very existence. The only route to easing their condition lay in the factory and as unacceptable as that was, it was all that was left to them. Now the factory was gone and they were alone. Jacks's betrayal was left behind like some deadly virus to invade the room.

The cry went up again for John Evans to address the meeting and fill the void of hope that Jacks had imposed upon many of these workers. Reluctantly, he began to walk towards the small stage at the head of the room, recalling the general view of the previous evening that this was exactly what would happen. Then his head filled with gentle memories of Dan Hawkins that drifted carelessly over events in the room. *Why isn't he here,* he thought to himself. Washed in the warmest of dreams, he ignored his own actions, walking disinterestedly towards the front of the hall. Its mundane predictability filled him with despair. A hard core of lackeys would always get into the factory and do what the boss said, no matter what happened. The thought depressed him even further and he tried to erase it with joyful images of his friend Dan Hawkins. How could he speak knowing the simplicity of avoiding the actions that now confronted the workers before him? He reached the platform and he too spoke as if on some automatic pilot, he called other members of the strike committee to join him. McCabe and O'Toole sat in a stillness of realisation that they were condemned, but unlike Jacks they could not exit this sorry situation, for both men were inextricably caught within these events as prisoners in a courtroom, and they knew that whilst those in the hall may wish to act as judge and jury, they were powerless to respond.

Both men hung their heads low, avoiding all contact with their accusers, and as John Evans arrived on the platform their only punishment was the vague hostility their treachery had always invoked upon the man who now rose over them. Eventually most of the members of the strike committee made their way to the front of the hall, and despite calls for McCabe and O'Toole to be thrown out, John Evans indicated that they should be allowed to stay. Their fate, he told the meeting, 'rests with the decisions we are about to take and we should never take away any workers' right to be involved in all matters which affect their livelihood.'

The hall was now choking in a thick smog of cigarette smoke that hung above the heads of the workers, almost obliterating the faint lights that shone sparsely over them. They choked on the words of John Evans—it was a compromise too far. Noise filled the air constantly, sweeping dramatically in volume in response to events inside the room like an uncontrollable tide that pushed against the walls of the room. John Evans stood awaiting the momentary silence that would allow him to address the meeting. Eventually, the storm of noise that followed Jacks's departure calmed enough to allow him to speak and be heard. The noise from the front rows had now increased substantially once they had realised that they had commanded no preferential rewards as a result of their crossing the picket line. It was to this group that John Evans spoke first.

'We can't isolate any worker in this room because of actions they have taken.' Calm seemed to settle in the room.

'Show me the man or woman who never makes an error of judgement. No. Sisters and brothers, this is what falls to all of us at some stage. We have to put our differences behind us and concentrate upon things, as they are not what we would like them to be.' People leant forward to pick out his words and their meaning.

'Jacks has spelt it out. Perhaps not as clearly as we deserve, certainly not in an honest manner. He told us nothing new.' He was speaking almost quietly, and for many it was a strain to hear.

'The blame for everything always falls upon the worker who challenges the authority of the boss and the union. Jacks denies the existence of the fact that he knew that the factory was going to close, that he did not oppose the employer and he did not inform the workers. No point exists in analysing this nonsense. This is what he did. Now he wants to place worker against worker to see how many of you will crawl back in to work to dismantle the machines you have worked on all your lives so that they can be exported abroad. When you have completed that task you will be sacked again. What irony exists in the fact that you men,' Evans spread his arms to the front of the hall, 'have been dumped like everyone else, because that is what it's all about. You have a use, and once that use is finished you too are finished.' The men in the front shook their heads.

'A product, no more or less than those churned out on the machines you once worked. So even the employer fails to distinguish between a striker and what he might term a loyal employee. We should learn from the bosses. Not much, I admit, but still it's important to realise that every man and woman in this hall is simply a mass in the eyes of the boss. A mass of labour value, a mass of potential surplus value, a mass of potential profit, good workers, bad workers, craftsmen and labourers, toolmakers, drill shop workers, all these lines of demarcation and separation that the boss imposes to divide us all mean nothing to him, really, because even they recognise that we are all part of the same process,' he said.

'What irony to be seen as a united entity by the enemy that does everything to destroy solidarity and unity amongst the working class. They fear that unity as much as the union has learnt to undermine that very principle from which it was born. I don't expect every man or woman in this room to agree upon everything, but the one concept that we must accept entirely is that the principle of unity, of solidarity.' A small noise eased its way towards the platform.

'It is all we have that gives our class its strength. The boss class know this, the creeping corruption inside our union knows this, the least we should expect from ourselves is that we should also know this.'

John Evans was now speaking as if he was in his living room addressing a few friends in conversation about the iniquities of life under capitalism, and the workers in the hall responded in the attention they paid. Occasional interruptions echoed around the room some in disagreement others bored with talk and wanting a conclusion—any conclusion. So that they could vote either way and be liberated from the stifling suffocation of the hall and their predicament. Leaning forward, John Evans sensed the need to reach such a conclusion himself.

'Sisters and brothers, all the discussions we have had over the last few days have failed to arrive at some definite recommendation that would free us from the condition we find ourselves in. The situation has always been clear in so much as we collectively decided to challenge the employer, knowing full well that he would respond. Certainly, during the occupation we found the evidence of Stevens's decision to close the factory, but this information only confirmed the justice of our struggle.' He paused for a second as if to catch his own thoughts.

'We can't buy the factory ourselves, we can't plead against the injustice of closure and beg to be taken back on. The option to surrender does not exist. All we can do is to continue our struggle to keep the plant open and to indicate to other workers and employers in this area that the workers will not just accept any decision imposed upon them as if they had less rights than the machinery they operate. In the morning some workers in this hall will enter the factory.' Loud shouts rang through the hall at this declaration, and John Evans waited until they subsided before continuing.

'I think we all need to realise this before we continue any further.' His eyes scanned the room. 'People will enter the factory and be interviewed by Jackson and they will sell themselves as to why they would be the best worker to dismantle the machinery and pack it ready for export. The worker will sell his labour at any price, and once he or she has entered the factory then in their solitude and isolation the boss will know that he has regained the power he lost. The ultimate power. And in this inhuman process some workers will fail to be chosen even after having surrendered their dignity for all to see,' he concluded.

Again the room resounded to cries of disagreement and for some of the workers John Evans was little better than Jacks, for all they sought was the comfort of a deal, a way out, a return to the abnormality that work in the factory represented for them as a deformed normality. Evans knew this more than anyone else. He could have lied or fabricated what in the short term may have had the appearances of a deal but this was not reality, and in a coldness that belied his character he pursued the capacity for treachery that is in all of us and that is as much a part of the human struggle as anything else.

'Jacks will be there sitting alongside the employer, sifting through the troublemakers even though they had betrayed themselves, and he will discuss the finer points of workmanship and skill available to the boss to ensure that the disconnection of the plant was carried out as efficiently as if the plant itself was in full production. I don't expect you to be happy with what I am saying, but you can be sure these events will unfold unless we, and that means everyone in this room, remain united and carry this struggle forward. Because despite everything that has happened G.P. Stevens is a factory like any other factory, and their decisions will be based upon what they can get away with. If we are capable of stopping that process then our struggle will take on a different dimension than the one that confronts us today. The occupation will continue. The struggle has to continue and you have to have the confidence to see it through to its conclusion!'

Many of the workers cheered and clapped whilst others remained silent or just shook their heads in open despair. Some workers in the middle of the hall shouted, 'Sell-out,' others preferred to call upon the union the make the strike official. John Evans asked if any other members of the committee wished to speak. Margaret Harvey spoke to confirm that the committee had exhausted all their discussions in the knowledge that no other option existed other than that laid out by John Evans. She appealed for unity and called upon all workers to ignore the call to re-apply for work in the factory.

'Better to close it down for good ourselves, because the alternative is too dreadful to consider. Talk about gravediggers digging their own graves,' she said, 'to enter the factory in the morning would bring shame upon everyone in this room. It is a choice that does not exist. Not one woman entered the factory to break the occupation. None will be there in the morning. So all you men had better realise that it will be down to you and no one else,' she yelled at the top of their voice.

This brought another round of shouts and indefinable insults from the floor of the hall, but the woman from the cutting shop was a match for any of the men and they knew it, but this did not stop them distinguishing the men from the women as factory workers who only worked for 'pin money'. On hearing this she rounded squarely upon one of the men whom she identified as the guilty party.

'How dare you insult the women in this factory? What the fuck do you know about pin money?' she screamed. 'What the fuck do you know about anything? You scabbed the last fucking strike and you dare to even open your stupid fuckin' mouth. Let's see where you are in the morning.'

Cheers and laughter rang from the back of the hall as all of the women workers welcomed this opportunity for retribution. For it was an unwritten rule in the factory that female shop stewards, being a rarity anyway, could only look after the interests of women workers. Many of them now stood and taunted the man from the drill shop who had challenged their leader, and within a moment the women became involved in a general taunt of all the men in the room, pointing random fingers and challenging them to declare whether they would enter the factory in the morning. Other members of the committee laughed and smiled to each other. Margaret Harvey sat down and Annie Reilly shook her hand vigorously as if to reinforce their solidarity for all to see. Hasaan was the only black representative on the platform; in fact he was one of only twenty or so black workers in the hall. Most of the black workers at the factory were much older than Hasaan, and it appeared to be the policy of G.P. Stevens to ensure that non-white employees did either labouring or menial metal shaping tasks. Backbreaking tedium and the latter work just pure tedium. It involved placing lengths of metal in a vice and pulling a long metal handle with a metal ball attached to it until the metal bent to the required angle. Most of the black workers in the factory had close working relations with the women. They seemed to share a lot in common. Hasaan and Annie sat at the end of the platform talking quietly to each other. John Evans looked along the table to see if any other members of the unofficial committee wished to speak, and when his eyes fell upon McCabe he offered the opportunity to address the meeting. McCabe refused but acknowledged the fact that he had been asked. Frank O'Toole appeared lost in another world, no doubt wondering why his puerile polemics focused upon the theoretical struggle of the working class had been so roundly ignored at the meeting. It was now customary for the meeting to be opened to the floor, and as usual a tangible reluctance to speak emanated from within the hall. Then the man who had spoken first at the meeting condemning Jacks's betrayal of trade unionism stood up. He wanted to state his support for John Evans and the truth that 'fighting injustice was never an easy task…. The key for us all is to stand together, shoulder to shoulder, so that the corruption of the union and the employer knew that at least…' pausing for a moment, he looked around the room, 'at least they'll know that we and others will continue to struggle against them until we sweep them aside!' Exhausted, the frail man sat down while he received the acclaim of the workers.

The meeting continued into the evening as workers stated their solidarity, pledging not to enter the factory. Willing to continue the struggle to the bitter end. Just as the meeting appeared to be reaching a natural conclusion, the young apprentice revolutionary rose to his feet rather nervously, ushered frantically by his political mentors, who were sitting either side of him. An audible groan reached out towards him as workers expressed the view that everything that needed to be said had been said. The time for political sectarianism was well past. It was now a time to be judged by actions, not words. Ignorant of the nuances of such affairs the boy called towards the platform.

'Comrade Chair! Comrades!' he shouted until some people on the platform looked his way. 'What kind of leadership have we had this evening?' he asked. 'A leadership that ignores the advice of the official trade union?' he answered. 'We cannot win this heroic struggle without the support of our official trade union. I've thought about this and if we don't go into the factory in the morning we will all be left outside, without an employer. Unemployed!' Some people started to clap sarcastically at the boy's revelation.

'How can an unemployed worker struggle against an employer he does not have?' he told them in all sincerity. At this point workers in the room called out to remind him that they were all unemployed now, so what did it matter? The boy ignored them and continued. 'The history of our movement rests with our official organisation, the trade union. Yes. They have their faults, but we must struggle within the union, not outside it,' he stated.

Collective questions now filled the room, ranging from how and what to the more blunt 'have you been fuckin' listenin?'

The boy strove forth in his own rhetorical mode. 'Yes. You can make fun, but where was the platform when we tried to occupy the factory again?' he asked his fellow workers. Now he spread his arms to embrace his two comrades sitting next to him. They were clearly immersed in their comrade's speech. 'Talking, that's what,' he said.

It was at this point that workers began to stand and scream at him, because most of them were attending the funeral of Brian Atkins at the time, but these arguments mattered little as more workers called for the boy to 'sit down and shut up' and amidst the fury that now reined down upon him he called for John Evans to order 'an immediate occupation of the factory! Victory to the working class!' he called to no one in particular.

The young boy had succeeded in returning the hall to the state of chaos that Jacks had left it in some time earlier. Nevertheless, the young revolutionary was proud of his contribution, which was warmly clapped by his two mentors as the rest of the room attempted to strangle him.

Throughout the boy's contribution John Evans's mind wandered to his first introduction to the boy he had so misjudged. Not for the first time he had witnessed the extraordinary human transformation that so often willingly inflicts itself upon those so eager to adopt the roles of self and public delusion. A falseness that invades the soul of individuals who conclude that the sublime act of pretence, the true evasion of the self, somehow mystifies the group into assuming that they are in the presence of greatness and in their wonder great cavernous opportunities open themselves to meet the betrayer. This metamorphosis can be as dramatic as it is subtle. Knowing no barrier than the base market value of personal treachery. It tempts and teases the individual to cast off the rags of honesty for a cloak of indebtedness, patronage and servility. Like a pact with a darkness that shimmers temptation, only to be replaced by a cold rage of hated isolation. Once the pact is cut the deal is done, and so the circle is complete and the food chain of the beast is thus increased. To move up and beyond, to leave the class, to better oneself, to reach one's full potential, to rise above the dismal, to sell one's soul to the lowest bidder, to escape the futility of being the lowest denominator. To adopt a label, any label, that is the key. So the innocence of youth that first set foot in the factory had now embarked upon a journey that had begun in his separateness from those around him, adopting the pose of the radical worker revolutionary. Where such a journey would end only time would tell, and yet John Evans still pondered the contagion of stupidity carried by the smallest flattery. How he wanted to speak with the young apprentice just to see what would result from such a discussion, but now a sea of workers marked the distance between the two, and as he rose to respond he could see the three figures huddled, as ever, in a dialectical morass.

'Sisters and brothers, we have to allow comrades to speak,' he said.

One worker who had crossed the picket line a day earlier stood up at the front of the room and shouted out that the boy had 'only been in the union for a week. He wants to learn some respect first.'

'I just want to say to our young brother that perhaps the answers to his questions will be found in the morning. The recommendation of the committee is that we reject the union's position as put by Jacks and that we continue the struggle to keep our factory open by any means necessary. And that includes occupation,' he paused for a moment, 'does anyone require any further discussion or clarification?' he asked.

A rush of talk filled the room, yet no worker raised any doubts as to what they would be voting upon. John Evans waited until the call to 'take the vote' resounded in the hall.

Evans continued. 'Before we finish can I just urge on behalf of the committee that in the morning we all meet at seven o'clock outside the factory? OK. All those in favour of the committee's recommendation.'

A sea of hands rose above the heads of the workers that ran from front to back.

'All those against?' A scattering of hands in the front rows lifted in the air, but they were overwhelmingly in the minority. It was the three hands voting against the committee raised from the middle of the room that caused the commotion that finally brought the meeting to an end. The hands belonged to three revolutionaries.

Chapter Eighteen

And through it all moved the Iron Heel, impassive and deliberate, shaking up the whole fabric of the social structure in its search for the comrades, combing out the Mercenaries, the labour castes, and all its secret services, punishing without mercy and without malice, suffering in silence all retaliations that were made upon it and filling the gaps in its fighting line as fast as they appeared.
—Jack London, *The Iron Heel*

Johnson had arrived in the factory at around six o'clock, having been given a police escort from his home. His assistant, Carberry, travelled by bus, arriving shortly before six thirty to endure the ridicule and hatred of around one hundred workers outside the factory. The ignominy of his journey reached its conclusion after he had spent some fifteen minutes explaining to the police who he was and why he should be allowed into the factory. As he entered Johnson's office, the silence of a man staring bleakly into the blank wall that faced him offered little solace. Both men hated each other and shared no relationship other than that imposed by the demands of their role. They were the shop floor agents of the factory owners. Instructions conveyed to Johnson were passed down to Carberry on a purely need to know basis. Excluded from any real management role, Carberry found himself despised by the workers and despised by those who shared office or lower management positions in the factory, and that morning he did not expect to receive any information or instructions about his role as Johnson's assistant nor did he get any. In the overwhelming drabness of the office both men had shared for almost twenty years Carberry sought the solitary comfort of his bench stool situated in the far corner of the room from where he could light a cigarette and wait in obedient silence.

Eventually, Johnson turned his head and without looking at the figure behind him stated simply that he would handle matters today based upon his orders from 'the boss's secretary'. He wanted no interruptions and no comments. Carberry lit another cigarette from the last remnants of the stump he held between the fingers of his huge hands. Smoke engulfed the small room as Johnson lit his umpteenth cigarette since his arrival in the factory, and both men coughed and winced and waited as the brown stained clock on the wall noted the time. It was seven thirty. Johnson's instructions were to leave the factory at nine o'clock if no workers presented themselves for hire by that time. Jacks had also received the same instructions from the factory boss directly. Stevens had rung him at home that evening to disclose the final position of the company regarding its closure. At approximately a quarter to eight Jacks knocked on the door and, receiving no response, entered in all the subservience his presence could summon and amidst the absence of any greeting he proceeded to place a chair next to Carberry. Both men spoke in hushed monologues as if the back of Johnson somehow deserved a unique reverence in respect of the responsibilities he was to carry out. They could but wonder at the heavy burden of his role and in this nonsense both men wished like children that one day they would reach this level of achievement. Johnson was thinking to himself what role he should adopt if any workers entered the roomm and in his limited perception he likened his situation to that of a four-star general awaiting the surrender of enemy troops. How he would make them shudder in his presence, the physical representation of capital, the vanquisher of human labour. He beat time with a battered pencil as the second hand clicked its way around the circumference of the office clock. Only a deserted factory floor lay between them and the noise of police and workers that flickered into the room with each burst of activity.

The dismal weather of the last few days had cleared and in the sullen darkness that gouged out their features some of the factory workers had begun to gather. The police presence was measurably larger than previous days, establishing a military pattern in the double lines laid out in protective formation surrounding the factory of G.P. Stevens. Police on horseback blocked each end of the street. From around six o'clock groups of workers had begun assembling in the strained emptiness that now echoed with every brusquely amplified movement or conversation. The two armies eyed each other with suspicion across the bleak terrain. An air of nervous expectation prepared both groups to gauge every detail of their environment for fear that they might miss the vital catalyst of inevitable conflict, and in the customary repetition that a thousand early mornings imposes most of the workforce had arrived by seven o'clock. Within time the loose affiliation of workers outside the factory had increased in number until almost the entire factory workforce of some eight hundred now stood across the road from at least twice their number in police stationed to the front of the factory. The call for a minute's silence passed along the line in memory of Daniel Hawkins. Almost instantly the entire workforce stood facing the police, head bowed. This silence defeated all in its path. And when the moment seemed right to all, John Evans casually led the march across the road. Now this perfect line of workers stood face to face with the police. No one knew if this was the moment of conflict, but both sides knew that within such situations spontaneity would ensure the ultimate spark that would ignite conflict like a much needed symbol of both sides' existence.

Margaret Harvey, Annie, Hasaan and Fred Williams stood alongside the unofficial strike leader attempting to watch every movement of both police and pickets. As daylight etched itself reluctantly on the roofs of nearby buildings, most of the workers appeared to be in a fairly sombre mood, waiting and looking for the first signs of movement; not from the police but from their fellow workers. Each grouping had opinions on 'the ones to watch', those most likely to cross the lines into the factory. Mistrust saturated all concentration as eyes swivelled amidst the ranks of workers towards the looming clock tower above them as its cast iron fingers lunged towards eight o'clock. Under orders from the ranks above them, and the interests of capital that ranged down forever upon them, the police also eagerly watched the movement of the clock, mindful of the instructions to make way and provide safe passage to any workers who wished to enter the factory that morning.

Some distance from the main entrance to the factory John Evans noted the resigned figure of McCabe, who seemed to be at the head of the largest contingent of workers along the line, those from his own drill shop. Frank O'Toole stood discreetly behind him, holding animated court with some of the older workers, and those around them hid their immediate assumptions that would have this phalanx of workers as the most likely group to cross the line first. Suspicion as ever fuelled confirmation that they were moving gradually towards the police lines and that the police themselves seemed prepared to allow them passage into the factory. Surveying the line still further, John Evans could see the young revolutionary with his attendant supporters distributing leaflets and shouting some slogan that the cold air refused to communicate any great distance. As the hour approached the lines of workers merged with the police and the inevitable humanity heaved backwards and forwards. Now clarity imposed itself as if sound and vision had been suddenly amplified in the wake of some deadly event. The audition had now been replaced by 'real life', and in the awaited confrontation insults and fists were now exchanged with the police, who were already beginning to make arrests. Some workers counted the seconds towards the hour, then the clock tower took command, striking the hour amidst the retort of distant factory klaxons. Then the sirens wailed. Motion visibly slowed as the anticlimax of the moment impressed itself upon the roles of both pickets and police, and it was at this instant that tempers calmed in collective relief. Eyes glanced wildly down the line towards the factory and upward towards the clock tower as if confirmation of the hour was still needed. No doubt seemed to exist that the line would be crossed at some point, such was the lack of confidence felt by this class so long inhibited by their rulers. Other workers exuded the real solidarity of their class and knew no cause for concern as calls to 'hold the line!' rained down the picket line, spitting in the face of immovable police obedience. They held the line and the workers held the line and nothing moved for an impenetrable age, frozen in the mists of cold air as it glistened under the morning sunrise. Granite figures, standing face to face, locked in some expectation that their roles dictated. This literal stagnation was to last for another half an hour.

McCabe appeared unusually stoic, standing in silence amongst the men he so often bullied into submission when they worked in the drill shop. A temptation to speak out did exist along the line with workers wanting to settle old scores, especially with those eighty or so men who regained the factory for the boss only a day before. The women stood together, sure of their solidarity whilst the fragile unity amongst some of their fellow male workers forced them to bury shared hatred in the vain hope that a unity could be forged and, most importantly, upheld at this crucial milestone of their struggle. Some workers lacked both the judgement and discipline to hold their tongues, embarking upon sporadic arguments in the hope that the line might be broken so that they could have the excuse to enter under the guise of the weakness of others. Around eight hundred workers and their supporters spread out along the full length of the factory and it was difficult to make out what was happening from either end, and those workers in the middle had little idea of events as they unfolded to the left or right of them. Some members of the strike committee walked the line and reported back to John Evans and Margaret Harvey, who now stood by the main entrance to the factory. As the half-hour left them, tensions rose again as the cries of 'hold the line!' evolved into a chant that had its greatest momentum in the centre of the line. Despite the distance between them McCabe and John Evans shared one inadvertent glance at each other, and it was then that Evans concluded to himself that McCabe held no threat to the unity of the line. His expectation was that a threat would undoubtedly emerge in the maelstrom of the workers' condition so afflicted by the demands of the system that their construction of reality could never conceive of life without it. Of a life beyond the factory.

At the furthest end of the line some commotion was detected, with police running to reinforce the line at this point as a large cluster of workers matched this movement, pushing past others who appeared merely as observers for much of the morning. There but not there, waiting, watching, hedging their bets between capital and labour, awaiting the moment at some stage of the struggle so that they may side with the victor—whoever that may be. These people were generally known to most of the workers and they were swept aside whenever they got in the way as events in such situations tend to happen with both a rapidity in action and a slowness in observation. Highlighted by the confusion invoked as bystanders pondering their failure to either comprehend or want to comprehend what is happening. McCabe's huge figure dominated the action at this point in the line as he crumpled one of the leaflets being handed out by the hyperactive young revolutionary. His voice boomed.

'This is men's work, lad, and I'm fuckin tella ya no clever arse theory's gonna break this line, so take yer leaflets and yer mates and fuck off!' he screamed.

Turning to some of the workers gathered nearby, he told them the same, but it all seemed too late. The revolutionary had done his damnedest in a short space of time, proclaiming the need to support the union at all costs, for the union was the true representative 'organ of the working class and without it organised labour could never challenge the power of capital.'

'Workers have no power outside of the production process,' he said, 'you can't fight the employer from outside the factory. The history of the class was that the unemployed were excluded from the struggle with capital by their very absence from the factory system,' he shouted, half submerged into the line.

The words rattled from the boy, urging, tempting workers to cross the line, and without admission his appraisal was shared by some of the workers. McCabe was soon shouting at a moving line of workers. Annie Reilly had been watching events closely and she threw herself into the crowd, grabbing the young revolutionary by the shoulder. He turned quickly, refusing to look her in the eye. She pushed further into his face, threatening him, daring him to cross the line. But as with McCabe, she also was talking to a moving tide of workers and it was here that the line broke. Led by the young boy, workers jostled their way through, encouraged and willed on by the police. McCabe was knocked to the ground by at least three policemen and Annie Reilly found herself on the receiving end of one worker's elbow as he forced his way through. With the line broken those frightened, non-committed workers took strength from this movement and fell into the space that now opened up before them, swallowing them whole like some biblical whale. Within minutes a whole section of workers from this part of the line had crossed behind the police and into an area of no man's land immediately in front of the factory. Fighting began along the line as the workers clashed head-on with the police in an effort to stop any further breach in this human wall. But in a momentary event the line was thus broken and a small band of strikebreakers had already disappeared into the warm, familiar protective embrace of police, authority and factory.

Annie Reilly, her face was covered in blood, helped McCabe to his feet and he thanked her, and for a moment the brutal exterior of this man that she had long despised graced itself with a humane warmth that she could never have expected. She wanted to get back to John Evans, and McCabe helped her through the throng of pickets whose animation did not reflect the reality that the conflict had passed with even the police now calling for restraint. When they arrived at the main entrance to the factory they saw John Evans surrounded by workers who wanted to know what had happened. Why had the line broken? Where was the unity? Why did he not prevent this from happening? Stupidity and ignorance hung in the air like an excuse that needed no explanation from the accusers, for blame rested solely with their unofficial leader. One worker spoke for many as he screamed at the chargehand as if he were the employer.

'That little bastard was your charge, wasn't he, John? How did you let that little bastard take control like that? You should have known what he was like,' one yelled.

Others followed while the man before them listened impatiently, as if time would bring its own answer. Some shouted back that it was just stupid to blame one man for what had happened. McCabe bluntly told the men to 'fuck off'. They saw the leaflets. They knew what was happening down there. Why didn't they do something about it? 'Go on fuck off and don't come back until you've got some sense. Stop looking for someone to blame,' he said. One worker sheepishly shouted from the back that McCabe had changed his tune and if he had stood up to the boss when they were in the factory none of this would have happened. McCabe's response was to knock three or four workers out of the way in an attempt to strangle the man who had spoken. Being held back by Annie and John Evans, all McCabe could do was curse and swear at the faces in front of him. John Evans asked McCabe how many men did he think crossed the line.

'It was difficult to see, I don't know exactly, about fifty or sixty perhaps,' he said.

'You lost some down here as well, didn't you?' Evans cut in.

'I'm not sure, maybe Annie saw better?' one of the men said.

The young girl had finally stemmed the flow of blood from her nose. 'Yes, that's about right, from what I could see,' she said.

Evans looked around, noting the workers who still clung to him as if he would still pull some solution from inside his pocket. Turning to McCabe and Annie, he concluded that the figure 'was enough to dismantle the plant'. In a lasting sigh he leant forward to state under his breath that 'the bosses seem to have what they want'. McCabe and Annie nodded their agreement. Their estimates were correct, and away from the picket line inside the empty cavernous factory this group gathered in isolation and shame without McCabe, without anybody, they were leaderless except for the police sergeant who told them to stay where they were until given further orders. Even the young apprentice turned revolutionary, who had provided the political excuse to cross the line, remained silent as the enormity of his actions dawned upon him. Like the condemned men they were they cowed in fear; the fear of what lay both inside and outside the factory.

Absence from anything lends itself to new interpretations that may alter fundamentally one's understanding or memory of a wide range of experiences. Often it is difficult to imagine the kaleidoscope of change that can be superimposed upon a familiar place once some alteration has been enacted and made invisible through absence. Like seeing something for the first time. A parallax. So this unlikely unity of the weak, self-centred and political pranksters saw their factory for the vast non-industrial canyon that it was. Silent but for the distant echoes of the eight hundred men and women whose human labour fired up everything from furnace to lathe for over thirty years in the plant that was now beyond their reach forever. The vast space around them dwarfed their existence, reinforcing in them the shallowness they now felt. The beings they had now become deserved this humiliation. The grand masters of production threatened more humanity than they felt within themselves, and vacant though the factory may have seemed its lifeless machinery evoked more dignity than any one of them as they lay in their regimented lines, secure under the protection of the police, State and capital. This inanimate machinery bathed in a newly discovered self-respect as they now awaited the promise of new labour to disentangle their engines so that they could once more become the vanguard of capitalist production in some distant corner of the planet. Wretched and ashamed, no man spoke to justify their action. These workless workers stood lifeless and imprisoned behind the lines of police that now corralled them on the edges of the factory. Outside they could hear the clock tower thud its realisation. It was now nine o'clock and in the empty roof space above them they heard the dullest of chimes saluting time from some invisible distance. For the first time they heard distant church bells ring in the factory. Johnson looked at the clock on the office wall and pulled out a pocket watch from inside his jacket, confirming that his instruction of nine o'clock had now been met. It was the first time he had ever heard church bells ringing when he was inside the factory, and for a few moments he thought upon this fact. He then turned to Carberry and Jacks to issue his second instruction of the morning.

'See if any of the bastards have turned up,' he ordered.

Carberry carried on smoking as he peered into the back of Johnson's head. Jacks rose immediately and went outside. Looking over the metal balcony that straddled some twenty feet above the factory floor. The union official was pleased to see that a number approaching the needs of the employer had now gathered in the half-light of the factory. Perhaps some of the workers would have expected their paid union official to come down the staircase and speak with them, explain what was happening; provide some advice, whatever. Jacks signalled to a police sergeant who measured a military walk to the foot of the metal staircase, speaking to Jacks as if he were a member of the local constabulary.

'Yes, Mr. Jacks,' he said firmly.

This pleased Jacks, who asked the officer to send the men up one at a time. 'OK, Mr. Jacks,' replied the obedient officer, no doubt convinced that some element of promotion might have rested upon this act.

For Jacks it was his inbuilt assumption that he would make senior officer grade in whatever line of work he would have chosen, and the officer's response recognised this quality or so he thought. In matters of law and order, discipline, power and retribution everyone becomes the police, and even Jacks short walk back into the office took on the plod of the dutiful officer serving Queen, country and capital. Johnson looked up as the hungry figure of Jacks entered the room with a satisfied air that declared his happiness. The execution of his main order from the boss 'to ensure that workers volunteered to dismantle the machinery' had been accomplished, and his part of the deal had been delivered for free as normal.

'Send them in,' mumbled Johnson.

Jacks turned, left the room and waved to the policeman to let the first worker up to the office. At the bottom of the stair stood the police sergeant with one of the workers at his side like an arrested felon, a condemned man. The worker adopted the role of the guilty man with all the necessary culpable mannerisms. The police officer held on to his arm as if fearful that he may escape. Any normal human observer would have looked upon this sight and drowned in a sea of sadness for the wretched being who was now being pushed up the stairs. As each step stole cuts of human dignity. Each step taking him ever closer to the shadows of the gallows that raged above him. Even the crime of crossing the picket line may have paled in relation to this punishment. But this was the real world and no excuses or sorrow could erase the self-inflicted shame that each man inside the factory had imposed upon himself. He carried a sorrowful burden. Dressed in the shabby uniform that working poverty designs with its emphasis on ill fitting and ragged. Each step on the metal staircase tore upon his trousers as they wore against boot heel and metal. Stooped even further by the weight of this new humiliation, the worker knocked on the door. Johnson turned his back again and spoke to Jacks and Carberry.

'Nobody speaks,' he said, and to the man behind the door he grunted a noise that may have mistakenly been understood as 'come in' or 'yeah', but it was a grunt all the same. On the other side of the door the man regretted his life and opened the door. By now the room was full of cigarette smoke, and with no real natural light it took the man some time to locate his own presence within the grey brown void he had entered. Eventually he was able to focus towards the ashen figure of Johnson sitting behind his desk. Only the red embers of Johnson's cigarette, as he pulled hard on it, allowed some vague outline for the man to recognise. He was now able to make out the two figures sitting in the corner of the room. After taking one step into the room the man was unable to move any further nor was he allowed to. He stood alone. Confirmed in his inferiority. Johnson confirmed his superiority by ignoring the man before him.

'Name?' he grunted disinterestedly.

'McKinley.'

'Age?'

'Fifty-two.'

'Trade?'

'Labourer,' the man said.

Johnson looked up and examined the man. Despite the man's vanquished state he was known to Johnson as a hard worker.

'The work is on a temporary contract, three weeks or so and pay on the rate agreed with the union. You start now. Report to the supervisors downstairs. Is that understood?'

'Yes, Mr. Johnson,' came the response. The man left the room.

At the bottom of the metal staircase another worker waited with his police guard. As the worker McKinley negotiated his way down from the office the other man was released to climb the stairs. The policeman told McKinley that he had to now go to the group of men who could be seen near the centre of the factory floor by the drill shop. When he looked ahead of himself only the white shafts of light that shimmered from some small bulbs fitted to nearby lathes and drills cast light. Thirty or so men dressed in white tunics gathered in huddles like surgeons considering the nature of their next operation.

One of them broke off his conversation to tell the worker in that casual manner that a surgeon could well adopt towards an incoming patient, arms loosely folded across his chest. 'Just wait over there, McKinley.'

The worker knew all the supervisors and like most in the factory he hated them, for they were the shock troops of the management pursuing the measurement of time and motion on every job. They had the power to cut men's wages by inflicting unattainable production targets, whereby once the worker failed to reach a given productivity level he would then have to work unpaid time to catch up on the bonus target. Supervisors, although in the union, did not consider themselves linked at all to the workers on the shop floor. Only one exception to this rule existed and that was Fred Williams, who was now standing outside the factory on the picket line. His fellow supervisors in the factory called him 'Quasimodo', and that was about as original as these automatons could be, for their only skill, if that was what it could be called, was to carry out the orders of the boss and inflict them on the workers. They despised the workers because they did not have the same aspirations or loyalty as them, but they saved their collective hatred for Williams, a foreman who never left the shopfloor. When they took on the job they were clearly told that they were crossing a 'bridge of no return from worker to management', and whilst their pay did not reflect their superior status, to all of them it was simply the prestige they craved. To be able to say that they were 'part of the management'.

Their responsibilities were now to collate a full inventory of every piece of machinery, every tool, every raw material. Indeed, anything that could be removed from the factory packaged and sold. Essentially, all the production machinery was to be exported to India; after that, anything left would be auctioned on site, and the supervisors were now discussing the most efficient method of recording all this information; the most productive means to close both the factory and their livelihoods down. Above all else they wanted to please their boss, hoping against hope that their devotion to servitude may result in some reward. They too knew the futility that now engulfed them. So it was that they continued with their role as supervisors with all that entailed, and should the factory crash to the floor around them then they would still act out their role. McKinley accepted his latest order and ambled in utter desolation across the factory floor as his role dictated. The supervisor who delivered the order was relieved that his power had been recognised so he could return to his company with his role intact. This satisfied the other supervisors, who felt comforted that their authority still held dominion. He looked over his shoulder at the lone figure grateful that they could both, despite adversity, act out their defined roles. Normality has been resumed. So the process of hiring workers to dismantle the factory continued and within one hour over thirty men found themselves corralled in the heart of the factory. Every so often one of the white-coated supervisors would march over to the men and take charge of a team of six who would be set to work on particular pieces of machinery. Others were delegated to construct wooden cases, ready for packing the dismantled machines.

In the far corner of the factory the young revolutionary had had time to consider his condition in the absence of his political bodyguards. Gone was the precocious confidence of the last few days as he surveyed the broken debris of a once proud workforce. No conversations took place as they awaited their fate in the cold, silent vastness of the factory turned prison. And in this isolation the young boy struggled to express his regret. Nobody wanted to know him now. For some he had simply provided the calculated excuse to cross the line. He was their distraction. Other workers were less sophisticated in their actions and simply followed those around them. Now, in the emptiness that filled him, freed from the brainwashing processes of the last few days, regret drained his very being. Thoughts of his first day in the factory calmed his panic. The support and friendship given by John Evans, Dan Hawkins and Brian Atkins. Two of his friends were now dead. He missed Annie and the love she gave to him. But everything he did was for them; it was their fault that they did not have the political vision that he and his comrades had. Then he questioned this thought, because only at this moment did he realise that he had been tutored to hate his friends, the very people who protected him and his political task-masters spread their hatred until he wallowed in the world where only they could be right. Talk of the power of the rank and file had somehow been turned to exclude people like John Evans, Margaret Harvey and Annie, as his two political tutors drilled into him 'they were now part of some elite, separate and distant from the workers.' But how could this be so? They still worked on the shop floor, how could they not still be considered part of the rank and file? They had lost their jobs like everyone else. Yet his political mentors saw no contradiction in their own support for a traitor like Jacks and his corrupt union, because whatever the situation, the union was the only representative of the working class that they could contemplate. That was why they urged him to cross the line, to get back into the world of work, bosses and unions. Like an obscure religious sect to which he had been kidnapped into membership, the young boy lost all contact with the real world. How he wanted to recapture his friends and explain how mistaken he had been. He wanted to rejoin them on the picket line. Above all else he wanted to rejoin Annie. The apprentice began to walk over to the steel door that would allow him to re-enter the world he now longed for. Just to stand on the picket line next to his real comrades. One of the policemen stopped him and asked him where he was going.

'I just want to leave, that's all,' he said in a voice soured with resignation and shame.

'No. My orders are that no one enters and no one leaves. That's what the manager said anyway,' the policeman said as if these were not his own words.

He was preoccupied with his main function of that morning, which was to send up each worker on the given instruction from his fellow officer at the foot of the steel staircase. The boy tried to ignore the officer's restrictions upon his freedom, but it was all to no avail and within seconds he found himself back in the company of others who crossed the picket line that morning. Each man, although grouped together for the purposes of Johnson's unnatural selection, stood alone, sharing no companionship, no conversation, no human concern for others. Stripped of all dignity, they stood vanquished, contending with the humiliation that seemed to consume them all. Since entering the factory no man was heard to defend their actions, as the time for talk had been overtaken by the declaration of their choice. Yet each man would probably have some reason, some justification, no matter how tortuous, for their actions that morning. Captured in the collective despair that encircled him, the apprentice began to survey his opportunities for escape, and it was then that he saw the dishevelled features of a worker sitting someway from the rest of the group. At first he paid little attention to the elderly man who sat half hidden behind some of the wooden planks brought into the factory to make the cases in which each machine would be packed for export. The man sat in a world even more distant from those around him. It was the storekeeper with the copperplate handwriting who had catalogued every nut, bolt, screw, drill piece, tool and raw material that was ever used in the factory. Listed in all their specificity. Listed in all their perfection. A unique inventory that provided his employer with an extraordinary grasp of stock fluctuations as well as the knowledge that production targets would never be impaired through loss or shortage. In consequence this man performed a number of functions, from financial management to stock control, thus saving the company huge sums of money, least of all in the general contribution made to productivity levels resulting from his undoubted efficiency. The apprentice remembered the first day he tried to sweep up inside the stock room as a foil to stealing bars of copper. This was also the man who spoke with such compassion at last night's meeting about the need for unity. The man who spoke of the historic spirit of trade unionism that rose above the individual. Now he sat in the factory as an individual, a loner in the company of loners. As the boy approached him the storekeeper looked away, as if by this act he could elude the shame of his condition.

'It's Mr. Turner, isn't it?' the boy asked.

The old man continued to look at some space on the floor in front of him as he ignored the boy. Then he spoke without the confidence or assurance of his contribution the night before.

'I'm no scab, lad,' he said, 'don't be thinking that you or the rest of them in here have anything in common with me,' he said quietly. 'No,' he said as if to himself. 'And that's true enough. So get on your way.' His hands ushered the boy away.

'I never said you were a scab,' the boy replied.

'I watched you out there, son, and nothing's more clear than the fact that you're a scab,' the man's voice raised itself, pushing air into the boy's face.

'That's were you're wrong again then, isn't it?' retorted the boy, rejecting immediately the thought that his actions were motivated through any alliance with the boss.

'Well, your sisters and brothers out there would have a different opinion,' said the man without feeling any need to look at his interlocutor.

Indignantly the boy sought to justify his presence in the factory that morning. 'I was misled and I didn't understand the politics of what was happening. I thought we should fight the struggle from inside the factory at whatever cost,' he said, almost shouting in the silent gloom of the factory.

'At whatever cost? Crossing a picket line?' the man asked. 'Now that's some cost,' the storekeeper said. 'Don't ever claim you're too young, or too inexperienced. Once you start work you're a man and you've got no excuses, so don't give me any of that, lad. I started in this factory thirty years ago when I was your age. They were the war years, and this place turned out armaments. No man or boy could make any excuse if they produced wrong measurements or damaged productivity because they couldn't read a blueprint. Once you enter that door you leave your excuses outside,' he said.

'What you've done,' now he spoke more resolutely, 'quite simply, lad, you've fucked up badly and it's irretrievable. But you can rest assured that's some record you've achieved. A scab at what? Fifteen? Sixteen? How long had you been here? Two days? Three days? Oh. You're a one off,' he laughed. 'That's for sure. That is for sure.' The old man's schoolmasterly charm had left him and a bitterness took over as he glared at the boy.

'I just tried to get out of this place and you wouldn't know what my plans were for being in here. I know what I'm doing and I know what I'm gonna do soon. What's your story?' He returned the old man's stare.

'What's your excuse?' he asked the man.

At this the man appeared to become unsettled as his eyes glazed in self-doubt. The tone of his voice softened as his eyes returned to an undefined point on the floor in front of him. Suddenly movement and noise began to reverberate throughout the factory as small groups of workers were set to work dismantling the machinery inside the factory. Startled by the noise, he seemed confused as to what was happening, forgetting the very reason why workers were in the factory that morning. Now on his feet, he spun around in as many directions as he could in an attempt to catch sight of the demolition now underway somewhere on the far side of the factory. It was an act beyond his comprehension.

'Where are they? What are they doing? If I find anyone in my store I'll kill them,' he shouted.

And in that instant the measured control he had exuded was lost. His role escaped to some other place as he screamed abuse at the unseen noise beyond him. A policeman came over and told him to shut up or he would be thrown out of the factory. The boy offered himself for expulsion but instead received a makeshift grin that secured itself around the boy's throat. Meanwhile, the old man was inconsolable. He staggered to his makeshift seat, mumbling under his breath, talking only to himself.

'All my life. All my life,' he cried into his hands, 'and they think they can just go in there and dismantle a lifetime's work as if it never took place, as if it never existed. Making my life's work irrelevant. No one has the right to do that. No one ever should. Not one day off in thirty years. No one ever interfered in my stores. Everything filed and catalogued like no other engineering plant in the country. No one could do what I did and they think that they can just break it down. Empty it out.' His hands covered his face.

'That's why I'm here, to stop those filthy bastards getting into my stores!' he told the boy. 'And to do this I had to cross the picket line. That's how much it means to me. Can you understand that? Can you?' Tears streamed down his face. The boy was comforted in this reasoning.

'You see,' the boy said, 'that's why I'm in here as well. To stop them. To fight against them.'

The boy spoke like a priest taking confession. The man wept in his despair and rejection. The apprentice tried to console him as he unfolded his life. And if the truth spoke out this was the case for all of the workers. The factory was their life. Even those that knew the robbery of this system relied upon the factory to feed their families. The power of capital could never be ignored. And those who devoted their lives to struggling against this criminality recognised the beast they fought against. It was an 'upside down' world in which the opposites of reality held power. Now most of those who entered the factory that morning had been processed. Only a few had been rejected by Johnson for reasons best known to this unintelligent, cynical and ruthless man. Perhaps a whim; to set an example to Jacks that it was he who had the power. Or just to settle some obscure, outdated score with a worker who may have crossed him in the past. Now these two secluded figures found themselves at one with each other. A situation to which they would never agree. But by their actions they were now the centre of attention of their police guard.

Chapter Nineteen

They fuck you up, your mum and dad. They may not mean to, but they do... Man hands on misery to man. It deepens like a coastal shelf. Get out as early as you can.

—Philip Larkin, 1974

'Which one is it to be then?' the policeman asked. 'Make your minds up.'

The policeman walked away in that self-satisfying manner, confident that his order would be obeyed. It fell to the old man to respond to the call of authority and he strove menacingly behind his custodian. He ignored the conventions imposed that morning, failing to stop at the foot of the steel staircase, marching directly into Johnson's office. Now he stood before Johnson, who ignored his presence. Carberry and Jacks sat in the murky atmosphere some distance behind their master. Before Johnson could speak the old storekeeper bludgeoned into the figure of Jacks, who had spent the morning in a smoke-filled anonymity, shielded by the back of his alter ego. With forefinger pointed directly at the union official the worker demanded to know what Jacks was doing there. Then he answered his own question.

'But that's a stupid question,' he said as he looked around at the three men in the room, 'because this is where you spent all your time when you should have been on the factory floor. This is your place because you act and think like them.' He began to walk around the room as he spoke.

'Workers are just an embarrassment to you. Reminding you every day of what you once were. Now you sit in judgement or rather watch others make like judge and jury while you just rubber-stamp any scrap that's thrown your way.' Jacks gave his usual look of disinterest. But the storekeeper ignored him with an intensity that fired fear in Carberry and Johnson. The storekeeper continued.

'What's so amazing is that you do it without any shame or remorse. No guilt. And that,' he moved towards Jacks, 'well, that is the trick.'

The old man's voice was almost conversational until Johnson broke his silence, and for the first time that day he addressed a worker by his first name.

'Let's not get too distracted, Jim, whatever you've got to say to your union official you can do another time. I hear you had a lot to say last night at the meeting. Well, that's your democratic right, as they say. You know we'd always have a place for you and I'm just pleased that the loyalty you have shown to G.P. Stevens and Son over the last—what is it, twenty or so years...?'

'Over thirty years,' interrupted the storekeeper.

'Well, I knew it was a long time,' Johnson said almost apologetically.

'Look, Jim, we need you to do an inventory of all the stuff we have in the lock-up. You know, tool pieces, drills, lathe parts, raw materials. The whole picture. God, I can tell you not one of my supervisors has a clue what goes on in those stores.' Johnson began moving the paper on his desk. 'Even the log went missin—stolen more like. And the bastards even removed all those fancy signs in the stores telling you what was where and what was what. Sabotage, and that's a police matter,' he said indignantly. 'That's where you can help us out. I'm prepared to take you on, you know. Let you record or list or whatever it is you do. Well, then we can pack it up and ship it out. That's what we can do. So let's forget about all this nonsense. Out of our control. Business pressures. It's trade. One day you think everything's OK, then.... Well, not my fault or yours. It's those other bastards who destroyed this company. So.' The pause rang out in the tiny room.

'How about it, Jim?'

The storekeeper stood defiant in front of the three men and allowed a silence to evolve unnaturally following Johnson's question. The three men now looked up at him, resenting his calm, thoughtful manner that exuded a quiet dignity so out of place in that office that it challenged, threatened, all three of them. A void opened, swallowing all three up in the chaos that refused to acknowledge their power. Johnson understood the game that was unfolding for it was his role to play the vanquisher and yet this old man now sought to reverse the roles. Johnson's temper ignited the darker side of him while the man wrestled with himself, knowing that once out of control the old man would realise his victory. What was even more annoying was the fact that he needed this worker's skills. His voice boomed towards the worker.

'Look, we haven't got all day. Let's get on with it, you're hired. Send the next one in,' he shouted into the door.

'I'm hired, am I? No. Not now, not ever. I'm fired. That's what I am,' the storekeeper said,' you've set me free,' he said joyfully, 'do you know how free I am?' he asked them all. 'All my life I've spent archiving bits of metal and I hated every moment of it. But to do it, day after day, week after week, year after year, I imagined that the place was a library, my library, and I was the librarian and those bits of twisted, pointed, curved, flat, round, square, spiralled, well, you name it, every piece of metal.' His words welded together. 'Well, they were my books. That was how fucking insane this factory made me. You see, I always wanted to be a librarian but I couldn't because I had to leave school and go to work, and when I saw the madness of this place I knew that all factories would be the same so I ended up in the stores and,' his eyes roamed around the three figures in front of him, 'well, to stop me going fucking mad I had to become fucking mad. Can you believe that?' The three looked vaguely through him as he spoke.

'Now I have my books at home and some time to read them. You've done with me over the last thirty years, now it's my turn to be done with you. I suggest you go down the stores and sort that mess out yourself. That's how free I am.' The storekeeper awaited a response. It never came. He pushed his jaw forward.

'I'm a librarian,' he announced proudly. At that moment he left the room, seconds later he re-entered. 'I took down all my references in the stores, all those copperplate signs that everyone laughed at, I took them home, all my indexes and it wasn't sabotage, it's what's known as intellectual property. My intellect and my property. Something you never, ever respected me for or paid me for.' He turned and left the room for the last time. The three men sat in absent silence until Jacks spoke for the first time that day.

'Well?' he exclaimed. 'What an ungrateful little bastard he was,' Jacks said to his comrades.

Johnson turned around, still seated, and glared at Jacks. Carberry looked ridden with guilt. The storekeeper reached the bottom of the steel staircase and was directed by the policeman on sentry duty to join the gangs of workers in the centre of the factory. Instead, he walked towards the exit of the factory, where he was promptly intercepted by another policeman, who he simply ignored and within seconds he opened the steel door to rejoin the picket line. The clean air bathed itself against his body. Most of his fellow workers doubted very much that a man of his calibre would ever cross a picket line and some of them had seen him dismantle his life's work in the storeroom during the occupation. He made his way towards John Evans in order to report back what he had seen and heard inside the factory. Back on the line his thoughts drifted as he made his decision to live his dream to become a librarian once the struggle had been concluded. Outside the plant attitudes had begun to harden as the workers realised the extent of their failure to maintain unity on the line.

Inside the factory the apprentice struggled with his reclaimed reality that impressed upon him a longing to be beyond the confines of the plant, on the picket line standing alongside Annie. His thoughts were shattered into the smallest of fragments. 'OK, son. You're the last. You know the script,' said the policeman, 'over there. Up the stairs and get your job back,' he said with an air of disinterest as he leant over the boy.

'I don't want my fuckin job back,' muttered the boy to no one in particular.

'Well you must be like those nutters outside. Either they're loaded or Commie bastards. Whatever. I couldn't give a fuck,' the officer said.

The boy shook his head stood up and began making his way towards the staircase walking past the second policeman as if neither existed. Now he was in Johnson's office correcting his mind as it flashed back to his first day in the factory; the encounter with Johnson and Carberry, their office and the dismal brown half-light that they existed in as if they might die should fresh air or light be allowed to invade their sealed lair. Only the despised figure of Jacks altered his original recollection, and it was to his presence that he concentrated his gaze. Johnson had been well informed, as always, of matters relating to the shopfloor. A network of company agents amongst the workforce had always reported back to supervisors, Carberry or even Johnson himself. It was a system he encouraged. This process continued inexplicably even as some workers stood on the picket line. But it was fundamentally flawed as some workers sought to ingratiate themselves by telling the management whatever they thought they wanted to hear. Johnson prided himself on his spy network, confident that this knowledge served to augment his power, especially when dealing with individual troublemakers in the factory. Information on individuals or activities had a number of uses for people like Johnson and Jacks as they played their role games in the full knowledge of their outcome. Jacks knew of the plans to close the factory long before the workers revolted in response to the company's strategy of invoking industrial chaos as justification for closure. Similarly, Johnson knew full well how to extract maximum influence and power from a wide range of information sources within both the factory and the union. '*It*' hid behind unique dossiers that wove the impression of ability, intelligence and power to those who spied on their fellow workers. Johnson could cast off webs of deceit in pursuance of the greater goal whilst his victims suffered in wonderment. This exercise of power was never enough to satisfy their iron will to destroy all opposition, to break those men and women who did not worship in equal 'wonderment' at the imaginary awesome governance of capital. Capital was built upon the backs of traitors. In Johnson's predictable assessment the storekeeper was simply 'too old and too mad with no servile toil left in him'. The apprentice warranted a different diagnosis. Now the dark cynicism demanded to fuel the engines that turned the social, political and economic cogs of capital came into focus. For its punishment protocol, if anything, did not lack for creativity. Johnson lightened to the task before him wrapped in the role of the local magistrate. The boy entered the room. 'So. You know what's on offer and despite everything I'm prepared to give you a second chance to work in this factory,' Johnson said with undue gravitas. 'We're not as bad as you've been led to believe and I'm prepared to give you an opportunity you should think about,' he said. 'Do you understand what I'm sayin to ya, lad?'

Behind him Carberry threw a look of astonishment towards Jacks. Carberry's mind was extraordinary if only for its limitations and he could not comprehend the reasoning behind Johnson's conciliatory offer to the useless troublemaker before them. Johnson smiled benignly, awaiting the boy's response. Now the apprentice began to feel his feet sink deep into the floor beneath him as the weight of doubt pressed down upon him, for he fully expected Johnson to kick him out of the office once he showed his face. In a momentary thought he became lulled towards the idea that he merited the respect of this manager, that he had a value and to this end he was being offered some place in the scheme of things. These headlamps of self-doubt, of weakness, blazed into his eyes and he felt a comfortable breeze blow gently across his face, removing all conflict, presenting a door through which he felt he could pass. Pass into a compliant world in which life appeared so structured, calm and peaceful. Was this the offer to join the '*it*'? To cease being an individual, joining the collective source that fed the system, and in the instant that he considered the warm easy breath of betrayal he was satisfied with his worth. Then the coldest shiver racked his body and sweat pushed itself from his forehead as images of John Evans, Brian, Daniel then Annie cut through his memory. The newspaper article, the death of Che Guevara, who would live on through the heroic struggle of all revolutionaries; the endless political tutorials given by his odd political commissars. The immeasurable struggle of good, honest people who stood up every day against the scourge of capitalism across the world. His wish to be out of the room crushed all these thoughts that made his ears suddenly aware of the noise outside the factory as pickets and police heaved towards each other in combat. Noise rang through his head, mixing sound and image flashing in front of him, and he could no longer make out the figures of the three men as they stared into him watching the colour drain from his body. To him their faces merged into one. His feet were cemented to the floor. He could not move, even though the nausea that swallowed him up kept telling him to fall, to collapse amidst the echoes of the three men's voices calling out to him. Fear ground into his face that the guilt he was now immersed in should release itself and expose his crimes to his three accusers. Like a dog. Yet here was his chance to confront capital and this is what he had intended to do, yet a hidden force deep inside him captured a weakness to which he

259

wanted to succumb. Father, mother, teacher, priest, spewed up from his past and ran around him, convincing him to do what the three men wanted. Clearly seeing the boy's distress, Johnson told Carberry to get a chair. This broke the numbing silence upon the apprentice, who, from somewhere inside himself, was able to indicate that he was all right, but this was as much a sham as the proceedings upon which the boy had fallen. He lifted his head towards Jackson and spoke.'No, I don't want your fuckin job.' The words came eventually with unexpected ease. He moved toward the door.

Johnson stood up. Deep inside himself the boy was proud of his stance. 'Before you go,' Johnson said, 'you had better know that we've got police evidence on you.' The boy turned to face Johnson. 'We know what you've been up to and if you walk out of here then by the time you get home your mother will be sitting with a policeman who won't be there to tell you the time. Do you know what I mean? Jacks knows what you did and we've got all the evidence we need. The police. Well, they just want to know if we want to press charges. You better get yourself back in here, lad, and sign up for work or spend the next few months of your life fighting against prison guards. That's right,' he said in self-praise of the power he thought he had.

'That's right. We've got all the evidence we need,' he said.

'Jacks! Tom! You tell him.' Johnson looked straight ahead as the two men behind nodded in agreement. Jacks was so committed to his role as class traitor that he felt compelled to underline his servility.

'That's right, lad. Mr. Johnson is offering you a way out and as your union rep I think you'd be a fool to ignore his offer.'

He held up these words as if meant for some higher being and the substance of his words fell towards the floor like dead metal. As always in his life it was taken as meaningless babble.The boy's shoulders hunched forward as he turned and faced the three men. His eyes betrayed his submission. Suddenly he looked older. Now he looked like Jacks. Now he remembered his father's fatal look of resignation. Now he was no different than them. All three men in the room recognised that the boy had been broken and if it was only for that instant then the interests of capital, the interests of '*it*', had been adequately served. Now the boy struggled to hold back the tears that welled inside him as the dark realisation that he would not stand up to these three figures dawned upon him. He could not, or so he felt, stand up to them, as the fear instilled by the threat of police action was enough to force him to heel. It was enough to seek to protect his mother from any shame he might bring to her. And to his father no thought entered his mind. How wrong he was, yet the threat mingled with his inbred sense of overwhelming guilt. This threat was meaningless. But little was needed to push this burden he carried over the edge. Perhaps he could have dealt with such matters. Now, as he stood alone in all his contradictions, he wanted to surrender. The four figures stood silently in the room together, and in those few moments the boy wiped his face roughly with his hands, turned, then left the room. At the bottom of the staircase he obeyed the lone policeman and walked towards the men in their white coats. His name had been written into their notebook, instructions unfolded as to which gang the boy would be working with. The five or six men he had been assigned to work with all crossed the picket line, all worked in the drill shop and all despised McCabe for not being with them that day. They stared venomously at the boy but no conversation was struck amongst them as if they had all taken on a vow of silence. It was only then that the boy realised that the factory was now void of all human communication, with the only noise being that of the dismantling of the machines. One of the workers threw a hammer, spanner, and large screwdriver to the boy. Eventually one of the supervisors broke the silence, dictating to the apprentice that his job was to release the drill machines from the floor while the other workers loosened then secured them for packing. So here he was in the heart of the drill shop surrounded by over one hundred machines working alongside the men who used to earn their living from working these giant iron cast Victorian antiquities. It took at least five men to physically move each drill machine from its secured position. Once loosened, they had to tilt the machine until enough space appeared underneath it to enable a steel trolley to be placed under it. Then the machine was tilted backwards onto the trolley with its total weight being taken by three men. Each machine was to be removed and placed near the centre of the factory, where other teams of workers set about the task of packing them for export. The boy watched as the workers struggled with the dead weight of the first machine to be unhinged from its resting place. Standing a full seven feet high, these mammoth drills towered over the men in a wholly disproportionate contest of physical strength, and the strain that this placed upon them was clear for all to see. Yet they continued while the supervisors watched calmly from the centre of the factory, arms folded in casual conversation, and when the workers struggled against this colossus one supervisor would amble over and referee the contest. Useless and irrelevant as they were, this industrial pantomime was to be repeated throughout the day. When the first machine had been removed from its plinth the young boy went to examine the perfect shadow of grease and grime it had left in its wake. One of the supervisors came over again and remonstrated with the boy to get about his business, and prompted by this call for industry the workers in the gang shouted from across the floor of the factory for him to unloosen the next machine. This was all done as if their very lives depended upon it. He had forgotten the darkness in his soul as the rigours of physical work blanked out his brain. After all, this was its function. The worker had to blank it out. Even more strangely, he found himself wanting 'to do a good job'. Not for himself, nor the other workers or supervisors. He wanted to do a 'good job' because that was what he had been brought up to fulfil. His one and only function to take on the role of the moment if only to satisfy the roles of others; he had to play his part and he wanted to prove, without any logical explanation whatsoever, that he was a 'good worker' even to those who would 'scab' their way through life based upon the assumption of the individual above all else. Even to these people around him, these people who hated everything he stood for, he wanted to show them that he could be just as productive, just as hard working. But now he did not know what he stood for. His mind fought against itself and his thoughts strangled each other. In this madness the dismantling of the machines that provided them with work for over thirty years appeared negligible. Bent over double, the boy attempted to release one of ten large bolts that secured the second drill machine to the factory floor. It would not budge. He banged the spanner with a hammer and still it would not budge. One of the workers came over and snatched both tools off the boy and began to squirt oil from a rusty can over each of the bolt housings. Without speaking to the boy he placed the spanner on the first bolt and, tapping it resolutely with the hammer, released it from its mounting. The first bolt was free and without and further gesture or communication with the boy the worker dropped the tools to the floor and returned to the other workers, who were still struggling with another cast iron burden as they edged it towards the centre of the factory. The boy picked up the tools and began to repeat the process established by his silent tutor. As in the production of any final product it appeared that repetition and the most minuscule division of labour seemed to exist as a natural law of work for all workers irrespective of the circumstances. Without instruction or debate they organised themselves according to some Darwinian principle so that the strongest of the men fulfilled their maximum efficiency and the weakest, such as the boy, also achieved his maximum expenditure, all being determined by weight, size, age and intelligence. No different than the machines they now dismantled, human labour equated at least for the capitalist as no different an entity than the cast iron beasts they were expected to remove from their personalised locations on the factory floor. The key was to establish its function, its use value and its optimum efficiency. Within all its ironies the workers did this themselves, free of charge, as if this was all part of the package purchased by the employer once human labour was hired. That they so organised themselves was a factor not lost upon the employer, but lest the scam be exposed bosses always ensured that fat layers of management stood over the workers, taking away from them any concept of independence, self-management or control.

So our young apprentice observed the way work tasks silently imposed a detailed hierarchy upon the group and in this shamed speechless acquiescence they toiled. Looks and grunts communicated the requirements of their work. A veil of soundless activity echoed to the occasional thrust of hammers on reluctant bolts or the weighted scrape of machines as they were shifted across the factory. This was no longer the heaving mass of men and machine that created its own industrial universe whose atmosphere was a concoction of oil, smoked and sweat. The giant extractor fans remained still, as redundant as the workers who laboured beneath their weary gaze, and they were as empty as the great shell they now functioned within. No longer did the ritualised formalities of factory work apply as the eighty or so 'demolition' workers were excused the need to clock on or respond to the wail of the factory siren. Only the sly inspection of the factory superintendents sought to represent the interests of capital. In his observations the boy could see the emptiness reflected in the eyes of those around him. For the first time he understood the meaning of that expression and it was at that moment that he began to understand the reasons for his father's malaise. Every bolt he removed, every machine he helped dislodge from its aged foundations added to the number of bleak blank spaces that moved gradually across the floor of the factory. Within hours over twenty machines in the drill shop had been removed, and as the vastness of the space they vacated dawned on those who performed this destructive act they realised that they were witnessing the death of their factory. Each function they performed drew the life from the vast architecture that had once provided work for over eight hundred workers and their families. In their silence they knew full well what they were doing, and as each machine was unhinged another sigh was unleashed within the factory, and the boy gasped at the unforgivable shame of it all. At six o'clock two buses backed into the loading bay and the workers were herded onto them by their white-coated superintendents. The plan, or so they were told, was that they would be taken from the factory, away from the picket line, and returned in the morning. This happened. Outside the factory the cold night air encircled the pickets, breathing an icy despondency through them all. When the privately hired buses pulled out from the factory the police and the pickets performed their designated duties, one fighting to defend the scabs, the other seeking to attack, and within this confrontation the buses drove past indifferently as its passengers hid in their humiliation. The apprentice leaned his head against the dirty condensation of the window, comforted by the damp coldness as it vibrated hard against his skull. In the momentary tumult that flashed by the factory gates he caught sight of John Evans and Annie in the darkness and he knew that they could not see him, but this only heightened his own feeling of abject desolation. On his arrival home, little had changed except himself. As normal his mother displayed a forgetful concern that questioned the events of his day whilst preparing the family meal. Nothing altered, whatever the circumstance, for she believed her home to be of a dimension capable of excluding the real world, and whenever its rancid tentacles clawed their way through her door her mind refused to admit it existence. The boy swallowed deep on his guilt whilst his mother wandered from one personalised conversation to the next, halting sporadically to ask the boy if he knew 'what she meant'. A phrase that had boundless use in any context, spurning any real sense or meaning. Only the softness of her voice displayed her real feelings. At seven o'clock his father walked through the door. For over thirty years he had worked as a skilled lathe operator at a small engineering shop close to the larger factories on the edge of town such as Stevens and H.A. Brambell. These two huge plants dominated not only the physical landscape but also the livelihoods of most of the families in the area, and the smaller producers all depended on them for specialised work. Perhaps it was the nature of his work, the pressure of production targets, the constant demands of precision that forged his personality, and above all else, the ever-present spectre of lay-offs that hung over his trade. Casual work imposed casual attitudes to all matters, for this man took refuge in his isolation from his class. It was in his eyes that the resignation of his life exposed itself like some dark deceit from which he had permanently sought to escape. Resignation followed him wherever he went and preceded him into his home. Routine in all things preserved the frugal rigidity of his life. Each night he would fill the kitchen sink with cold water, unbutton his overall and shirt and free his arms from its sleeves, leaving clothes to fall around his waist. Standing in his vest and hanging work clothes he would punch the water against his face, scrubbing fiercely as water flashed in every direction. Sitting in his vest, he would take his place at the kitchen table and wait for his wife to present his meal. Over the years this had turned into a monotonous strain for the father and son whilst their mother dismissed its misery as being the only time the family were together. In silence they would sit compact and unsatisfied and the son's eyes reflected the emptiness that had once been the sole domain of his father. It was at this moment that the father pulled out the local evening paper from the back pocket of his overalls. He opened it with a rare glint of satisfaction, as if discovering some sad misfortune that gave him a newfound status that made his life somewhat better than that of others. He rummaged through its crumpled pages, then he spoke, continuing to examine the text before him. 'That's praise indeed. Even this local right-wing rag,' he said directly to his wife, 'thinks it's wonderful that sacked workers at Stevens's factory have volunteered to dismantle machinery.' His speech slowed deliberately as he read directly from the article.

'Says here that the workers are "behaving in a sensible way after the closure of the plant due to the value of the pound ... lost orders ... and the activities of a small group of militants who recently took part in an unofficial strike and occupation of the plant." What crap!' he shouted across the kitchen. He continued to read from the paper.

'"When will these people learn the damage they are doing to Britain's manufacturing base? Early today over one hundred sacked workers began dismantling industrial machinery inside the plant that will be exported to an unknown buyer based in India. Yet another lesson in the damage that union militants cause to local employment."' He turned to his son.

'Headline here says, "Workers aid export drive," suppose you spent the day on the picket line? You know my views but those lads had no choice, all this wage cutting and it all rebounds on the small makers,' he said with as much conviction as his son had ever witnessed before from his father. His son looked at his father and saw a fire in his eyes and his own soul filled with shame. How he wanted to run from that room. He hoped his father would stop. But he continued, unaware of his son's guilt.

'Yes. Once they broke the back of the big players. So you stick to your guns, son. You know, I heard today that the union knew all along that the factory was gonna close. Shut down and they didn't tell anyone. Nothin new in that. That's for sure, but what on earth....' He looked in disbelief at the newspaper. 'One hundred volunteered to go back in the plant and strip it down,' he laughed mockingly, 'that's just about the lowest treachery any worker can do. Sacked, then go back in to close the place down.' He looked at his son and his love for him cascaded heavily upon the boy. His mother smiled in infinite innocence and her husband's love filled inside her.

'So. Was it cold down there today?' the father asked his son.

The boy stood up and went to leave the kitchen and the father looked into the answer that spoke from his son's eyes. He grabbed his arm, pulling him back into the room. His face blazed with anger as he struggled to control himself in the vain hope that he was wrong.

'You're one of them! You?' he screamed.

His wife continued to eat silently as if these events held no meaning for her. The peaceful love that had entered the room had escaped. It was lost forever and she knew it as she looked towards her son. The hatred he had for himself had festered for days like some tumour that he could feel spreading throughout his body until it needed to release itself, but he contained it within himself, hoping that some event would wipe out the shame that now entombed him. He remembered the empty expression that haunted his childhood whenever he looked towards his father for some hint, some inside knowledge as to what life held in store. This was the trust he placed in the one man he thought could guide him, and it never came. In his innocence this was his expectation that fathers held these great secret formulas to life, and even if he doubted its truth the thought gave him comfort and strength. When he became older this dream gently faded, evaporating as every month brought age and new obstacles to the once sheltered life of a child. Then he became aware of things previously unknown to him that could no longer hide in the half-light of a baby's gaze. He was no longer invincible. Age toiled on both the father and the son that shattered the delicate balance of trust and belief. A grey heaviness weighed upon the father, who was resigning from life at the moment his son was entering the industrial abyss before him, and he resented his father for not protecting him from it, for not warning him about it. He was to blame for everything and now it was he who turned upon the son to accuse him, to blame him. But this naïveté had been imposed by others more concerned to protect the corruption they fed off. His father was not responsible for a society that placed profit above humanity. Yet the boy felt that he could have done more to fight against the system that now shattered his existence. His father was more revolutionary than he would ever know. He shouted his response, expecting the noise to drown out his humiliation.'When did you last go on strike? You gave in years ago,' he shouted, 'surrendered! I'm doin' what you told me. *Keep yer head down, don't cause any trouble.* That's what I'm doin now. You a militant all of a sudden? Reclaiming your working class roots?' he asked his father sarcastically. 'No!' he shouted again. 'Don't tell me about what's wrong when you wouldn't fight it yerself. I'm like you. I've given up. Sold out. Yes, boss. No, boss. Three bags full, boss. I thought you'd be proud of me. I'm one of them in the paper helping the export drive. I'm fuckin famous.' He cried into his father's face. His father stared at him. 'Aren't you proud that I've followed in your footsteps. Like father like son?'

In his silence the father's eyes renewed their lost intensity and his fists raised to the ceiling as his body shook in the struggle to stop him raining blows upon his son. Fear was not lost upon the boy as his father towered before him, then a sudden calmness took over the man, whose face pressed and contorted towards the boy. Now only his head shook in careful denial. 'You're a man now,' he said as if he wanted to put an end to the confrontation. 'Don't go blamin others for yer actions. Whatever I've done is down to me. But I'll tell you this, I never crossed no picket line. I never scabbed no strike.' He was angry at saying this, but the words flowed uncontrollably. 'And I never demolished no factory. That's bastard's work!' He was talking to himself.

The boy had left the room and the man sat down to finish his meal. The mother looked on and life continued as ever.

Chapter Twenty

I remember well my attitudes and confusion at the time. He can't be too much different since our development was forced along similar lines. Of course he has had a slightly better chance or atmosphere to build the things necessary for the changeover from man-child to man. That school Mama was sending him to did him great harm but not irreparable harm since in his case you were on the job after school sowing pride and knowledge of self and kind, and explaining the promise and problems in acquiring self-determination and control over all the circumstances surrounding our existence. Of course you have been explaining that this control must never be allowed to remain in the hands of strangers or incompetents, etc.
—Soledad Brother. The Prison Letters of George Jackson,
September 1ˢᵗ. 1967

The cold wind spiralled off the surrounding buildings, forcing gales of frozen rain against the worn faces of the pickets and the indifferent scowls of the police. A point was reached in the night where both armies began to peel away from their thinning lines. By eight o'clock a token picket had been left outside the factory. As normal some of the men and women from the line decided to go to the local pub for solace, comfort and company. Those without money found it whilst those with money shared it. This was and always would be their way. The usual group of John Evans, Margaret Harvey, Annie, Hasaan and Fred Williams sat together with other members of the strike committee scattered around them. They had been joined by McCabe, who sat next to John Evans, uncomfortable and silent, a feeling shared by many in the group, but this was a time to respect everyone involved in the struggle although McCabe's past made it almost impossible for some to forget. But McCabe was now on strike, on the picket line, and for the moment his past was forgotten. Discussions and argument flowed like rivers raging and calm as the workers assessed the nature of their struggle and how they could defeat their enemy. Some had lost the will to continue, others wanted to fight to the bitter end whatever the consequences. But this was the normal run of things, and the bar that night eased with the repetition of other nights. John Evans looked physically exhausted though his faith in the struggle of his class remained; undiminished as ever. His eyes surveyed his friends and comrades in the rich contradictions that embraced them all. McCabe held himself in deep conversation with John Evans and the two acted at times like long-lost comrades. Their history together made such things possible, much to the restrained contempt of others around them. Hasaan and Annie listened intently but felt matters had moved beyond this group. As was normal, workers came and went with promises of support and hopes of solidarity, and this process rolled from picket line to pub, raising expectations and the potential of disappointment. These evenings followed the same pattern of highs and devastating lows. Every moment was fuelled by the hope that some event would unfold, another factory joining the strike or the union making the strike official, some event, any event. Some realised the futility of hope when reality dictated the pure simplicity of their condition run in cliché, locked in endless historical paradigms of workers' solidarity, union betrayal, state repression and defeat. Hasaan was losing patience while Annie tried to hold back his frustration with her trust and belief in those older and theoretically wiser than her. Without the realisation of solidarity action being taken by the surrounding factories all was lost. This they all knew. This being the fundamental principle of workers solidarity.

As the evening wore on a maelstrom of confused emotions entrenched themselves in the workers who sat quietly around the room while at the bar victory was only days away, and the more they drank the more they celebrated. Talk of the workers' struggle against the beast that was capital shouted political rhetoric into stranger's faces. For some their strike provided a bizarre link with machismo as some shouted what they would and would not do. Often these calls came from people still working in local factories. Across the room other workers tried to stumble through a logic that might explain how their crisis would end. In the corner an unknown group of supporters sat huddled in intrigue, and amongst them Annie made out the shrunken intensity of the two 'politicos' who had worked their spell upon her young apprentice. As ever they indoctrinated the air around them. She resented their existence, their intrusion in a struggle that they lived off and not for. Once they had tried to recruit her, and for a while she was lost in a black hole of contradiction, hatred and sectarianism. She had been at a few of their meetings organised in different followers' houses, where the party line was speared through their skulls and whose poisoned tip decomposed free thought. The demands of party work eradicated the individual, leaving only a vacuous shell, drawn, haggard and worn, incapable of human relevance, incapable of talking about anything else but the triumph of the party over life itself. She was of a mind to confront them again but the thought passed through her mind absently as she caught sight of other comrades whose political work gave untold support to the struggle. They had a line but it was not the reason for existence; the struggle for them was. And if they had a line it was 'workers right or wrong'. Every so often John Evans would get up and answer a phone call from one union branch or another. McCabe rang his contacts, sometimes calling upon John Evans to detail the struggle or call for direct action. When the calls finished Evans and McCabe released no emotion, just the occasional comment that disclosed nothing of note. Hasaan merged his frustration with Annie's fading hopes as they both looked upon the dwindling unity before them, and as their hearts collided head-on with the incessant promise of some event unfolding that would bring a conclusion they realised that in the midst of everything nothing was happening. It was a room full of people just waiting for something to happen. Then they concluded that John Evans and the others recognised that now their struggle was fatally flawed, decimated by the failure of other workers to take direct solidarity action. Hasaan was older and more cynical than Annie; he also held a deep jealousy, resenting that she had chosen the new apprentice as opposed to himself. Now he reminded her of what a class traitor he had turned out to be in that falseness hidden behind the rhetoric of political theory. That same theory that resulted in the apprentice going into work to dismantle the factory. Annie ignored the persistent references to the boy, thinking it merely to be a distraction, and she knew Hasaan held no great political perspective other than his often-repeated justification for stealing from the firm as some contribution towards the redistribution of wealth. The humour had long since elapsed for her as she urgently studied the lost momentum of her struggle, for all the talk of the evening seemed to conclude that the picket line had to dig in and for her this meant a strategy of waiting for something to happen. A pointless activity irrespective of where it took place; on the street, in the pub or in the home. An infinity of inaction lay before all of them, and she saw it in the eyes of those around her. In her concentration Hasaan's voice echoed around her head, compounding the futility that she now saw unfolding that evening, and a fearless anger grew inside her, then she looked towards Margaret Harvey, who was deep in conversation with McCabe and John Evans. The former she hated the latter she loved. What kind of contradictory leadership would unfold in the days ahead? How much could McCabe be trusted, she thought to herself. But perhaps trust was irrelevant, as the room for further betrayal seemed impossible. Her mind was closed to all but revenge.

Outside, the apprentice had been walking the cold night alone and impoverished, shamed by his father, trapped by the circumstances of his political ignorance and naïveté. All he wanted was to clear his name, explain his guilt, seek forgiveness. To make a new start and rebuild the foundations of shattered human respect. Above all he wanted to escape the stigma that had been inflicted upon his soul as his head shook with anguished rage, lost in self-imposed exclusion. The night rain slashed against his body as he took shelter near the factory. Towering over him like some huge oak, the clock that crashed time for all workers rumbled above. Now he could see the factory shimmering in the light reflected against the rain as it cut diagonal swathes across the boy's deadening eyes. That evening the bankers, assessors, scrap metal merchants, demolition companies and those characters who, without any real title, simply appear, as if from nowhere, to see what coin could be turned from the misery of others. These vultures meandered in grotesque unity around the plant, picking over the bones of dead profit. Nature had taken its course, proving that even the corpse of capital could still produce a profit for those with an eye for such things. Now his mind was closed to all but revenge.

The eighty or so sacked workers rehired by Johnson had been split into two shifts that day, some even worked overtime as if nothing had changed. When the cast iron clock hit the eleventh hour the boy hid in the shadow of its structure so that he could observe the blackened cowed figures trudge into the closure of the night. Once this rump of servile humanity had been lost to his sight the boy dug his hands into his pockets to continue his unintended journey. The cutting from the newspaper he had bought on his first day at work was still in his pocket, and he tugged it out as if to confirm not only what he had read that fateful morning, but more importantly the meaning it now held for him. His mind flashed through memories of recent events, and he relived those moments whilst simultaneously changing them so that he could preserve a more satisfying recollection. Che had become his conscience. How he wanted to be just like this man. To die for the people's revolution, and in that fraction of a second his thoughts captured his own commitment to that cause. He knew what he was capable of, and his short life had always been dictated by principles he held cradled in his heart. His thoughts broke down as he recoiled from the brutal casual critique of Che stammered from the two party members whose malign influence had done so much damage to his brief working life. How stupid he had been to assume that he could live his life by unlocking the truth. Truth did not exist, it never existed. His head flew back—his mind closed to all but revenge. Carefully folding the fragile document, he placed it back into his pocket, shielding it from the rain. As the auctioneers completed the dismal business before them they too left the factory and its lights turned off. Within minutes he found himself outside the bar where many of the strikers continued to reason their condition. For some time he stood in the beating rain, excluded from the light and warmth that blazed against his eyes whilst his hands pressed against the brass plates of the door. Not knowing how he had arrived there, he watched the rain cascade from his body, causing small pools to originate around his feet as a damp steam rose from his clothes, blending with the oppressive smoke that layered the inside of the bar. His arrival went unnoticed. Head bowed, he edged and pushed his way through the room, catching the eye of John Evans, whose blank acknowledgement momentarily unnerved him, but his search continued until before him sat a group separate and beyond, *outcaste from everyone else around them. They were as he was. Pushing forward, his two former 'comrades' ignored his presence, preferring to continue their endless lecture to an equally intense cadre of new potential party members. He was even being excluded by the excluded. What madness had overcome them all? Now he was being watched, and the people watching him knew that he should not have been there, yet there he was. He looked and felt like death. This was what he thought, and the sensation satisfied his guilt. Hasaan and Annie stood speechless at the sight before them while John Evans, McCabe and the others remained seated, as if fearful that this expression of broken youth might impact into the stale resignation that had now been democratically elected as the weapon capable of fighting the employer. They sought and got anonymity while the young party members rambled aimlessly upon matters they had never really known. He was happy playing the victim. Hasaan laughed and made some unheard comment to Annie, who moved forward, away from him, and in those moments that can never be measured the apprentice represented one statement that in its stupidity both revolted and confirmed an unknown feeling within her. In the bedlam that he had created he too had become anonymous. This allowed the boy to move silently towards the girl. Shouts and laughter from the bar provided further camouflage as the two met at the edge of the room, her anger was clear, her face was incapable of dishonesty. He knew this and loved her for this ultimate weakness in the world of falseness and dishonesty that he had learned to hate.

Her voice was quiet and clear. 'Just what do you think you're doing?' she said.

He responded as she spoke. 'Annie. I just want to speak to you. Please. Just come with me. I want to show you something. Explain.' He stopped himself for a moment. 'Annie, please,' he implored her.

Behind them Hasaan broke into their conversation. 'What the fuck do you want?' he asked the boy. 'Fell out with yer Party members? This is a workers' pub, not a scabs' pub,' he said.

The boy ignored this expected intrusion that partially distanced him from

Annie. She seemed angrier than he did as if Hasaan was assuming to speak for her. But he persisted, unaware, ignorant of events, being rooted to the spot like some unwanted guest at a wedding or, more aptly, a funeral. As if to free herself from everything the girl, left the two of them together. She gathered her coat from where she had been sitting. Margaret Harvey and John Evans both asked in unison if everything was all right and the question was nothing more than a response. Nothing more than any response people make to an event when they have nothing or no comprehension worth articulating. She knew that and they knew that. She smiled, grabbed her coat, and in that instant she was gone. Hasaan stood proud and alone for this was the opposite of what he really felt, but others were watching so he maintained the pretence. This was the role he chose. Outside the bar the apprentice helped Annie with her coat, shielding her against the force of the rain that challenged them. He fussed and worried about her as she pushed him away, allowing the cold rain to embrace them both instead.

Chapter Twenty-One

If they could make me stop loving you—that would be the real betrayal.... It's the only thing they can't do. They can make you say anything— anything—but they can't make you believe it. They can't get inside you.... If you can feel that staying human is worth while, even when it can't have any result whatever, you've beaten them.
—George Orwell, *Nineteen Eighty-Four*

The night was black and carried them concealed along vaguely lit pavements towards the factory. Neither of them spoke as if both had a sense of destiny, a guiding trust despite all that had gone before. They walked, heads bowed against the fury of that night. She knew they were heading towards the factory and as they passed the small industrial units that served the larger plants dark yellow hues of light exposed their presence. Men were working nights in almost all these small factories, and the irony insulted their existence. Above them the giant clock tower loomed accusingly above them. Its role to guard the factories it served. It was almost midnight as they stole into the shadows and back alleys, making their way towards their destination. Freed of the need to explain their actions to each other, the two stooped figures had reached the broken wire fence that reluctantly marked the boundaries of G.P. Stevens and Sons. Within seconds they were outside the lean-to that housed the acid baths where Daniel Hawkins used to work. In the next instant they were inside the factory. Crouching down behind one of the huge concrete baths, a fragile light illuminated their faces, then the boy spoke, whispering while he surveyed the blank canvas of half-light that spread before them.'It's OK,' he whispered, 'no police. I don't even think they've got security guards now.' He stood slightly. 'It's all over as far as they're concerned. No need to worry about any threats now. I picked that up today. The arrogant bastards. But we should be careful,' he said to her. Annie remained silent as she too looked beyond her concealment. Still crouching as low as they could, the two figures made their way into the factory hidden from any searching view with only the bleak frames of light that speckled in the unseen vastness of the factory, providing any sense to the route they

273

crawled. In time they reached the metal staircase that led to the offices and raised platform that encircled the plant, and with silent steps they eventually found themselves a vantage point from which they could gaze down upon their former workplace. They were in awe of what confronted them as they scanned the power that belonged only to the factory. The longer they stared the more its clarity enforced itself. A brightness that only they could perceive enriched their inspection, which marvelled in the intensity of a night sky that now radiated all before them. Over the glass roof that carpeted itself high above the factory floor a unique and magical light cascaded gently down upon its subject. A secret light that required intense concentration rewarded them, and they could see inside the darkness and hear the sounds that stillness creates. Only the crash of the night's rain upon the glass roof reminded them of their mortality. Vast open spaces unveiled themselves where once the chaos of metal dominated as if some colossus had swept everything aside in gigantic swathe of the giant's arms. They could not comprehend the cleanliness of the scene, its flatness, its resolute emptiness that seemed to crave the opportunity to echo its reclaimed dominance so long subdued by the presence and majesty of the machines. Their youth and inexperience amplified the immensity of what they saw. How could over thirty years of industrial production be obliterated in little more than a day? What power lay behind such a process? For Annie and the young apprentice had been born to a world of certainties, of longevity, a world of continuity instilled into them with security assured of the provenance of the system, of '*it*', to provide stability, a life that follows rigid deliverance of infinite production, work for all with no uncertainty.

'What happened here?' the boy whispered to the girl. 'How could it be that the very life of such a place be obliterated overnight? They've done it. Christ,' he exclaimed. 'They've only been at it a day and look what they've done. The drill shop just doesn't exist. The tool room's been stripped. Look at the stores, half the cage has been torn down. Annie,' he turned towards the girl, 'looks like your job's gone, where's the cutter? How could they work like that? You'd think they would spin it out, make it last. My God, you'd think they were on a bonus. What makes them do it?' he asked repeatedly. 'Do it to no one but themselves, after all they've been through there breakin fuckin records like their lives depended upon it. It's upside down,' he murmured under his breath.

She did not respond. Her face contorted and he could hear her grinding teeth while her hands gripped the metal bars, turning the rolled steel in their brackets. He was talking too quickly, too excitedly and too much was filling her head to comprehend anything. To look down on the devastation and attempt to comprehend what it meant took her breath away; sickness overcame her and the boy's incessant talk compounded her nausea as he appeared intent to answer imaginary questions that failed to break through the girl's tortured silence.

'Johnson said it would take weeks. Those stupid bastards have done it in a day. How could they wrap up their lives like this? It's like an experiment that's finished and they're dead ... they're fuckin dead, and their executioner couldn't be arsed making their gallows or digging their graves. So what does he do? It doesn't matter. If they execute themselves and dig their own graves,' he said to her, pleased at the profound nature of his analysis. He thought himself that the girl would be truly impressed.

Annie's head spun like it would if she were to faint or vomit, so intense was the verbal onslaught of the boy. He continued in the failed belief that she was content to listen. Now he moved on to lecture and impress his singular audience. What he attempted to describe went beyond his own limited comprehension, and above all it was the transformation, the change from what it once was to the empty shell it had become. Like a truth instantaneously exposed as a lie this crushing of a religion left him speechless, but he pursued his quest to communicate at a level of political maturity in the vain hope of further impressing the girl. *Winning her back,* that was what he thought.

She became angry at the boy's rambling.'What are you talking about? You crossed the line. You went in with them and started all this,' she said.

The apprentice caught his breath after being cut and jolted into silence. How he wanted to cry away his shame. His voice slowed. 'Annie. It wasn't like that,' he pleaded, 'I didn't realise what I was doing. Now I can see it all. I thought I could have changed things. Kept the union inside. Kept the union fighting. I was wrong. I made a mistake,' he admitted.

She shook her head, engulfed in the charade of confusions that were being discarded by the boy. It was uncomfortable on the metal gangway as the apprentice, assuming to continue, picked up the pace of his discourse.'You can change things, make them better, prove that—well, prove that we don't have to live with our mistakes. Prove that we can break free,' he was begging forgiveness from the girl. 'You know, I watched a programme on the television a few weeks ago. It was like a natural history thing but it was really interesting, about these tribes in the Amazon or somewhere, and Pirelli, or one of those big tyre manufacturers.... Well, they'd built a factory near this rubber plantation and they had the local tribesmen working there. They said it was good for them and the people. Just imagine the money they were saving on a plant like that making tyres with workers having no industrial history. And it was their own culture and society that they had to destroy to force them into the factory. So they had these native people who had been lured to work in the factory with promises of money and they had to sign a contract with the company to say they would work for a minimum of three years and most of them hated it because they were used to working their land. So they got this pathetic wage and they had to spend the money in the company shop. Like slavery—like when the factory system started here during the industrial revolution. So this tribesman's speaking to the camera and he's sitting in this jungle clearing. He has got this portable radio … and he's explaining how long he worked in the factory … the long hours. And they enforced a discipline upon these people who only really knew the freedom of the land … they imposed a time clock that no one knew. You see … it was like the transition from agrarian to industrial economy, they work the land with no clocks, no time; it was sunrise to sunset and the farmers worked to their own speed, free of the whip-hand, free of the boss. I don't think we can imagine the transformation, it's incomprehensible because we have been brought up with the capitalist clock … their obsession with time and money. Well, he's sitting there and he holds up this portable radio and says this is all he has to show for three years' work. Then he looks around his land and says that in three years he could have cleared and planted crops for his family and neighbours. In his terms they would have been enriched by this labour. The man starts to cry and he grabs this fuckin radio and after a few minutes silence he says it doesn't work. He hasn't got any batteries and because he left the factory he doesn't have the money to buy new batteries and he cries at the futility of it all and in his tears he says he will never leave his land again.' Annie leant back,not betraying her interest in what the boy was saying. Casting snatched glances at the girl, the boy continued. He was winning her back, or so he thought. 'Nothing is new in all of this. It's the system. So it continues like some endless disease, incapable of alteration—it mutates. Like starting with one formula that must never be altered and so it continues, and when the formula is profit then it's simply the process of extraction that determines its reality. That man, the tribesman, wherever it was, whatever the company, it doesn't really matter. It's like measuring an injustice, a crime against humanity, the murder of a culture. Once it has happened then you can't sit back in amazement when it happens again. All the quotes from some Party pamphlet or revolutionary work are gonna alter or explain away the crime. Annie, the system's fuckin corrupted from birth and it's not gonna change. Because if you look at what's happening here then it's the same in India or anywhere.' He looked into the bleak distance ahead of both of them.

'How many families are gonna end up like that man?' he asked, 'taken off the land. Not because the country needs to industrialise but because some fat bastard capitalist knows he can make more profit from exploiting cheap labour across the globe. What work do we do then? What's left for us then? How can it be cheaper to make this stuff in India and then sell it back to us? I think it's all inevitable anyway. The work is goin and it's goin fast. Would we be free then? Free of the filth and drudgery?' he asked himself .

The girl had closed her eyes in the darkness, listening to the rambling voice that spoke softly now without any real location. The boy continued, no longer conscious of his original need to explain his actions to the girl as this was his confession to himself, hidden beneath a half-light of guilt. He rode on the back of his words, remorselessly.'You know, about a day after I started work in the factory they were discussin' things like, like everything is forever. Nothing could possibly change to affect their lives and work. Everything would stay the same, as if it had been written somewhere, and they had this agreement. Like workers had to work and the boss had to provide the work—oh, with the usual ups and downs but work all the same—and the union?' He paused for a moment. 'The union comes with the package and they take all this as if they have to accept it because they can do nothing about it cos' that's written in the same concrete as all the rest of the crap. So there they are, everyone in their place and a place for everything, like some perfect entity in perfect harmony, complete symmetry. The key to it all is that nobody can rock the boat. For the whole deceit to work good people had to swallow it all. Have you heard that sayin, *for evil to triumph good people have to remain silent*?'

Annie remained silent to this question and the boy continued to plough ahead regardless.

'It's something like that, but it makes the point, and in this factory too many good people kept their heads down, no different than anywhere else, and they think that the need for lathe operators will last until the end of time while cheap labour and technology march forward. I read about Marx, John Evans gave us one of his books, and it was all about human labour and things like when "labour power" is taken out of the production process by machines and everyone's a consumer and producer, except the capitalist. Just think about the future when we're the same age as people like John Evans. Will all the factories be in India or Africa? Annie, I haven't got a clue. I want to learn. I want to learn about that future. If machines replace human labour do we get paid for doin' nothing? It's fucking crazy talk, only kings and queens get paid for doin' nothing.' He was begging forgiveness again and the girl was bored with his guilt; nevertheless, he was unstoppable. She was immune to his ramblings.

'But they never taught me. I didn't expect anything like this when I began work. I thought it would be just like school. No one told me what to expect. One minute I'm at a desk and the next minute some bastard's forcin' me to do something I didn't want to do,' he said.

The girl opened her eyes and turned towards the boy, she spoke with a cold bluntness that cut through the boy's pleas.'What are you saying? No one should work? That you're too good to work in a factory?'

'No. I'm not saying that. We have to challenge the boss,' he said.

'So why didn't you challenge the boss and stay on the picket line?' she countered.

'I did! I fuckin did! I thought I could get back in here and fight the boss from inside the factory, not standing outside watching the place being fuckin dismantled. Watching the work disappear forever. I didn't think....' His voice trailed into the darkness of the factory as if he knew the futility of his stance.

'You didn't think?' the girl interrupted. 'Well, that's original. Was that the problem you had at school?'

'No. If you want to know I thought too much at school and the teachers didn't want any of that. They wanted to teach me how to do what I was told. Because that was what they were told to do. To make sure that they turned out enough automatons to serve capital. So I wasn't that bright. Was I?' His question hung in the air like some unwelcome thought.Both figures now lay back against the office wall with their feet dangling over the edge of steel gangway that encircled itself above the factory floor. A tangible silence breathed amidst them that relieved both of them of the need to talk or listen further; they needed this break, this release, and in this brief respite their eyes surveyed the scattered detail beneath them. The drill shop no longer existed, almost every drill machine had been moved to the centre of the factory, and there they languished in regimented lines as if they themselves had just been manufactured off some invisible production line. Now they stood gleaming in a half-light coated in vivid industrial paints of red and green, each machine standing over seven foot in height bent over their huge cast metal frames like giant fairground boxers waiting to strike an opponent. Flat lathes packed themselves as mortician's slabs, solid and still. Smaller lathes, drills and cutters broke into random spaces, punctuating their presence amongst the machine elite that still held dominance over the factory. Thrown around this central arc of cast metal, the angular contours of manual machines used for bending shapes into lengths of steel or iron could be seen like scales of justice with their solid steel ball counterbalances raised high above the drooping cast bars that provided the powerful fulcrum of force required to impress the central tool head which would ultimately contort shape to all manner of metals. To the furthest corners of the factory floor wooden crates, ready for dispatch, tossed casually without form so as to give the impression that encasing machines was a difficult task that was released from the luxury of conformity. The factory no longer existed. It had been transformed into the final scene of *Citizen Kane*. Wooden crates and straw jostled for space amongst this vast auction of industrial heritage as closure filled the air with an age of finality. A finality that hovered long ignored and now in dark retribution pressed forward its reality, its inevitability—in their minds all was assured, and in the silent darkness Annie held his hand tightly. Nothing in life prepared them for the cold finality that danced beneath them. No logical explanation existed, for this was beyond logic. What was displayed beneath them was the system that dumped food at sea whilst two-thirds of humanity starved. What rose up before them was the celebration of profit above all things. A full hour passed without either speaking, and for some of this time they slept undisturbed. Yet the factory creaked and banged like a ghost ship. Despite its emptiness the factory was echoing its past in distant hollow noises whose haunted cries confused the senses. Like a brewing storm the noise raged behind them until one clash, that seemed to reach through the highest apex of the glazed roof, woke both of them. The young apprentice stole searching inspections across the floor beneath him. She joined him, both on their knees, both looking for an enemy that did not show itself. An enemy that did not exist outside their own fear, for the enemy was within them. 'It's empty, no security, no police,' the boy repeated again, 'come on, Annie, let's go,' he ordered confidently.

The boy stood up and ran towards the staircase, leaving the girl behind. He bounced down the metal stairs and each step reverberated around the whole of the factory with each crash transcending the other in waves of noise that rolled forward, descending and ascending somewhere in the farthest corner or the highest point of the dead factory. Annie called after him, intent that they maintain their anonymity, but by now he was standing amongst the discarded industrial debris calling her name as she gently negotiated the stairs.

'What are you doing? You'll have us arrested!' she called as quietly as she could.

He looked towards her and shouted at the top of his voice, arms outstretched. 'No! This belongs to us. To our class. Fuck the police, fuck the boss and fuck the bosses' union. It's time to make our statement. To express the solidarity of the international working class. Long live Che Guevara!' He moved forward and jumped on a small crate. 'Good evening ladies and gentlemen,' he called out, 'welcome to the sale of the century. What bids do I have for this entire drill shop?' The boy seemed happy in this moment.

'Madam,' he bowed towards the girl, 'would you like this drill shop? No? Perhaps you'd prefer to buy the families of the men and women who sweated their lives out on these machines in the true pursuit of profit for the ruling class? It's a job lot then, men and machines sold to the young lady with the fur coat.' Now both of them were laughing.

'But remember, once you have purchased these wondrous gifts you get a free gift, yes, you've got it, the working class will be truly liberated. Truly free,' he called out, 'can you cope with that? What an offer, Madam, an offer you can't refuse.' His voiced echoed around the building. Annie jumped up on another crate and took a bow towards the boy.

'What do you say to this wonderful lathe,' she called out to the boy as her laughter rang out through the cavernous building like church bells. Her voiced echoed dramatically, endlessly multiplying, mixing with the faded trace of the boy's shouts.

'A finer piece of technology not seen this side of the globe. Buy it now and take it home. Take it to another continent. For a special offer on this extraordinary piece of northern industrial heritage I will kindly throw in a lathe operator. Not very young. But a lathe operator all the same. Now who will accept this fine piece of mild steel, three-speed drill?' she asked.

'A bench micrometer?' As she spoke the young apprentice called over to her, picking up this once magical symbol of status off the floor where a day earlier John Evans had thrown it. 'Madam! I want one of those bent arthritic workers chained to that machine and it's a deal. Throw in a crooked union official and you,' his voiced bellowed against the empty factory walls, 'and you! Madam. You have got a deal. A doubleplus deal,' he screamed out like the master of a circus ring urging the crowd to applaud the celebrated acts that paraded before them.

Annie ran towards one of the tall metal bending machines whose base had been precariously balanced upon two wooden rickets. One hefty push and it crashed into the concrete floor. The whole factory shook with the rage of this felled giant, and in the aftermath of its spoken force slivers of glass from the roof window, loosened by the shock, crashed to the floor like tingling exclamations. The action of the girl released an energy in both of them that fed upon the shock that proclaimed the power of her deed, the fact of its existence and their own mortality. That the machine could be toppled so easily injected an exhilaration that pumped fear through their veins, as all they had been incarcerated to respect was now exposed for the great deception it was. Now both of them placed their full weight behind one of the giant drills kept for the heaviest work in the factory. Its weight crushed down against them, refusing to yield. The girl pushed a length of timber between the four metal plates at the base of the machine. Within seconds they both watched the tool rock from side to side, and the more they applied themselves to their work the greater the machine tilted. Like some immense drunken statue whose precarious balance had been removed. Then the huge edifice that towered over them lightened its load upon its fulcrum until it had passed the point at which no further movement other than down existed. Its fall brought other machines to the floor in one catastrophic clash. Yet more glass and debris rained upon them, and the pigeons perched sombrely on the roof rafters flew wildly off and away from any danger.

Within seconds they had inflicted irreparable damage on these great beasts of industry that had once ruled over them as if all their imagined dragons and demons had been slain, wasted at their feet. Mixes of oil seeped onto the floor from broken pipes like the gaping wounds of a murder victim choking thick blood in the shape of a final black oily shadow, and this was what they saw when they looked down upon the wreckage before them. Acting as one, they both gathered rags, straw and wood, anything that would burn. He had the matches. Both of them crouched over to watch closely as infinite wafts of grey white smoke fanned gently amongst a pile of debris. As yellow flames licked inside the small mound they had constructed, and with a serious air of professionalism about them and their task, they surveyed the tiny fire that now took its hold; tendering it with matchwood until the flames made the wood crackle and spit, offering golden sparks which ordained the first real moments of the fire until it was established enough to allow them to repeat the process in other areas of the factory. And as they watched the child's flames of each individual beacon the fires unfolded their immense potential before them, allowing both to glimpse nature's great equaliser as she gave birth to the tiny sparks that were to grow into an inferno. More than anything it was his act. A cleansing apology to the girl, and she just played along with his game of extremes. Neither cared. A mutual madness captured them. His madness masqueraded as an act of sublime liberation. Her madness was revenge. But it was she who indulged the boy in his fantasies.

Eventually they worked their way back to the acid bath shop from where they could see the violence of the flames engulf different sections of the plant, and with time these separate fires merged as one. Paint blistered and blackened as thick pales of smoke raised solidly towards the roof of the factory. Large sections of the glass roof exploded in every direction, raining shards of blackened glass downwards like silver rain. Now they were one, acting in complete unison. Without speaking they left the factory and made their way towards the field that rolled gently away from the rear of the factory. Sitting beneath one of the trees that marked the boundary to the other factories in the area they watched in silence as the blackness of the night failed to embrace its shadow over the brilliant lights of flame that flickered their caress inside the building. He lit a cigarette and gave it to Annie as if it were a rare gift. Settling back into the comfort of the tree they watched the factory gradually disintegrate before them. As it surrendered to the power of the fire great explosions peppered the night skies. Flashes of immense light reflected down upon them like a hundred suns and they were warmed in its glow. Now they could hear the force of their action and see its destruction, and from the distance they watched the futile speed of fire engines and police cars as they bundled with officious urgency towards the factory, just in time to watch helplessly as the roof cascaded in on itself. The recoil of this implosion uncoupled the sign that proclaimed that this was once a factory owned by G.P. Stevens and Sons Ltd. In the field two distant, unseen figures drifted into innocent sleep. And they were free from any sense of guilt.

That morning bright sunshine glistened over a canvas of damp meadow grass. Rolling sheets of golden light and grey black shadows tumbled loosely across the ground before them as the sun poked itself through broken covers of cloud. Eventually these intermittent rays caressed the two young faces that rested against each other, as one and in time they awoke, silent for the moments in which they languished in the warmth of the fresh sunlight. Before them lay the ruins of the factory and finally they began to walk slowly across the field towards the burnt-out remains of the factory, where they could see the devastation that had been visited upon their former workplace. The destruction of the factory had been complete. As they edged their way around the front of the building the phoney serenity before them transformed itself as police and firemen waged a war of roles in their haste to act out their perceived responsibilities. To no great avail, for their moment of crime-fighting and fire-fighting had long since evaded them in the sparks and smoke that chased the factory's air to starve it and consume it whole. The culprits remained hidden from detection. The fire smouldered in the exhaustion spent to bring a once mighty building to its knees. From the front of the building the immensity of their act called out to them, identifying them in the crowd, blaming them, pointing towards them. But they knew the guilt was only in their mind. What passed for street normality skirted the burnt-out building as if it was pulling away from the shamed failure of it all. The area was blighted with an industrial suicide whose shattered remains continued to accuse the two figures with their own guilt. Yet still they felt no guilt, only pure innocence.

A police cordon encircled the boundary at which the debris of the factory neatly ended. In this restricted space staff and management were thus forced to stand alongside some of the sacked workers. They signified their detachment from this mass, because that was expected, by squandering their presence at the furthest point in the line. This disaster did not bring any level of equality. Every so often one of their number would push forward towards the picket line proper to snatch a glance at some passing vehicle scurrying back to present detailed updates on proceedings to fellow employees. Expectation mingled with the bright cool air as every human present appeared to await instructions from some higher body, so used were they to the everyday diet of order and obedience, and it was an unnoticed anarchy that now rose out of the damp white smoke of the fallen factory. This fraction of freedom was invisible to everyone at that moment and would soon be thrown discarded in the ruins that made it all possible, that made anything possible if only they could see it. John Evans shielded himself from some invisible weather melting into the anonymity afforded by the equality and freedom that such disasters donate in their immediate aftermath; if only to those who look for such things. For he now adopted the role of the collective and all eyes filled with the realisation of disaster. Not the physical destruction of the building. No. Much more than that. It was the same emotion that the perpetrators discovered as they set light to the building a few hours earlier. It was the realisation of the truly fragile nature of the beast that dominated them all their lives, and it was this realisation that shamed them further. Although they would not admit this even to themselves, they feared the finality of the destroyed buildings before them; which brought mortality to the system they had been forced to revere as infinite. This factory no longer existed, and it frightened them that no others would exist for them to re-enter the world of normality as it had been defined for them throughout their lives. But it was within their eyes that a scale of things could be measured. Vacancy and fear filled them as though blindness had transfixed them. Rooted them to the spot before the mighty altar of capital weighed down by an invisible yoke that drew their heads towards the ground as their imposed guilt demanded. How they waited for their punishment and how brave they stood. With no thought to elude their condition or escape from their imaginary prisons how brave they stood, now that its walls had collapsed. These brave men and women.

Despite the seminal scale of this event nothing much was really happening. Just lines of people. Lines of people facing each other, some in workers' clothes, others in uniform, motionless and silent. Annie and her young accomplice sat invisible under the band of shadow cast by the clock tower. The boy awaited the acclaim of the workers. It never came, and he did not have any comprehension of this. Surely their oppressors' symbol of power and control had been razed to the ground and in its place stood now a monument to workers' power, and yet they acted as if this was something they never wanted. Perhaps they could not remember that they had been sacked and that the tools of their livelihoods were about to be sold to the highest bidder. Perhaps they had forgotten how they had suffered the indignity and poverty that work in the factory always imposed upon them. These thoughts belonged only to the boy. The girl understood what the reality of work meant for the majority. It provided their basic needs and this could never be confused with subservience or defeat. The majority of workers measured their exploitation, knew its worth and knew the price of revolt. Revolt would come—this they also knew, for they were part of the contradiction of capital.

A nothingness embraced all until the familiar red Jaguar of Johnson rolled into the void that lay between the redundant workers, the police and what little remained of the factory. The dwarfed fat figure that was Johnson waited for the driver to open his door before he pushed himself up from the back of the vehicle, and for a brief moment he stood in the middle of the road trying to pick out particular workers so that he might express his hatred for them, but as much as the arrival of his car focused some levels of attention, the line of workers before him drilled their eyes further into the ground, further into the obscurity of the servile. Turning quickly, he walked towards the police lines, searching for the most senior officer available. Some time passed before such an officer appeared, providing both men with the opportunity to display their authority before their assembled clients, providing the opportunity for Johnson to rest his chins in a stubby hand whose elbow came upon the support of his crossed arm in a look of ruling class stoicism. Whilst this meaningless display of role and hierarchy unfolded Johnson's slavish chauffeur stood by the car, occasionally polishing an invisible blemish on the paintwork with his handkerchief, checking the safety of its tyres, looking into the reflections of each mirror. He appeared diffident towards the workers who lined the edge of the road, being no doubt convinced of his own superiority in the great scheme of things. Johnson took one final look at the building and shaking his head made his way back to his car. From amidst that calamity of police and workers Tom Carberry, Johnson's lifelong friend and assistant, rolled forward, hand outstretched to greet his erstwhile colleague. Johnson stared down at his hand for what seemed like an eternity to the overweight manager. And with Carberry's hand still reaching out into the depths of rejection, Johnson turned away. The chauffeur performed his role, as chauffeurs do. The car sped off, and in a final act of incomprehensible defiance some of the workers began to shout abuse that subsided almost as quickly as it had been released. 'It' ceased to exist, yet they failed to realise this as they stood on the road examining the wasted mortar and twisted metal that once dominated their lives. The police knew 'it' was over, at least in this location, so they left and they took with them their orders and in their absence the workers began to fold away from the line. John Evans and the rest of the strike committee kept their anonymity and they too folded into an invisible distance away from the factory. The two revolutionaries who maintained their dispassionate watch over events since the strike started looked into the ashes and saw the domination of all their dogma burning, and it filled them with hatred as each said to the other, under their breath, 'Anarchists.' And poor old Carberry examined his diseased hand and winced at the futility of it all.

Annie Reilly walked slowly with the apprentice huddled together against the pointlessness of their act as it reflected amongst the workers. But this was not their problem, they had released themselves from a life of servitude if only in their minds, and it was their intention to stay amidst the debris of their act for as long as possible as no fear of discovery weighed upon them. Annie was hungry and she wanted to get some breakfast. Then, she thought, they could decide what to do next, and in silent weary agreement they left the scene of their crime to go to a nearby transport café. The place had been in the same location for decades, and the workers from the surrounding area provided sporadic custom. It was a dirty, depressing place that sold 'fry-ups' all day and night. From outside its wooden boarded façade it appeared deserted except for a single sign that advertised its most singular menu. Given a free choice, much like the factories that encircled it, the café would be avoided, as Karl Marx once wrote, 'like the plague'. But free choice did not exist, so subsequently trade came in repetitive spurts three times a day. The manager of the Green Baize Café reflected the ambience of the place, dirty, smelly and rough. Some years earlier he had been a cook in the army but was forced to leave after a food poisoning episode of epidemic proportions. Theft was also involved. Nevertheless, it was with these credentials that he opened 'his' café as he so often proudly reminded his disinterested customers. Thick, greasy air repulsed all that entered. Annie put her hand to her mouth and looked for a place to sit. Eight tables edged the room down either side, and between them a black grease-laden floor led the way to a plastic cabinet covered in an immovable film of filth, and it was behind this blockade that Higgins, the owner, performed his black art, poorly supported by his identical son. His body filled the space behind the cabinet and the first thing you noticed about this man was the unnatural width of his neck as if his head was a continuation of his shoulders. Dirty tattoos covered his arms, mixing the Union Jack with the Red Cross and various references to his mother. Unsurprisingly, love and hate covered the fingers of both hands. Dressed in a filth-ridden overall Higgins was a man who thought himself far too intelligent for the tragic role life had dealt him. His business, as he told people, was 'doin very well' and soon he would be moving into one of those 'posh snob places in the town'. A friend to everyone, or so he thought, and yet he treated everyone with a spite left only for the worst of enemies, no one trusted him and most feared him, for the threat of violence was served up with every meal. Only strangers made complaints. Army motifs and a decrepit Confederate flag formed the back-cloth to his front of house service assisted miserably by a son who, being aware of the man's unpredictable rage, spent much of his life absent of speech and cowered by fear.

The Green Baize Café was half empty that morning and at the counter Annie ordered tea and toast in the sad hope that such an order would be delivered in an edible form. The routine was to order the food then take a seat, and another unwritten rule was that Higgins did not speak and was allowed to scowl or curse as much as he wanted to. Annie followed the routine even though she hated Higgins and agreed with most that the man was a fascist. Both Annie and the apprentice sat wordless, exhausted, surveying the uniquely dismal environment that Higgins had managed to recreate like they were in his mind, looking at the world through his deranged eyes, and in this insipid silence they drank the weak, soapy tea that the son brought them, and after examining the toast dropped before them their hunger was forgotten. Some country music crackled from behind the bar but the distortion made it impossible to decipher as it merged forlornly with the hiss of stale fat coming from the four pans that constantly rested on the flames of a grubby pre-war gas cooker. Conversations in the café became clearer as the couple picked out people in the room making assumptions as to who and what they were. Furtive talk of the fire, the sackings and the occupation at G.P. Stevens lingered in the greasy air. Half sentences travelled across the room, supplying the impression that the few customers in there were taking part in a general discussion. One old man sitting by himself had intervened in the discussion being held by four workers from a nearby factory, and he kept saying, 'That's bollocks,' while the four men dressed in regulation overalls ignored him, talking louder in an attempt to drown out the man's interruptions.

'They sacked themselves,' one said, 'that's what happened. Everyone knows what that Evans is like. A communist,' he spat, 'everyone knows that. He did McCabe in. Now there's a good man. A good trade unionist. Think about it. Jacks, the union official, a wealth of experience behind him. Think about it,' he repeated. 'He told them what to do. Bloody political, that's what it is. A working man has to work and the factory's the place that gives us all a good standard and it's the union we have to thank and without the union yer nothing.' The other men at the table nodded in agreement. On the next table two young workers talked quietly, trying to ignore the noise around them while in the corner two other men silently studied their newspapers.

'Whoever lit that fire cost those men their jobs,' continued the man at the table, 'it's a fuckin scandal. I'd like to get my hands on the bastards. Let's hope the police get them and throw the fuckin key away.' All the time the man spoke the others kept up his pace, agreeing, repeating ends of sentences, endlessly nodding. One of the men reading a newspaper lifted his head and turned towards the table. He spoke deliberately, raising his eyes over his glasses.

'Whoever lit that fire knew what they were doing. Good luck to them. Let's hope they don't stop there,' he said. The page he was reading proclaimed, 'vacancies for library assistants'. The words were circled in red ink.

The four men stopped talking, looked towards the man and his newspaper, then continued. The old man smiled to himself. Outside a delivery wagon pulled up close to the café and before the lorry had stopped the driver was out of his cab and walking towards the door of the Green Baize Café. Everyone turned around and Annie could see a Confederate flag like the one in the café hanging behind the driver's seat in the lorry. She then examined the driver as he walked towards the bar checked shirt, blue jeans, boots and a knotted red handkerchief tied around his neck. He was a cowboy, or at least that's what he thought he was. It was his undoubted role. But he was a lorry driver, and this made her smile. On his right arm she could just make out a tattoo that proclaimed 'Free to Roam,' now she started to giggle and her young apprentice could not see the joke until she nodded in the lorry driver's direction. The cowboy was direct and to the point as he faced up to the manager of the café. And in a dubious American accent made his declaration.

'OK, fella. That sure smells good. Full English an' a coffee,' he said.

Higgins glared at the cowboy, examining him from top to bottom, fixing his gaze through the man's eyes as if attempting to read his mind and drill through to the back of his head.

'You takin' the fuckin piss or what?' he spat.

The driver looked nervous but held his ground as his accent became more of a Southern drawl.

'Nope. It sure looks good,' he reaffirmed.

Higgins withdrew as he too caught sight of the flag in the driver's cab. His attitude towards the man seemed to change. 'Sit down and I'll bring it over,' he ordered.

Following his instructions, the driver sat down at the table nearest the bar, but before he did he appeared to wave to the rest of the customers as if he were a person of some celebrity. 'Howdy,' he called to everyone and no one in particular.

Conversation begun over again, and in the meaningless clatter of the cafe's customers the cowboy shouted to the manager as his breakfast was being prepared. In a matter of moments Higgins stood over the man tilting the plate just enough to allow hot fat to pour onto the table, which he wiped with a dirty rag, leaving a proud stain upon the already gangrenous table. At a rigid angle the plate was dropped before the man. His coffee followed, and in an exclamation that defied reality the man in the check shirt saluted the plate of congealed meat and fat laid before him, causing an air of false

modesty, unknown to Higgins, to emblazon the monster face of the cafe
manager. The cowboy greedily sampled the food. Then he spoke confidently
to Higgins, spitting fat and gristle across the table.

'Com up to take some machines or sumink to the docks,' he said, 'then
there it is, this goddamn burnt-out wreck. You people been bombed here?' he
asked as his accent swung from New Orleans to Walsall. Higgins seemed
unusually interested.

'Fuckin Communist Anarchists,' he screamed, 'lazy bastards shut the
place down,' he told the cowboy. 'A fuckin good job it wus. Sum' o me best
customers. Big breakfasts!' he exclaimed as if this was the answer to life
itself. Higgins physically stopped, stood still and seemed impossibly to think
about his words. Customers took notice of this fleetingly momentary episode.

'I fed em every day and that's the fuckin tanks. No respesks for nothing.
That's why the boss did the right thing.' His bull head glared around the
room looking for dissension. 'Sacked the fuckin lot of 'em. Then the bastards
burnt the fuckin place down,' he said by way of an explanation.

'Why's the machinery going down the docks?' asked the cowboy.

'Gonna go to the Indians,' Higgins stated.

Checked shirt spat his interruption carelessly, 'Gonna go to the Indians,'
he said. 'Indians?' he repeated more clearly. The cowboy leant forward
imposing a better American accent.

'Yeah … fuckin Indya,' cried Higgins, 'our machinery gonna go to India.
What the fuck does that tell ya?' Higgins screamed without any need. By now
everyone in the café was transfixed by the conversation.

'Nope. Don'know,' admitted the cowboy in all innocence, 'I thought all
the Indians had been wiped out.'

'Indya,' the word fell with distain from the manager's mouth into the sea
of grease that layered the café floor, 'think abah it. Our Brit machines goin
all over there. It's our fuckin work. We gonna start growin fuckin rice or
wha'. Think abah it,' exclaimed Higgins.

Thought now etched itself all over the cowboy's face as if the contagion
has passed from Higgins to his erstwhile customer. But the more he thought
the less he understood the moronic thud of the manager's racial hatred.

'So what's that?' asked the cowboy innocently.

Higgins's face reddened instantly. 'Ya don't know what it fuckin means?'
he screamed.

Like a man instantaneously disillusioned, robbed of a soul mate, the
brother he never had, a true doppelganger. He had been deluded and tricked
beyond a solidarity that never really existed. The man was not the immediate
friend he thought he was. Not the bizarre twin of desperation who could offer
justification for Higgins's own brutal existence. Often customers would

predict the telltale signs of the manager's wild rages gauging carefully, identifying each element that would eventually combine and erupt in a dark violence that held no preference, and today would be no different. Silence mingled with burdensome conversations until the threat of bloodshed flushed into the room like too many street gangs and only Annie kept on talking while the boy listened, and when the silence reached its crescendo Higgins cracked. Slowly and softly he cracked; rumbling uncomfortably, he cracked until his distressed hatred for everything released the beast within him. Leaning towards the cowboy, he lifted the half-eaten plate of food away from the table and threw it across the room. With knife and fork still in his hands the cowboy looked at the manager. Higgins towered over him with one huge thick monkey wrench of an arm pointing towards the door.

'You haven't got a fuckin clue, ave ya,' he screamed, 'Confederate flag and ya haven't got any fuckin idea what's it abah. Get out! Get out of my café and don't ever show your fuckin face in ere agin,' he shouted, forcing the windows of his café to rattle. Speechless, the man stood, and within seconds he was being marched out of the café by its manager. All eyes locked upon the manager.

'What the fuck are ya lookin at!' he spat as he walked the length of the café in between the tables, inviting someone to speak, waiting for someone to comment whilst all the time his son cowered behind the café bar. Fat began to burn behind the stove. Those customers who had the misfortune to be skilled in such matters now knew that it was normal for all to leave the place until such time as Higgins's violent temper had been replaced by manic depression.

'Go on, get outta my fuckin café. We're fuckin shut!' he screamed.

He did not have to speak, customers were already leaving. Annie carried on talking softly to the boy, whose eyes began to close and gently open with the weight of exhaustion and the dirty heat of the café. Then the boy noticed a fly feasting on some wasted fat on the edge of the table. Oblivious to the manager's ranting his mind had been lulled by the girl's soft voice, his mind dreamed with past images and broken hopes for the future and then he became aware of the futility that engulfed him. The café was empty now. The bluebottle struggled to leave the table but it had gorged itself and was unable to lift its wings to free itself, and in the end the boy smiled towards the girl who loved and understood him. He pulled out the newspaper article that had lain in his pocket since he bought it on his first day at work. So close was he to the girl he could read to her, murmuring the printed message from the page as if unloading some heavy secret, and as he did this his eyes prodded in the direction of Higgins.

'Annie,' he whispered, 'listen to this,' he began reading from the cutting, "'the American agent made desperate efforts to keep off the crowds. He was a very nervous man and looked furious whenever cameras were pointed in his direction. He knew that I knew who he was and he also knew that I knew that he should not be there, for this is a war in which the Americans are not supposed to be taking part. Yet here was this man. The body of Che Guevara was flown into this small hill town in South-Eastern Bolivia at five o'clock last night. He was a Marxist.... He was perhaps the last person who tried to unite radical forces everywhere in a concerted campaign against the U.S. He is now dead, but it is difficult to feel that his ideas will die with him.'"

He smiled at the girl as if the words conveyed a mysterious totality, a reason, an explanation, a remembered dream breathing its way towards them as the paper crumpled gently within his hands. The boy seemed to think that by reading this piece, by association, he would be released from any crime of strike-breaking or supporting the union's bureaucracy. But still, he knew nothing. But it was really the Christ-like image of the revolutionary that captured the imagination of the boy. The magnitude of the words were lost upon him but he maintained the charade. Jesus looked him in the eye and he was dead again. Priests hovered over the boy. If he had acquired any knowledge it was in duplicity.

'For the real people. For the real revolution,' he stated softly.

And this made Annie fill with a momentary happiness and contentment as she kissed the boy. But only she understood the meaning of the text and the role of the man known as 'Che'. She despised the Christ-like image of the corpse whilst worshipping the true image of the real revolutionary. How she celebrated his life and words. How she truly adored the revolutionary struggle of Guevara and Castro. How she differed from the boy.

The dry paper lit easily, burning naturally in his hand as the apprentice eased it towards the decaying rubbish that lay at his feet, and in moments a long, dirt-ridden curtain, that clung to the floor where they sat, was alight. A pyre of burning words and image. All the time the cafe manager stared at them incredulously. Then they both stood up to leave the café, ignoring him. Outside they could see smoke escaping from the building. The manager could be heard screaming at his son and as they came out of the building they were both coughing and spitting and all the time the manager's palace of brutal, hateful spite burnt behind him.

Martin Cloherty had arrived at his destination, directly ahead of him stood the smouldering remnants of the factory and behind him the wretched cafe was catching light. For the first time the sky that loomed above him was crystal clear, and the faint call of birdsong cascaded gently.

At that moment they held on to each other. Held on to their

innocence—basking in a warm sun, unaware that it was all proclaiming the power of '*it*'.

Time passed effortlessly from this day. Only Annie truly understood the real meaning of freedom. She made sure she was free.

The boy could never be free and as he wondered what had become of her he held out his hand and took another brown employment card from the hand of Mrs.Hyndle.

'Be there at seven o'clock on Monday morning, don't be late,' she ordered without looking him in the eye.

And he? Well … he simply obeyed—Martin Cloherty had arrived at his destination.

*

Printed in the United Kingdom
by Lightning Source UK Ltd.
101158UKS00001B/151-228